Animal Rites

Primordial Press
A division of Uprising Communications Group
P.O. Box 490
Laguna Beach, CA 92652
Visit our website at:
www.michaelpanno.com

UPRISING

ANIMAL RITES

Michael Panno

Primordial Press
Laguna Beach

My paw is sacred. All things are sacred.
Sioux Bear Song

He makes a solitude and calls it peace.
Byron

for
Lauren

ONE

Home at last. Took me two trips to bring in all the supplies and though it is only a two mile hike, it can be difficult after dark. Sometimes I wish the road came closer to the cabin, but of course, that would eventually be disastrous. Didn't expect to be gone for so long, but there were so many things to take care of. Picked up my checks from the P.O. Box—so far, so good on that; I was afraid Daniel might not handle things, what with my quick departure, but I guess I was wrong; he is a good brother, a kind and gentle man.

I spent a whole day in the library reading up on the black bear. There has been much more written on them than I had imagined. Here's an interesting fact: The black bear can detect a man upwind ten miles away; who could ask for a better watchdog?

I hate the city and I hate going in there at all; in time, perhaps (as I become more self-sufficient), I can stay away completely. The place grows filthier by the day, and the people...what's happening to this society? There are children walking the streets at night in Hollywood, selling themselves; thirteen, fourteen year-olds; many are on drugs, some have guns, they kill for fun. They're all so lost. So hopeless. Where are their parents? Who's protecting them?

Buildings are crumbling, entire neighborhoods seem to sag under the weight of desperation; doors and windows are covered with iron bars. People living in cages! So many years I spent among them, thinking I could make some kind of difference. How could I have been so blind? Our society is collapsing; it's too late to start erecting pillars.

A man cut me off on the freeway today, almost hit me. I honked just to let him know I was there and he flipped me off. I was overcome with rage; I could feel my pulse increase, could hear my heart beat, couldn't get a breath. I followed him right on his tail for ten miles, watched him glance to his mirror. I couldn't see his eyes but I know he saw me; I could sense his fear. It was like being in the jungle on patrol and you can feel the enemy out there and your heart is pounding because you're certain they know right where you are and any minute they're going to fall on you and wipe you out. Yes, I know the fear,

1

and that guy felt it today, believe me. He exited the freeway somewhere in the Valley and I let him go. If I had had my gun, I think I would have continued after him, maybe I would have shot him, maybe it would have taught him a lesson.

My fuse has gotten very short, I know that, but there seems to be nothing I can do to control it. Even if there were, I'm not sure I would. It's best I just stay out of the city as much as possible; I can't afford any trouble now that I have the bears to take care of. It's funny, after Nam and being with the Agency for so long and everything that went with that. I used to see those faces in my sleep—and why shouldn't I? Not one of them had ever done anything personal to me—never flipped me off—but this guy today, this one was different. I think I could have killed him and come right home and gone to sleep. No guilt.

My father was right, it's just like the bible says. We have fallen from grace. Being out here in the woods, I can see just how far we've fallen. Everything here is in order. There is violence but no cruelty, pain but no anguish. Each creature protects its young, defends its own space, but none are greedy. The animal kingdom is just that— a kingdom. They move on instinct and seem to want nothing more than to survive. The rules are simple.

I can't wait to see the bears, tomorrow. I've brought some new music, some Mozart and Schubert. I'm sure they'll like it. It may seem ironic that the same species that created this music is also orchestrating the destruction of this society (this planet!), but I have to remind myself that this music is from another period, a better time when men still had character. Still, I'd rather be out here with nature than next door to Mozart, any day. I don't know what I'd do if I didn't have this place, and the bears; most importantly, the bears. All I wanted when I came out here was some peace, but I've found much more than that. I've found a life.

I'm tired and it's late and I want to get up early tomorrow. Haven't seen Bones around anywhere, but that's not unusual. Feels like rain is coming. I hope so. I worry about fires out here. Can't wait to see the bears.

Frank Noble closed his notebook and slid it back into its place next to the others on the wooden bookshelf beside his bed. For years he had planned to condense them, perhaps even attempt to have them published—wouldn't people be interested in a close up account of a decorated soldier, a veteran Secret Service agent? But those thoughts were gone now; they belonged in that other life. No, his journals would not be published, they would sit there on his shelf, a row of dusty reminders of a world he had left behind. If someone were to find them after his death, perhaps learn something of value from them, they were welcome to them, but he would have no part in it.

He untied his boots and kicked them off, then removed his filthy socks and lay back on the bed, staring up at the ceiling. A small fan hung by a rope from a beam directly overhead. A window was open and an intermittent breeze kept the fan in motion. Frank focused on a solitary blade and followed its circular path until the blade became solid and still in his eye, then his focus shifted and the blade merged once again into the blur of the fan.

He smiled; the room was cool but comfortable, and he felt good, better than he had...well, he couldn't remember *ever* feeling as good. He'd been living out here in Big Santa Anita Canyon for a little more than six months now, but he'd known of the house all his life. His grandfather had built it himself, laid every stone, hammered every nail. That was back in the thirties. The government had set up a "recreation residence" program designed to allow citizens access to the national forests. For a nominal yearly permit fee, cabin dwellers were allowed to build and vacation on national park grounds. Many, including Frank's grandfather, ended up living there year round.

Frank and Daniel had spent a whole summer there when they were boys. By then, the old man was living there full time, all alone. He taught them how to fish and hunt, how to track an animal. Daniel had liked it okay, but for him it was just a vacation, a good childhood memory, nothing more. For Frank, that summer had been an awakening. It was as though he had been living in a false world and had suddenly come home. Everything out here was new to him and yet somehow familiar. He spent each day exploring the terrain, familiarizing himself with the land, the plethora of

3

vegetation, the wildlife; especially the wildlife. By the end of those three months he could wander from the cabin for miles in any direction and know exactly where he was, examine any animals feces and know not only what kind of animal it was, but also what it had for breakfast. When that summer came to an end he swore he'd be back, that someday he would come there for good.

It was that summer, those memories, that he kept in the back of his mind his whole life. It had gotten him through his tour in Vietnam, had been the light he saw himself moving toward during his twenty years with the Secret Service. And yet, he'd waited almost a year after he retired before moving out there, had gone up to Eureka instead. He'd told himself it was because Daniel was up there, he was his only family, he needed to feel connected. The usual stuff.

But it never felt quite right. He kept thinking of the cabin, kept seeing himself there in the woods, alone (always alone), until finally one day he just packed up and left, wrote a note to Daniel saying he'd be in touch and just disappeared.

The house was made almost entirely of stone; his grandfather had brought them in by mule and wagon all those years ago, back when there was a discernible trail to follow. The floors were hardwood. Frank had refinished them, and nailed some of the loose boards to get rid of the squeaking (it was amazing how few needed it) when he first moved in, and then covered sections with thick throw rugs. The only heat came from a large fireplace in the living room. He had considered putting in a vent to direct heat to the bedroom, but opted for extra blankets in winter. On exceptionally cold nights—there weren't many—he would make a bed on the couch and sleep in front of the fire.

The furnishings were very sparse: An overstuffed couch, a large reading chair, a small wooden dining table with two chairs, a couple of low tables with kerosene lamps. In his bedroom sat a simple pine-framed bed, a desk and chair—all built by Frank—and one electric lamp that he used for reading. He also had a portable CD player that he ran primarily on batteries. The kitchen had an apartment sized refrigerator and one small basin for washing dishes. Frank had hooked up a generator to handle his electrical needs and to pump water from the well. There was also a large cesspool dug years ago for the toilet; he had already begun digging a new one, for the old one was about full and there was no way to bring in a truck to clean it out.

He lay there now, thinking about the new hole and how much deeper he'd need to go. As far as he could tell, that was probably the most serious problem he had to deal with at this point in his life, just pick up a shovel and dig. He could feel himself drifting off to sleep and considered getting up and undressing, but he felt too comfortable now in his half sleep and the thought quickly passed.

Soon he was deep asleep and with the sleep came a short dream, a dream that started there in the freshly dug hole with Frank waist deep, the sun beating down on his bare back, dirty sweat stinging his eyes. Then the shovel became a rifle and the sun fell behind a cloud and Frank ran from the ditch across an empty field; there was noise and confusion and a predominant feeling of fear, but just as quickly as the fear came it subsided. It was as if a wave had washed over him and then receded and now the rifle became a baseball bat and Frank was ten years old. That part of the mind that tells you you are dreaming tried to replay the dream for Frank, wanted him to remember it for the following day, and it seemed as if the dream ran through his head half a dozen times until he told himself he had it, that he would remember it all, the incidents, transitions and most importantly, the feelings.

There were other dreams that night, but none so vivid, and when Frank awoke the following morning he would do what he had been doing off and on for over twenty years. He would sit at his desk and try to piece together as much of the dream—the important one—as he possibly could, sometimes with success, sometimes with none. One thing was certain, they were coming less often and they were much less painful since he'd come out here.

They had been on the dirt road for over half an hour. The passenger, a borderline anorexic whose head was swallowed up down to his eyebrows by a black ten-gallon hat, had a cigarette in one hand and a cup of coffee in the other. Every time he'd raise the cup to his lips, the driver would purposely veer into a pothole on the right side of the road and the coffee would lap over the edge and splash down onto his lap.

"You think that's funny?"

"What?"

"You know damn well, what. Knock it off."

"Can't help it if there's pot holes."

"You can help hitting them. Fucking moron."

The driver was much bigger than the passenger, but he recoiled at the harsh tone in his partner's voice. He reached down to the seat and grabbed a can of beer and opened it. "Shoulda got yourself one of them lids with the little holes in it for your coffee." He took a swig of beer.

His partner took a quick gulp of coffee. "You sure this is the right road?"

"Positive."

"Positive, huh."

"I've been out here four times."

The forest seemed to grow thicker with every curve in the road. There were no stars or moon to light the way, only the narrow beams from the old pickup's headlights. Small drops of rain had begun to fall, just enough to smear the dust on the windshield but not enough yet to merit turning on the wipers. The driver leaned over the steering wheel and squinted, but he didn't bother slowing down, even though he couldn't see more than fifty feet in front of him. He was having fun, like some kid on his way to go fishing. The passenger pulled himself up a bit, too, and glanced over at the speedometer. They were only going forty-five, but out there on that narrow road, with the forest so thick you couldn't tell where one tree left off and another began, and pine branches scratched the fenders like the claws of a hungry beast, it seemed

6

more like sixty, and the truth of the matter was, it was more than just a little spooky.

They came to a fork in the road and the driver veered to the right. "Yeah, this is it, I remember the fork, and that little cabin. Should be just another mile or so now."

The cabin he spoke of was set back away from the intersection, nestled in the trees, and indiscernible in the darkness but for two small yellow blotches of light—like a wildcat's eyes—and a pale stream of ascending smoke. The road straightened out a bit now and grew a little wider and both men sat back in their seat. The passenger twisted his head and caught a final glimpse of the cabin.

"What time is it, Freddie?"

Freddie, the driver, checked his watch. "Quarter till four."

"Wonder why the lights are on?"

"Where?"

"That cabin back there."

"People get up early in the country."

The passenger looked back toward Freddie and shook his head. "Fucking idiot, getting up at this hour. Bad enough doing it for money. And a lousy five hundred bucks at that."

"I kinda like it in the morning. Everything's so quiet, nobody around. You'll see, once we get to huntin'."

"This ain't my kind of hunting, especially at this time of the day."

Freddie shrugged his shoulders. "Was your idea to get here early."

"Well, we couldn't exactly do it in the middle of the day now could we? Especially with the weirdo hanging around playing his fucking records."

"I don't think it was records, Cleve. Looked like a CD player."

"Whatever."

"Was real nice music, too."

"Well, that's just grand, Freddie. Maybe we'll get lucky and he'll show up. Put on a concert for us."

They hadn't hit a pothole in quite a while and the passenger,

Cleve, was getting pretty relaxed with his coffee drinking, taking large swallows now instead of little sips, but when he held the cup up to his lips a second too long, it happened. The right front wheel hit a hole, a deep one, and coffee went flying everywhere, mostly in his face. To make matters worse, he jerked his head back to avoid the coffee, and in doing so smacked the back of his head against one of the rifles mounted behind the seat.

"Goddamn it, Freddie! Pull this fucking truck over, I'm gonna kick your fucking hillbilly ass." He took off his hat and started rubbing the back of his head. "Damn, fucking idiot."

"That time it really was an accident, Cleve, swear to God. Almost hit a deer."

"Fuck the deer, Freddie." He was still rubbing his head. "It's starting to swell up."

"We're here," said Freddie. There was a small cul-de-sac at the end of the road and Freddie took a minute to turn the truck around and back it up against the wooden barrier that marked the dead-end. Cleve used his shirt to wipe the coffee from his face then he opened his door and tossed the empty cup out onto the ground. He stepped out, then, almost as an afterthought, reached back in, opened the glove-box and pulled out a large knife encased in a leather holster, and began attaching it to his belt.

Freddie got out now and grabbed one of the rifles off the rack. "Ain't you takin' a rifle?"

"That's your job." Cleve pulled the knife from its holster. "I'll do the carving."

"Well, you oughta take one with you, anyway, just in case."

"I thought you were mister hot-shot hunter."

"Well, I'm a crack shot, for sure, but you never know when something can go wrong, Cleve."

Cleve shook his head in disgust. Two weeks earlier he was sitting on five grand and like a fool he went and took one of those cheap flights to Vegas and got himself into a poker game. He was doing all right, too, was up a couple of grand, till he got stuck with a sixty-four in a high-low split game. Figured he had a wrap on

8

the low hand; his hand was hidden pretty well and the guy across the table was betting heavy on a seven. The only other person left in the game had a pair of aces showing, so he was definitely going high, and if Cleve got lucky and drew a five, he might just get the whole pot. At least that's what it looked like. Turns out the guy with the aces had a three and a four in the hole. He drew a deuce on the turn and got Cleve's five on the river, took the whole pot with a wheel. Cleve was left with barely enough money to get back to L.A. Now here he was, four o'clock in the morning with Freddie, doing a job way beneath him, and all for a lousy five-hundred bucks.

"Just what is it you expect could go wrong, Freddie? You think maybe the rangers are issuing guns to the bears now?"

Freddie had busied himself with loading his rifle. "Bears are smart, Cleve, and fast. I'm just saying, I wouldn't go after one without a rifle?"

"I ain't afraid of no fucking bear, okay, so let's just get this shit over with."

"Whatever you say. You better put out that cigarette, though. Start a fire."

"Hey listen, fuck your bears and fuck your fires, okay. If I wanna smoke, I'll smoke. It's fucking raining out anyway."

Frank woke shortly after dawn with a start. It seemed as though there had been a noise, a loud pop like gunfire. He wondered if maybe it was part of a dream. He got up and went to the bathroom and threw some water in his face. It wasn't a dream, there had been a noise, a distant one, hard to tell just how far away, but his guess was, maybe a mile. His next thought turned to the bears; their den was at least two miles away. Would he even be able to hear a rifle at that distance? At this time of the morning, and coming out of that canyon, most definitely.

He took a long hard look into the mirror. He was fully alert now, he could see it in his eyes; he could see the worry, too. Two years in Vietnam and twenty with the Secret Service had taught him to be very conscious of his own state of mind, to read the messages his body was sending him. Right now his stomach was jumpy and his heart rate was up. Your panicking, he thought. Don't jump to conclusions. Yes, there had been gunfire, but that wasn't so unusual out here. Even though the area was pretty remote, there were others living in the vicinity; many of them had guns, some hunted their own food.

He'd never met any of his neighbors—the closest one was a mile away—but he had seen people now and then, had seen their houses. They all seemed to keep to themselves and that was fine by him. He'd never seen anyone around his property. It was a long hike to the nearest dirt road and there was no clearly marked trail to his house; at least, not anymore. There had been one, years ago, but much of it had become overgrown with bush. Frank fashioned a new one, using sections of the old one along with new carefully marked and well-hidden portions so that even if a casual hiker were to stumble onto a section of it, after a hundred yards or so it would just disappear. You'd have to know there was a trail and that it led to a house and then you'd have to be a damn Eagle Scout to find it.

No, no one had ever stumbled across *his* place but plenty of people did come out to these woods from the city. Most just to hike or fish; usually a father and young son. They'd pick a spot, more often than not a bad one, and the father would set about showing the boy how to bait his hook—they'd use all kinds of concoctions, from caviar to cheese; Frank got a kick out of that—and the boy would inevitably prick himself with the hook and start crying, prompting the father to start in with the lecture about being tough and bearing up to the conditions. Then he (the father) would start into his first beer of the day and the boy would sit there feeling useless, losing patience and interest until finally, an hour or so later, they'd start packing it up, the father shaking his head in disappointment, playing out the scene just the way it had no doubt been played to him when he was a kid, the son doing his best to hold back the tears as they'd slowly disappear into the bush; then Frank would come out from his hiding place and clean up the empty beer cans and potato chip bags.

There were exceptions. Now and then he'd see it done right. There would be a father who really connected with his kid, one who'd broken the cycle, made a commitment to be different than his old man, and it was funny because they were the same ones who would clean up after themselves when they left. It was a pleasure watching them, almost as good as watching the bears.

Others came too, some just to target practice but some to hunt. The serious ones were looking for deer, and although it bothered Frank that they would kill any animal, he tolerated those who knew what they were doing, the ones who only hunted the bucks and took their kill with them for food. There were others though who would shoot and kill anything that moved, that were there for sport. Frank didn't find it sporting at all and he would do everything he could to dissuade them from returning to his little kingdom. He had destroyed tents, smashed out truck windows, left threatening notes on their vehicles. When one hunter killed a young doe, Frank fired a round over his head and then others at his feet until the guy finally got the hint and cleared out of there.

He was pretty sure whoever fired the round that morning was a serious hunter; the others were too lazy to come out at that time of day. Someone had most likely bagged a deer, and although he felt a slight pang in his heart he managed to reassure himself that the bears were okay. He had a quick shave, and downed a cup of tea and a piece of toast. It was his routine to do an hour of exercise each morning but he settled on some stretches today. In the six months he'd been out there he'd dropped ten pounds and honed his body to a fine machine, six-two, one hundred eighty pounds of muscle. He might have been pushing fifty on the inside, but outside he was the picture of youth.

He hadn't been to see the bears in over a week and as he loaded his backpack with food and various CD's, Frank couldn't help but feel excited—he had forgotten all about the gunshot—though it was an excitement held in check.

Expectation breeds disappointment. He'd learned that as a child, anticipating Christmas, only to find little under the tree, except for maybe a shirt or a new pair of pajamas. His parents didn't have much money and what little they had they were not inclined to spend on anything as frivolous as toys. Had it not been for his mother's insistence, they would not even have had a tree. She was Catholic and held much reverence for the birth of Christ, even went to great effort to build her own nativity, and in fact was not opposed to the concept of gifts. One year she had slipped the boy two dollars to buy himself whatever he wanted, so long as he kept it from his father's sight. But his father was a strict Calvinist with little time for rituals. His weakness was his love for his wife, a love that she would use whenever possible to get her way; but there were limits. He would allow the tree, but no lights or other decorations, and it had to be a live tree, one that they could take out and plant the day after Christmas.

And so Frank had learned early in life not to get his hopes up, and of course the lesson had served him well over the years, for disappointment had reared its ugly head many times, enough to destroy a more naive soul. For Frank, each instance merely served to strengthen his resolve to the point where he believed the axiom "that which does not kill me makes me stronger," had sprung from his own mind.

Still, he was excited this morning. The bears had shown a strong preference to classical music and he had recently purchased these new CDs, including a compilation that encompassed within its titles, a piece by Geordani, entitled *Caro mio ben*. It was a short piece with a simple melody, but one strong with emotional depth; the rich texture of the strings filled Frank with an unexplainable longing and yet also left him feeling soothed, as if the music had somehow bathed his soul. He had listened to it half a dozen times at the record store, each time with the same effect; in fact, its power seemed to increase the more he listened. He was sure the bears would like it too.

It was by accident that he discovered their fondness for music

12

in the first place. The mother had been coming around his cabin for quite some time, but every time he tried to approach her, she was quick to take up a defensive stance, and he was smart enough to back off and leave her be. His father had instilled some qualities that served him well, and patience was one he used most often.

He began leaving a pan of leftovers for the lone bear, every few days placing it a step or two closer to the cabin so that after a few months she was eating right off the porch. Then, late one afternoon—it had rained all day and only cleared up just in time for Frank to catch a quick glimpse of the sun before it settled behind the hills—as he sat on the porch listening to Chopin's *Piano Concerto No. 2*, she walked right up to him, close enough to touch and just stood there, her head cocked to one side, her eyes shifting back and forth from Frank to the little black box. She was not huge as far as bears go—less than five hundred pounds—but Frank knew she would have no difficulty separating his head from his body if she were so inclined, and so he just sat there frozen for the entire eight minutes of the piece, wondering what would happen when it finished.

As the sun sank further behind the mountains, the remaining clouds lit up with intense shades of orange, pink and blue, and these bright colors reflected off the glass in the cabin windows and into the huge brown eyes of this mesmerized creature. For Frank, it was as though he was witnessing the birth of creation and as the final few gentle piano notes faded into the cool autumn air, he thought he saw a tear form in one eye of the beast, and then she quickly turned and ran away.

Frank sat entranced. He had come to these woods six months earlier to start over, to leave the world behind. He had seen too much, done too much, more than God had intended, he was sure, and had come looking for peace. He'd had no ambition, just a vague longing for a purpose. He'd long ago rejected both his parents' religions, had even—for a while—abandoned God. Now, sitting here alone on his porch, with only the tiniest remnants of color remaining in the sky, the trees receding into the forest and the image of a solitary tear running down the cheek of this gentle creature, he felt...reborn.

He hadn't gotten more than a hundred yards from his cabin when Bones ran up to greet him. An older mutt—Frank figured Lab and Australian Shepherd—he could still get around pretty well. He was there when Frank first moved in, and behaved from the start as if he belonged there; perhaps a drifter had used the cabin and left the dog behind. The two took to one another right from the start. Frank put food out for him, even let him sleep inside, and Bones continued on probably like he had before Frank had arrived. Sometimes he'd disappear for two or three days, then come walking up, tired, hungry, his coat littered with pine needles and thorns. Frank would feed him and take him to the creek for a bath and then Bones might spend the next two days sleeping. They were good for each other; neither one made any demands.

Today he seemed anxious, lunging toward Frank, then backing up, his barking loud and aggressive. Frank was not one to take Bones's antics lightly for he knew he was smart and not inclined to bark or raise a fuss over any little thing. Some dogs would go crazy every time a squirrel crossed their path, but not Bones. If he was upset, there was good reason, and he was very upset today.

The gunshot from earlier echoed now in Frank's head.

"Okay, Bones, I hear you," he said. "Let's go." Bones took off ahead of him and Frank broke into a run. He was in good shape and had jogged the two miles many times, loaded down with a full pack, but he had never moved this quick, even in Nam. Something was wrong, he knew it in every bone of his body. Damn, he thought, don't let it be so. ❧

It only took him twenty minutes to reach the area where the bears had their den, but Bones didn't stop there. He continued on to the north as Frank followed him through some thick brush. Bones was a good fifty yards ahead of him, barking frantically. As Frank drew closer to the old dog he slowed his pace to a fast walk. The barking had stopped, replaced now by an intermittent whine. Frank approached slowly, afraid of what he would discover. A light mist had been falling when he left the cabin but it had stopped now. He wiped his face with his sleeve. A few vultures flew up around Bones; he growled at them and they started squawking, too. Frank crept toward the commotion until he came upon a small clearing, and there at Bones's feet he found him, one of the cubs, lying in a pool of blood, a gaping wound in his head made larger still by the ravenous birds. Frank pulled his pistol from its holster and shot in the air towards the birds and they flew a little higher. He knelt down to the dead bear and checked his body. He had been shot once in the head and there was another gunshot wound in his shoulder.

There was more. A large chunk of flesh was missing from the small of his back and it looked like someone had dug deep into his flesh with a knife and cleaned out a section of his insides. Frank put his hand to his head and turned the cub just enough to allow him to gaze into his open eyes. It was a look he had seen many times before, in the jungle, on the faces of soldiers, some of them still kids, a look of disbelief, a look of shock, a look of sadness as they had contemplated their own pending death. That look, that last final moment of life, was exactly the same on the face of this young bear as it had been on those dying soldiers; it asked why, why me, why now?

Bones moved in close to Frank and the dead bear—Frank had named him Stumble, for he was very clumsy—and put his paw up on the carcass. Frank dropped to both knees, and gently laid his head on Stumble's lifeless belly. Bones licked Frank's face then backed up a few feet and began barking again. Frank ignored him for a couple of minutes; he was far away, back in another land, another time. Bones persisted until finally Frank raised his head and looked at him, then slowly rose to his feet.

"What is it, Bones?"

Bones ran to the edge of the clearing, stopped and barked again. Frank followed him back through the brush again, a short jaunt, maybe fifty feet, and there he found Gladys—he'd named her after his mother—the mother, sprawled out on the forest floor. There were vultures on her and Frank fired his gun again, this time emptying his pistol, firing randomly into the air and screaming as loud as he could, but not at the birds, and not any discernible word, more a primal yell of pain directed toward the gray sky, and beyond.

His examination of Gladys had revealed but one bullet hole; it had entered her left eye and exited the back of her dead; death was most likely instantaneous. But she also had a hole, like Stumble, cut in her back and she was missing one of her paws. Whoever had done this had done it for more than sport; they had taken parts of her body, mutilated the two bears and then left them there to rot. Who could do such a thing, and why?

Frank pulled himself together and began inspecting the scene. The area immediately around Gladys was completely disheveled, as would be expected; when Gladys hit the ground she would stir things up. He found his first clue less than two feet from her outstretched arm. The ground was still wet and there were footprints, clear enough to tell someone with Frank's skills a lot. He followed the steps back a few yards then dropped to his knees. There had been two of them. The bigger one wore hiking boots and had a wide stride; Frank figured him to be at least six-foot, and heavy, judging from the depth of his imprint. The other one was very light footed and wore a pointed toe boot, a cowboy boot. His steps were close together. They had come in from the east, had most likely parked their vehicle at the end of the dirt road a couple of miles back. Somewhere between here and there he would find something to lead him to them.

He turned and considered the proximity of the two dead bears. Gladys had been shot first, no doubt about that. She had come after the two men, had confronted them face to face and the bigger man, the one in the hiking boots, had shot her. He was good. Frank could see where the man had stopped and planted both feet firmly to take his shot. He had been thirty feet away when the bear started her charge. It took courage to hold his ground and make such a clean shot. A bear at full speed can run faster than a horse and could cover that thirty feet in a matter of seconds, and Gladys had in fact made it across the clearing before she dropped right at the feet of her assailant. Frank felt he knew a lot about this man, already.

But the scene after that got a little fuzzy. Stumble had been shot from behind and it had taken two bullets to bring him down. Or had it? The wound to his face was much larger than the one in his shoulder, suggesting a close range hit. Frank checked the area for spent cartridges. He found one close to Stumble, three at the edge of the clearing and one more by Gladys. The casings were all the same; only one rifle had been used. The shoulder wound had brought Stumble down and then she was finished off close up. But something didn't add up. The shooter brought down a charging Gladys with one shot but it took him three for Stumble. Or had the same man done the shooting? There were two shooters, had to be; the second guy was an amateur. Why hadn't the hunter brought down both bears?

There was work to do. The bears would have to be buried, and there was Mozart, Stumble's brother. If he were still alive, Frank would have to figure out how to take care of him. But, first things, first. He would need to follow their trail back to the road, see what he could find that would lead him to these two killers. His heart felt like it was going to break. It was as though he'd come across his own children, butchered. Part of him wanted to lie down next to them and just quit, give it all up right there and then, but that other part, the part that got him through Nam, the part that kept him in the front line with the Secret Service, putting his life at risk day after day for twenty years, that part wouldn't let him quit. He'd had hundreds of missions in his life, many he did with no emotional commitment at all; it was merely his job. But this, this would be different. This was personal. This he would do for Gladys and Stumble, and yes, for Mozart, too. It would be no bigger or smaller than that, not for bears, not to uphold the law, just a man whose life had been taken from him out to set things straight. He left Bones behind to keep away the vultures and set out toward the dirt road.

The sun had begun to break through the fog; it should have been a good day, just he and Bones and the bears listening to his new CDs, enjoying the brisk fall afternoon—perhaps he'd have caught a few trout for lunch—but all that was gone, perhaps forever. He could feel the sun, but it didn't warm him; could hear the chatter of busy squirrels, but paid them no mind. There was only the broken trail before him, and the promise of revenge in his heart.

Frank's summation of what had taken place was pretty accurate. Freddie and Cleve had left their truck at the end of the dirt road then headed off on a narrow trail, Freddie leading the way. He had spent a week in the area searching for bears before finally coming across Gladys and her cubs. It was actually the music that had led him to them. Freddie had no idea what was being played other than the fact that it was classical, but he had liked it and so had followed his ear toward its origin. When he had finally arrived at the source, he could hardly believe his eyes. There they all sat (the three bears, a scrawny looking dog and some guy) close enough to touch each other, the older bear picking stuff out of one of the cub's hair, all of them circled around the ghetto-blaster with this beautiful music coming out.

When he had told Cleve about the scene all Cleve said was yeah,

yeah, so what about this guy, and Freddie explained that the guy came every morning for a couple of hours and then disappeared, but that he hadn't been there for a couple of days so Freddie figured maybe he'd gone away. That was when the two of them decided to make their move.

So they had gone out there that morning, Freddie with his rifle and Cleve with his knife, hoping to get in quick, kill the mother bear and get out before this stranger got back. Freddie had also mentioned to Cleve that this man carried a rifle and a pistol and didn't look like anyone they'd want to fuck with. This only served to piss Cleve off. He wasn't afraid of anybody, least wise not some nutcase that listens to music with bears.

The first half-mile of the hike wasn't too bad. The trail was fairly wide, the ground level. But then the trail ended. Freddie plowed his way through the brush. He was completely prepared for their venture, decked out in his boots and army surplus fatigues. To him, this was fun, it was what he'd done all his life, he and his old man back in Arkansas getting up before the sun, going out hunting rabbit or possum, or now and then even bagging a deer. It was how they had gotten most of their food. Most people went to the grocery store. Freddie went hunting. Cleve, on the other hand, didn't find it at all amusing. He'd worn his cowboy boots and hat and a pair of Levi's and his good leather jacket. His Levi's fit him pretty tight and so every little thorn managed to pierce through the cotton and stick him in the leg. The jacket would have protected him okay, but Cleve had taken it off early on in their hike so as not to tear it. That put him down to his t-shirt. He was cold and getting scratched and torn all to hell.

"How much fucking further is it?" Cleve was getting out of breath. They'd been climbing for the last quarter mile.

"We're half way. You wanna rest?"

"Fuck you, just get us out of these bushes. I'm getting ripped to shit."

"Put your coat on, Cleve."

"Listen, asshole. This coat cost five hundred bucks. Whoa,

fuck!" Cleve stepped on a wet boulder with his leather-soled boots and went down hard on his behind.

Freddie stopped and turned around. "You okay?"

Cleve got up and brushed himself off. "What a bunch of shit."

And that's how it went for the next mile, Cleve falling down, Cleve scratching himself on branches, Cleve freezing his ass off. Then, just as they came upon a small clearing and Cleve started putting on his coat, Freddie came to an abrupt halt and raised his rifle. Cleve started to say something but Freddie quickly hushed him and pointed across the clearing.

"Jesus Christ," said Cleve.

There it was, twenty or so yards away, huffing and puffing and slapping at the ground. Cleve just froze in his tracks, one arm in his jacket, the other groping for his knife. Freddie widened his stance and the bear started into its charge, storming across the clearing like a tornado with teeth, growling and flapping its arms in a maniacal quest for blood. Freddie took sight and fired. The giant creature took a few more steps, and Freddie's world became eclipsed by a fury of teeth and mangled fur. Freddie quickly stepped aside and the bear crashed down hard to the ground, snagging Cleve's arm with his paw on his way down, tearing through the sleeve of the new leather jacket and shredding his arm from the shoulder all the way down to the tips of his bony fingers.

"Fuck! My arm, Jesus Christ." Cleve grabbed his arm and started dancing about in pain. Freddie was staring out toward where the bear had emerged from the trees.

"Be quiet, Cleve."

Blood was running down Cleve's arm. "Fuck you. I'm bleeding."

"There's something out there. I think it's another bear."

Cleve grabbed the rifle from Freddie. "Give me that fucking gun. Mother fuckers." The rain had turned to drizzle and the sky was lighting up significantly now. The two men saw some bushes move and then another bear dashed away from them. It was smaller than the first. Cleve gave chase.

20

"Let it go, Cleve, it's just a cub." But Cleve was already hot in pursuit. Freddie followed after him. He got about twenty yards and then the firing started. Two quick ones in a row, then silence. Freddie caught up with Cleve and up ahead, maybe twenty feet away, he could see the smaller bear lying on the ground moaning, blood spilling out of its shoulder.

"Put him out of his misery, Cleve."

"Let him suffer. Look at my arm. Look at my coat!"

Freddie grabbed the gun.

"Can't leave him like that." He walked over to the wounded animal, aimed the rifle at his head and fired. There was no more movement after that. Freddie went back to Cleve. "You didn't need to do that."

"Yeah, well, you killed him, not me. Besides, now we'll get two bladders. Maybe we can make this trip worth our while."

"You better let me bandage that arm for you." Freddie set the rifle down and removed the pack from his back.

Cleve was examining his coat. "Man, look at this, it's ruined."

Freddie pulled out a first aid kit from his pack and opened a small container. "This is gonna hurt," he said and poured it over Cleve's wound but Cleve was too angry to feel any more pain. Freddie wrapped
his arm with some gauze, taped it and gave Cleve a shirt from his pack to wear.

"You been holding out on me. You had that shirt in there all along, you made me walk through all that shit with just a t-shirt."

"It's for emergencies, Cleve, like now."

Freddie showed Cleve where the gall bladder was located and Cleve did the carving on the large bear. Then he whacked off the animal's paw, the one that had ripped him open. Freddie just stood there shaking his head. He'd done a lot of hunting in his life, but never anything like this. Then Cleve went over to the smaller bear and started cutting him up.

"Oh, man, Cleve. That's not cool."

"Shut up, you moron." Cleve yanked the small bladder from

21

the still warm creature. He was about to cut away his paws, too, but Freddie grabbed his shoulder. "Listen," he said. "Someone's coming."

Cleve stopped momentarily. "I don't hear nothing."

"Be quiet." There it was again, this time Cleve heard it, too, a dog barking and moving closer.

"It's just a dog," said Cleve.

"There might be someone with him. I'm leaving, Cleve, you can stay if you want."

Cleve stood up and gave the small bear a kick. "Fine, let's go," he said, and handed the bladder to Freddie. "Here, take care of this."

The trail left by the two men was easy to follow; they had made no attempt to hide it. Frank found blood along the way; evidently, Gladys had gotten a piece of one of them. But there was nothing else to help him, no clothing or papers. It was amazing, the things he'd usually find after someone had come out there: driver's license, pictures, money. People couldn't seem to hold onto anything. But these two, having just poached two bears and probably in a hurry to get away, had left nothing behind.

He followed the trail to its source, the end of the dirt road, and found what he hoped might be his first break, a Styrofoam cup; there was still a small amount of coffee in the bottom. There were fresh tire tracks, large tires with a deep tread, probably off of a truck. He decided to follow the road out to where it turned off from the paved highway. Halfway there he came to the fork, the other prong of which led to the west, toward his cabin. There was a small cabin set back off the road; Frank had seen it before on his trips to town, had seen smoke coming from the chimney. Perhaps whoever lived there had seen something. He'd had virtually no contact with humans in six months and dreaded the idea of approaching one now, but the picture of Stumble and Gladys lying in their own blood, tore at his heart. He'd have to do it; he'd have to do a lot of things now that he'd rather not do.

22

He had brought his rifle with him from the sight of the killings, had been carrying it in one hand, ready for use in case he were to get lucky enough to run across the killers. But as he approached the cabin he slung the gun over his shoulder so as not to alarm the inhabitants. He made a point of making a fair amount of noise as he approached the front door. Most people living out in the woods have guns and know how to use them. He certainly didn't want someone taking a pot shot at him.

As he drew closer to the cabin he couldn't help but notice something odd about the construction. All the windows seemed to be cut very close to the ground. In fact, he could see where they had been moved from their previous height. It was as if they had been cut out for children. The cabin was wood, tongue and groove, and had a wooden porch cut from logs and a small low-hung swing off to one side. He stepped up on the porch. The door was open and there was a small motorbike next to it. Frank set his rifle down next to the bike and gave a holler.

"Hello. Anybody in there?" He could hear some noise from inside. He pushed the door open a little more and took a step inside. "Anybody home?"

"Come on in." The voice came from another room.

Frank stepped inside. The cabin was small, very clean and appeared to be neatly organized, but, like the windows, all the furniture seemed to be made for children. There was a little couch and chairs, end tables that couldn't have been more than a foot high. Even the refrigerator was tiny.

"Make yourself comfortable, I'll be right out."

There was something odd about the voice, too, like someone with laryngitis; it was scratchy and, well, small. Frank continued his perusal of the house. There was no place he could see where he could make himself comfortable except for one large wooden chair that had been placed against the wall in the kitchen. He thought about grabbing it and sitting down, but decided against it.

The place had a very soothing atmosphere. A soft diffused light

23

poured through a large skylight in the kitchen, casting an amber glow onto the wooden cabinets. The kitchen walls were papered in a woodsy theme and upon close inspection Frank could see numerous animals playing in the woods or sitting in the trees. The overall effect was that of an enchanted forest, something out of a fairy tale. There was a small catalogue on the table. He picked it up and began leafing through it. Inside was an odd collection of clever inventions, products designed to ease everyday tasks. There was a pill crusher for pulverizing pills and a pill alarm for scheduling medication. There were gadgets to help you hold your pencil, extensions to help grab things out of reach, walkers, wheel chairs, leg extensions for chairs, bed readers, cervical pillows, urinary leg bag kits. Some of the items could be useful for just about anyone, but most appeared to have been designed for those with some type of disability.

He set the booklet down and took a few steps through the kitchen and into the living room. If Frank's place was Sparta then this was surely Athens. The room was painted a soft blue color, the walls adorned with numerous pictures, mostly black and whites of circus animals and clowns. Against the far wall, stood a small table with a television and stereo system and next to it, an oak desk replete with computer, printer and various books. Closer to Frank was a wooden bookcase filled with hardback books, most of them older looking but still in good shape. Frank bent down and examined them. Most were recognizable: Dante's Inferno, numerous editions of Shakespeare, *War and Peace*, *Crime and Punishment*; some of these he'd even read, himself. Others, newer looking books, were completely foreign to him: *A Confederacy of Dunces, Tourist Season, The Secret Life of Algernon Pendleton*. This last title intrigued him. He pulled the book from the shelf, opened it randomly to somewhere in the middle and began reading.

The right of absolution was superstition. Childishness. Both heaven and hell were misconceptions. Souls moved from world to world in a twinkling of an eye.

Frank closed the book, set it on top of the bookcase and turned his attention to one of the photos on the wall, a black and white of a group of people standing in front of an elephant.

The door to the bedroom opened and the man behind the voice came out. "Mr. Noble, yes?"

Frank was stunned. The man couldn't have been more than three feet tall, and his body was all deformed, his head seemed huge. He waddled like a duck when he walked.

"Do I know you?"

"I don't believe we've had the pleasure. That's me in the picture. Third from the left. I was twelve when that picture was taken. Long time ago. Do you like the circus?"

Frank couldn't get over the voice. He'd never heard anything like it in his life, like somebody trying to speak through gravel. "I don't know, I mean, I haven't been in years, since I was a kid."

"Well, it's a world onto itself. I can tell you all about it someday." The little man noticed the book sitting on top of the case. "You a Russell Greenan fan?"

"No, no, I was struck by the title. I didn't mean to pry..."

"Ah, curiouser and curiouser! Don't worry about it. You're welcome to borrow it if you like. He's very underrated, if you ask me." He stuck the book back in its place on the shelf then extended his hand to Frank. "Pardon my rudeness. The name is Marcell. That's it in its entirety, like Madonna or Cher, except that I can honestly say it's all the name I've *ever* had."

Frank hesitated then gently grabbed the small hand in his.

"Don't worry, you won't break it. I'm a dwarf, not a piece of china." He laughed a hearty laugh.

"I..."

"It's okay. Most people wanna know. Just what exactly is he? Is he a dwarf? Is he a midget? Actually, the politically correct term is short statured. These days, they got us broken down into a hundred different categories. You got your proportionate short statured, disproportionate short statured, achondroplasia, hypochondroplasia, diastrophic dysplasia; you name it.

You have to be a scientist just to know what you are. But, everybody's thin-skinned these days, like a bunch of tomatoes. I prefer dwarf, myself. But you didn't come here to learn about dwarfs, did you Mr. Noble. From the look on your face, I'd say you're here about the bears. And it isn't good." ⁊

THREE

Freddie Diddlesby sat at the kitchen table in his apartment staring at Gladys's gall bladder, trying to figure out exactly what it was about it that made it worth so much money. Some people liked bear meat—he'd had some himself—and lots of people liked having a genuine bear skin rug, but a gall bladder? It was only nine in the morning, he and Cleve had just returned from their kill, but Cleve was already into his second beer.

"I don't get it Cleve, I mean, do you know what this thing is for. It holds bile."

Cleve was sitting on the couch. He had removed the bandage Freddie had made and was inspecting the wound on his arm. Some of the gouges were deep and still oozing blood. "Man, I have no fucking idea. You're the hunter. This arm is all fucked up. What do you mean, bile?"

"Bile. Puss. It has something to do with regulating body fat."

Cleve looked up at Freddie. "Yours is obviously not working right."

"Well, why do you suppose somebody would want it?" asked Freddie. The insult had gone right over his head.

"I don't know, but I'll tell you one thing. I been thinking, Veronica is just gonna take that thing to the guy who hired her to hire us, and she's gonna get paid and then that jerk-off 's gonna sell it to somebody else and somebody's gonna end up paying a lot of money for it. We do all the work and get a lousy five hundred bucks each. Not to mention my arm."

Cleve got up from the couch, walked over to the kitchen sink and poured some beer over his wound.

"What are you doing?"

"It's alcohol, ain't it. I'm sterilizing it."

"I don't know if beer will work for that, Cleve. I got plenty of stuff in the bathroom. I can clean it up for you, but I still think you should go to a doctor, make sure you don't get infected."

"Well then, get the shit and do it."

Freddie went into the bathroom and got some gauze, tape and a bottle of disinfectant from the cabinet. He set it all on the counter and washed his hands in hot water. One thing his father had always impressed upon him was the need for hunters to have plenty of first aid around, and the utmost importance of cleaning a wound; you never knew when something was going to happen. Freddie had heard the horror stories about guys who'd accidentally shot themselves while cleaning their gun or out on the hunt and then bled to death for lack of a first aid kit; or had bandaged themselves out in the wilderness with a dirty rag, gotten an infection and ended up losing a limb.

So Freddie was well prepared with bandages, tape, alcohol, even some morphine he'd lifted during a drug store heist. He gathered up his supplies and returned to the kitchen. Cleve had removed the smaller bladder from the box and put it in a separate container, an empty milk carton he had ripped in half.

Freddie sat across the table from him. "Give me your arm."

Cleve stuck his arm across the table. A tattoo of a naked woman ran from the middle of his biceps down his forearm, her toes coming to rest just above his wrist. The scratches from the bear cut through the woman, dicing her into vertical sections.

Freddie opened the bottle of disinfectant. "This is gonna sting." He poured the fluid onto Cleve's arm, and Cleve recoiled in pain.

"Jesus..."

"Sorry." Freddie gently dabbed the scratches with cotton while Cleve finished off his beer. "Why'd you take that out of there?" Freddie was referring to the second gall bladder.

"The way I figure it," said Cleve, "why should Veronica get a piece of the action on this one. She sent us to get one; the second one is ours."

"Well, what are we gonna do with it?" Freddie had begun wrapping the wound with clean gauze.

"We're gonna find out, stupid, who she's selling it to, and take it to them ourselves. Then we'll get more money. Man, look at this tattoo. It's ruined."

"Listen, Cleve,"—Freddie's voice was shaking—"I don't think you should be calling me stupid. I'm the one that found the bear, not you. If it wasn't for me, you wouldn't be getting any money."

"So you know how to hunt, big fucking deal. You're a moron, Freddie, that's a plain and simple fact, and if it wasn't for me, you'd probably be cutting this thing up right now and frying it for lunch."

Freddie stopped working on the bandage and stared across the table at Cleve, thinking he wanted to reach over and strangle the skinny bastard, but Cleve, like he was reading Freddie's mind, reached down and pulled out his knife and set it on the table. The two men sat there for a couple of minutes, Cleve tapping his fingers on the knife, Freddie just staring a hole into Cleve until finally Cleve put the knife away and spoke.

"Don't take it personal, Freddie, you're just not bright, okay. Too much inbreeding. So let me do the thinking and you take care of whatever it is you can do, like patching me up."

Freddie waited a few seconds then started working on the bandage again. "I just don't like being called stupid, that's all. No reason to do that."

Cleve took a deep breath. "You finished crying now?"

"Ain't cryin, just sayin, that's all. So how are we gonna do it?"

"Do what?"

"Sell the other bladder?"

"See what I mean. Let me worry about that. Hey, get me another beer, will you?"

Forty miles away from Cleve and Freddie, Frank Noble sat on a wooden chair under the soft yellow light of Marcell's skylight, listening to Marcell explain what had happened that morning. Marcell sat across the table nursing a cup of tea. He'd offered some to Frank but he had declined.

29

He had gotten up early, as was his routine, to work on his computer; he had to make a living, he had said, and then winked at Frank and told him maybe he'd let him in on his little secret some day, and Frank had said fine, but about the bears.

"I heard this truck come by around four-thirty."

"How did you know it was a truck?"

"Well, I didn't, not for sure, but I could tell it was a big motor, probably an eight cylinder and most likely a truck, way out here, and as it turns out, I was right. Anyway, I knew it didn't belong to anyone out here—I know all the vehicles in this canyon by sound and sight, including yours—so I decided to check it out. I like to keep track of everything that goes on around here. Kind of like you, really. Oh, yes, we're a lot alike, you and me. Where was I? Oh yes, I finished some work I was doing and then started hiking down to the end of the road, and let me tell you, that's no small accomplishment with legs this short. But, I like to exercise.

"Well, I didn't get far when I started hearing these gunshots, first one by itself, then three more, bam, bam, bam, right in a row, which is rather odd, don't you think, for a hunter? I mean, I could be wrong, but I always think of a hunter taking one, maybe two shots at something, not this rapid firing. Sounded more like a drive-by. Then there was one more shot—what's that, five, altogether? Anyway, I started running, and I was right."

"About what?"

"The truck. It was a truck, just like I said. A blue Chevrolet, an older one, fifteen, twenty years old, covered with rust and all dented up. Some people don't take very good care of their possessions; don't you agree? And I don't believe that bit about people taking better care of their things if they've had to work for them; I think it runs deeper than that."

"The truck..."

"Oh, yes, sorry. I get carried away sometimes. Though I'm anything but clever, I could talk like that forever." Marcell paused a second for Frank to respond, but Frank just stared at the little man inquisitively.

30

"That's a little poem...by Gilbert? Doesn't matter. So, I wrote down the license plate number and then I hid in the bushes and waited. That was the worst part; it was damp out there this morning, and cold. And I was afraid I might get poison oak; can you imagine? You may have noticed I have very short arms. There are parts of my body almost impossible to reach."

Frank was slightly mesmerized by Marcell. When he told his story he seemed to glow, or maybe it was just the light in the kitchen, but there was something about him, something almost magical, Frank wasn't sure what it was. It was as though he had been a storyteller for thousands of years, had sat around a million campfires telling the history of the world to anyone who would listen. When he told his tale, he dressed it with melodrama, his hands flinging about, his scraggly voice rising in pitch at just the right moment, his eyes aglow with the unfolding of events, as if he too were just now experiencing them.

"So you were waiting in the bushes."

"For whomever it was to return. I heard the shots about forty minutes after the truck went by my house, so I figured it would be coming back another forty minutes later, maybe sooner if they were in a hurry to leave."

"What made you think they'd be in a hurry to leave?"

"Because, they were in a hurry to get there. That truck went by here going at least sixty miles an hour, stirring up dust, scaring the animals. You sure I can't get you anything? Coffee?"

"No, no, I'm fine. So, they came out..."

"Two of them. One was real big, bigger than me, ha, ha. Actually he was a little bigger than you, except not in as good of shape; nowhere near. He had a big belly, and kind of an all around soft look to him, but big and probably pretty strong. We always had strongmen in the circus and to look at them you'd just think they were fat, but let me tell you, Frank,"—he leaned forward—"they could squeeze the life out of you just like that." Marcell snapped his fingers.

"The other one was skinny and pale, smoking a cigarette,

probably on some kind of drugs. My guess would be speed. Lot of speed freaks work in the circus, easy to spot. Always skinny with long greasy hair and lots of tattoos, and almost always white. Don't think I ever saw a black speed freak, come to think of it. Anyway, the skinny one was bleeding. His left arm was bandaged. The big one had a rifle. He must have been the one doing the shooting. Which brings me back to my question. Did they kill the bears?"

"You've seen the bears before?"

"I told you, Frank, I know everything that goes on out here. I've seen you with them, playing your music out there. I've been very moved by it; I particularly like the Chopin numbers. I don't get out there very often; it is quite a hike. We used to have bears, of course, in the circus, lots of animals. Lions, tigers. And bears, ha, ha." Marcell got very quiet all of a sudden, then started up again but in a much more somber mood. "I could tell you stories, Frank, about the animals, sad stories that would break your heart. But then, it's already broken, isn't it. I can see that in your face." He perked up again. "Yes, sir, we're a lot alike, you and me."

Frank got up from his chair. He was still holding the Styrofoam cup he'd found on the road. He crunched it up and tossed it onto the table. "If you've got the license number, I guess I won't be needing this."

"Oh, I've got more than the license number, Frank. I've got the name and address of the driver."

"And how did you manage that?"

Marcell looked into the living room. "I told you, I'm very adept at the computer. That's how I got your name, though I must say, I haven't had much luck getting any further information on you. My guess is, you're with the government, C.I.A. maybe, very clandestine. I haven't been able to penetrate those files yet, but I'm working on it."

"I'll save you the trouble. I was with the Secret Service, but I'm retired. So, why don't you give me the information on these guys and I'll be on my way. I've got work to do."

"Oh, no, no, Frank, that would never do. I broke this case, my friend. Is that the lingo? I'm in on this, too. I want to help."

Frank stared down at the tiny man. The last thing he needed now was some dwarf poet slowing him down. "I'm sorry, Marcell, is it? This is something I need to do alone."

Marcell grabbed the styrofoam cup, hopped down from his chair and carried the cup to the burner on his stove. He seemed very agitated. He lit the burner and quickly melted down the cup. "You better get out there and hunt for some more clues, then, Mr. Noble. And don't bother thinking you can get the information from my computer. It's all up here." He pointed to his large head. "And if you think torturing me will do you any good, you're wrong. I have a very high threshold for pain. So, what's it gonna be?"

Frank smiled. "I think we can forgo the torture. But you need to understand something, Marcell. What they did, they didn't just kill the bears. It's much more than that and whoever is involved is going to have to answer for it. What I'm saying is, I don't know where this is going to lead me, but I'm going all the way, wherever it is. Do you understand what I'm saying?"

Marcell smiled. "Oh, yes, all the way. I like that. I'll tell you a story sometime, about going all the way. I think you'll like it. But first, we should give the bears a proper burial, don't you think? Pick some music for them. I have a great collection of music, although most of it is on vinyl; I prefer the sound of vinyl over CD. No matter, you probably have something special you want to play, anyway."

"And the address."

"We'll get to that. There's no hurry. They're not far away."

By ten o'clock that night, Cleve was passed out on the couch in Freddie's living room—he hadn't left it all day—a pile of empty beer bottles strewn about the floor below him, spent butts overflowing the ashtray onto the couch, the TV blaring in the background. He'd finished off two six-packs plus a half-pint of bourbon, trying to deaden the pain. Freddie had even broken out the morphine and given him a small dose.

Freddie was at the kitchen table cleaning his rifle and flipping through the pages of a magazine looking at pictures of guns. He'd had his eye on a Weatherby .340 magnum and now that he'd picked up this extra money he figured on treating himself. They had ordered a pizza a little earlier but Cleve had passed out before it arrived, which was fine by Freddie. Every now and then he would wipe his hand on his pants, reach down and pick up a slice and stick as much of it as possible into his mouth.

She came in without knocking, startled Freddie and woke Cleve from his sleep. "Don't you guys ever lock your doors?"

Cleve sat up, still half asleep and groggy from all the booze and drugs. "Try knocking, bitch."

"Fuck you," she said, and then turned into the kitchen.

Freddie got up from his chair and went to the fridge, then returned to the table with a box in hand. "Got your bladder right here, Veronica. You wanna see it?" He set the box on the table, then bent over and picked up an empty beer bottle.

The place was filthy; Cleve's empties were everywhere and a bag of trash had overflowed onto the kitchen floor, including a half-eaten TV dinner. Veronica, dressed up in a short red skirt and high heels, entered the kitchen slowly, sidestepping through the mess while Freddie made a futile effort to clear a path.

She was Chinese or Vietnamese, Freddie wasn't sure which, ninety-eight pounds, good looking but not beautiful, black hair down to her ass and possessed with enough sex appeal for three girls. Not that it mattered to Freddie; he'd never given it a second thought. Cleve, on the other hand, thought about it a lot, especially her lips. Veronica had a small face, small features, except for her lips, which she had had implanted with silicone. She kept them highlighted with bright red lipstick and had a tendency to wet them now and then with her tongue. Cleve wanted that tongue and those lips to go to work on him.

Cleve got up from the couch, steadied himself for a minute

then slowly walked up behind Veronica and pressed himself against her. She quickly recoiled from his touch.

"Don't touch me, you pig." She looked down at Freddie. "No, I don't want to see it. Just put it in a bag. I'm in a hurry, someone waiting in the car." She shook her head in disgust. "This place is sickening."

"Got a hot one lined up, Kieu?" Cleve was breathing down her neck.

"You disgust me. Why don't you take a bath?" She looked down at the bandages on his arm. "What's this?"

"He got hit by the bear," said Freddie.

"Too bad he only got arm."

Cleve grabbed her by the arm and spun her around. "You got a nasty mouth. Maybe you oughta put it to better use."

"You fuck with me, I tell Rudy, he cut your dick off, cock sucker."

Cleve released her. "Ooh, you're a nasty one, I like that. Suppose you keep my five hundred and we go a round."

Veronica smirked. "You take five hundred dollar, go fuck whore. I no fuck charity case."

Freddie wrapped the box containing the bladder in a brown paper bag and set it on the table. "Hey, Veronica, Cleve and me were wondering just what you're gonna do with this."

"That none of your business, Freddie." She opened her purse and handed him an envelope, which Cleve quickly plucked from Freddie's hand.

"I handle the cake, sister. Now, what's the big secret on this thing?" He opened the envelope, counted the money and handed half to Freddie.

Veronica grabbed the bag and tried to push her way by Cleve but he blocked her path.

"I asked you a question?"

Veronica smiled at him, ran her hand along his groin and up his stomach, then quickly grabbed his wound and dug in with her long red nails. "There's your answer," she said.

"Aah! God Damn it!" Cleve raised his good arm above his head and was about to smack her, but Freddie grabbed his arm and stopped him. Veronica removed her nails from the wound and Cleve's blood squirted out. Then she pushed by him and opened the door.

"Get me some more, Freddie. One thousand dollar. And clean your house. You live like pigs."

Veronica stormed out of the room. Freddie let go of Cleve. "Don't wanna be hurting her, Cleve, get this Rudy guy upset. Look at your arm; it's bleeding again. You better let me fix those bandages."

"Just get me a towel to wrap around it. I'm gonna follow that little slant-eyed bitch. Hurry up."

Freddie ran to the bathroom and came back with a towel. Cleve wrapped his arm, then grabbed his jacket and stuck his good arm in and wrapped the coat around his shoulders. Then he grabbed the carton with the second bladder in it.

"I'll be back in awhile, and Freddie, you ever fuckin get in my way like that again, I'll be selling your bladder."

Cleve hurried out the door after Veronica and Freddie sat down at the table and grabbed another piece of pizza. People out here in California sure were uptight. Sometimes he wished he was still back in Arkansas. He took a large bite of pizza, wiped his hand on his jeans and turned the page of his magazine. Yes sir, folks were a lot different out here. ☙

FOUR

Rudy Carlyle thought his apartment was swank; swank like Elvis's sequined jumpsuits, or Jackie Gleason's billiards room. Swank like Sammy's hair. Ever since a clerk at a seven-eleven told him he looked a little like Elvis—from the side—he'd completely remade himself; got a black wig, let his sideburns grow long, started wearing shirts that were all collar. He even tried to talk like Elvis, low and sexy, but he wasn't much good at it, always falling out of character in the middle of a sentence. Was there a resemblance? Maybe a little; the Vegas Elvis. He had the gut and his upper lip did tend to twitch a little now and then, but Rudy was only five feet six inches tall and his teeth were yellow from years of smoking Camels; one of these days he was planning on getting caps.

His apartment was decorated pretty much like him. His black leather couch floated on a bed of plush red carpet, and surrounded a thick glass coffee table. Right in the middle of the table stood a two foot flesh colored statue of an erect penis, so that from the air (if possible) or by lying on one's back and gazing up into the mirrored ceiling, it appeared as though the couch had been tossed around the penis like a horseshoe.

There was more; more glass, more leather, more mirrors, and in particular more shall we say "art." Each item was chosen with an eye toward the erotic: garish nudes done in hellish combinations of blacks, purples and vibrant flesh tones that seemed to drip off the subjects like excess body fluids; cheap statues of lovers in various positions; black and white photos of bodybuilders in different stages of nudity. Rudy had hand picked each piece, thinking they would serve as aphrodisiacs for both himself and his sexually bored clients, but there was so much and it was all so gaudy that the opposite effect was achieved, leaving one feeling as though they had entered a museum of low-class decadence rather than the desired sensuous boudoir. The whole place was an X-rated joke.

Rudy stepped out onto the deck—one of those little four by eight jobs you see plastered across the sides of high-rises like too many bulging pockets on a cheap suit—and stared down at the street. It was getting late, almost eleven, and there was not much activity below him; that suited Rudy just fine. Location was the main feature that prompted him to rent the apartment in the first place. He wanted something close to the action but not right in the middle of it, and of course, the place had to be ritzy. Hollywood Boulevard was just three blocks away, so if Rudy got bored and wanted to get out among the freaks he could be there in a matter of minutes.

He especially enjoyed the slumming after sex. He'd have one or two of his girls over, do his thing, then do up a couple of fat lines, put on his wig and take a stroll. It was best after midnight, when all the fiends' drugs began to wear off and they started craving for more. Rudy liked to watch people in their weakened state, liked remembering how he used to be, how he'd pulled himself up, made a life. He'd amble down Hollywood Boulevard, maybe dart into a tattoo shop, watch some speed freak cover up that last ten per-cent of virgin skin with another hideous rendition of a dragon. Or maybe he'd stop at the corner and talk to a couple of whores—older, washed up girls, probably carrying the bug—tell them he was looking for some quality women, just like them, to add to his stable, and maybe he'd get back to them. "Here's a hundred bucks," he'd say, "just to let you know I ain't bullshittin you," then he'd shuffle away, feeling important.

When he didn't feel like walking, he'd just go out on his deck. He liked being up on the seventh floor. It gave him a feeling of security—no whacked out crack head would be coming through a window—and added to his feelings of superiority, like a king keeping vigil over his subjects. Up here on his deck, snuggled in one of his silk robes, cocktail in hand, he *was* the king— with a view.

38

Of course, it helped having a telescope, and Rudy did not contain his voyeurism to the streets. The deck was completely paneled, enabling him to stick the end of his scope over the edge and peruse the windows of the surrounding apartment buildings with little risk of detection.

There was much to see. Like the lesbian couple directly across the street—fifth floor, fourth window from the corner—that seemed to enjoy being watched; they made it a habit of drawing open the shades and lighting candles just prior to engaging in sex. And what sex it was. Though neither of the two women had what Rudy would consider to be good bodies—one was a good forty pounds overweight, the other skinny and flat-chested, almost boy-like—they more than made up for their anatomical shortcomings with their prurient imaginations. Rudy was particularly entertained by their selections of objects of entry, everything from carrots to the head of a bass flute. One night, he almost fell off his deck laughing when the fat one— right in the middle of some heavy oral gratification—reached under the bed and brought out a clarinet. From the gestures, it appeared she wanted to use the flanged end. The skinny one kept shaking her head no but then finally acquiesced. It took some doing but she managed to get the contraption inside of her, at which time the heavier girl started blowing into the mouthpiece and fingering the keys. Rudy wondered what she was playing. He also wondered if she knew how to play the tuba. Why, he wondered, if they were so interested in mimicking a penis, didn't they just try the real thing? Like his, for example.

But tonight he wasn't interested in voyeurism. He'd been expecting Veronica at ten and here it was pushing eleven and not a word. Not that Veronica was known for her promptness—it would be just like her to pick up a John on her way over—but dammit, he'd been waiting for this for weeks, had put up a fair amount of money in advance, and his clients were getting impatient. If she'd taken off with his cash she'd be one sorry bitch.

He'd made that perfectly clear to her right from the beginning.

His customers were important people who were used to getting their way. They would not be toyed with and they did not have any qualms about cutting up some Asian whore when it came to their money. She may have thought that changing her name to Veronica made her a class act, or gave her more value in the eyes of her rich American clients, but of course all that ended at the foot of the bed. She was meat, pure and simple. They might adorn her perfect body with pearls and furs, and stuff hundred dollar bills into her panties but, like any piece of meat, she was there to be consumed, and, like any piece of meat gone bad, she could easily be thrown to the dogs. The amount was irrelevant. They had impressed this point on Rudy in a way that he understood it was not just her life that had no value to them, but his as well. You can make a lot of money off us, they had told him, but fuck them just once and that was it. And of course Rudy had passed the message on to Veronica and the others. They all seemed to understand, but right now, Rudy was beginning to wonder.

The smell of something burning drew him back inside to the kitchen. The concoction atop the stove was sizzling in the pan. "Damn," he said and slid the pan off the burner. He had added some vanilla and cinnamon to try and mask the horrible odor but it wasn't doing a lot of good. And now it had overcooked. She better show up, he thought.

Rudy grabbed his phone and dialed Veronica's house. Her machine came on. He was pissed. "Damn it, Kieu. Where the fuck are you?" There was a knock at his door. "That better be you," he added, then slammed the receiver down. He hurried to the door and jerked it open. Veronica marched past him. She had a paper bag in hand and behind her was a young girl dressed in torn jeans, tennis shoes and a dirty long sleeve shirt.

"Where the fuck have you been?"

"Oh, fuck you, Rudy. I had to pick up girl and go get your package." She took off her coat and laid it on Rudy's couch, pulled a cigarette from her purse and lit it, then took a quick glance around the place. "What smells in here?"

40

"I was trying to make some tea with that little piece of bladder you gave me. I thought we'd try it out."

"You think I drink that, you're nuts."

"I wanna try it, Kieu. It's supposed to be great." Rudy's voice took on a whiny tone. He could never stay angry with Veronica. None of the other girls would ever see this side of Rudy. It wasn't fear, and it definitely wasn't love, but there was something about Veronica that brought out the little boy in him. Maybe he sensed her strength, the feeling he got from her that she had no fear, not just of him but anyone else; she could not be intimidated.

"Oh, you're fucking crazy, Rudy. That shit no good. You sell that to your rich friends. I don't need it. Any man I fuck don't need it."

Boy, she was right about that. All she had to do was walk in the room and Rudy started getting hard. She was great looking sure, but so were plenty of the other girls. Some had better bodies. Some were younger, much younger, but none of them had that thing like her. If he could bottle that and sell it, now that would be something.

Rudy put his arms around her. "You don't want to try just a little," he said, his lip twitching.

She pushed him away. "Fuck no, Rudy. Besides, I got an appointment, remember?"

Rudy tried to get stern. "But I told you it was gonna be you and me tonight."

"That was for ten o'clock. It way past eleven."

"Well, whose fault is that?"

"It's your fault, Rudy. You make the appointments. Not me."

"That's right. And I told you to be here at ten."

"You also say don't come over without bladder, or Mister O'Neill be very angry. You also say bring over new girl. You always say too many things, then you forget. Not my fault. Now give me my money. And give me some Valium. I can't face that stuffy fuck tonight without something."

Rudy reached down for his pocket, and then realized he was

wearing a robe. "Just a second," he said and walked into a little alcove off the living room where he had set up his office. There was a computer on the desk, a couple boxes of floppies and some books. Rudy opened the top drawer of the desk, pulled out some money and went back into the living room.

"Here." He handed the money to Veronica who quickly counted it, then tucked it away in her coat. The young girl was walking around the room, checking out the pictures. Rudy turned his attention to her. "Hey, sweetheart, do us a favor and go wait in the bedroom, okay?"

The girl just shrugged her shoulders and left the room. Rudy turned back to Veronica.

"You shouldn't be calling him by name, you know, especially in front of her. What's she on, anyway?"

"I'm not her fucking pharmacist, Rudy. What's the big deal about O'Neill?"

Rudy walked over to a cabinet, opened a drawer, grabbed a small jar and removed a few pills. "The big deal is, one of these days you're gonna slip up. I told you before, you don't wanna fuck with these guys."

Veronica had gone to the fridge and grabbed a beer and now returned to Rudy, grabbed the pills and quickly downed them with the beer. Then she grabbed Rudy and gave him a long wet kiss. "You plenty big asshole," she said, doing a parody of an Asian right off the boat. "But I like you, okay. I have friends, Rudy. Very mean friends. So, fuck Mr. O'Neill. Where is he, anyway?"

"He's at the Bonaventure."

"He's supposed to be here. Now I have to drive all the way over there."

Rudy picked up the box with the gall bladder in it. "Hate to tell you this, love. But he's planning on cutting this up and trying it out tonight. So put on a good show, okay?"

"He has to pay extra. You told him, didn't you."

"Don't worry, you'll get yours. What's the kid's name?"

"I don't know, I think it's Penny. What's the difference?"

"Hey, I like to be close to my girls. This her first time?"

"I just find them for you, Rudy, I don't do biography."

"Don't get testy, I gotta know these things. My clients don't want no virgins making a big mess, you know. They want them young and innocent, but not too much."

"That your problem, not mine. What you want me to do with her. I don't have time to take her to the house."

"Leave her here. I may as well start breaking her in."

"Lucky girl. Maybe you should put on your wig."

"And cut me off a piece of that thing. I burned up the other one."

Cleve had had an easy enough time following Veronica to the apartment building, but getting into the building would take some doing. Veronica had used a card to open the main door and by the time Cleve reached the door it was closed. He could see the elevator from outside and watched the numbers as it rose to the seventh floor and then stopped. His arm was bleeding through the towel and Cleve was getting pretty angry standing out front trying to figure out what to do. He considered smashing the glass but it was a good half-inch thick and was most likely tied to an alarm system.

A man and a woman approached the building, then stopped short at the sight of Cleve. They were dressed nice, she was a real looker, he was all clean-shaven and well pressed. For a moment, Cleve considered robbing them—he might be able to pull a couple hundred bucks out of this guy—but he quickly recalled why he had come there. He tried his best to turn his smirk into a smile.

"I lost my card," he said. "Think you could let me in."

The woman clung to the man's arm and the two of them took a step back. Cleve had had a long day and was not looking his best, but he was wearing a nice pair of jeans and his jacket wasn't cheap. He tried widening his smile; it felt like calisthenics. The man quickly sized him up and seemed to be willing to accept the possibility that he might be telling the truth. The man spoke.

"What apartment are you in?"

Cleve hesitated, then, "I'm on the seventh floor."

"What apartment number?"

"We just moved in. I think it's apartment twenty-three."

The man looked at Cleve's arm. The towel was almost completely red, now. Cleve tugged at his jacket in a lame effort to cover up the wound.

"Got bit by a dog." Cleve lost the smile. "Well, come on man, whadaya say?"

"There is no apartment twenty-three. I think you better leave before we call the police."

Cleve started to get angry. "Listen asshole," he said as he put his hand on his knife—he was back to thinking about the possible two hundred. Then he glanced into the entryway and noticed the elevator was moving down from the seventh floor. Probably Veronica, coming back down. If he hit this jerk for his money, he'd have to do it quick before Veronica got down there and saw him; she wouldn't like being followed.

He pulled out his knife. "Okay, punk, let's have the wallet and make it quick."

"Oh my God." It was the woman. Cleve jerked her away from her date and put the knife to her throat. "Not a word out of you, bitch. Come on, man, give me the wallet."

The elevator stopped at the fourth floor. The man pulled out his wallet and handed it to Cleve. Cleve had to grab it with his wounded arm, which only served to make him more angry. The elevator was on the move again. Cleve pushed the woman into the man.

"Next time somebody asks you to open the door, open the fucking door!" he said, and ran off toward the street.

Cleve got to his car and quickly scanned the contents of the wallet. There was less than fifty dollars cash, a couple of credit cards and one other card, a white plastic one with a few numbers on it and a long blue arrow. Cleve kept the cash and the credit cards and tossed the wallet into the street, and then he realized what the white card was and quickly retrieved it from the discarded wallet.

In the excitement of the robbery he'd almost forgotten about Veronica, but as he was about to pull away he saw her come out of the building, alone. The couple he had robbed tried to talk to her but she just waved them off and walked away. She was still carrying the bag that she had taken in with her. Cleve's wound was really starting to hurt but he decided to stay with her. She got into her red Mercedes and pulled away from the curb and he swung a U-turn and gave chase. One thing was certain, as soon as he finished his business, he was going to a doctor and get this thing fixed up right, and somebody, somewhere, was going to pay for all his pain and aggravation.

Marcell had pleaded with Frank to let him skin the two dead bears. He realized, he said, that it seemed like a macabre thing to do, but if Frank would just trust him on this, he would eventually see it his way. "We're not talking about trophies here, Frank, I promise you."

"What *are* we talking about?" asked Frank.

"Justice. Poetic justice. And maybe a little terror."

"The answer is no. Please don't bring it up again."

Frank dug one grave for the two bears. The ground was pretty firm this time of year—there hadn't been any significant rain in six months—and the digging went slow, but after a long arduous afternoon he finally got a hole big enough to suffice. Then he and Marcell rolled the bears into the hole. They looked so fragile in death, especially Stumble, lying there on top of his mother, his limbs tucked beneath his lifeless body.

Frank started shoveling, slowly at first, then frantically, until at last the carcasses disappeared beneath the dirt. When the hole was filled, he put a CD into his portable player. He chose a piece by Beethoven, *Adagio Sostenuto*, from *Moonlight*, a short, delicate selection done on piano. He had played it many times for Gladys; it seemed to calm her during those rare occurrences when she became

45

over excited.

Frank stood motionless over the grave as the soft piano notes washed over him and drifted off into the woods. Marcell dropped some wild flowers atop the mound of dirt and whispered a short prayer. When the piece ended, Frank selected one more, a Mozart Fugue in C minor. He had hoped Mozart the bear would hear it and show himself, but if he was around he was staying well hid.

By the time they finished the funeral, the sun had dipped below the peaks of the surrounding hills and a series of large cumulus clouds had moved into the area. In the distance, Frank thought he heard thunder and wondered if there would be rain. All summer he had fretted over the possibility of fire, had waited through early fall as the overgrown foliage turned brown and dry, had stayed up late when the Santa Ana winds hit, knowing everything could go up in flames in an instant. Now, as the huge clouds gathered around him like a curtain and the thunder drew closer with each roar, the air thick with the promise of rain, he realized his worrying had been in vain. It was not lightning or a careless match that would destroy his world, but two small chunks of metal, forged by men, with one purpose in mind.

The two men made a silent retreat from the grave, and then started their hike back toward Frank's cabin, Frank leading the way. His pace grew quicker and more deliberate with each step, Marcell doing his best to keep up with him, at times having to break into a jog, but somehow managing to stay close.

Frank did not utter a word all the way back. When they reached the cabin, he tossed his shovel to the ground and just stared off into the distance until the first drops of rain fell. He offered to heat up some soup, but Marcell said no, they should go to his cabin and he would prepare a meal; besides, he said, he was going to need a shower—he was covered in dirt—and some fresh clothes. Frank was exhausted and could barely keep his eyes open.

"We don't have to go tonight," said Marcell.

"What?"

"To L.A. We can wait till tomorrow."

Frank had leaned his rifle up against a tree. He reached over now and picked it up. "No, we go tonight. If I wait...we go now. I'll get some things. We'll change at your place."

It took them a little over an hour to find the apartment building. It was an older structure, just one building, maybe twenty units in all, and in need of serious repair, as were most of the buildings in the area.

Frank parked his Toyota truck across the street. "What's the apartment number?"

"Four."

"Okay, you wait here, keep an eye out. I won't be long."

"Oh, no," said Marcell. "I didn't just come along for the ride. I'm going in, too. That was the deal, remember? All the way."

"All right, but remember, you don't do anything unless I say."

"Oh, sure, Frank, absolutely. You're the boss."

The two men got out of the truck and started across the street toward the apartment building. An older car drove by very slowly. It sat so low to the ground, the bumpers almost scraped the road. Loud music blasted through the open windows. The young men inside the car gave Frank and Marcell a long hard look then continued on.

"Bangers," said Marcell, a tone of excitement in his voice. "They're kind of like us, don't you think? Protecting their turf."

Frank glanced toward the car then back to Marcell, but said nothing.

The apartment they were looking for was on the ground floor, facing the street. The number four tacked to the door was missing one nail and was hanging sideways. Frank pushed the number into an upright position then let it drop. It swung briefly like a pendulum, and then came to rest again in its original cockeyed position. He gently grabbed the knob and gave it a slight turn; it was unlocked. He nodded down to Marcell and both men readied their guns. Then Frank grabbed the handle again , pushed open the door and stepped inside.

The man seated at the kitchen table started to reach for his rifle, then, glancing over at the row of shiny bullets, pulled his hand away. Frank walked over to him and stuck his pistol right in his face.

"He's the one," said Marcell, pointing his finger at the man. "That's him, that's Freddie."

"Where are they?" asked Frank.

"Who?" Freddie was relatively calm for having a loaded .38 pointed at him. "What do you want?"

Frank cocked his pistol. "You have a nice hunt today?"

"I don't know what you're talking about?"

"Let me cut him," said Marcell. He pulled out a large hunting knife and began prodding Freddie with it.

"I'm gonna ask you one more time. You killed a couple of bears today, and you took some parts with you. I want them back, and I want them now."

Freddie shifted his eyes back and forth from Frank to Marcell. "Okay, okay, just take it easy with that knife."

"Put the knife away," Frank said to Marcell.

Marcell stuck the knife up to Freddie's throat. "You're lucky I don't cut your heart out. Maybe I still will." Then he pulled the knife away. There was a pizza on the table. Marcell stabbed a piece. "Do you mind?"

Freddie just looked at him, didn't say a word.

"The bladders," said Frank.

"And the claw," added Marcell. "Don't forget the claw."

"Listen, mister, all I did was shoot the mother. I didn't take no bladders."

"Where are they?"

"Veronica." Freddie told Frank about this girl, Veronica, and how she had hired them to go out and get some gall bladders, said she would pay them one thousand dollars for each one they got. He had only shot the mother bear, he said, but his partner, Cleve, had killed the little one and had done all the cutting.

"Where is this Veronica?" asked Frank.

48

"I don't know where she lives, I swear. It don't matter, anyway, cause she was taking the bladders to someone else."

"Who?"

"Some guy named Rudy. I think he lives in West Hollywood. That's all I know. I swear."

"This Veronica, why'd she come to you."

"I don't know, I guess cause I'm a hunter. She said Jack gave her my name."

"Jack who?"

"Jack from Jack's Rifles. I go in there a lot."

"Where's your partner?"

"I don't know."

Frank looked over at Marcell, who was into his second piece of pizza. "Let me see your knife." Marcell handed Frank his knife and set his pizza on the table. "Call 911, tell them where we are, tell them there's been an accident."

"Sure," said Marcell. "Happy to help." Marcell walked into the living room and picked up the phone.

"You right handed, Freddie? asked Frank.

"Yeah, why? What do you mean, an accident?"

"I'm going to give you a choice. You shot Gladys right through her left eye and you used your right hand to squeeze the trigger. So what's it gonna be?"

"What do you mean. Oh, man, no, you can't do that. She's just a bear."

Frank grabbed Freddie by the neck. "Just a bear! Just a bear! She was a beautiful animal. She had two children. She loved Chopin and strawberry ice cream and she liked playing tag with her cubs. All she wanted was to roam the woods and fish and be left alone, and you took it all away. Now I'm offering you your life, but I'm quick running out of patience, so you can choose the eye or the finger or I'll just put a bullet through that little fucking p-brain of yours right here and now. Choose!"

Freddie looked across the room toward Marcell, perhaps thinking he would get some sympathy, but Marcell only smiled and dialed the phone. He set his right hand on the table, examined it for a few seconds, then slowly pulled it away.

Marcell hung up the phone and returned to the kitchen. "They're on their way," he said. Then he went to the refrigerator and starting rummaging through it. "Don't you have anything to drink?"

Frank looked down at the sobbing Freddie. "What's it gonna be?"

"I don't know. How am I supposed to make a choice like that. It's crazy."

For a moment, Frank felt sorry for him, and a voice inside his head said maybe he should let him go, call the whole thing off, but then the picture of Gladys and Stumble filled his brain and he raised the knife up above his head. If Freddie wasn't going to make the choice, he'd make it for him. Then he heard the gunshot, followed by a dull thud as the bullet tore into Freddie's face and blood started dripping from his left eye. The large man didn't utter a sound, just keeled over in his chair, and fell hard onto the cheap linoleum floor. Frank looked over at Marcell. He had a paper bag in one hand and the gun—smoke rising from the barrel—still pointed at Freddie, in the other.

"What the fuck...why'd you do that?"

"He moved his hand off the table, I figured he was making his choice. Or maybe he was reaching for his knife. Check it out; in his boot. Sometimes being short has its advantages."

Frank checked Freddie's boot. Sure enough, there was a knife, but it was still in its case; not much chance of Freddie using it.

Marcell held out the bag. "Besides, he was lying to us. Look at this."

Frank took the bag from Marcell and looked inside. He slowly lifted Gladys's hand out and then quickly returned it. "Jesus...what kind of people are these?"

"Well, I'd say that one's a dead one."

"We better get out of here," said Frank.

"Wait. I have an idea. Give me the bag."

50

Frank handed Marcell the bag. He reached inside for the paw and set it on the table. Frank gazed down at the dead man. Blood was pouring out of his wound and onto the floor. He felt Marcell remove the knife from his hand and as he looked over at the paw, Marcell raised the blade over his head and quickly whacked off one of the claws. Then he walked around Frank, reached down to Freddie and laid the claw on top of his forehead. "A little message for the others."

Marcell stuck the paw back in the bag. "Time to go, Frank."

"Yeah, yeah, let's go."

The two men ran out of the apartment and crossed the street to their truck. A light rain had begun to fall. When they had arrived, the street was full of commotion but now everything was silent. Frank was amazed that no one had heard the gunshot, had come out to investigate. He started the truck and pulled away.

"There's no ambulance yet."

"I never called one," said Marcell. "Couldn't see the point."

"We're murderers, now. You know that, don't you?"

"Isn't that what you meant when you said 'all the way' Frank?"

Frank stared out at the darkness. All he really saw was the road ahead of him, as though he were in a long tunnel. He could feel the adrenaline pumping through his veins and the all too familiar churning in his stomach. He had tried to put all of that behind him, had gone to the woods looking for peace and he had found it Now, with the squeezing of a trigger that peace was shattered and there would be no putting it back together. Not in *this* life.

"I don't know," he said. "I don't know what it meant." ❧

FIVE

Cleve had followed Veronica to the Bonaventure hotel, had gone inside and watched her take the elevator up to the penthouse suite, had even attempted to reach that floor on another elevator, but of course there was no way he was getting access without a key. His arm was in a lot of pain and the bleeding had increased, so after a heated exchange with the concierge—a French gentleman who kept looking over the top of his bifocals at the bleeding arm—about his right to get onto any floor of the hotel, he got back into his car and went looking for a doctor.

It was late at night and the calls he made were all met with either an answering machine or an exchange. A girl from one exchange told him the doctor could see him first thing in the morning, to which Cleve replied he might not have an arm by then, and the girl suggested he go to the emergency ward of any hospital, or any one of a thousand walk-in clinics. She had said the word *any* with just the right inflection to suggest *any* idiot would already know that.

Cleve slammed the phone in her ear, got back in his car and started looking for a hospital. He went racing through the streets of Hollywood, cursing out loud at the bear, Freddie, the lousy five hundred bucks he got paid, fag doctors, Veronica and the fucking Bonaventure Hotel, all the time not having the faintest idea where a hospital might be. He'd only been in California a couple of months, and though he was sure he had driven by a hospital now and then, he certainly couldn't remember where one was. He was feeling like, well, like he wanted to kill somebody, anybody, just to give him a little satisfaction for all he'd been through that day.

It was at that moment, when he felt like maybe just running his car into a drunken pedestrian, that he saw what looked like a large red cross a block ahead. He slowed his car a little as he approached the neon sign. It *was* a red cross, lit up with a white background and at the bottom of the sign, in small red letters, was the word Mergicenter. It wasn't a hospital exactly, but fuck it, he thought, it'll do.

Cleve burst through the front door of the Mergicenter in a foul mood. Blood was dripping freely from the wound as he placed his bad arm on the counter.

"I need to see a doctor. Now!"

The receptionist was an overweight girl, borderline obese, maybe thirty years old; it was hard to guess her age, what with the drooping jowls and baggy eyelids. There were no other patients in the waiting room and she was obviously taking advantage of this quiet time to eat a meal, take a break. She had a couple of cheeseburgers, some fries and what looked like a milk shake all laid out before her. She bit in to one of the burgers.

"What seems to be the problem?" Ketchup was running down her chin.

Cleve stared at her in disbelief. "I have a headache. Oh, yeah, I also have one arm that's about ready to fucking fall off!"

The girl looked down at his wound, reached under the counter with her free hand and retrieved a slip of paper, which she placed in front of Cleve. "Fill this out. The doctor will see you in a moment."

Cleve picked up the sheet of paper, read the first line then gently set it back on the counter. The girl was now sucking whatever was in the paper cup through a straw. The straw rubbed against the hole in the lid and made an irritating screeching sound. Cleve reached down and grabbed the cheeseburger that had not yet been bitten into and began unwrapping it. He took a huge bite.

"Hey..."

Cleve set the burger down and pulled his pistol out from beneath his jacket. "Okay, fatty, here's what we're gonna do. You go lock the front door, then you take me back to see the doctor. Don't make any noise, and don't do anything stupid, all right, cause to tell you the truth, right now I'd just as soon put a bullet in your fat ass as look at your ugly face. Now move."

The girl set her drink on the counter, grabbed the key and tried to hand it to Cleve. "Could you do it?"

Cleve stuck the gun right in her face. "Get your fat ass up and go lock the door. And wipe the ketchup off your face."

The girl wiped her face with a napkin then slowly extricated herself from the chair and waddled around from behind the counter toward the door. Cleve stuck the gun in his pants, picked up the burger and took another bite. For a minute he considered shooting the girl; something about her weight really pissed him off. Here she was working in this mini hospital, walking around looking like Orca, eating all this crap; it was disgusting. Still, he couldn't just start shooting, at least not before he got his arm fixed. But, goddamn it, she better keep her mouth shut, not aggravate him in any way or he'd put some holes in her, no hesitation, drain out some of that fat.

The girl locked the door then flipped the sign over to read 'closed' from outside. Then she led Cleve down a narrow hallway to a small office. The sign on the door read, Dr. Aurivello.

The girl tapped lightly on the door before opening it. "Dr. Aurivello, there's a patient here that insists on seeing you."

Cleve pushed the girl into the room and stepped in behind her. The doctor was sitting at his desk. He had a small stack of papers in front of him, which he appeared to be working with. He dropped the papers and looked up, first at the girl, then at Cleve. Cleve had his gun out.

The doctor stood. "What's the meaning of this?"

"It's like Bertha says, doc. I need some attention."

The doctor was a frail looking man, late sixties, thick glasses. He went with Cleve and the girl into another room and had Cleve sit on the edge of a narrow, cushioned cot. He started gathering supplies from a cabinet and instructed the girl to remove Cleve's old bandage. All the time, Cleve kept waving the pistol back and forth from the girl to the doctor, who both, surprisingly enough, managed to stay relatively calm.

"That's a nasty looking wound, young man. What did you run into?"

"That's none of your business. Just fix it up."

"I'll need to give you a local before I stitch that up."

"No needles. You ain't slippin something in on me, get me to pass out."

The doctor got the syringe ready. "You'll have plenty of time to pull the trigger if you feel yourself passing out. If I try stitching you without this, you'll be jerking your arm around. I might puncture an artery. Then we'd really have a mess."

Cleve cocked the gun. "Okay, but I'm telling you, I so much as yawn, she gets one,"—he tapped the end of the pistol on his forehead—"right here. Understand?"

"Clearly. You know, you didn't need the gun. I would have patched your arm for you. That *is* why we're here."

Cleve thought about it for a moment. "The gun, asshole, says I don't pay. The gun says you don't tell anyone I was here. Besides that, I like my gun. I like showing it to people. I like to share. Now shut up and get to work."

Detective Kate Mallory was crouched over the body, her shoulder-length brown hair pulled back in a ponytail to keep it out of her face while she worked. Kate was thirty years old, seven years on the force, five as a detective. An attractive woman, her parents thought she'd become an actress or at least a model, but Kate knew by the time she was ten what it was she wanted. She loved solving mysteries, didn't matter how simple or complex, she just always wanted to get to the bottom of things. Once, when she was twelve, she saw a flyer stapled to a telephone pole with a picture of a missing white kitten. Kate went to the owner's house, spoke to them and then started her investigation. It took her two weeks, but she cracked the case. Seems it was the father who had gotten rid of the thing, took it to the pound. She learned her first big lesson on that one: never overlook the obvious.

Today's victim was lying on his side, one eye totally obliterated by the bullet, along with part of his cheek. There was a trail of dried blood that led from his eye socket down the side of his face to the linoleum floor, where a pool of blood the size of a large Frisbee sat coagulating. There was a splattering of blood on his unbuttoned shirt and more on his chest. The detective reached around to feel the back of the dead man's head. No hole there.

"I'm looking for Detective Mallory?" The voice sounded out of breath.

Kate stood up to greet the man behind the voice, got a whiff of his breath and quickly turned her head to the side. "You must be Lawrence."

"Yeah, that's me. You Mallory?"

"I'm Kate Mallory. Welcome to Hollywood." She removed her latex gloves and extended her hand to the detective, who took it briefly and gave a limp shake.

"Do me a favor, call me Tulary, okay?" He let go of her hand.

"Sure." Kate turned her attention to a couple of uniform police. "I'm through here."

"So what do we have?"

Kate gave the detective a quick once over. He wasn't a bad looking guy, still had a full head of hair, although there were streaks of gray among the brown. He was a little overweight, maybe twenty pounds, and his face seemed like he'd either been a smoker and a drinker all his life or spent too much time in the sun. She figured him for around forty-five, but he looked over fifty. No, it wasn't surfing in Malibu that had aged him; it was hard living, plain and simple.

"Freddie Diddlesby," she said, "minus one eye. No exit wound. I'd say he's been lying here at least four hours. Manager called it in."

Tulary laughed. "Diddlesby. What the hell kinda name is that?"

"Guy's got a rap sheet, minor stuff, B & E, petty theft. Kate grabbed a small plastic bag off the table and handed it to Tulary. "This was on the ground, next to the body."

"What is it?"

"Open it."

Tulary opened the bag and pulled out a small claw. "What the hell is this?"

"Well, it looks like a claw to me, or somebody's got some really bad teeth. Maybe it's a calling card."

Tulary dropped the claw back in the bag, then reached inside his jacket and removed a cigarette. "Diddlesby," he muttered, then stuck the cigarette in his mouth.

Kate looked at the cigarette. "You know better than that."

"You don't see any smoke, do you?" He stuck the cigarette behind his right ear. There was a rifle lying on the table, along with some cleaning utensils and a row of polished bullets. The rifle looked completely assembled.

"Bad timing for Mr. Diddlesby."

"How's that?"

Tulary pointed to the rifle. "Well, look at the gun. It's been cleaned and reassembled. If the shooter comes in a minute later than he did, the rifle is loaded and our boy here has a chance."

"Well, your assuming he keeps the rifle loaded. This is a guy who didn't even lock his door. Maybe he took them out of his pocket."

"Maybe. Has he got other guns in the house?"

"There are a couple of rifles in the bedroom."

"And…"

Kate began to feel a little agitated. "And, one of them was loaded and one wasn't."

"Well then, I guess it's a draw. So what else we got?"

"We pulled plenty of prints. My bet is none of them belongs to the bad guy, but we'll check them out. We've also got a shoe print in the blood, or I should say half a shoe. From the markings, I'd say some kind of hiking boot, but the funny thing is, it looks like it belongs to a kid, or maybe a woman; can't be bigger than a size four. Looks like our vic was into hunting, stacks of hunting magazines all over the place. I thought we'd check some local gun shops; start there. Somehow I don't think we're going to get much help from any of the neighbors."

Tulary smirked. "In *this* neighborhood. Strictly here no evil, see even less. So what do you think, robbery?"

"Well, I'd have to say yes, and no." Kate bent down by the body. Look at the pattern of blood behind his head; it's a nice clean circle. It looks to me like he landed on his back, then somebody else came in a couple hours later, after the blood had started to dry, and flipped him over on his side to get to his wallet, which, by the way, is empty." She stood up again. "We found an empty white envelope with Freddie's name scribbled on it."

"So, somebody had recently laid some cash on him."

"Looks that way."

Tulary reached down to the table and flipped open the lid to a pizza box. There was no pizza left.

"Dominoes."

"What?"

Tulary pointed to the empty pizza box. "The pizza. Maybe the deliver boy saw something."

"I think it's safe to assume he was murdered *after* he ate, by which time a Dominoes driver could probably have finished the Indy five hundred."

"Well, that may be true, but unless our boy here was real hungry, I'd say somebody else was here when the pizza showed up."

Kate got another whiff of his breath, definitely alcohol. "Or maybe our perp ate it; it's a hungry business, killing. Tell you what, though. I'll start with the gun shops; you can follow up on the pizza. Maybe get yourself some breakfast while you're at it."

"Not my style."

"No. I figured you for a pizza and beer kind of guy."

"Actually, I prefer Pizza Hut, but I'm sure that's no reflection on your ability as a detective. Are we gonna have a problem here?"

"With what?"

"I'm sensing an attitude, you know. Are we like moving into that wrong time of the month or something."

Kate noticed a couple of police watching them. She lowered her voice a little. "Can we go outside a minute?"

58

Tulary smiled. It was a boyish smile but one filled with irony. "After you," he said.

Once outside away from the crowd, Kate started in. "You show up here half an hour late, stinking of booze and you want to know if I'm starting my period. I don't know what you've got going, but don't dump your shit at my door, okay. I've got a homicide to solve, and I don't have time for some drunken, fifty-year-old, chauvinist asshole. Are we clear on that?"

Tulary shifted his weight back and forth, looked down at the ground, then rubbed his hand through his hair. He pulled the cigarette from behind his ear and lit it. "Like vodka, lady."

The bears have been moving closer to the house every day; I think they're starting to trust me. One of the cubs (I call him Stumble) is constantly tripping over himself. He is the most uncoordinated animal I have ever seen; it's amazing. He gets into everything and I have had to tie down anything I don't want destroyed lest he take it apart. A few days ago he fell into the hole I've been digging for the new cesspool. He couldn't get himself out and started crying right away. I started moving toward him to try and help but the mother chased me away and quickly removed him from the ditch. Then, I swear it's true, she actually started lecturing him; I could tell by the tone in her voice. Incredible.

I know no one would ever believe this but each of the three bears has a definite preference in music. The smallest one prefers Mozart, and there are certain pieces he prefers over others; he seems to be particularly moved by the flute. The mother, Gladys, is a Chopin lover. She is the most dedicated listener of the three and can sit still for as long as fifteen minutes listening to a piece. But here is the most amazing thing of all: the three of them, especially Gladys, respond to the music with the appropriate emotions. I have seen Gladys cry (violins always do her in) smile and even start to dance, and always at the right spot in the number.

I have followed them on occasion when they leave here, but Gladys has not yet allowed me to see her den. Once we get a mile or so from the cabin, she stops and turns toward me and gestures in a way that I have come to understand means 'far enough.' I must go into the city and see what I can find

59

in a library about these creatures. I am learning much about their habits but I am sure I could benefit from any research that may have been done.

Here's the big question. How could anyone even consider hunting one of these incredible animals? They are so like us and yet so unique. These woods are full of other bears and I know the hunters will always be out there. I can't protect them all, but I will not let anything happen to my family, no matter what.

Frank set the journal in his lap and stared out the bedroom window. It seemed like only yesterday when he wrote that entry, and now Gladys and Stumble were dead. He had vowed to protect them and he had failed. And Mozart, what would happen to him without Gladys to protect him? That must be his priority. He must find Mozart and take care of him.

He thought of the man, Diddlesby, and how he had been reticent to kill him. Now he was glad Marcell had done it, and promised himself he would not waver in the future. Something beautiful had been taken from him; that was reason enough. But this was bigger than that. He'd lost people in Vietnam and had felt that pain until he thought it would destroy him, and had managed to survive, to continue on.

But in a way, this was even worse. In Vietnam, everybody had a gun, everybody made a choice to be there. Even the draftees had a choice. They could have left the country, gone to Canada, faced the consequences of that decision. But what choice, what chance did Gladys and Stumble have. Someone, somewhere decided it would be nice to kill a couple of bears and have some of their body parts around as souvenirs. These people had no appreciation for life of any kind. They weren't out fighting for some ideology, right or wrong; it was merely sport, a way to keep oneself entertained. Since they placed such small value on life, Frank would allow them the same consideration. They would give up their lives, each and everyone of them involved in this pointless slaughter, and the world, somehow, would become a little bit better place.

He flipped through the pages of his journal to the end of his last entry and started writing.

Gladys and Stumble are dead; mutilated. I have met someone, a neighbor—a dwarf—named Marcell. He is an odd sort, and I don't mean just his dwarfism. He recites poetry—or rather injects bits of poems into his speech—and lives in a cabin close by, a cabin filled with books and pictures and music. He seems, how do I put it— magical. Even now, I'm not quite sure he wasn't just a dream. Tomorrow—if he does indeed exist—we search for Mozart. I have but two goals now: Protect Mozart and find the rest of the killers responsible for the murders. I am overwhelmed with grief. Words are no good. I will have my revenge. ❧

SIX

They were driving through Malibu Canyon in his Jag. The girl, Penny, had her dirty tennis shoes up on the leather seat and her arms wrapped around her legs. She wore the same Levis and shirt from the previous night. Her short blonde hair was uncombed and still wet from an earlier shower, and yet on her it looked good.

As they drove along, she stared out the side window. The thunderstorm from the previous night had moved through the area and left but a fraction of an inch of rain, but it had cleaned the air and made for a beautiful fall morning, the sky dotted with occasional clean white clouds.

Rudy was smoking a cigarette and had all the windows rolled up. He had on his wig and dark wrap-around sunglasses and a loosely fitted gold bracelet that rattled against the steering wheel every time he turned a corner. His potbelly rubbed it, too. He had the radio tuned to his favorite station, no music, just talk. The topic was violence on television and in the movies, and the host, Jerry Porter, was talking to a congressman. Rudy reached over and turned up the volume.

"There have been numerous bills brought before the legislature, Jerry. I introduced one myself last year. But you have to remember, Hollywood has a powerful influence in Washington, especially with the current administration. These people take the constitution and twist it around to suit their own needs..."

"Are you saying, sir, that freedom of speech should not apply to Hollywood?"

"What I'm saying is, we've got gratuitous sex and violence on the screen and it is directly effecting the morals of the youth in this country. Something has to be done."

Rudy glanced over at Penny. "Do you believe this shit? That son-of-a-bitch has been to the house a dozen times. Politicians. They don't come any hornier."

Penny just sighed, and continued staring out the window. Rudy turned off the main highway onto a narrow blacktop road. "Jerk-off," he said to the radio and shut if off. He reached over and gave Penny a nudge.

"Hey, cat got your tongue?"

Penny pushed a button and lowered her window, and then she stuck her head halfway outside where the air was cool.

"Hey, it's cold out there, roll up the window."

"I can't breathe."

"I don't give a shit. Do what I tell you."

She pulled her head in and glared over at Rudy. He reached down on his panel and raised her window.

"I can't breathe. Do you have to smoke?"

Rudy reached over and smacked her in the face with the back of his hand. "Let's get something straight, little girl. You're not a bad piece of ass, but you start giving me shit, I'll fix it so you never wanna look in a mirror again. You understand? And what's with the fucking ring in the nose? You some kind of Watusi, or something?"

Penny rubbed her face with her hand and started fidgeting with the small silver ring in her nostril. She had white, flawless skin, not a blemish to be seen; if you got rid of the bright red lipstick and purple eye shadow you'd have a real looker. Her gift was one of natural beauty but she was ruining it trying to look tough.

She rubbed the tears from her pale blue eyes. Rudy took his cigarette and squashed it in the ashtray. "There, you happy now? You want something from me, you ask me nice. You'll see, I can be generous. But you start with an attitude, we're gonna have problems. You talk to the other girls, they'll tell you, Rudy's okay. Just don't forget, I'm the boss."

They drove along for a few minutes in silence, Rudy glancing over at her now and then, Penny pretending not to notice as she gazed out the window. He turned onto a long dirt driveway that ran through a stand of eucalyptus trees. "Veronica's gonna take you shopping, get you some new clothes. How does that sound to you?"

Penny sighed. "Yeah, that's terrific." she said.

"Don't get too excited," said Rudy. "This is it, we're here."

He pulled the car to a stop in front of a large wrought iron gate. A tall stucco wall stretched out in both directions from the gate and disappeared into the trees. Rudy honked the horn, then opened his door and waved up at a camera mounted on the wall. The gate opened and he got back in the car.

The house was set back a good fifty yards from the fence. It was a large ranch style building with a red tile roof and white plaster walls. The driveway inside the gate was all brick and led to a large circular parking area in front of the house. In the middle of the circle stood a beautiful fountain of Venus de Milo. Two men with rifles sat on the edge of the fountain, smoking cigarettes. As Rudy pulled the car to a stop, one of the men got up from his seat and approached them.

Rudy opened his door and got out. The man peaked around Rudy and into the car at Penny.

"Hey, Rudy, got some new talent, huh." The man was much bigger than Rudy, and well built. In addition to the rifle, he had a pistol holster strapped around his shoulder.

Rudy looked back at Penny. "Let's go, sweetheart, out of the car."

Penny got out of the car and walked slowly toward the front door. Her clothes were almost rags, yet all three men watched her move as though she were parading down a ramp in a beauty contest.

"Hey, Rudy, man. When are you gonna let me be in one of your movies?"

Rudy looked the large guard over, and then he let out a short high pitch laugh. "I don't do fag flicks, Roberto."

"Hey, mother-fucker. That ain't funny."

Rudy patted him on the shoulder and went into his best Elvis. "Sure it is. Relax, I'm just kidding. I'm looking for a special girl, just for you, and when I find her, you'll get your chance."

Rudy pulled his shades down and winked at the second guard,

and then made his way to the front door. He and Penny went inside.

Roberto turned to the second guard. "One of these days I'm gonna kick that fat fuck's ass."

"Take it easy. Why would you want to be in a fucking porno, anyway?"

"I want some of that young pussy."

The second guard got up from the fountain wall and flicked his cigarette into the water. He was much smaller that Roberto, and much better looking, his dark hair slicked straight back, his face clean-shaven and tan. He removed his dark sunglasses, then pulled a hanky from his jacket pocket and began wiping the lenses.

"You don't have to be in a movie to get laid, Roberto."

"Yeah, Rudy'd never let me get close to any of his girls."

"Well, like you said, Rudy's nothing but a fat fuck. You want one of those girls, you let me know and she's yours."

"Really, Arnie, you can do that?"

"Really."

Roberto thought it over for a minute. "What if she doesn't want to?"

Arnie laughed out loud. "What's that got to do with anything?"

Penny had been somewhat impressed as they pulled into the driveway and she saw the red tile roof and the large fountain in the middle of the courtyard. This was Malibu Canyon, home of the stars, playground for the rich, and she was moving right into the middle of it. Things looked slightly different inside. The walls were off-white and badly in need of paint; the carpet, an old, green shag—older than Penny—the curtains worn and saggy, the color of tobacco stains. The living room had been turned into a studio of sorts. There was a king-sized bed in the middle of the room, a few erotic pictures on the walls and plenty of lights.

Rudy's pornos were all shot in here and they were all basically the same, no script, no story, just one or two young girls—the younger the better—and a guy, their instructions simple: get into the bed and have sex; make it as wild as possible. The films were all short, twenty minutes, and all shot with one video camera. They were cheap to make and easy to reproduce. Nothing was changed but the sheets, and not that often.

One of the bedrooms had been set up with a dozen VCRs. Once a film was shot, Rudy's photographer would spend an afternoon making copies, box them up and send them off the very next morning to Rudy's distributors. When things were going good and Rudy had a large stable of girls, he might make as many as five films a week, each of which was guaranteed to sell between three and five hundred copies, at a profit of three dollars apiece. And that was wholesale! Rudy had a list of two hundred regular customers who bought direct and paid upwards of ten bucks each.

His biggest problem was keeping fresh talent around. He catered to a special clientele, mostly older men—and some women—who wanted to watch young girls (children) being initiated into the world of sex. After the girls had been in ten or twelve flicks, they would start getting jaded and the element that attracted the customers in the first place—their innocence—would vanish and Rudy would have to retire them and bring in some fresh faces.

The routine went like this: A new girl arrives, she makes movies for a couple of months, maybe pulls a few tricks in-between pictures, then she's retired from films and put to work doing Johns or the occasional private film. The older the girl gets, the less valuable she becomes until eventually Rudy either sells her to any one of a dozen pimps, she overdoses on drugs, or, if she has become a real nuisance, she is sold off to Mexico. A couple of girls had even found a permanent home right there in Malibu Canyon; bodies *that* little didn't require much digging.

Typically, Rudy would pick his girls up when they were around thirteen and was through with them before they were old enough to drink. Some stuck around longer. (Veronica was twenty-six.) As long as they could turn a profit, they had a home with Rudy.

He showed Penny around the house, told her how she was

going to be in the movies, make a lot of money, meet some interesting people; hell, with her looks, she might even become a star. He showed her to her bedroom—she'd be sharing with two other girls—and told her to relax, enjoy the house. His photographer would be back in a week or so, and she could get started in her first film. In the meantime, he'd put her with a few Johns, get her broken in; teach her a few tricks of the trade.

Before he left, he pulled out his wallet and handed Penny a couple of hundred dollar bills. "Here, a girl's gotta have a little spending cash. If you need anything else, just ask Arnie or Roberto. They're always around. They'll take good care of you."

Veronica had had a long night. It was bad enough she had to pick up the girl, Penny, and take her to Rudy's, then turn around and go over to the Bonaventure for her appointment with O'Neill; but O'Neill had brewed up some tea from the bladder and either the stuff had worked like it was supposed to or just believing it would had turned him into a new man, for he managed to keep her going until four in the morning; the guy was usually only good for one pop, and that never took more than half an hour. To make matters worse, along with his improved sexual prowess came a bit of rough play, leaving Veronica with some bites and bruises she hadn't counted on. He had slipped her an extra five hundred, thinking it would make her happy, but when she left there she promised herself she'd be back, only next time not for sex.

She was still half asleep now, it was almost noon, and her cool silk sheets felt good against her sore body. She thought she heard someone knocking at the front door; then it quickly turned to a pounding. She dragged herself out of bed and slipped into a robe. There was a bruise the size of a grapefruit on her thigh and she cursed out loud. The pounding at the front door got louder.

"All right. I'm coming!"

Veronica peered through her peephole. She couldn't believe her eyes. It was that fucking asshole friend of Freddie's, Cleve. She double-checked her chain latch, and then she opened the door a couple of inches.

"What the fuck you want? You don't come to my house."

"Open the door."

"Fuck you, go away."

"Open the door, bitch. Freddie's dead. I need to talk to you. Now!"

"That's bullshit. Freddie not dead."

"Listen, I'm telling you, he's dead. He's got a huge fucking hole where his eyeball used to be. Now, you either open this door or I'm gonna knock it down."

Veronica gave Cleve a long hard look. He was crazy enough to do it— knock down the door. Could Freddie really be dead?

"Just a minute," she said. "I have to get dressed."

"Well, make it quick. And don't try anything cute."

"Rough night, huh?" Cleve was referring to the large bruise on Veronica's neck. He was sitting on her new white couch sucking down a beer. His injured arm was in a sling and he had his jacket wrapped part way over it, the empty sleeve dangling at his side.

Veronica put her hand up to her neck to feel the bruise. It had been a long time since anybody had gotten rough with her and she wondering if maybe there really was something to all that gall bladder business. O'Neill was kinky, had even tied her up a couple of times, but nothing like this. The thought of it all pissed her off and now she had this cretin sitting on her brand new sofa, drinking her beer.

"If it's rough play you like, you should have told me..."

"Cut the shit, Cleve. What you want? What happened to Freddie?"

Cleve set the empty beer bottle on the coffee table and belched. "Freddie, my dear, is no more. Freddie is kaput, history, out, of, the, picture." He got up from the couch and headed toward the kitchen. "Mind if I have another beer?"

"Okay, Freddie's dead. So what. Why you tell me?"

"Oh, well," Cleve yelled from the kitchen, "it's not his death that's important,"—he returned to the living room and leaned down and half whispered in her ear— "it's who killed him that matters." He returned to his seat on the couch.

"You probably killed him. Take his money."

"Oh, I took his money, all right. But I didn't kill the poor bastard. But I know who did. Boy, what a mess it was, too. Shot him right through the eye. Poor Freddie."

"How you know this?"

"Because, I went over there last night, after I got back from the doctor." He lifted his wounded arm. "Remember this?"

"So, who killed him?"

"The way I see it, that's on a need to know basis. And you ain't got any needs that really concern me. However, your friend at the Bonaventure, he has needs, and I'm the guy that can fill those needs for him, and you're just the slut to take me to him."

Veronica laughed. "Oh, you are fucking crazy. I no take you anywhere, especially not there."

Cleve sat up on the edge the couch and looked around the apartment. A lot of money had been dumped on furniture and art, nice looking stuff, very classy; even Cleve could see this. "This is a nice place. I like what you've done with it; everything is so...coordinated. Did you do this all yourself or did you hire a decorator?"

Veronica just stared up at him.

"Yeah, real nice." He took a long drink from his beer then grabbed the bottle by the neck and smashed it against the edge of the coffee table, beer and glass flying all over the couch and floor. Veronica jumped out of her seat.

"What are you doing!"

Cleve went over to her. He had half the broken bottle in his hand, which he promptly stuck against the side of her face. "You think that joker last night hurt you. You don't know hurt. Me, I like hurting things; it makes me feel...well, I guess happy would be the best word for it. So, if you want to make me happy, then let's not go over and see your friend. Let's stay here and play. Is that what you want? You want to make me happy?"

"Yes...no. I take you, I take you."

Cleve lowered the bottle from her face. She was staring him right in the eye, a look full of hate. "Now, just one more thing. Perhaps you recall our conversation, the one in which I offered you five hundred dollars for your services. Well, I've changed my mind. I think I want it for free. Yeah, I definitely think free is a much better price. Call it restitution for what you did to my arm. That would be—how do they say it?—full value for my dollar."

Veronica reached up and ran her hand through his hair. "You pretty tough guy, huh? Maybe I like tough guy."

Cleve dropped the bottle on the floor, then grabbed her hand in his and slowly started to squeeze it until Veronica began whimpering with pain. "You're hurting me. Let me go."

"Let's get something clear. I ain't one of your chump clients you can fuck with. Fact is, I'd just as soon cut you as fuck you, so watch your step around me. Understand?"

"I understand. Please, let me go."

Cleve released her hand. "That's better. I like that tone. You learn quick. Now, pick up the phone and call our friend, tell him you're coming over."

"He not there."

"What do you mean, he's not there?"

"He not live at hotel."

"Well, where does he live?"

"I don't know. I only go to hotel."

Cleve grabbed her by the arm and gave it a twist. "If you're lying to me..."

"I'm not lying. I see him again in a couple of days."

Cleve let go of her arm. "Fuck! Okay, okay. Here's what we do. I'll give you the number where I'm staying. You call me when it's time to go over there. And don't fuck around with me. I don't hear from you, I'm coming back here and you're gonna be one sorry whore. Understand?"

Veronica shook her head, yes.

"Good, now get your clothes off."

The door to Lieutenant Horton's office was open but Kate Mallory gave a light knock before entering. He looked up briefly, waved her in, then continued with his paperwork. "With you in a minute," he said.

William (Billy) Horton was a former linebacker turned cop who had worked his way up in ten years from pounding a beat to running a division, one of the first black lieutenants on the job. He'd worked for Davis and Gates and now Williams, had been through the Watts Riots in sixty-nine, the Rodney King fiasco in ninety-three and everything in between. Everyone said he was tough but fair, and honest; maybe too honest for his own good. He had the brains, he could have kept going up the ladder, maybe even gotten into politics, but Billy Horton wouldn't play the game. Hell, even being a lieutenant was sometimes too much. He envied his detectives, out in the field, putting the pieces of the puzzle together, somewhat removed from the public relations bullshit. But the promotions kept coming and he needed the money; and, if pressed, he'd admit, he did it partially for his race. He never intended to be a hero, but damn, somebody had to get in there and take on those positions, open the door for the next generation. Whenever he'd start feeling sorry for himself, he'd think of Jackie Robinson, how all the man wanted to do was play baseball—which he got to do, no denying that—and ended up having to be some kind of role-model and public figure. Damn near killed him.

"Let me guess," he said. "You're here to talk to me about Tulary."

Kate had been studying a picture on the wall. At the sound of Horton's voice, she turned around. "Yeah, Billy, I am." She pointed to the picture. It was of a group of young black men dressed in football gear. "Is that..."

"O.J. Simpson. That's me in the middle. Long time ago. How's it going on that shooting last night?"

"Well, it's a little early. We've got a few leads we're going to run down. Do you think he did it, Billy?"

"Who?"

"Simpson."

Horton looked very distraught. "I don't know Kate. I don't want to believe he did. I just don't know. Tell me about this claw you found."

"Some animal claw; I think it was left there on purpose. I've got the boys in the lab checking it out."

Horton gestured to a chair. "Have a seat. And close the door, will you?"

Kate closed the door and took a seat across the desk from the Lieutenant. She had on a pair of light blue Levi's, a white shirt and a dark blue sport coat. She usually tied her hair back in a ponytail, but today she let it hang free down to her shoulders. Lieutenant Horton took a long, hard look.

"My, you are a sight for sore eyes, detective. If I wasn't so damn old and happily married I might try out some of that sexual harassment I been hearing so much about."

"I've seen your wife, Billy. I'm sure she gets harassed enough for the both of us."

"Amen to that. So, what's up?"

"Well, I'd like to know what the story is with Detective Lawrence. I don't want to start trouble for him, okay, so, think of this as off the record, but, he showed up at the scene this morning slightly tanked and, quite frankly, I think he has an attitude about working with a woman. If you don't mind my asking, what's he doing in West Hollywood, and why did you put him with me?"

Horton leaned back in his chair. "How long you been on the job now, five, six years?"

"Seven."

"You're what, thirty-two?"

"Thirty, thank you. What's your point?"

"Well, let me just give you an overview of the situation. Tulary's been on the job now, well, close to twenty-five years. He's a bit old school, but he's a good cop. Now, I don't want to go too deep into

72

his personal life, but let me just tell you, he's got some problems at home, you know, his wife left him not too long ago, problems with his kids, stuff like that. Now, I can tell you this, it ain't easy reaching fifty even under the best of conditions, but for a cop who's been out there on the line most his life, it can be pure hell. Hopefully, you won't experience it."

"So we're talking mid-life crisis here. Is that it?"

"Well, I don't go much for labels. I can tell you that when I was thirty, fifty seemed like a long ways away, and then bamm, I woke up one morning and there it was. You start thinking to yourself, if those last twenty years went by so quick, how about the next twenty, and before you know it, you're afraid to go to sleep for fear you'll wake up an old man and your life will be over. I don't mean to get melodramatic about it, but it's a pretty serious thing. You take Tulary, he's been married a long time, now he's alone, he's a little overweight, his hair line's receding, maybe he sees a young woman like you, maybe he's attracted to you, maybe he wishes he was young enough to do something about it..."

"Jesus, Billy, he's fifty, not seventy."

"That's my whole point. I think he thinks he is seventy, not literally, but, you know what I mean. He's not seeing a lot out there in his future, right now."

"Well, what am I suppose to do, resurrect the guy? Is that why you put him with me?"

Horton laughed. "No, no, of course not. I put him with you because you're a good cop, one of my best. Tulary won't work with someone who's not up to snuff. And, you know, I thought maybe you might be a good influence on him, you being kind of a health nut and not drinking and all that."

Now it was Kate's turn to laugh. "Billy, the guy needs professional help. I'm just a cop. This guy, he's...he's a walking disaster."

"Will you try, Kate, as a favor to me?"

"He must mean a lot to you."

"We go way back. Listen, this is his last shot. Just between you and me, nobody else would take him. You're right, he is a walking disaster, but I have to give him this chance. What do you say?"

"Well, I'll try, Billy, for you. But I have to tell you, I'm not gonna kiss the guys ass, just because he's troubled. And the drinking part, I can't have somebody watching my back if they're not a hundred per cent."

Horton stood up from his desk and extended his hand out to Kate. "I'll talk to him about the drinking, Kate. I appreciate your help."

Kate got up from her seat and the two shook hands. "One question, Billy, just curious. Where did the Tulary name come from?"

"Larry Lawrence. Two Larrys."

Kate rolled her eyes. "What genius came up with that?"

"Actually, that would be me."

"Oh."

"I'm working on a name for you too."

"Terrific."

"Oh, listen, about that claw. There may not be any connection here, but, we had a call early this morning from this Emergicenter over on Robertson. Seems a man was treated late last night for a wound on his arm. According to the doctor, the wound looked like it had been inflicted by a large animal."

"I'll check it out."

"One other thing. You should know before you go over there. The doctor and his nurse were discovered this morning by a custodian. The patient had left them tied up all night in a closet."

"It could have been worse."

"Well, actually, it is a little worse. They were nude and, how can I put this, in a rather odd position."

"Odd, how?"

"In a word, doggy style. I'm telling you this ahead of time so you don't get yourself in an embarrassing situation."

"You're kidding me."

"No, and it's even worse, Kate. Evidently, the doctor got

aroused by the whole thing and..."

"Don't. Don't even say it. Thanks for the info, boss. I'll check it out."

"Yeah, great. And Kate, thanks again..."

"Don't thank me yet, Billy, I might end up killing the guy." ❧

SEVEN

Two days after her visit from Cleve, Veronica drove out to the Malibu house to pick up Penny and take her shopping. Rudy had told her he did not want to see Penny in her ragged jeans one more day; he didn't want any of his girls looking cheap. Veronica had not bothered mentioning the incident with Cleve to Rudy, who would of course not be happy to find out somebody knew about O'Neill, had in fact demanded to meet the man. This would bring much heat down on Rudy, which would in turn bring even more trouble for Veronica. It was a sticky situation, and yet, Veronica felt confident she could figure out some way to deal with it. She was not one easily frightened.

She had come to America a few years after the Vietnam war, had in effect, been sold to a rich couple in exchange for helping get them into the country. She was only ten years old at the time. It was all part of the Amerasian policy. Children of American G.I.s were allowed into the country, even had their flight paid for, and could bring their adopted Asian parents with them. Rich Vietnamese wanting to migrate to America simply found an Amerasian orphan—or one whose mother was desperate—and agreed to bring the child to America, be his or her parents, take care of the child once they got here in exchange for helping them get in. Unfortunately, many of them abandoned their "children" as soon as they reached this country, leaving hundreds like Veronica to fend for themselves.

And so Veronica found herself alone in a new country at age ten, no money, unable to speak English, no way to survive. Small wonder she was selling herself by the time she was eleven, had slit a man's throat at fifteen, had been an alcoholic and drug addict by sixteen. But all that was in the past now. She'd been clean over ten years, had worked her way up as a prostitute to her present day position with Rudy, bringing in over a hundred grand a year. She was—and Rudy knew it—the backbone of the whole operation. She found the girls, trained them, weeded out the duds, even directed for some of the pornos. A few more good years and maybe she'd retire, perhaps even return to Vietnam, find her mother.

She would have to deal with Cleve, there was no doubt about that; he was not one to just go away. But in the meantime she had a job to do. Penny needed grooming, needed clothes, and she needed a lot of work if she wanted to be one of Rudy's girls. Most of these girls show up with a few hours experience in somebody's back seat and they think they've got what it takes, and when it comes to a horny sixteen year old boy from Kansas, maybe that's true. But most of Rudy's clients were not that easily satisfied. Many were older and not easily aroused, their libidos beaten down by age and gravity. It took a lot of work to breath life back into those old bones.

Veronica picked up Penny around noon and the two of them took off in her Mercedes through Malibu canyon. Penny wanted to put the top down but it was overcast and cool and Veronica said no, causing Penny to pull her legs up under her chin and begin to sulk.

"You take feet off seat. This nice car."

Penny rolled her eyes and slowly moved her feet off the seat. "Can't do anything."

"You want put feet on seat I take you back to bus station. You like better there?"

Penny remained silent.

"You lucky girl, I find you. Life very hard on street."

"Doesn't look so great at that house. What's with those morons with the guns?"

"They protect you."

"I don't like the way they look at me."

"They won't do anything. Rudy won't let them." Veronica looked over at the young girl. She was biting at her fingernails and spitting out the pieces. Veronica reached over and slapped her hand. "That very bad habit. Look at my hands. See how beautiful. Cheap whore bite nail, not beautiful woman."

Veronica did have beautiful hands, her nails were long and painted red, her fingers slender and graceful, like her mothers. She had trouble picturing her mother's face now, it had been so long, but she would never forget her hands. Veronica had been so frightened that day, she could not look into her mother's eyes but chose instead to watch her hand, thinking if she kept her eye on it, it would not let go. It had held onto Veronica right to the last minute, when the new "father"—what was his name?— separated the two of them and dragged the sobbing young girl from her shack. It was an image carved in her mind forever, her mother's hand clinging to her tiny arm so tight that it hurt, the unpainted fingernails, short and plain, worn down from hard work, the fingers, long and slender—they could encircle Veronica's arm— the huge veins that ran like rivers through the dark, rough field of skin.

"Why do I have to have sex with Rudy?"

"Rudy's the boss. If he wants sex, you give him sex."

"He's so...horrible."

Veronica let out a tiny laugh. "Never tell Rudy that. He thinks he is very sexy, like Elvis Presley."

"I can't stand to have him touch me."

Veronica pulled the car over to the side of the road and turned off the motor. "Maybe you should go home...while you still have a choice. Maybe this not good job for you. I drop you off in town, tell Rudy you ran away."

"I'll never go home." There was a determination in her voice, a strength not displayed prior to now. "There is no *home*."

"Okay. If you don't want go home, then I teach you everything about men, teach you how to make plenty money. You pretty girl. All men want to fuck pretty girl. I teach you how to fuck them so they pay plenty. It's not so bad, once you get used to it. You do everything Veronica tells you."

"Have the other girls been there long?"

"Those girls, stupid girls. They snort too much cocaine, too much party all the time. You don't be like them, you end up on street again, or dead. Today we buy you some clothes, some lingerie. Then we get you a manicure and a haircut, turn you into beautiful woman."

"Just like in Pygmalion."

"No, no, not like pig."

"No, Veronica, Pygmalion. It's a book. A play from school."

"Oh. You like books?" Her tone was very serious.

Penny shrugged her shoulders. "Sometimes. You have to read them in school. Some of them are okay. You know."

"No. I never read books."

"Really. Even in school."

"I never went to school."

"Well, you didn't miss much."

Veronica looked over at the young girl. She wanted to tell her just how much she did miss, how much better off Penny would be if she were still in school. She wanted somehow to save her and yet felt helpless to do so. She even wanted to love her, but had learned long ago to love was to make oneself vulnerable, to jeopardize ones own survival, and she was, above all else, a survivor. Love was a luxury Veronica couldn't afford. Love had broken her mother's heart, the longing for love had caused Veronica to make a lot of mistakes on the street, had led her to booze and drugs. Love was dangerous. She would teach Penny what she could, protect her if possible, but she would be—like all the rest—on her own. She seemed smarter than most of the girls on the street. Perhaps she would make it.

Rudy Carlyle handed the keys to his Jag to the parking attendant and proceeded into the Bonaventure Hotel. He wasn't wearing his wig or his sunglasses, never did when he came to see O'Neill. It wasn't like O'Neill had said something to him about it—he'd never even seen Rudy's wig—Rudy just figured he wouldn't care for it.

O'Neill hadn't said much on the phone, just that he wanted to see him right away. Rudy thought maybe he was going to offer an explanation for the rough play with Veronica, which Rudy was more than a little curious to hear. If anyone was going to be slapping his girls around it was going to be him. Still, he couldn't play it too hard. It was basically O'Neill's operation. He owned the Malibu house, he supplied most of the customers. Rudy had made a lot of money off him in the last year; he didn't want to upset the apple cart. And of course, there was always fear.

He would let O'Neill say his piece first; maybe he'd be apologetic. If not, Rudy would have to bring it up, lean on the business angle, how it only hurts everybody involved if the merchandise (Veronica) gets damaged. He rode the elevator up to the penthouse, running different scenarios through his head, figuring out the best way to present his case. Semantics was the key, he decided. Gotta use the right words at the right time. Gotta be smart, earn the man's respect.

A guard greeted him at the door and let him in and a young man dressed in slacks and a white silk shirt escorted him to the living room. Rudy did not recognize the houseboy; seemed like every time he came up here there was a new one. They all had one thing in common—they were extremely good-looking; too good-looking if you asked Rudy. He couldn't help but wonder if O'Neill was doing them; wouldn't put it past him.

It was two in the afternoon but O'Neill was still in his robe, a bright gold with black trim; Rudy figured silk. He was sitting in a black leather-upholstered chair, smoking a cigar with one hand and stroking the back of a white Cheshire cat with the other. The drapes were pulled back and O'Neill was admiring the view, though it really wasn't much of a day outside, a hazy afternoon, thick with smog.

"You wanted to see me, Mr. O'Neill?"

O'Neill set his cigar in an ashtray and gave the cat the full attention of both hands.

"Look at that sky, Rudy. It's brown. Ugly. Filthy."

"Yes, sir. Well, that's L.A." Rudy tried to be upbeat.

O'Neill turned his attention to Rudy, eyeing him inquisitively, then shook his head as if in disgust. Rudy wondered if the look was for him or the sky.

"Have a seat, Rudy. Steven, get Rudy a drink."

Rudy tried to wave him off. "Nothing for me..."

"Nonsense. Let me think. You're a gin drinker, right?"

"Uh, yeah, yeah, that's right." He lied.

"Gin and tonic for Mr. Carlyle, Steven, and a club soda for me."

Rudy took a seat on the couch, also black leather. The cushion sank beneath him but it did not make Rudy feel particularly comfortable. Being around O'Neill always brought out the worst in him. He felt like some obsequious waiter, ready to do anything to please, unable to control his inferiority. He was so...self-conscious. Steven returned with the drinks then quietly left the room without saying a word.

O'Neill sat in his chair directly across from Rudy, staring a hole right through him, his cat curled up in his arms like a young lover, his fingers disappearing beneath the thick white fur. Rudy tried his best to relax, but the staring, as if O'Neill were reading his mind, unnerved him terribly. He had to speak.

"What was it you wanted to see me about?"

O'Neill set the cat down on the floor and took a sip from his club soda. "Do you always drink in the middle of the day, Rudy?"

What! He was the one that suggested the drink. Rudy didn't even like gin. It was a test and he had failed, or maybe it was a test he couldn't possibly have passed. If he'd rejected the drink would O'Neill have chastised him for being rude?

"No, no, actually I rarely drink at all."

"Oh, I see," said O'Neill, but very condescending. "Well, I certainly hope I haven't started you on some new trail of vice."

Rudy tried to think quickly. "No, no, it's just, you know, sometimes something can just sound good at the moment. The gin sounded refreshing."

"Well, let's not dwell on it. As long as it doesn't get in the way of business. I wanted to talk to you about the gall bladder. I must say, I was a bit skeptical, that is, I've sold quite a few in the past, but until the other night I had never really tried it out. You know, that stuff is big with the Orientals. Naturally, I just assumed it was all hocus-pocus stuff—you know, they're a strange group of people—but, let me tell you, Rudy, there is something to it." He smiled and shook his head. "It was quite an experience."

"Yes, uh, Veronica mentioned it to me. In fact..."

"She did, well, terrific." It was a throw away comment.

O'Neill stood up from his chair. He was a tall man, over six feet, thin and in good shape, still handsome at sixty. He walked over by Rudy so that he stood above him staring down.

"To the point then. I want more of them, as many as you can get. And I want you to look into other animal parts. I hear Rhino tusks are quite potent, and monkey brains, they say they make quite a delicacy. Do we have monkeys in California?"

"I, uh..."

"Well, you check it out. It's always good to diversify. Oh, and, one more thing. I have a client coming in this weekend from Hong Kong. We're going to do some business, make some money. Anyway, he'll need to be entertained. He wants the movie treatment, something young, not too worn out. You got something good for him?"

"Yeah, sure, I can take care of him, but I don't have anyone to shoot the video. My guy's on vacation."

"I'll send somebody with him." He pulled an envelope from his robe pocket. "This is for you. Thanks for coming by."

Rudy took the envelope and stood up. He started to extend his hand to O'Neill but he had already stuck both *his* hands in his pockets. Rudy wasn't sure what to do. Nothing had been said about beating on Veronica; and what was all that stuff about monkeys? He had to mention Veronica, he knew it, it was now or never.

"There is just one other thing...if you have a minute."

O'Neill seemed taken aback by Rudy's bold behavior. "Yes."

"Well, it's about Veronica. She kinda mentioned, well, I guess you got a little rough with her the other night."

"And."

"Well, you know, Veronica has other customers and it doesn't look good if she shows up all black and blue."

O'Neill put his arm around Rudy and slowly started escorting him toward the door. "Tell me something Rudy. Do you make a lot of money off of me?"

"Oh, yeah, sure. No complaints in that department."

"And this, Veronica, she basically works for me, right? That is, you set the schedule, but I am the one who has financed this operation. Correct?"

Rudy nodded.

"Well, then, why are we having this discussion?"

"Well, it's just, Veronica is very valuable to me, to us. If something should happen to her..."

O'Neill laughed out loud and slapped Rudy on the back. "Now, what could happen, Rudy? Worse case scenario, you get another girl. She's a whore, for Chrissake."

They reached the front door. "Work on that stuff for me Rudy. Oh, and one more thing." His tone became very serious. "You ever question me again about my behavior, I'll have you run through a meat grinder and feed you to my cat. Understood?"

"Yes, sir."

"Good. Now get out of my sight."

Kate Mallory was in her office with Detective Lawrence. He had his feet up on her desk and was flipping matches into her trashcan. It looked to Kate like he was wearing the same suit from the night they first met; in fact, it looked as though he had maybe been sleeping in it. But from her side of the desk she couldn't smell any alcohol. That was something.

"I checked with the kid who delivered the pizza," he said. "Said there was another guy there and he thinks maybe the guy had some kind of wound on his arm."

"He thinks?"

"He delivers pizza, you know. Let's not expect too much. Said the guy had his jacket thrown over his arm, but that he might have had it in a sling. And, he was sitting on the couch having a beer, like he belonged there, while our vic sat cleaning his gun. Anyway, we went through some pictures but he didn't pull anybody. I put him with one of the artists, see if we can come up with a sketch. You know, I used to deliver pizzas, back when I first got married. I'd forgotten all about that. Shitty job."

"I'll keep that in mind. This sounds like the same person that robbed that couple outside their apartment, and played matchmaker at the Mergicenter.

"Busy boy," said Tulary as he flipped another match. It was like he had split himself in two, the smaller portion going to Kate.

"The couple said he was trying to get them to let him into their building, they refused and he pulled a knife. His arm was bleeding pretty bad."

"Why do you suppose he wanted in?"

"I don't know. I can't figure it. The doctor that worked on his arm says the wound was caused by some kind of animal, which fits very nicely with the claw we found at Mr. Diddlesby's apartment." Kate reached into her desk and retrieved a plastic bag with the claw inside. She tossed it on the table. "Fish and Game says this came from a black bear. Ursus Americanas. " She stared at Tulary's feet. "Are you comfortable?"

Tulary removed his feet from the desk, pulled a cigarette from his pocket and stuck it in his mouth. "Don't panic. I'm not gonna light it. What about prints?"

"Couple of partials, nothing to work with. The shoe print in the blood came from some kind of hiking boot, size four and a half or five."

"Well," said Tulary, "maybe it's a father-son team. Never too young to learn."

One of Tulary's matches hit the side of the trashcan. Kate glanced over at it then back to Tulary. "Anyway, I'm thinking the one with the bad arm went out to run his errands, and while he was gone our perps came in and gave Freddie an eye exam."

"And they leave the claw as a message for the partner, a warning. They're coming for him next." Tulary removed the cigarette from his mouth and leaned forward. "Then Freddie's pal returns, takes Freddie's money, wipes the place down and clears out."

"Exactly." Kate couldn't quite figure Tulary. One minute he's far away, indifferent, bored, the next he sounds like a man eager for his work.

"But the claw was still there."

"Maybe he didn't see it. Or maybe he was too stupid to figure it out."

"I don't know," said Tulary. "Doesn't make sense; none of it. Freddie's partner gets cut up by the bear, then he stops to commit a robbery on his way to the doctor. Why strong-arm the doctor? And why do a couple of small time thugs kill a bear in the first place?"

"Well, the last part is easy. Evidently, there's big money in gall bladders, paws, things like that."

"How big are we talking?"

"Millions."

"Millions, huh. How many bears does it take to make a million bucks?"

"Well, according to this lieutenant with Fish and Game—Wilko, I think was his name—a gall bladder can go for twenty, thirty thousand dollars. They're real big in the Asian community."

"For what?"

"Medicine, herbs, aphrodisiacs."

Tulary sighed, shook his head. "Man, it always come down to sex" He leaned back in his chair and rubbed his hands through his hair, stared up at the ceiling for a few seconds and then brought the chair down on all four legs. "Well, I suppose we should check with a few of our local animal rights whackos. I'm sure they have some strong opinions about gall bladder stew." He stuck the cigarette back in his mouth.

"You think somebody has to be a whacko to care about animals?"

"Gee, detective, I thought we were talking about a murderer."

"Let me ask you this. What would you do, somebody came into your back yard, killed your dog and sold his parts for money? What would you do if you caught him?"

"Well, that would depend on whether or not he went inside the house and finished off my wife while he was at it. Of course, he'd never make any money off *her* parts; not for an aphrodisiac."

Kate smirked. She had promised herself she wasn't going to get into it with Tulary, wasn't going to let his drinking or his attitude disrupt her, but there was something about him, the way he slouched into the chair, and that look on his face, like he knew better than anybody about everything, his cigarette hanging from his lip a constant reminder to her and anyone else that he would do what he wanted, when he wanted; something about him that made her want to lash out. And maybe that's just what he wanted, keep her and everybody else on edge, let them be a part of his suffering. She pulled a pack of matches out of her desk, lit one and leaned over to him.

"Here, I don't want to get on your bad side."

Tulary stood up from his chair, took the cigarette from his mouth and stuck it in his shirt pocket. Then he leaned over and blew out the match.

"I'm trying to quit." ❧

EIGHT

"I need to stop and rest a minute, Frank," said Marcell. They were out in the woods, had been all day, and Frank had been keeping a pretty good pace.

"It'll be dark in a few hours."

"I'll be dead by then if I don't rest."

"I guess we have been pushing it. We'll stop for awhile."

Marcell removed the small pack from his back and opened it. He pulled out a couple of packets wrapped in aluminum foil and handed one to Frank. "Here."

"What is it?"

"Sandwich."

"You eat it, I'm not hungry."

"You need to eat, Frank, keep up your strength. Come on, I made them myself, they're good."

"What is it?"

"Wheat gluten."

"Sounds great."

"Try it, tastes like roast beef."

Frank took the packet and unwrapped it. Inside the foil was a layer of wax paper and inside it another layer of paper towels, and then finally the sandwich. "You think you put enough wrapping on it?"

"They each have a function. The foil regulates the temperature, the wax paper keeps the food fresh and the paper towel is to wipe your face when you're finished."

Frank opened the sandwich, inspected the ingredients for a second, and then took a bite. Marcell found himself a seat on a large boulder. He took a swig from his canteen.

"It's okay," said Frank. "I don't know about the roast beef part, but it's good. You're a vegetarian?"

"I can't eat meat. I'm allergic to it. Besides, I don't want to end up with that mad cow thing."

Frank was too full of nervous energy to sit still, and practically swallowed his sandwich whole, all the time pacing the ground, staring off into the distance in different directions. From their position on the side of a hill, he could see quite a ways. To the north, the sky was blue and clean but as he checked the west and then to the south the color turned to a yellowish brown from the smog in the city.

Marcell sat nibbling away at his sandwich, his legs tucked under him, his body crunched forward. A beam of sunlight cut through the trees and lit up the right side of his face. His complexion was not good; a couple of pimples were so smooth they actually shone in the light as though they had been polished.

"It's been three days, Frank. Do you think he's left the area?"

"I wouldn't think so. This time of year their metabolism starts to slow down, they get ready to hibernate. But who knows, without Gladys to find a den and take care of him...anything could happen."

It was starting to cool off a bit now. Frank grabbed a long sleeve shirt out of his pack and put it on. He looked out to the north once again. "Let me see those binoculars."

Marcell reached into his pack and pulled out a pair of binoculars and handed them to Frank. He peered through the glasses for a moment then handed them back to Marcell. "Here, take a look, about a mile off." He pointed. "There, just below that rise. Is that smoke?"

Marcell stood up on the rock he had been using as a seat. His back was stiff and he stretched out to limber up a bit. Then he looked through the glasses. "I don't know. Maybe. My eyes aren't so good. Nearsighted, I think. I get them confused."

"It's just like the word says, Marcell. If you're nearsighted you can see things close up—near, sighted." Frank removed a canteen from his belt, took a long drink then quickly replaced it. "I'm gonna go down there. Why don't you stay here and rest."

"I can make it."

"No. I'll go alone, check it out. While I'm gone you can check this area. Work out from here in a circle, check the trees. He likes to climb. If you come across another bear, just back away slowly. They won't bother you unless you threaten their cubs."

"We had bears in the circus. Bears like me. All animals like me."

"I know, just, be careful, okay? I shouldn't be gone more than an hour or so. If you get in any trouble, fire two shots, close together."

"Two shots," said Marcell, "bang, bang."

It only took Frank half an hour to get down to the area where he had seen the smoke. As he got closer, it had begun to dissipate, and he figured whoever had lit the fire would be gone when he got there. Still, he wanted to make sure it was completely out. All he needed now was a forest fire to start; that would be it for Mozart, not to mention thousands of other inhabitants in the valley.

He could smell the smoke now; he knew he was getting close, and he thought he saw some movement among the trees. Not taking any chances, he slowed his pace and carefully moved in on the spot. He could hear voices, men's voices; they were laughing and taking no precautions to hide their presence.

Frank moved in close enough to see them. There were two men dressed in jeans, t-shirts and boots. They were breaking camp; their tent had been brought down and was still in a pile. One of the men tended to it while the other gathered up their supplies. From the looks of their equipment, Frank figured they could easily have been out there for a week or more. Perhaps they had seen Mozart.

Frank came out from behind a tree, his rifle lying across his arms. "You fellows have a permit for that fire?"

The man gathering up the tent dropped what he was doing and stood up to face Frank. He was stocky, six feet tall with a full dark beard. There was a tattoo on his right forearm. It looked like some kind of ship with a ribbon running across it. There were letters on the ribbon, but Frank couldn't make them out. The man's partner glanced at Frank, and then he grabbed a sweatshirt and stuffed it into a backpack. He was younger than his partner, tall, skinny and very pale. His brown hair was long and greasy and he made no effort to brush it away from his face.

"Didn't know we needed one," said the tattooed man.

Frank perused the campground. He hadn't seen any rifles yet and that made him a little nervous. He kept glancing over toward the skinny one, making sure to keep him in his field of vision.

"Real dry around here, this time of year. Things can happen fast."

"You some kinda ranger or something?" said the skinny one.

Frank didn't like the guy's tone of voice. He shifted the rifle in his arms so that his right hand was gripping the stock, ready for action if necessary. "No, I'm not a ranger. I'm a guy with a gun, asking questions."

"Don't pay him no mind, mister." The heavy-set man looked over at his partner. "Just shut up and keep packing." He turned back to Frank. "We didn't know about no permit, but we're leaving now, so no harm, no foul, right?"

"What have you been doing out here?"

"Just camping out. Doing a little fishing, you know, that kinda thing."

"How long you been out here?"

"Just a couple of days. Why all the questions, mister?"

"I'm looking for a bear, a cub, actually. You two haven't seen one in the area have you?"

The two men looked at one another. They seemed nervous. The big one spoke.

"Ain't seen no bears. You seen any bears, Karl?"

Karl glanced over to his pack then back to his friend. "No, I ain't seen none." He started moving slowly toward the pack. He walked with a limp.

There it was, the rifle, leaning against a tree next to the pack. Frank pointed his rifle at Karl. "That's far enough, friend."

Karl stopped.

90

"Listen, mister, we told you we ain't seen no bears. What's the problem?" said the man with the tattoo.

"The problem is, I think you're lying to me and unless I get some answers real quick, we're gonna have ourselves a situation. Now, one more time. What are you doing out here?"

"Maybe we should..."

"Shut up, Karl. It's like I told you, mister, we're just fishing and camping."

Frank moved in close enough to read the tattoo on the big man's arm. It read 'Anchors Away.'

"I don't see any fishing poles and even if I did, there's not enough water in the stream along here this time of year to float a cork." Frank cocked his rifle and pointed it at the man. "I'm not gonna ask you again."

"All right, we're out here hunting, okay. There ain't no law against that..."

"Depends on what it is you're after."

"Well, it ain't no animal, least wise not the four-legged kind."

"Go on."

"I'm looking for the man killed my brother. I think he might be living out here somewhere."

The skinny one laughed, then said, "half a man be more like it."

"What's he mean by that?" asked Frank.

"Means, the man we're looking for's a midget; name's Marcell."

Frank still had his rifle pointed at the larger man. At the mention of Marcell he glanced away briefly, then quickly collected himself. "I've been living out here a long time, and I can assure you, there aren't any midgets around."

"Well, if it's all the same to you, we'll just keep on searching."

"No, I don't think you will. Things are peaceful out here, and we like it that way. I think you better just break camp and go back wherever it is you belong. I see you out here again, we're going to have a problem. You understand?"

The two men looked at each other. "Yeah," said the big man.

"We got ya. We'll be out of here in half an hour."

"No, you'll be out of here in two minutes. And leave the rifle."

The big man moved up closer to Frank. "You don't know who you're fucking with, mister."

"Neither do you. Now get your stuff and get out."

By the time Frank returned to the spot where he had left Marcell, the sun had dropped behind the hills and it had cooled down considerably. Marcell had curled up between two large boulders and fallen asleep. Frank gave him a light nudge.

"Marcell. Marcell, wake up."

Marcell opened his eyes and slowly sat up. "I fell asleep."

"Come on, we have to go."

"What is it? Did you find Mozart?"

"I'll tell you all about it. Right now, we have to get out of here."

Marcell gathered up his things and the two men took off toward their cabins. It took them two hours to get back. Frank purposely hiked a mile out of their way to where a small creek ran with water—it was shallow, but deep enough to hide their tracks—then the two of them hiked down stream in the water, away from the cabins, another half mile, then doubled back on land in the right direction. Marcell kept pressing Frank for information but all he would say was, keep up the pace, keep to the water.

They reached Frank's cabin a little after dark. They were both exhausted and Marcell's feet were badly blistered. Frank got him a bucket with hot water and poured some Epsom salt into it. He heated some soup and buttered some bread and gave Marcell a bowl full to eat while he soaked his feet. Then he told him about the two men in the woods.

"What was the tattoo?" asked Marcell.

"A ship. And there were words. 'Anchors Away'."

"Anchors Away. You're sure that's what it said?"

"Positive."

Marcell sighed. "Bartelli."

"Who's Bartelli?"

"It's a long story, from when I was with the circus." The soup in Marcell's mouth actually improved the quality of his voice, softening the normal gravelly tone. "Now that we're partners, I guess it's okay to tell you."

Frank didn't say anything. Marcell continued. "We had this elephant, it had been with us ever since I was a boy, and it didn't know very many tricks. For years her only job was to walk around in a circle, giving people rides. I used to ride her all the time. She liked giving me rides. I think it was because I was so little, it didn't bother her to have me on her back. And I always brought her things, like peanuts and pieces of fruit. Every time we'd get a new trainer, they'd try to teach her some new tricks to perform but Dinky—that was her name; I don't know who named her—she either wasn't smart enough to learn or maybe she was just too lazy, I don't know.

"She was getting to be pretty old, when we got this new trainer by the name of Bartelli. He traveled with his brother, who was a mechanic. Anyway, this Bartelli was supposed to be kind of famous for training elephants and he decided he was going to teach Dinky a bunch of new tricks; said we needed to spruce up the acts, that people were losing interest in the circus. Like a few elephant tricks are going to change all that."

Marcell paused a moment and stared out the window. Frank thought he saw a tear form in his eye but Marcell quickly wiped his face with his hand and continued on with his story. "Anyway, this trainer, Bartelli, he would take Dinky into one of the large tents at night and he wouldn't let anyone come in there. For weeks he kept working with her and every night I could hear her crying inside that tent. A couple of us went to him and asked him what he was doing to Dinky and he said to mind our own business, said he didn't need any freaks telling him how to do his job. So we went to the boss and he said Bartelli was the trainer, it was up to him to handle the animals.

"Well, Dinky wasn't learning any new tricks and it seemed like Bartelli was getting more and more angry about it all the time, said he was gonna teach her or kill her trying. One night—we were camped just outside of Pittsburgh. You ever been to Pittsburgh? People think there are a lot of freaks in the circus; you should try going to the Pittsburgh bus station around midnight sometime— anyway, I sneaked over to the tent where he kept Dinky one night, and cut a hole in the canvas so I could watch him. Frank, you wouldn't believe what I saw. He was trying to get her to stand up on her rear two feet, like a horse, you know, and every time he'd give her the command he'd zap her front legs with an electric prod, but she refused to lift them. I watched him for an hour, Frank— I could see tears coming from her eyes, I swear it's true—until I couldn't stand it anymore, then I went back and told my mother about it and that's when we decided what we would do."

Frank took a seat on the bed and watched Marcell intently now as his story unfolded. He opened the window to get some air; a light breeze gently turned the overhead fan. It was quiet outside, as if all the creatures of the night were trying to listen in on Marcell's tale.

"Bartelli was a drinking man, and when he drank he would put on this friendly persona, coming around our buses trying to get us to have a drink with him, all smiles and how-do-you-do crap. I think he was just trying to get to my mother."

"What do you mean?"

"Sex, Frank."

"But..."

"Oh," Marcell started laughing. "You were thinking maybe my mother looks like me."

Frank recoiled in embarrassment.

"No, it's alright, I can understand your confusion. I never told you. My mother isn't a dwarf. She's a very beautiful woman, a trapeze artist. But that's a whole other story. Where was I? Oh, yeah, so, Bartelli was coming around her bus being all nice and shit. He'd slept with every good-looking woman in the circus except my mother. She despised him, and not because of his looks or anything like that. He actually wasn't a bad looking guy, though

94

he was completely bald, and had a ridiculous looking mustache that twisted up on the end into two little circles. People spoke of him as being charming; I suppose he had that aspect to his personality, but I can tell you, Frank, he was a cruel, evil man. All the freaks stayed away from him, believe me, but some of the workers would drink with him on occasion, mostly, I think, because he always provided the booze. Usually, though, he would just sit in his tent alone, or with his brother, and drink himself to sleep.

"A couple of nights after I saw him with Dinky, my mother invited him into our bus. He came in with a bottle of vodka and started passing it around. There was me, my mother, Gordy the contortionist, the Peabody twins—Tiny and Karl..."

"Karl?"

"Yeah, Karl and Tiny, Siamese twins; joined at the hip. Why?"

"Nothing, go on."

"So there was Gordy, the twins and Mary; she was billed as the tiniest woman in the world. She was only two and a half feet tall and weighed less than forty pounds. She was so pretty and delicate; you never saw such a beautiful creature.

"Anyway, Bartelli came into the bus, half drunk already, and started right in how he was so misunderstood, that he loved animals, and that the animals loved learning tricks and pleasing people with their performance. 'I don't like inflicting pain,' he said, 'and besides, animals don't really experience pain like a human does.' Every time he spoke he stared directly at my mother, and kept reaching out for her hand with his. She'd let him hold it for a few seconds and then slowly pull it away. He went on for an hour, sobbing and complaining, drinking all the time, passing the bottle around to each of us. We pretended to drink, too, and we smiled and tried to reassure him that we understood. Meanwhile, Mary slipped some powder into his bottle to make him sleep."

"Wouldn't the alcohol do the trick?"

"You would think so, Frank, but this guy could drink a lot, and we didn't want to take any chances. Anyway, he finally passed out and I told everyone to wait outside. Karl, one of the Peabody's, tried to talk me out of it, said he was afraid we'd all get in trouble. He and Tiny got in a big argument about it, right there in the bus—they were always arguing—until my mother walked over and slapped Karl right in the face and told him he should be ashamed of himself, that we were all family, that Dinky was part of that family and we had to protect her. That shut Karl up.

"They all went outside and left me alone with Bartelli. He was lying there on his back, snoring like a large hog, still clinging to a half bottle of booze. There was a part of me that wanted to get his prod and start torturing him like he'd done to Dinky, but to tell you the truth, I didn't have the heart for it. I climbed on top of him and stared down at his face. His mouth was wide open and every time he breathed out his mustache would wiggle. He was so pathetic. I have to tell you, Frank, I was nervous, sweat was pouring off my face, but I had made up my mind to go through with it, so I reached down, thinking I would strangle him with my bare hands, but, as you can see, my hands are small, and wouldn't fit around his neck."

Frank stared at the small man. He had a huge grin on his face and the large spaces between his teeth were full of bits of bread. He noticed for the first time just how short his fingers were; short and thick. The sleeves of his shirt were rolled up to his elbows, exposing his forearms. They were thick too, all muscle, like a body-builder. Frank imagined if Marcell's hands *could* fit around somebody's neck, he could easily choke the life right out of him.

"I stood up on his chest and considered jumping on his face, maybe break his neck, but I was afraid it would only wake him up. The Peabody twins stuck their heads into the tent and asked me if it was over yet and I told them my problem, and Tiny said we should let Dinky do it, just carry him over to her cage and stick him inside. So we did. The five of us, six actually, if you count the Peabodys as two—although Tiny did all the lifting for the both of them—the six of us started dragging him across the grounds toward Dinky's cage; me and the Peabodys had one leg and my mother, Mary and Gordy..."

"The contortionist?"

"Right. They had the other leg. Mary wasn't much help, being so small, but she wanted to contribute. We all loved Dinky."

"I understand."

"It was hard going, must have taken us close to an hour, but we finally managed to get him to the cage. There was a lock on it, but I found the keys in Bartelli's pocket, so we opened up the door and dragged him in. We set him right at Dinky's feet and backed out of the cage and waited. We waited for two hours, but Dinky just stood there looking at Bartelli, then out at us, like she didn't understand what was to be done. I think she was afraid, maybe she thought it was a trick, but she refused to touch him."

"So, what did you do?"

"I got the hammer, the one they use to ring the bell—you know that game?"

Frank nodded yes.

"It's all in the swing you know, timing. I could ring the bell every time. I've seen men bigger than you couldn't do it because their timing was off. Anyway, I got the hammer and I went in there with Dinky and Bartelli. Dinky had her trunk down in Bartelli's face, kissing him I guess. That would be just like her, to kiss that monster. So I moved her away and just stood there for a minute looking down at Bartelli. You ever notice how *innocent* people look when they're asleep? There was a second there where I almost changed my mind. I thought, gee, Dinky doesn't seem to hate him. Then, he let out this big snore and his mustached twitched and his face contorted just enough to wipe that innocence away. I raised the hammer up over my head, and just then he opened his eyes and looked up at me. He looked very confused, but he was awake and I was happy about that. You know what I did, Frank, I smiled at him and said 'watch this trick, Mr. Bartelli,' and then I brought that hammer down as hard as I could, right on his Adam's apple, crushed his larynx, did it with one blow. He laid there twitching, trying to suck in air, staring up at me in his half-dead drunken stupor, trying to figure out what was happening to him, but he didn't have a chance. It was an awful thing to see, a painful death, but he had it coming, he really did."

Marcell lowered his voice, almost to a whisper.

"We left him in there, thinking when they found him, they'd think he'd passed out drunk and Dinky stepped on him, you know, and crushed his neck, which is pretty much what they thought at first. The problem was, after they removed him from the cage, they led Dinky out and chained her to a post. At first I thought they were just going to clean the cage; there was some blood, not much, but some. Then, Bartelli's brother came out with a rifle. We were all there watching him load the gun, yelling at him not to shoot her, that it wasn't her fault. I tried to grab the rifle from him but he let me have it right in the gut with the stock and I fell to my knees. Dinky must have known what was going on, Frank, cause when he came close to her, she reared up on her back legs, like she was trying to tell him she could do it, she would do the new trick."

Marcell paused for a moment and stared down at the floor. "She must have been up on her hind legs a full minute. Then he shot her, right between the eyes; the sound of the rifle going off was deafening. She hit the ground so hard I fell over from the shock. Bartelli just turned around and smiled at all of us and walked away. I think he was happy his brother was dead; it gave him an opportunity to kill something.

"Later that day we heard they were going to do an autopsy on Bartelli, said they suspected maybe some foul play. That night, I packed my things and left. Left my mother, all my friends. Told them if things got too hot, just tell them I did it. That was two years ago."

"You've never heard from anyone since?"

"Last year, the circus was up by San Francisco. I went up there and sneaked in one night to see my mother perform. She was fantastic."

"Did she say anything about Bartelli's brother being after you?"

"I didn't talk to her. There was a guy waiting for her after the show. I didn't want to get in the way."

"Get in the way?"

Marcell shrugged. "I got to see her. That's enough. And I got to talk to Mary; she's still as beautiful as ever. I told her how to get hold of me. Anyway, we know they're after me now. If they come, I'll just give them what I gave his brother. I'm curious about the other guy. What did you say he looked like?"

"Tall and skinny, walked with a tilt to one side, like he had a bad back. And I think his name was Karl."

"Hmm. Sounds a little like the Peabodys."

"This guy only had one head. In any case, you better stay here for awhile, Marcell. Your place is too exposed."

"I'm not afraid, Frank. Besides, no offense, but you live like a Spartan. That's not my style. I need to be home; need my TV and my computer. Forget about them. What I want to know is, when do we go after the others?"

Frank grabbed Marcell's empty soup bowl. "You want some more?"

"No, no that's plenty."

Frank took the empty bowls into the kitchen and then returned. Marcell was wiping his feet with a towel.

"How are your feet?"

"They're okay. I think I will stay here tonight though; too tired to walk any further. I appreciate what you did out there."

"Well, we're partners, right?"

"All the way."

"Good. Tomorrow we'll look for the girl. But, just so you understand, I'm not killing any women. We'll just find out about Freddie's partner and see who this Rudy fellow is."

"That's fine with me, Frank. I like girls. But what if she won't talk?"

"Let's hope she does." ❧

NINE

We had to escort a group of politicians through the area today. American politicians, that is, senators and congressmen. They said they had come to see Vietnam in person, to understand better what it was we were fighting for. I spoke to one of them myself, a senator from Texas. He was a pleasant enough man, and seemed sincere in his concerns. His name was McCoy and said he hoped someday to run for president. I drove him and two others around in my Jeep and there were two other Jeeps traveling with us.

We drove out to a small village—it was supposed to have been secured the night before their arrival—and we walked around speaking to some of the residents. I could tell Senator McCoy was moved by the humility and sincerity of these people. Who wouldn't be?

We were walking past a small hut. There was a young girl, maybe seven years old, sitting on a stool by the entryway; she was very beautiful, her hair was long and flowed freely down past her waist. She was biting her nails. I was trying to explain to the senator what I had seen in this very same village just a week earlier. Some South Vietnamese troops had been questioning the villagers, accusing them of aiding the Viet Cong. They had a teenage boy on his knees in the mud and were jabbing him with the butts of their rifles. Every time the boy would fall down, one of them would jerk him back up on his knees and start hitting him again, all the time screaming at him in Vietnamese (liar!). I wanted to intercede, but my lieutenant stopped me. Then—it all happened so fast—one of the soldiers pulled out his pistol, stuck it right up against the boys head and fired.

As I finished my story to the senator, the young girl stood up from her seat and lofted what at first looked like a rock in our direction. I followed the object out of the corner of my eye as it hit the mud a few yards away from us. It was green and had a small handle. I instinctively threw myself in front of the senator and knocked him to the ground. There was an explosion. The concussion knocked me unconscious. When I awoke, I was on a stretcher in a helicopter. I had taken some shrapnel in the leg, but it wasn't too bad. They told me the senator was unharmed, but that two other soldiers had died from the grenade, along with the young girl who had thrown it. How are we supposed to fight this kind of war? Just who is the enemy?

"What are you doing?"

Marcell looked up from the notebook. "I didn't think you'd mind," he said. "These are very fascinating. To think, that whole thing was over before I was born. You must have a lot of stories to tell."

"You're welcome to read the journals, Marcell, but I have nothing to say to you about Vietnam. We better get going; we've got a lot to do. How are your feet?"

Marcell closed the book and set it back on the shelf. "They're fine. What's the plan?"

"We need to get supplies and some special equipment to set up a security system at your cabin. Then we're going to see a man about a rifle."

Marcell hopped off the bed and began rubbing his hands together. "Now you're talking. Say, Frank, you're not sore at me are you, for looking at your diary?"

"No, no, I'm not sore."

They sat outside Jack's Rifle Shop for an hour, waiting for the place to empty out. It was dark now, after six, and most of the shops had already closed for the day, the clerks eager to lock up and escape the inner city. Iron grated doors slammed shut, dead bolts snapped into place, alarms were set. After three hours of madness the work traffic on Fairfax had finally begun to subside. Frank and Marcell had watched in awe as an endless parade of cars raced through the streets of L.A., each good citizen making his own desperate attempt to get home a few minutes earlier than the rest of the crowd.

After a full day of dealing with bosses, coworkers and demanding customers, they were free. And they had power; it was right there at their feet, a little pressure on the gas pedal, a slight turn to the steering wheel and two tons of crushing metal was at

101

their command. Nobody gave an inch. Battle lines were drawn at each intersection, drivers speeding up to prevent others from making left turns, tightening up the line to keep anyone from making a lane change, blocking the intersection long after the light turned red, all set to a cacophony of screeching brakes, piercing horns and X-rated insults.

Some battles were more personal than others. The drivers of the older, beat-up cars seemed to particularly enjoy terrorizing those in newer, more expensive models. Mercedes, BMW, anything luxurious, was open game. This was the one place in the city where poverty ruled. Nobody in his right mind would pit his brand new Lincoln Towncar against some dented up, spot-primed sixty-eight Pontiac.

Marcell rather enjoyed the circus atmosphere but for Frank it was almost too much to bear. He sat there behind the wheel unable to catch his breath, the chaos of the street unsettling his nerves. Plus, the bearskin he was wearing was beginning to itch. Well, it wasn't a real skin, but it itched nonetheless. Frank had forbidden Marcell from skinning the bears, but that wasn't about to stop Marcell from implementing his plan. He knew a guy at a costume shop in Hollywood who reluctantly agreed to loan him a couple of outfits.

There had been times, with the circus, when they would not have a bear and one of the clowns would dress up in a bearskin and perform the act. It was very effective; people would flinch in fear even though they knew it wasn't a real bear. It would be, he said, as if Gladys and Stumble were there with them, revenging their own murders.

The outfits fit the two men well—it was eerie just *how* well— and with the exception of a few spotty patches of missing hair, were in perfect condition.

A couple of men came out of the gun shop, got into their pickup truck and drove away. Frank gave Marcell a nudge. "Let's go."

They got out of their truck, grabbed the bear heads from the bed, put them on, then ran across the street, a pistol holster draped over Marcell's shoulders, a rifle in Frank's hand. A couple of cars honked and somebody yelled something out a window, but most people didn't pay them much mind. It was, after all, Los Angeles, and Halloween was just a week away. So a couple of bears carrying guns ran across the street and into a rifle shop. So what?

Which was probably what the man was thinking when the two bears entered his store. Couple of hunters coming in to show off their kill, maybe get some work done on their rifles.

"I'm closing up, fellows, so make it quick." He was an older man, late sixties, with white hair and beard to match. Frank moved slowly through the store, examining the walls on either side of him as he went along. The wall to his right was decorated with stuffed heads: deer, elk, bear; beautiful creatures all of them, each stalked and killed before their time, then mounted on a wall as a souvenir, a trophy, a reminder to the hunter of his great conquest.

Frank understood the concept well. There was something about keeping a part of your kill's body around that gave a man a sense of power, as if he could sustain that feeling he had at the moment he had pulled the trigger and brought a life to an end. He'd seen guys in Nam cut off the ears or fingers of Viet Cong soldiers they had killed and wear them around their neck into battle. It kept them focused, maybe even kept them alive. Frank knew of one man in his platoon who had gone through two tours without so much as a scratch, only to die in a helicopter crash on the day he shipped out. Earlier that morning he had handed over his string of ears to a friend.

The other wall was covered with rifles, all kinds, from semiautomatics to old Winchester bolt actions. The floor was wood and covered in spots with bearskins. Frank walked up to the counter and slammed his paw down onto the glass counter.

"You Jack Pepperton?"

The man looked down at the paw. "That's an expensive case, mister."

"I asked you a question."

103

"I'm Pepperton. What do you want?"

Marcell had stayed by the front door, flipped the sign to read "closed," and drawn the shade. He then started taking rifles off the racks on the walls and inspecting them.

"I'm looking for a girl named Veronica," said Frank.

"I sell rifles, mister. You want a girl, Hollywood Boulevard's just up the street. I'd suggest you change your outfit first." He looked over at Marcell. "Hey, those are expensive guns, kid."

Marcell walked over to Frank. He had a rifle in his hand. "This looks like a very expensive rifle." His gravelly voice sounded cryptic through the mouth of the bear.

Frank took the rifle from Marcell. Then he leaned in real close to Pepperton. "I'm looking for the woman who hired Freddie Diddlesby to kill a couple of bears, and I'm not gonna ask you again."

"Look, asshole, I don't know any Veronica. Now get the fuck out of my store."

Frank backed away from the counter, grabbed the rifle by the barrel, raised it over his head and smashed it down into the glass case, shattering the case and breaking the stock of the rifle.

"Are you out of your mind!" Pepperton started to reach for a gun but Marcell drew his .38 from the holster and pointed it right at his head.

"I'd love to do it, " said Marcell.

"Veronica," said Frank.

"All right, all right. I'll get you the phone number. That's all I have. I don't know where she lives."

"Get it."

"It's in the office."

Frank raised his rifle. "I'm right behind you." He turned to Marcell. "While we're here, we could use some things."

"Terrific. A shopping spree."

Frank followed Pepperton toward the back of the store till the two men disappeared into another room. Marcell cleaned out the cash register—there wasn't much, a couple hundred dollars—then he dug around behind the counter, found some paper bags and began filling them with weapons and ammunition. He wasn't sure what bullets were for what guns so he just took everything he could get his hands on: .22 shorts, longs; shotgun shells; a derringer. He even grabbed a couple of semiautomatics. He quickly filled three large bags and was carrying one of them toward the front entrance when a shot rang out from the back of the store, startling him and causing him to spill the bag of goods all over the floor. He turned and dropped to the floor and pointed his pistol toward the back of the room.

For a minute, all was quiet. Then, the door to the office swung open and a solitary figure stepped out, silhouetted by the dim light of the office. Marcell squinted, trying to see who it was, but at that distance and with his poor eyesight he couldn't tell for sure. He was nervous and sweaty. He hadn't felt like this since the night he'd killed Bartelli. He slowly, carefully, stuck one paw before the trigger of his pistol; it was a tight fit and wouldn't require much pressure to fire the weapon. As he lay there sprawled out on the dirty wooden floor, surrounded by boxes of ammunition, the image of a newspaper headline crossed his mind and he started to laugh: 'Store Owner Dies in Shootout With Bears,' or maybe there would be a picture of him in one of those tabloids with a caption reading 'Half-Bear, Half-Dwarf Creature Killed in Robbery Attempt.'

The figure started moving toward him.

"Frank, is that you? Frank?" He was laughing so hard now he started to tremble. And then his gun went off. The figure at the other end of the room cried out in pain and then fell to the floor.

Penny had laid three dresses out on her bed, trying to decide which one to wear that evening. She had been in and out of each of them half a dozen times, checking herself in the mirror, thinking she'd made a decision, then changing again. One thing was certain: she looked great in each of them, each one made a different statement, each powerful in its own way. The red one was silk, cut low in the front and back and fit skintight. It was the sexiest of the three but Penny thought it would work better on someone with larger breasts, though that could be remedied with a push-up bra. There was a white knit one that clung to her skin and exposed her stomach, one of her better features, and then there was a black evening gown that hid her body but added a look of sophistication. Considering her age, she felt perhaps this would be the best one for tonight's work. Her customer was an older man and Veronica said they would be having dinner together at his hotel. The dress would add a few years to her, make her feel less out of place.

She put the black one on again, added some pearls and a gold bracelet then stood back and checked herself in the mirror. Who could ever guess she was only fourteen? She recalled dressing herself in her mother's clothes when she was a little girl—how fun that had been—and pretended that was all she was doing now, playing grown-up. There would come a time, later in the evening, when the pretending would stop and she'd have to do what he wanted her to do, have to find ways to please him— whoever he was—have to feel his hands, his body, all over her. All she could hope for was that he was not too gross, and that he'd be gentle with her.

Veronica had spent an afternoon with her explaining how she should behave, what was and wasn't expected of her. Each customer had certain things they liked and if Penny wanted to make a lot of money, it would be good for her to become versatile. Some girls chose to specialize; maybe they were especially skilled in S&M or, like Angel, one of the girls living at the house, got particularly skilled with foreign objects, but the real money was in versatility. Veronica could switch from a little girl to a total bitch with a whip, in the beat of a heart; she was like a piece of dough, there to be molded to fit any man's desire.

Penny sat on the bed and began pulling on a pair of dark pantyhose. She heard a clicking sound then looked up to see her door open and a man step into her room. It was Arnie, one of the guards. He had been watching her everyday since she had arrived. She could feel his eyes on her even when her back was turned. He wasn't bad looking, but the staring, the hovering about, frightened her.

"You're not supposed to be in here."

"Getting ready for your big date, huh?"

"You better get out of here before Veronica gets here."

"Well, now, that's not a very friendly attitude." He moved closer to her. Penny let go of the pantyhose.

"Veronica..."

"I don't know where you get your information, little girl, but Veronica isn't taking you to your date. I am. That's what I do, you know, deliver the goods, make sure nobody fools with Rudy's property. I'm your protection."

Penny tried to get up from the bed but Arnie grabbed her and sat her back down.

"Thing you gotta understand is, everybody in this little family has a job to do. Rudy sets up the dates, Veronica takes you out and buys you new clothes—looks like she went all out this time—and me, I see to it none of the merchandise gets damaged. Now, my job, as far as you're concerned is the most important job here. You wanna know why?"

Penny sat there on the edge of the bed, trembling. Arnie squatted down on his haunches and put his face just inches away from hers.

"You see," he said, his voice low now, almost a whisper, "a lot of things can happen to a pretty young girl. Some of these guys, boy, I'll tell you, they can get pretty rough. But as long as they know I'm right outside, well, then, they're not so likely to get carried away."

He dropped his hand from her chin and let it fall to her shoulder. Then he slowly ran his hand down her neck and onto her breast. "So you see, it's very important to keep me happy. If I'm not happy, I might forget to come in and stop some guy from breaking your jaw or cutting you with a knife." He stood up and his voice got louder. "Hell, anything can happen. You could disappear. You wouldn't be the first, and nobody would know. Nobody would care. You understand what I'm saying?"

Penny sat motionless.

"I asked you a question?"

She nodded yes. He reached down and unzipped his fly, then he stuck his groin right up to her mouth.

"Good. Let's just measure the depth of your understanding."

"I thought you checked Jack's," said Tulary. He sounded irritated. Kate was driving and Tulary had his window rolled down and his hand resting on the edge, smoke streaming from the wind stoked cigarette. The moon was a bright yellow, almost full and low in the sky. They were headed right at it.

"I talked to him myself. He said he knew who Freddie was, had sold him some ammunition, but that was it. Are you almost done with that?"

Tulary shook his head. "Well, maybe it's just a coincidence," he said sarcastically. He took a drag from his cigarette, exhaled and then flipped the half smoked butt outside and rolled up the window.

"I guess this is the way it's going to be with us, isn't it?" asked Kate.

"Meaning what?"

"A struggle. I feel like it's a constant battle with you. What is it with you, anyway?"

"I need a drink," he said. It was the most sincere thing to come out of his mouth since they got in the car.

A half a block down the rode Kate pulled the car over to the curb in front of a liquor store. "Go on."

"What?"

"Go get your alcohol. Maybe you'll be easier to deal with."

"We're on our way to a crime scene, detective."

"Our vic's not going anywhere. Get your booze. I can't take this."

Tulary reached into his overcoat and pulled out a paper bag. He quickly unscrewed the cap to a small bottle. "If you insist," he said and took a large gulp from the bottle.

Kate couldn't tell what kind of booze it was. Not that it mattered. She had watched her father slowly drink himself to death over a ten-year period. By the end, he'd drink anything that had alcohol in it; they couldn't even keep cough medicine around the house. She pulled away from the curb and proceeded toward the rifle shop. Tulary put the lid back on the bottle and tucked the bag into his overcoat pocket.

They drove along for a good five minutes before Tulary spoke. "Thanks."

"You feel better?"

"It helps."

"You want to talk about it?"

"That doesn't help. Besides, we're here."

The area had already been taped off, an ambulance had arrived along with numerous police cars and the press, and a small crowd of civilians was gathered outside the tape. Kate shut off the engine and started to open her door but Tulary didn't budge.

"You coming."

"How long you been on the job?" asked Tulary.

"Seven years."

"In six months I'll have twenty-five years in. Twenty-five years of yellow tape and blood stains, and you know what I've figured out. It's like pissing on a forest fire."

"Well, at least you've got plenty of liquids in you. Maybe you should quit."

"Maybe you should," he said, "while you still like it."

He opened his door and got out of the car. It was a cool evening for L.A., and still, not a trace of wind, and that moon, it was huge. He couldn't keep his eyes off it.

"Beautiful, isn't it?" said Kate as she stepped into the street.

"What causes that, anyway?"

"What?"

"The moon. Look how large it is."

"I don't know. I think it has something to do with dust particles in the air; something like that."

"It looks so close."

"It'll be full by tomorrow. Then we'll really see some weirdness."

"Yeah, blame it on the moon," said Tulary.

The two detectives crossed the street and were greeted at the front door of Jack's Rifle Shop by a uniformed officer.

"You the first on the scene?" asked Kate.

"Yeah. Looks like a burglary. The cash resister is empty, along with the safe, and it looks like they took some ammunition. The vic's in the back."

Kate and Tulary went inside.

"Somebody got clumsy," said Tulary, referring to the bag of ammunition spilled across the floor.

The corpse was in the office, an older man with white hair and beard. A uniformed officer was standing next to the body.

"What do you have?" asked Kate.

"One shot, straight through the heart. There's a pistol in the safe. Looks like he was going for it when he got hit. Name is Jack Pepperton. He's the owner."

"How about prints?" asked Tulary.

"It's a store. Place is probably full of prints don't belong here."

"Concentrate in here and by the cash register," said Kate.

"There's also some blood just outside the door. Maybe the shooter's."

Kate looked down at the pistol in the safe. "Doesn't make sense. The guy never reached his gun."

"You're the detective," said the officer and walked out.

Kate bent down to the body. Tulary's words were echoing through her head. She wondered how many times she'd seen this before, how many lifeless bodies she'd inspected, pools of blood she'd seen mopped up.

"There's no claw," she said.

"It's probably just a robbery, Kate."

"Or this is the guy the message was left for."

"Doesn't fit the description of Freddie's partner."

"Excuse me, Detective Mallory." It was another uniformed cop, a female, young, attractive. Tulary gave her the once over. "We got a witness outside you might want to talk to."

Kate stood up from the dead man. "Imagine that, an actual witness."

"Don't get too excited, detective. It's some wino, lives behind the dumpster. Claims he saw the killers. Are you ready for this? He says it was a couple of bears."

"And you wonder why I drink," said Tulary.

The first thing Frank saw when he came to was a bear head sitting on a small chair next to the bed. It was dark outside and the only light in the room spilled in through the window from a waxing moon. The pale yellow light lit up the eyes of the fake bear, and for a second Frank thought Gladys, and that maybe her death had been a dream, a long sad nightmare. He tried to sit up but he was weak and disoriented. His eyes were beginning to adjust to the dark room, enough so that he could now see where the head left off and the chair began. His head was throbbing. He reached up to the source of the pain and when he brought his hand back down there was blood on it. He tried to remember what had happened, but it hurt too much to think. He looked down at the foot of the bed and noticed his legs were hanging over the end. He could hear noise coming from the other room and tried to call out. "Marcell." His voice was weak and scratchy. "Marcell. Are you in there?"

Marcell came into the bedroom. "You're awake."

"What time is it? What happened?"

"It's after midnight. You don't remember what happened?"

Marcell turned on the lamp.

"We went to the rifle shop." Frank paused and tried to recollect.

"You went into the back with the owner, Pepperton."

Frank glanced over at the bear head. "We were wearing the bear skins. The guy, Pepperton, he opened his safe. Next thing I know, I shot him. He must have gone for a gun...and there was a notebook. I remember a notebook."

"I got it. There's some interesting stuff in it, too."

Frank reached up to the wound on his head. "I came out of his office and, I thought I heard your voice...what the hell happened?"

Marcell explained about the accidental shooting, how he had started laughing and fired the gun. "I'm sorry, Frank, it just went off."

"How did you manage to get us back here?"

"Well, it wasn't easy, I can tell you that. First I had to drag you through the building and out into the alley. I'm pretty strong for my size but you're a big man, Frank. Then I had to run around front and get the truck. The hardest part was getting you into it. There was no way I was going to be able to get you into the cab so I had to just lay you down in the bed, and your head kept falling off..."

"The head came off? Did anybody see me?"

"I don't know, Frank. I didn't see anyone around but I was just trying to get out of there as fast as possible before the cops showed up."

"But, how did you drive my truck? I mean, you know, how could you reach the pedals?"

"I found a wooden box in the dumpster and set it on the seat so I could see out the window, then I set a small box of ammo on the gas pedal and used a rifle to push down on the clutch. It wasn't easy, but I've done trickier things in my life, believe me. When you're little like me you have to be creative. I made some soup. You feel like eating?"

"I think so. My head is killing me. You got any aspirin?"

"I'll get you some."

Marcell started to leave the room but Frank called out to him. "Marcell. the guy, Pepperton. Is he dead?"

"Oh, he's dead, alright. You got him good. Right through the heart. But I wouldn't feel bad about it, Frank. Wait till you see the notebook." ❧

TEN

After taking care of Arnie's needs, Penny had to ride all the way into the city with him, a big grin plastered on his face, his eyes hidden behind his Jack Nicholson sunglasses. And she'd had to change dresses thanks to the mess he'd made, had put on the red one without so much as a thought to how it looked, or whether it would be right for the evening. Arnie never said a word the whole way into town, but every now and then he'd glance over at her legs, then up to her face, run his tongue around the inside of his cheek and bob his head as if to say, "yeah, you're mine."

As it turned out, it didn't really matter which dress she wore. They were having dinner all right, but not in the restaurant. The man—he called himself Mr. Smith—had food delivered to his room, a high priced suite at the Beverly Hilton. He made Penny wait in the bedroom while the food was delivered so she wouldn't be seen.

The meal looked good enough, some kind of fish, but Penny didn't feel much like eating. She kept thinking of Arnie and how the taste of him had made her gag. The only thing she could even consider swallowing now were the raw carrots on the side of her plate; she sat there nibbling on one while Smith gobbled up his dinner.

Mr. Smith really didn't care if she ate or not. He kept pouring alcohol down her throat and drawing out lines of cocaine—mostly for her. He didn't want to get too numb, not be able to concentrate. He was an old man, he told her, closing in on sixty-five, and out of shape. He wasn't quite as virile as he used to be.

By the time he finished his meal, she was pretty drunk and pretty fucked up from the coke, which was just what he wanted. As it turned out, it helped her, too. The sex went by in a blur. He had taken her to different rooms, put her in strange positions, even made her watch some awful porno. After three hours of tumbling around together he finally had a climax, and not a moment too soon, for Penny was beginning to sober up. She wasted no time getting dressed while Mr. Smith diligently cleaned the sex from his worn old body.

"I could pay you extra," he said, "we could go again."

"I haven't got all night," she said and realized how cold it sounded. He had been nice enough to her, not like Arnie at all. But he was so pathetic.

Arnie was waiting right outside the door when she came out. It didn't make any sense, him waiting out there all that time with a John like Smith. Arnie wasn't there for her protection. Not for one minute. She was his prisoner, no doubt about it. Living on the street, she'd had to sleep with guys to keep herself fed, but she'd always picked them herself. This, this was much worse. She was going to have to figure out a way to get out. She'd have to be smarter than Arnie. Smarter than Rudy. That shouldn't be too difficult; she knew which zipper covered their brains.

On the way back to the house Arnie unzipped his fly and looked over at Penny. "Well."

She didn't say anything, just lowered her head to his lap and went to work. She was thinking about her mother's boyfriend. He had been the first. He was just like Arnie, cold, ruthless. It had gone on for a month. Penny would come home from school and Earl would be there waiting, take her upstairs and have his fun then tell her she says anything he'll kill her and her mother. And Penny finally figures fuck it, I'd rather be dead, and goes to her mother and tells her and Earl says no, it was Penny seduced him, and Penny's mother turns and slaps Penny across the face. It was a moment Penny would never forget, not because her mother believed Earl—she could see it in her eyes that she didn't—but because she chose him over her. Penny should have been full of hate for her mother but all she felt was pity. He's all yours, mother, she said, and walked out the door.

She pictured Earl, now, and thought about biting down, real

115

hard, give Arnie a blowjob he would never forget. It was so tempting, just lock on with her jaws and never let go, let the sound of him screaming be the last sound she ever heard. That's the commitment it would take. He'd either crash the car and kill them both or somehow get her off him, then put a bullet in her head. It would almost be worth it, she thought. Almost.

"His nose is too small. And it doesn't turn up so much." Louis Crumb was sitting at a desk with Linda Burroughs trying to describe to the artist the man he had seen in the alley behind Jack's Rifle Shop the previous night. It was hard to tell how old Louis was—he certainly couldn't remember—he had long filthy hair and a tangled beard, his face was tan and wrinkled from spending so much time outdoors. Detective Mallory promised him some new clothes and some money for a room for a few nights if he could help them out, but Louis said he just wanted the cash; his clothes were fine and so were his digs. There was an odor emanating from Louis, a combination of urine and sweat that kept both women gagging for air.

Louis had had a lot to drink that evening—like most nights— and had settled into his regular spot between the dumpster and the building for a night's sleep when it all happened. First thing he had seen was the small red pickup come racing around the corner and park right outside the back door to the rifle shop. At first he was afraid it might be some hunters. "Rednecks," he told the pretty young artist. "They think it's funny, kick a guy around had too much to drink." He pointed at the picture. "Yeah, that's better."

"How about the eyes, Louis?" asked Kate.

"Eyes were blue. I told you that. Big and round, and blonde eyebrows."

Then—and he swore on his mother's grave it was true—a little bear got out from behind the wheel and went inside the store. Kate looked at Linda and shrugged. Louis had told Kate the whole story twice already, and seemed determined to tell it again. A few

116

minutes later the small bear had come back out dragging a larger bear by the shoulders. "It was pretty frightening," he said, "seeing those two bears. I thought maybe I'd had too much to drink. I do that sometimes, you know. I've seen snakes before and bugs, lots of bugs, crawling all over me. Ain't never seen no bears.

"I put my hands in front of my face and wiped my eyes but I couldn't make them go away. When I look again, the bigger bear's head is laying on the ground, not more than ten feet away from me and it's staring right at me, growling and snorting. I figured my time had come, the good Lord had sent this bear to punish me. I was so frightened I couldn't move. I looked back over at his body and there's a man's head sitting on top of it. Good looking fellow, too. Then the little bear, he comes over and picks up the big bear's head and throws it in the back of the truck. Saved my life."

"Okay, Louis. Let's try out some cheeks," said Linda.

They sat there for another hour, various cheeks, chins and hairlines, Louis going over all the details he could remember, until finally they arrived at what Louis said was it. They had their face.

Kate picked up the picture and studied it. "That's interesting."

"What's that?" said Linda.

"Oh, just, this picture, it looks a lot like somebody I used to know."

"Well, remember, it's a composite, more a type of face than a specific person."

She set the picture down on the table. "Yeah, I know. I mean, there's no way it's the guy. He's with the Secret Service. We worked a case together a couple of years ago."

Louis picked up the picture from the table. "That's him. That's the man with the bear's body."

"Louis, it wasn't a bear's body, okay. It was just two people dressed up as bears. You understand?"

Louis smiled. "No ma'am. Those were bears all right. I heard the little one growling. Ain't no man sounds like that."

"The little one, could you make out what he was saying?"

"He was growling, like a bear. Bears can't talk."

"No, they don't Louis, that's true, but they don't generally drive trucks either."

"Maybe it was trained. Maybe it escaped from the zoo or the circus."

"How about his head, Louis. Did his head come off?"

Louis was starting to get irritated. "I told you. Only the big one lost his head, but the little one, he was all bear."

"Okay, Louis, listen. I've got your money here. Do you want to take a shower and get cleaned up before you leave?"

Louis got up from the table. He looked at the two women then glanced around the room. Then he looked down at himself. "I could use a shower," he said. "Wash my clothes. Damn bears scared me into pissing myself. I ain't always been like this you know."

Kate put her arm around his shoulder. "Of course not. If you want I could get someone from a shelter to come down, talk to you..."

"No ma'am, don't wanna talk to nobody. Think I'm crazy, try and put me away somewhere. I'll just take that shower."

Kate called out to a male officer. "Joe, can you help Mr. Crumb get a shower and get his clothes washed?"

Louis left with the officer. Kate took another look at the picture. She couldn't get over the resemblance. But there was just no way Frank Noble was running around dressed up as a bear, killing people. Not the Frank Noble she knew. She checked her watch. It was almost eleven and Tulary had yet to show up at the station. She thought about asking Captain Horton if he had heard from him but if he hadn't she might be getting him in trouble. Here she was again, covering for another alcoholic, just like she used to do for her father, telling her mother he had called and said he'd had to work late or calling his work and saying he was ill. He was ill all right. Maybe she was, too.

The beam of warm light on Tulary's face was clock enough to tell him he was late for work—way late. The sun never hit that window till after noon and Tulary was due in at nine. He opened his eyes and shifted his position to escape the dagger of light so intent on punishing him. He hadn't planned on drinking the night before, had in fact gotten into bed before midnight, downed one shot of bourbon to help settle his nerves and quickly fallen asleep.

Around two in the morning the phone rang. It was Sheila, his ex, calling to tell him their youngest daughter, Amanda, had been arrested for possession of cocaine and was being held in juvenile hall. Tulary was going to have to get up and go get her. Before Sheila hung up she had made sure to remind Tulary that it was his fault his daughter had become such a problem, that it was his drinking that had set such a poor example for the girl.

"Right, Sheila. Of course the pills you've been taking for the last twelve years have nothing to do with it."

"That's a shitty thing to say, Larry. Those are prescription drugs for depression, and you know it."

"If you did something with your life besides sit around and watch soap operas all day, maybe you wouldn't be so fucking depressed."

By this point both of them were ready to explode. They each knew how it worked, had been working for years, yet both seemed incapable of change. It was anger so buried, so twisted and camouflaged over the years, neither one would be able, if pressed, to put their finger on the source, to step through the wall of pain and say here it is, this is where it all started.

"I'm not going to have this argument with you. Are you going to pick her up or not?"

"Well what do you think," Larry said, and hung up the phone.

So he'd gotten dressed and drove down to get his daughter. It was after four by the time they released her. He'd reached out to the arresting officer and gotten him to drop the complaint, then sat in the waiting room half an hour while they got her ready to go. When she came out, she was champing on a piece of gum and tapping her hairbrush against her leg as if the whole thing was just way too boring. Tulary grabbed her by the arm and ushered her out to his car. Then he got in behind the wheel and just sat there for a few minutes staring out into the night.

"Are you gonna say something?" asked Amanda.

Larry looked over at the young girl. Her hair was dyed black and cut real short; she had an earring through one nostril and numerous others in her ears. But it was her complexion that bothered Larry more than anything. The two of them used to get down to the beach once a week and even when they couldn't make it, Amanda always made a point of lying out in the back yard, get some color. Now, she was as white as a dead Swede, as if she were trying to emulate one of the many victims Tulary had stood over; her bright red lips could be the blood, the pierced body parts the bullet holes. At least that's how Larry saw it and he had told her as much; she was trying to punish him. She just shook her head, told him he was lame.

"Why are you doing this?"

Amanda smirked. "Why do you care?"

"Why do you think, Amanda? You're my daughter for Chrissake."

"Right. Don't you have a murder to solve or something?"

"Yeah, like why did detective Lawrence kill his cokehead daughter? I should have just left you in there."

"Don't do me any favors. And I'm not a cokehead. It wasn't mine."

"It wasn't yours?"

"I was holding it for a friend."

"Well, now I feel better. You're not using coke, you're just an idiot."

Tulary took a deep breath then started the car and headed off toward Sheila's house, the house where he used to live, the house where both his daughters had grown up. He'd been gone a year now, but things had been bad for at least the last five. Except for him and Amanda. They had been close, much more so than he and Carol, the older girl. She was off in college now, studying to be a lawyer. She didn't like Tulary, never had, but the two of them

120

had managed to live under the same roof all those years in relative peace. But he and Amanda, they had been pals. They liked the same movies, listened to the same music. Tulary was a blues fanatic and had introduced Amanda to it early on. Sometimes he'd come home from work at three in the morning and he would hear Charles Johnson or Etta James coming from Amanda's room and he'd grab a couple of sodas from the fridge and sit up with her till dawn listening to the music, not saying much, not needing to. If it was a school night, he'd tell Sheila, Amanda was sick the next morning and not to wake her.

Everything changed after the divorce. Tulary tried to explain to her he couldn't take her with him. She was only fourteen, she needed a home, her mother; she needed to be in school. His schedule was crazy; it just wouldn't work. He tried coming around, tried bringing her over to his apartment whenever possible, but it just wasn't the same. Amanda pulled away, pulled away fast and hard. Started running with a new crowd, listening to a whole new type of music—a misnomer in Larry's mind—bands with names like Suicidal Tendencies, Social Distortion; cryptic, angry music, painful to the ear. Tulary had already been drinking; it only got worse.

Tulary pulled up in front of the house. He kept the motor running. "What do you want from me, Amanda?"

"I can't stand it here. She drives me crazy."

"Can't you try and get along with her?"

"Can't you?"

"That's different, Amanda."

"How? You couldn't take it anymore so you left. Well, I want to leave too. It's not fair."

"When you're an adult, you can make those kind of decisions..."

"Now you sound just like her."

"Listen. I'm quitting after this year. Maybe then you could come live with me."

She opened the door and got out. "You won't quit this year. You'll never quit."

"Now you sound like her."

Amanda opened the door and got out of the car.

"Amanda, wait. I'm trying, okay. Don't give up on me."

"Whatever, Larry." Amanda slammed the door and ran to the house. Tulary pulled a bottle from the glove compartment and took a long swig. Larry? When did he become Larry? He pulled away from the curb and drove back to his apartment where he finished off his pint of Jack Daniels and passed out on the bed, fully dressed.

By the time Tulary got to the police station, it was two o'clock. He had showered and shaved, even changed clothes. Kate Mallory was in her office talking on the phone when he walked in. She looked up and raised her hand.

"Right. Terrific. Good work." She hung up the phone. "New suit?" she said to Tulary.

"No, it just hasn't gotten much wear in the last year."

"I think we may have a couple of breaks..."

"Don't you wanna know why I'm late?"

"I think I have a pretty good idea. I had Parker cross check the phone records from Diddlesby and Jack's Rifles. We've got one number comes up the same, belongs to a Kieu Ho. Miss Ho is a working girl."

"Let me just explain about last night..."

Kate got up from her seat and walked around her desk, then sat on the edge of it, next to Tulary. "Let me guess. Something came up, something with your ex-wife, perhaps. You had a drink to calm down, but one wasn't enough. So you had another, and another. Next thing you know, the sun was coming up. Believe me, I know the routine."

"Well, you got all the answers, don't you."

"No, Tu, I don't. My father started drinking when I was eight years old and didn't stop until it killed him ten years later. To this day I have no idea why he drank. I spent a lot of years in therapy trying to figure that out, trying to find out if it was my fault. You

122

know what I finally realized? It doesn't matter what drove him to it. That's not what killed him. The booze killed him. It'll kill you, too. You wanna talk about your problems, I don't know if I can be of any help or not but I'm willing to listen. You want to justify your drinking, I've already heard it from the best."

Tulary quickly changed directions. "So, you said a couple of breaks."

"Well, in addition to Miss Ho, we've got a drawing of one of our perps. You mentioned the animal rights groups, so why don't you take that end and I'll go see Miss Ho."

"You don't think it might be better to switch that around?"

"Oh, I'm sure it would be. For you. Unfortunately, the last one to the table gets the scraps. Think of it as penance."

Frank slept till the noon and when he awoke it was to the smell of fresh coffee. He looked over at the bear head. Pieces of his conversation with Marcell the previous night began playing in his mind like segments of a song; one without a title. That conversation, those few minutes, had seemed so surreal at the time, he hadn't even realized he was in Marcell's house, but that was quite apparent now in the light of day. The room was an average size, maybe fifteen feet square, but everything in it was miniature: dressers, table, chairs, the bed in which he lay, contorted. Like the living room, the walls were covered with photos, black and whites, mostly from the circus. Frank searched the walls, trying to pick out Marcell's mother. There was one on the far wall of a woman— she appeared to be a blonde—with her arms wrapped around the trunk of an elephant. The woman wore shorts and a t-shirt. Frank couldn't make out the face from the bed.

His headache had subsided considerably from the night before but when he stood up, he became somewhat dizzy. He leaned against the wall for a minute to regain his balance, and then moved closer to the picture. If it was Marcell's mother, he was right, she was beautiful. Frank studied the other photos. There were a few more of the same woman, a couple of her on a trapeze, one with a crowd of people, but none of her and Marcell together.

He slowly made his way into the kitchen, stopping every few feet to rest against the wall. Marcell was standing in front of the stove, spatula in hand, half-dozen pancakes on the grill.

"Ah, Frank, you're awake. Sit down, I'll get you some coffee."

"You're up early." Frank eased into the one full-sized chair.

"Sweet is the breath of morn, her rising sweet, with charm of earliest birds." Marcell spoke the words in a lilting manner, affecting a slight British accent in the process.

"Shakespeare?"

"Milton. You want some pancakes?"

"Just the coffee for now."

"Black?"

"Sure."

Marcell delivered Frank's coffee, and then returned to the stove. "I went into Pasadena this morning, bought this coffee; it's supposed to be organic, no chemicals. Hey, I got some donuts, too. How about one of those."

"No, nothing. How did you get to Pasadena?"

"On my Moped."

"You mean it actually runs?"

"Sure, Frank. How do you think I got the bear outfits? Anyway, the circus is just outside Pasadena. They had flyers all over the place."

"And."

"It's my old crew. My mother will be there. We should go and watch her."

Marcell set a plate of pancakes on the table and sat down. In this house, around all this tiny furniture, it was Frank who looked out of place. Size, like distance, was relative. Marcell sliced off a half a cube of butter and slapped it on top of his stack of cakes and poured a good half cup of syrup on top of that. Frank watched in amazement.

"What about the men who were looking for you?"

"Well, I figured you could help me come up with a plan, being

124

as you're the big spy and all."

Frank laughed, then grabbed his head in pain. "I'm no spy, Marcell. I'm more of an armed guard. With a headache."

As Marcell attacked his pancakes, syrup and butter flowed down his chin and dripped back onto the plate.

"What's the hurry, Marcell?"

"Well, they'll only be there for a week."

"No, I mean with the pancakes."

Marcell's mouth was stuffed. "Pancakes..." He swallowed. "Pancakes must be eaten while they're still hot. Anyway, maybe you're not a spy but you know how those things work. You could help me figure a plan, couldn't you?"

"I can try."

"Good." Marcell pushed the notebook they had taken from Jack's across the table to Frank. "You should look at this."

Frank picked up the book and began leafing through it. Then he set it back down on the table. "The pictures in your room, are those your mother?"

"She's very beautiful, isn't she?"

"Yes, she is. I couldn't help noticing you are not in any of the pictures with her."

Marcell started fidgeting with his food. "Well, I, I have other pictures."

"Really. Could I see them?"

Marcell brought his fork down hard on his plate. "Why are you so damn interested in me and my mother?"

Frank was silent for a moment. He had not seen this side of Marcell before now. "I'm sorry if I upset you, Marcell."

Marcell got up from his chair. "You think my mother was ashamed of me don't you? Let me tell you something, Mr. Noble, my mother loved me as much as any mother loved a child."

"Marcell, I..."

"You think it was easy for her, with me? You saw the pictures. My mother is a beautiful woman, she could have had any man she wanted, she could have been rich." Marcell walked to the window

125

and stared outside. He lowered his voice. "When I was little—young, that is—men in the audience—important men; doctors, artists, politicians—would send her flowers and candy. After the show they would come around to see her. When they did, I always made it a point to stay out of the way. I was trying to do her a favor." He turned and faced Frank. "I knew nobody was going to marry her with this albatross around her neck. But my mother wouldn't have it. She'd find me or send somebody to find me and parade me around in front of her suitors. 'This is my wonderful son, Marcell,' she would say, 'he's the joy of my life,' and inevitably the guy would start to stuttering and before you knew it, he was gone." He returned to the table, close to Frank. "You want to know why I'm not in the pictures, Frank, it's because I stayed out of them on purpose, because my mother would have put them out for everyone to see. She would have blown them up into posters, smeared them across the walls. If it was up to her, there would be billboards all over the country of the beautiful Miranda and her wonderful dwarf son, Marcell. I tried to help her, Frank, but she loves me too much for her own good."

"Maybe she just loved you, Marcell. Plain and simple. Maybe she didn't see a freak when she looked at you. Maybe you just heard it so much from everybody else you started believing it yourself. Did it ever occur to you that your mother could never be happy with a man who didn't love and accept her child? You want to break her heart so you can make her happy?"

"Look at me and tell me you don't see a freak."

The two men stared at each other. "You're different, I won't deny that." said Frank. "But you're no freak. Not in my mind. Not for a second."

"Well, what do you think?"

Frank and Marcell were sitting on Marcell's porch. Frank had been looking through the notebook for half an hour and every five minutes Marcell would interrupt with the same question and each time Frank would glance over the top of the book at Marcell as if to say 'don't bug me' then continue on with his reading. This time, he set the book down on the porch. He was feeling a lot better now, though the dizziness still persisted. Another day or so and he figured he'd be back to one hundred per cent.

"It's just what you said, only more so. He's got a record of every transaction he's made in the last year, which hunter specializes in bears or mountains lions, how much each of them pay him for the referral and names of the clients. It's unbelievable. By my count, it looks like over fifty black bears were killed for their parts in this park alone last year. It's a huge business."

"Let's get 'em all, Frank. One by one. What do you say?"

"I'm interested in finding the people responsible for Gladys and Stumble's death. This is too big, Marcell. Too many people."

Marcell hopped down from his chair and began to pace. "Frank, what if we could get a group of these hunters together somehow. You know, we could wipe out a whole bunch of them at once."

"I'm not interested in killing every hunter who ever poached a bear, Marcell. That's not what this is about."

Marcell stopped his pacing right in front of Frank. He stood there now rubbing his chin, looking perplexed. "I don't get it. If you get the people you're after, there will still be a whole bunch of hunters out there killing bears."

"And if I kill everybody in this book, there'll be more to take their place. When I was with the Service, I spent three years chasing counterfeiters, and we put a lot of them out of business, but we never really made much of a dent in the counterfeiting business. But, that was my job, keep the banks from overflowing. I don't have time for that now, Marcell. This is personal. I'm through protecting the property and rights of my fellow Americans. These people took something from me and from Mozart. They're going to pay, each and every one of them and then that'll be it."

"Well, Frank, you're the professional, and I don't want to tell you what to do but, maybe the reason you never made a dent was you didn't punish them hard enough. Don't you think if a dozen or so counterfeiters had been executed, fewer people would be doing it."

Frank laughed. "We don't kill counterfeiters in America."

"Exactly! Did you know that in Kenya they have men whose job it is to protect elephants from poachers and they have orders to shoot to kill if anyone resists. We could be like them, only we wouldn't have to wait around for the poachers. We've got the list. We could send a message, Frank. Make a real impact."

Frank got up from his seat and walked to the edge of the porch. It was a warm afternoon and very calm. "It's dry, feels like a Santa Ana condition developing. I got a bad feeling. I wish I knew where Mozart was."

"We'll find him. What about my idea..."

"Marcell, there's no percentage in trying to change the world. And, more importantly, you don't want to be that person...have all that blood on your hands. Trust me on this. Let's stick to our plan." He quickly changed the subject. "I want to start setting up some surveillance equipment today, get your place secured. I'm going to have to assume I was seen last night, which means it won't be long before they know who I am. I can't use my P.O. Box anymore, so we're going to run out of money."

"Don't worry about money. I can move some around for us."

"Oh, yeah, I forgot. Listen, while you're at the computer, why don't you see if you can locate this Rudy person. That hunter, Diddlesby, said he lived in West Hollywood. How many Rudys could there be in that area?"

"I can do that. I can to it today. When do you think we could go to the circus?"

"Halloween is coming up. Might be a good time to go."

"Oh, Yeah, the circus is great on Halloween. Everybody will be dressed up."

"Are you going to visit your mother?"

"I don't know. Maybe." ❧

ELEVEN

Kate Mallory pulled up to the guard gate outside Kieu Ho's condo complex and flashed her badge to the guard, an older portly gentleman with well-trimmed gray hair. The guard pulled a pair of bifocals from his shirt pocked, examined the badge carefully then nodded his approval to Kate. He pushed a button and the iron gate swung open. Kate couldn't help but wonder just how effective the man could be if some undesirable really wanted to get in. I guess he can dial nine-one-one okay, she thought.

It took her a few minutes to find the building; they all looked alike, terra-cotta stucco with a dark green trim, wrought iron gates and fences and pale yellow canopies above the windows and doorways. Some architect obviously had an infatuation with Tuscany and Kate had to admit to herself it looked nice, if you liked that kind of thing. She preferred her little house at the beach in Santa Monica. It took a lot of upkeep, but it had charm and was reminiscent of better days.

She followed the curved walkway from the parking area to Kieu Ho's front door. It struck her as being a little odd, a woman living in such a nice, tidy place and associating with the likes of Freddie Diddlesby and Jack Pepperton. But then, Kate had never worked Vice, never really considered the bigger picture. Most of the hookers she saw were walking the streets in Hollywood or being dragged in to the station. One didn't associate them with the good life.

There was loud music coming from inside the condo; real upbeat, dancing music. Kate rang the bell. No answer. She rang it again, and then tried pounding on the door with her fist. The music turned down and a moment later the door opened.

129

"Kieu Ho?"

"Veronica," said the woman. She was wearing bright purple tights and had a yellow bandanna wrapped around her head. She was out of breath and sweating.

"You're not Kieu Ho?"

"I changed it. I'm very busy."

Kate showed her badge and asked to come in.

"I'm working out. What this about?"

"It'll just take a minute."

Veronica stepped aside and let Kate in. Kate glanced around the room. Expensive stuff, but too modern for Kate's taste. Miss Ho was either pulling a lot of tricks or had taken a step up the ladder somewhere along the line.

"Nice," said Kate. "What's a place like this run?"

"More than you make. I very busy, so..."

"I'm here about Freddie Diddlesby, and Jack Pepperton."

Veronica grabbed a towel from a chair and wiped the sweat from her face. "I don't know anyone by those names."

"Look, Veronica, we can either have this conversation here, or you can get dressed and we can go to the station. It's up to you."

"Okay, so, maybe I know them. So what?"

"So, when was the last time you saw either of them?"

"I don't know. Maybe two weeks ago. I read about Freddie."

"Tomorrow you can read about Jack."

Veronica put the towel around her neck. "Pepperton, dead?" She sounded genuinely surprised.

"Last night. Suppose you tell me what your connection was to Freddie Diddlesby."

Veronica sat down on the edge of her couch. "He call me up, say Jack give him my number, ask me out for a date."

"For a date. Listen, Veronica, we both know how you earn your living. I'm not with vice, so you can drop the euphemisms."

"He want to know how much I charge."

"Oh, I see. He wanted to hire you for your services."

"I too much money for him."

130

"What if I told you Freddie was walking on the other side of the street?"

"I don't know what you mean."

"Really. Well then let me be more precise. Freddie didn't like girls, Veronica. Not like most men do. You better get dressed."

"No, wait. Okay, Freddie called me. He say, Jack give him my phone number, he has gall bladder he want to sell."

"Why would Pepperton give him your number?"

"Because I Vietnamese. Everyone think Chinese, Vietnamese all the same. Pepperton tell him, maybe I know someone want to buy it. I told Freddie I would ask around, then I find out somebody kill him. That's all I know, I swear."

"What was your relationship with Pepperton?"

Veronica cocked her head and smiled. "Jack not walk on other side of street."

Kate pulled a card out from her pocket and handed it to Veronica. "Two men are dead, Veronica, and there's a good chance it has something to do with this gall bladder. I hope for your sake, you're telling me the truth. If you think of anything else, call me."

"You think same man kill Pepperton?"

"I think it was the same person. I never said it was a man. You call me."

Cleve had been holed up in a cheap motel in Hollywood all week, waiting on Veronica's call, growing more impatient with each passing day and quickly running out of money. (He'd gotten into a poker game in Gardenia and lost over four hundred dollars, had gone through another three hundred on whores and liquor, and was spending a small fortune on ice trying to keep the gall bladder from spoiling.) The dressing on his wound needed to be changed and he had actually driven back to the place where he'd gotten the stitches, fully intent on putting his victims through the same hell once again, but there was an armed guard posted at the front door to the clinic, causing Cleve's good sense to prevail.

There was something about revisiting his victims that really gave him a rush. Just the thought that they might be in their office or home thinking about him, worrying about his returning, made him feel powerful, God-like. The world was made up of weak, spineless victims, all waiting to be preyed upon by the strong; it was their fate and he was more than willing to accommodate them, over and over again. He thought about the couple he had robbed that night he'd followed Veronica. He knew where they lived but not which apartment. Maybe it would be on the mailbox. He could go to their apartment, rob them again, spend some time with the woman, some quality time, make the husband watch. Now that was an idea.

Cleve popped open another beer and reached inside his boxers and grabbed his dick. The thought of taking the woman in front of the husband had gotten him slightly aroused; he gave it a couple of shakes and then lost interest; masturbation was too much work, too much concentration. A cockroach crawled up over the edge of the bed. Cleve grabbed a glass off the end table, sat up slowly so as not to frighten the bug, then ever so carefully moved closer to it till he had the open mouth of the glass just inches above the unsuspecting creature. Quickly now, he brought the jar down over the roach, trapping it with the glass. He then manipulated the bug down to the bottom of the glass and set it on his table.

The phone rang.

"Yeah."

"They killed Jack." It was Veronica. She sounded upset.

"I don't know any Jack. I been waiting to hear from you."

"Jack Pepperton. He gave me Freddie's name."

"Well I'll be sure and send him some flowers."

"I think it was same men who killed Freddie."

"That's all the more reason Mr. Big and I should meet."

"I pick you up."

"Yeah, right. You think I'm stupid. I tell you where I'm staying, next think I know a couple of your pals show up try and rearrange my face."

"Okay, meet me at the Bonaventure, in the lobby.

132

Seven o'clock."

"Seven o'clock. And Veronica, no tricks."

Cleve hung up the phone and took a long swig off his beer. It occurred to him that "tricks" could be taken two ways. He felt clever and proud. What was that called? Oh well, it didn't matter. Point was, ol' Cleve was not only a badass; he was clever.

The cockroach was halfway up the glass jar now. Cleve picked it up and gave it a shake. "No you don't." He set the jar back down on the table, lit an entire pack of matches and dropped them into the glass. The bug tried to scurry up the side of the glass but Cleve knocked it back down into the flame until it caught fire and slowly shriveled up into a torched little pile of protein.

"Yeah! Gotcha, you little fucker."

Marcell's house was only a hundred yards from the road, making access to it relatively easy and securing it difficult. Frank considered setting up cameras along the road, but unless there was someone to continually monitor the screens, they wouldn't do much good. There was enough legitimate traffic on the dirt road to set off any alarm every couple of hours. Instead, he set up a system along the two trails that came closest to the cabin and another one that completely encircled it. The two along the trails were a good fifty yards away; the other one was closer, a last minute warning in case someone came through the bush instead of up one of the trails. The alarms were set at five feet off the ground so as not to go off every time a deer or some other creature passed by. Along with the alarms were cameras that would snap a picture of anyone or thing that triggered the alarm, allowing Marcell to check his monitor, make sure it wasn't an innocent hiker passing that tripped the system.

While Frank worked on the system, Marcell stayed busy on his computer, trying to find an address for Veronica Ho, and run down all the Rudys living in West Hollywood. When Frank was finished, they ran some tests, made sure everything worked as planned, then worked up the procedure they would follow in case of any intrusion. Frank had also purchased some walkie-talkies, enabling them to keep track of each other twenty-four hours a day, and had drawn up maps of the area between the two cabins and designated rendezvous points in case they somehow lost contact.

As he went over the system with Marcell, Frank remained calm and methodical, like a scientist explaining a simple experiment to a layman. He seemed to Marcell to be a man totally in his element, and for Marcell, though he felt it was all a little overkill, the entire process was exciting; he couldn't help but hope someone would come after him, that they would be able to play out this intrigue to its natural conclusion.

There was, however, one nagging question on Marcell's mind. With men like Frank setting up security systems and guarding over Presidents, how was it that assassins had been so successful in the past? He thought of Kennedy and the close calls with Reagan and Ford. Even that nut case—what was her name, Squeaky something—had gotten close.

He had to ask. They were in the kitchen going over the procedure for the third time, Frank making Marcell repeat each step.

"I hear the alarm, I check the screen. If I have any doubt at all, I contact you on the walkie-talkie, then retreat to area one and keep an eye on the cabin." Area one was a large boulder on the side of a hill about fifty yards from the cabin. It allowed for a good view of the cabin and could easily be defended against an attack.

Frank interrupted. "Unless the alarm comes from cameras three and four. You won't have time to leave the cabin if they get in that close."

"Right, I knew that. If the alarm comes from three or four, I move into the bedroom and take my position behind the bed where I can watch the windows and the door. What if they set the place on fire?"

"They're not likely to do that unless they know you're in there. The only way they're going to find that out is if they come inside.

134

Once they get in, it's up to you to see to it they don't get out. Remember, I'll be on my way. I can make it here in fifteen minutes."

"If you're at your cabin."

"There are a lot of ifs, Marcell."

"Is that what happened with Reagan—an if? Were you in on that?"

"I was there." Frank stopped and pondered for a minute. "I go there all the time, in my head, replaying that moment. You get outside, with hundreds of people around, so many things to consider, you can lose your edge, anything can happen, no matter how thorough you think you've been."

"What do you mean, lose your edge?"

"Just that. You're trained to look for certain things, but in the chaos you have to make choices, instantaneous decisions about people. Maybe you see someone who looks nervous and keeps looking around so you watch him for a few seconds, but then somebody else pops up, it's a warm day but this other person is wearing a bulky jacket so you turn your attention to him. Choices. I saw Hinkley coming, I saw his eyes; I should have read his intentions, but I hesitated. I don't know, maybe I wanted to be sure, wanted to see the gun, before I did anything. I looked away and the next thing I knew, there were gunshots, Reagan was hit and Brady was lying on the ground, bleeding. All our planning, all the precautions—you look away for a split second—that's why it's so important you pay attention to every detail. Things happen quickly. You have to be ready for the unexpected. Now, let's go over this one more time."

"I still have a lot to do, Frank, tracking down this Rudy fellow. So far I got fourteen Rudys in West Hollywood. Who would of thought there'd be so many."

"We may not need that. You got Veronica's address. We'll go see her tonight. Now, let's run this down again."

Tulary had spent the entire day getting educated on animal

rights. He had expected to find a bunch of rag-tag organizations, loosely run by fanatics, but had been met instead by articulate representatives, each eager to educate him on the realities of animal cruelty. He started with the most innocuous—Society for the Prevention of Cruelty to Animals—then worked his way through People for the Ethical Treatment of Animals and Last Chance for Animals, showing them all the drawing of the suspect, getting the same results: zero. He had hoped to make contact with someone involved with the Animal Liberation Front, but if anybody he spoke to knew anything about them, they weren't saying.

The one common message was this: They were there to protect the rights of animals, not to kill human beings. Nobody from any of their organizations would be involved in that kind of thing. Of course, none of the people Tulary talked to seemed very upset over the murders, and all of them knew about the illegal hunting of bears for their bladders.

"California and Alaska are the new hunting grounds." The man's name was Delaquoix. He was the head of a new organization called Save Our Animals. "China has pretty much wiped out their entire population of bears."

"Well, no wonder they have so many people."

"Yeah, that's real funny, detective. For your information, the gall bladders are used more for the treatment of hemorrhoids than anything else. The aphrodisiac aspect makes good copy—which is fine, whatever gets the word out—but it's not really used that much for that purpose."

"Hemorrhoids, huh. If only I'd known."

"Yeah, well, some traditions die hard. In the meantime, the bounty on California bears keeps going up. I don't advocate violence against these poachers, but I sure do understand it. If they're allowed to continue, we'll lose our bears, just like China. You may not care about the bears, detective, but keep in mind, even from a selfish point of view, these hunters are taking your property and selling it."

136

He went on to tell Tulary about the various projects they were involved in, how they had recently helped police bust a couple who had been stealing pets—cats and dogs—and selling them to labs for research. He showed him pictures of wolves caught in traps then bludgeoned to death for their fur, monkeys strapped to chairs with wires attached to their brains, elephants slaughtered for their ivory. And there were numbers. Seventeen million animals used in lab experiments every year, thousands of those, dogs, cats and primates.

Tulary kept trying to bring the subject back to the hunt for Freddie's killers, but Delaquoix was on a roll. He pulled out the pamphlets and started handing them to Tulary, articles by famous doctors and scientists disavowing the benefits of animal research. When Delaquoix ducked into a back room for some more literature, Tulary made a run for the door, his arms full of literature, a pin that read 'meat is murder' pinned to his lapel.

Cleve sat in the lobby of the Bonaventure, trying his best not to look conspicuous, which was hard to do with his arm bandaged, and the bandage being as dirty as it was. And there was the box with the gall bladder. The ice was melting and water was seeping out from the bottom and onto the seat. He kept pulling the sleeve of his jacket over the wound to hide it as best he could and kept his head buried behind a newspaper. He came across the article about the guy from the rifle shop being murdered. There was a drawing of a suspect along with the article. Cleve carefully tore away the picture and stuck it in his pocket; it was nice of the police to help him out. Now he not only knew the area where the guy lived, but he had a good idea what he looked like. All that much easier to sell his idea to Veronica's trick.

It was after seven and Veronica still hadn't shown. Cleve had been sitting there for half an hour and every ten minutes or so someone would come up to him and ask if there was anything they could help him with. Inevitably, they would glance down at the wet spot on the seat and then back at Cleve as if waiting for an explanation. It was really getting on his nerves. When a young woman from behind the desk came over for the second time, Cleve let her have it.

"What is it with you fucking people. I told you, I'm waiting for a friend, a woman friend. If she don't show up, I'll let you know and you can take her place. You're a little skinny for me, but I'm sure I can find some good use for you. Until that time, tell everybody here to quit fucking bothering me. You understand?"

The girl was young and obviously new at her job, for rather than call security and have him thrown out of the place, she quickly apologized and retreated behind her desk. Someone during her training had accented the need to treat their customers with the utmost respect, had told her there would be times when people would be rude and discourteous. Better to ruin a chair than risk upsetting an important person, maybe even a movie star.

Veronica showed up around seven-thirty. She was wearing a full-length fur coat and a pair of black high heels. She stopped next to Cleve just long enough to tell him to meet her at the elevator. He started to give her some shit about being late but she just kept on walking.

Veronica had to use a key to get access to the penthouse. On their way up she told Cleve he should not be pushy with Mr. O'Neill, not like he was with everyone else. He would be angry enough that she had brought Cleve in the first place. He should let her do the talking.

Cleve pulled back his jacket and revealed his pistol. "You don't tell me how it works, understand? I do my own talking. I ain't afraid of your Mr. O'Neill."

"Yeah, you big tough guy, all right."

Veronica wasn't sure what would happen when she showed up with Cleve. Anything was possible. She had seen a new side of O'Neill the last time she'd been over, the night he'd knocked her around. In a way, he was worse than Cleve. He didn't get worked up emotionally when he was hitting on her; it was more like sport. Cleve, well, he was hot headed, downright mean, but you could

138

understand his meanness. His emotions got out of control and he started inflicting pain. Veronica had known lots of guys like him, guys that liked to push their weight around. A girl just had to be smart, stay out of their way, head them off before they got a chance to get too worked up. Guy like O'Neill, you just never knew. He might listen to what Cleve had to say and hire him to take care of the problem, or he could just as easily kill them both, right then and there.

There was a guard in the foyer and as Cleve and Veronica stepped out of the elevator the guard stood up from his chair and placed himself in front of the door. He was a large man, all buffed out and showing off his muscles behind a tight black t-shirt. He wore a shoulder holster packed with a .44 magnum.

"Mr. O'Neill expecting me," said Veronica.

"He ain't expecting this clown."

Cleve put his hand inside his jacket and the guard reached down and grabbed his arm in his huge hand, quickly pulling it out into view. "You don't wanna be making those kinda moves my friend."

"I ain't your friend, asshole," said Cleve.

"You tell Mr. O'Neill I'm here and I have someone who needs to speak to him." said Veronica.

"He don't go in less I frisk him first."

Cleve extended his arms. "Do it."

The guard took Cleve's gun and his knife, and then he opened the door. "Wait here."

Veronica stood there shaking her head at Cleve who was now leaning up against the wall, picking at the gall bladder, water dripping from the box onto the floor. The guard came back after a couple of minutes and let them both in, and Steven showed them to the living room.

O'Neill was staring out the window, drink in hand. "Veronica, I'm disappointed in you," he said, as he turned around to face the couple. "I rather thought you were an intelligent girl, but this, you bring this,"—he gave Cleve a disapproving look—"vagabond into my home. What am I to think?"

139

"I can explain..."

Cleve jumped in. "I didn't give her much choice, and you need to listen to what I have to say."

"Really. You're here to satisfy my needs, are you?"

"I'm here to do business."

"Okay, Mr...."

"The name's Cleve."

"Cleve. Short for Cleveland, no doubt. I was in Cleveland, once. Ugly, filthy town. Suppose you tell me what you have in mind. I like what you have to say, maybe we do business. I don't like it, maybe I have my guys cut you up into little pieces, pack up your parts and ship them all over the country. Maybe even international. How's that sound, give you a chance to see the world, or at least let the world see you?"

"You're gonna need more than those Nancy-boys you got around here, you expect to do any cutting on me."

"Well, now I'm frightened. If you don't mind my asking, what is that you have dripping all over my white carpet?"

Cleve showed him the gall bladder he had brought and told him about the two murders. Then he laid out his proposition. He would deliver more gall bladders directly to O'Neill, and he would take care of the bear lover out in the woods. He wanted twenty-five hundred for each gall bladder—he'd throw in any paws for free—and ten grand to get rid of Grizzly Adams.

"Why should I pay you ten grand to do this guy?"

"Call it a hunch, but I think he's working his way up to you."

"Well, there's really nothing to lead him to me, is there?"

"I found you easy enough."

O'Neill glanced over at Veronica. "Yes, yes you did. Veronica, sweetheart, why don't you wait for me in the bedroom."

Veronica hadn't said a word throughout the meeting, but she didn't like the way things were unfolding, especially the last part. Wheels were turning inside O'Neill's head, wheels that were roaring right down the highway toward Veronica, high-beams lighting her up like a frightened doe. How could she have been so stupid, bringing Cleve here? Rudy had warned her about O'Neill. Rudy. Maybe he could help her, if she ever got out of here alive. She thought about making a dash for the front door, but Steven was in her path and there was that gorilla outside in the hall. She grabbed her purse and went into the bedroom. In his haste to search Cleve, the guard had forgotten to check her purse. Veronica opened it up and checked the contents. Good, it was there, a little two-shot derringer, loaded and ready if needed. She couldn't get all of them, but if O'Neill started something, damn if she wasn't going to take him with her. ✹

Well, he did it. This morning President Reagan actually sent a couple of F-14s into Lybia to bomb Qaddafi's house. The report is that Qaddafi was not even on the premises and escaped unharmed but that one of his children was killed along with other civilians. It's unbelievable! How can the President of the United States drop a bomb on the home of the head of state of another country, kill his children, and think it's okay? And the staff. Everybody's cheering and backslapping around here, like this was some major accomplishment.

I've always liked Reagan, on a personal basis, that is. He has always been very friendly towards me and the rest of the staff, but this, this is too much. Can you imagine what Americans would be saying if some country dropped a bomb on the White House and killed one of Reagan's children? We'd be dropping a nuclear bomb on the place.

I try my best to keep my political beliefs out of my work. My job is to protect the President, plain and simple, and I am very much aware of that, but sometimes I feel like I'm working in an insane asylum. The stuff that goes on around here. The politics! Terrorism is the new magic word, the new evil to be rooted out and destroyed. Nobody wants to see innocent people die and I certainly abhor some of the tactics used, the bombing of airplanes, the taking of hostages. But none of this is new. The colonists were terrorists in the eyes of the British. The Israelis, who are always screaming about terrorism, used the same tactics against the British after World War II. I spent two years fighting an undeclared war in Vietnam and if the things I saw happening there weren't acts of terror, what is? My God! The hypocrisy!

"Batteries must be going dead," said Marcell as he gave his flashlight a shake then turned it off and placed it in the glove box. He set the journal on the seat, next to him.

They were sitting in Frank's Toyota in front of Veronica's complex, waiting for her to show up. They'd been there over and hour and it was their third trip that evening, each time, Marcell getting out of the truck and ducking under the cross-bar that blocked the entry—it wasn't much of a duck—jogging up to Veronica's place, peaking through the crack in the garage door to see if her car was there, and then running back to report to Frank. Each time the report was the same: He couldn't tell if there was a car in the garage. The house was dark and it was quiet; it didn't look like anyone was there. Frank finally decided to just park it out front and wait for her return—much to Marcell's delight—hope nobody got nervous and called the cops.

"I remember when that happened," said Marcell.

"What?"

"In your journal, when Reagan bombed Qaddafi's house. I was pretty young at the time, but I remember it."

"Great day for America," said Frank.

"Do you regret it? Those years in the Secret Service."

"Regret is like guilt, Marcell. It doesn't change anything. I will say this: I think I could have found a better way to use my time." He checked his watch. "It's almost four, I don't think she's coming home tonight. Let's go on in, have a look around."

They got out of the truck and crossed the street. A little blue sports car zipped by and Frank instinctively turned his head away; they hadn't brought the bear skins tonight, just a couple of cotton ski masks to cover their faces—which neither of them had bothered wearing. Marcell ducked under the bar and Frank stepped over it.

Marcell led Frank to Veronica's condo where Frank quickly located the wires to the security system and disconnected it. He figured he'd have to pick the lock to the front door but when he gave the knob a turn the door swung open. He drew his pistol and the two of them stepped inside. The living room was dark but there was a sliver of light slicing through an open door at the end of a hallway. Frank motioned for Marcell to check the kitchen and he proceeded down the hall.

He gently pushed open the door then stepped inside the bedroom, both hands on his pistol. It was a mess—someone had rifled through it looking for something—drawers had been emptied out onto the floor, knick-knacks scattered off of shelves, pictures torn from the walls. The only thing still intact was the stereo, soft music drifting up from the overturned speaker. He reached down and cut the volume.

There was another sound now, coming from an adjoining room, like radio static or water. It was running water, a shower. He moved slowly in that direction, tiptoeing over the debris. He turned a corner and stepped into the bathroom. There was only one small window in the room and it was closed, and yet there wasn't any steam building up from the shower. He stood quietly for a moment, listening. All he heard was the water, no singing, nobody dropping a bar of soap; nothing. He grabbed the curtain in one hand and stood there frozen, reluctant to open it, afraid of what he might find. Maybe it would be better to just turn around and walk out, he thought, and he started to do just that. He released the curtain and turned away, then, knowing he really had no choice, turned back and grabbed it again, and quickly pulled it open. Now all he had to do was look down.

Veronica had gone into the bedroom and waited half an hour for O'Neill, thinking he would come in and put an end to her, or at least try. She'd gotten undressed and into the bed and slipped the small pistol under the pillow. But O'Neill tried nothing. They had sex, nothing too outrageous, no aphrodisiacs, no punching or biting or even name calling; O'Neill usually liked calling her names: bitch, whore, anything degrading, but there was none of that. Afterwards, he paid her extra, told her not to worry about Cleve, that the guy was a loose cannon and that he would have his guys take care of him. In the future, he said, she should let him know, somebody tries strong-arming her, don't just bring them up to see him. Certainly she could understand how he'd be upset over that.

So she'd left there thinking things were okay, that she'd gotten through the whole ordeal, though she couldn't help feel a bit anxious in her gut. Why was O'Neill being so nice, so understanding? She searched her mind for any previous hints of this type of behavior. They'd been together ten, twelve times. He'd always been nasty and often mean in bed and had beaten her up after using the gall bladder, but there was never any niceness afterwards. He was generous with the money, but then he'd quickly usher her out of the place, like a servant who had performed her duty and was due to leave. Not that Veronica wanted to hang around and get acquainted—in fact, she hated it when a trick would start getting mushy on her afterwards; just pay up and shut up, that was her motto—but a civil word now and then wouldn't kill him. So, why all the chatter this time?

She stopped at a 7-11 on the way home and got a pint of raspberry sherbet. The clerk was Vietnamese, about her age, and the two of them exchanged a few words in their native tongue. Then she got back into her Mercedes and headed for home. It was after midnight by the time she got back to the condo. During the day, there was a guard at the gate, but at night one gained entrance with a card. It seemed to Veronica that it would be better the other way around, have a guard at night.

She grabbed the remote from her visor and pushed the button. Her garage door slid open and the shiny Mercedes glided inside. Veronica turned off the motor and as she replaced the remote on the visor, she caught a glimpse of something in the mirror; it went by so quickly there was no telling what it was, a shadow perhaps, or a dog. She grabbed the derringer from her purse and sat their motionless, listening; there was not a sound. You're paranoid, she thought. She grabbed her purse and the ice cream and got out of the car.

She went inside, set the sherbet on the kitchen counter, turned off the alarm, and then checked the front door and the windows, making sure everything was secured. Then she made a room-by-room search until she was satisfied she was safe. She called Rudy. His machine was on. "Rudy," she said. "It's me. I need to talk to you right away. Call me when you get in tonight."

She hung up the phone. She remembered the sherbet and

considered going back in there and sticking it in the freezer but she figured it would keep long enough for her to take a shower and get changed, and so she put it out of her mind. She set the gun in the bathroom, on the counter, got undressed and turned on the shower. She liked long hot showers; sometimes she'd stay in there till all the hot water was gone, trance like, basking in the warmth of the water. It made her feel secure.

She cleaned herself, then lathered her hair with shampoo and rinsed it. A little got in her eye and she reached through the curtain for a towel. Her fingers touched the soft cotton but before she could grab hold of the towel, a hand grabbed her by the wrist. She opened her eyes just as the curtain pulled back. The soap stung her eyes and slightly blurred her vision, but she recognized Cleve. There was no mistaking that grin.

"Sorry, sister," he said. "Nothing personal."

In her mind's eye she saw the gun on the counter, but in the short time it took for her to process the memory, Cleve had the knife at her throat. She threw her hands up to protect herself but before they got half way, Cleve had managed to slice her from ear to ear. She grabbed her throat, her life pouring out in warm, red gushes, then quickly turning orange as the cooling water diluted it and spun it down the drain. Veronica tried in vain to hold back the blood with her hands but the blade had gone deep, severing the jugular. The more she struggled, the faster the blood gushed out, her heart growing louder with each beat, until it seemed as though it would explode. Her knees began to buckle under and she clawed at the tile in desperation, but the strength was going out of her hands; they plopped to her side as she collapsed into the tub. She glanced down at her shiny red nails; such pretty hands, she thought. She was losing consciousness; she could feel herself drifting away; she was dying and she knew it. The last thing she thought of, lying there in that cold white tub with the blurry shadow of her assailant standing over her, was her mother; only now it wasn't her mother's *hands* she saw, but her face. She could see it very clearly now for the first time since the day she'd left

146

home; she looked very much like Veronica. She was smiling, and there were tears pouring down her cheeks. "Welcome back," she was saying. "Welcome home."

Cleve rinsed his knife off in the cool water flowing from the showerhead, and then wiped it dry on the white cotton towel and placed it back in his belt. He saw the derringer sitting on the counter and stuck it in his pocket, and quickly set about searching for Veronica's phone book and any valuables she might have.

The phone book was easy to find. Veronica kept it in the top drawer of a small desk next to the bed. He checked the contents. Rudy was in there along with a host of others. This was for O'Neill. Without this there would be no connecting Veronica to Rudy and then Rudy to O'Neill. Whoever had hunted down Freddie and then the guy at the rifle shop would reach a dead end. There was a key tucked into a small pouch in the book's cover. Cleve examined the key briefly, then stuck it in the coin pocket of his jeans.

He tossed the book into a pillowcase along with a few other items: a watch, some jewelry, a couple of gold candleholders. Then he set about looking for the cash. There had to be some somewhere; every hooker kept a stash around the house in case she needed to get out of town quick. He tore pictures from the walls and cut away the backing, checked the bottoms of the dressers for taped packages, rummaged through every pocket on every pair of pants hanging in her closet. As he searched he became more and more angry, slicing things up with his knife, smashing knick-knacks against the wall. The fact that there was a dead body in the shower, that someone might hear him making such a ruckus and call the police, never crossed his mind.

He was about to give up the hunt when he came across a small wooden box tucked away on the top shelf in the very back of her closet. The lid to the box had a carving of a farmer and an ox working a field. The farmer wore a large straw hat and had no shoes. Cleve opened the box and pulled out a roll of hundred

147

dollar bills, then tossed the box to the floor. He counted the money; close to two thousand dollars. Not a bad haul for a couple hours work.

He stuffed the money in his pocket, grabbed the pillowcase with the rest of his booty and left the room. There was a pint of ice cream sitting on the kitchen counter; it was lying on its side and had started to melt, forming a small red pool around the lid. Cleve grabbed a spoon and dug in. It was sweet and tangy, tasted like raspberries. He took a couple more bites, wiped his mouth with his sleeve and burped. Then he set the container back on the counter and walked out the front door. Life was good.

It was just what Frank had feared. There in the tub, blood still oozing from the gaping wound to her neck, her eyes wide open and staring up at Frank, lay a small Asian woman, cold water pounding down on her very clean, very dead body.

He reached in and turned off the water, then knelt down beside the tub. The girl was already beginning to show the distortions of death: the flattened face, the pale bloodless complexion. He reached in and closed her eyes. He had fallen in love with the Vietnamese people from the first day he set foot in their country, had been moved by their beauty, struck by the irony of their size, so small and seemingly fragile and yet endowed with such a powerful will. He saw many, just like this one, dead before their time, cut to pieces by shrapnel, shot point blank in the forehead or torn to shreds by a bomb, or cut by an angry trick. Then, the bombs stop, the treaties are signed, everybody goes home, and twenty years later a young girl thousands of miles from home dies alone in a cold porcelain tub.

He felt a hand on his shoulder.

"I found us some sodas," said Marcell.

Frank turned his head. On his knees, he and Marcell were about the same height. Marcell got his first look into the tub and dropped the cans of soda onto the floor. "Oh, man," he said. "Is that Veronica?"

148

"It must be. We better get out of here."

Marcell couldn't take his eyes off the dead girl. "What about Rudy. The address?"

"There's no time. Besides, somebody has already been through the place. I have a feeling they were looking for the same thing."

"Let me just, check, by the phone. See if...maybe there's a book."

"Make it quick, Marcell."

Marcell didn't budge. There were tears in his eyes.

Frank put his hand on Marcell's shoulder. "Hey, you okay?"

"Yeah, yeah, I'm fine. She looks...it's so sad, Frank."

"Go on. Look for the book." Frank reached down and started lifting the girl out of the tub.

"What are you doing?"

"I can't leave her in here."

He carried her into the bedroom, laid her on the bed and pulled a blanket up over her cold body. Marcell began rummaging half-heartily through some dresser drawers—most of them had been emptied onto the floor—every now and then glancing over to the dead girl. He found the answering machine tucked half way under the bed. A small light was blinking. He pushed the message button.

"Veronica, it's me, Rudy. What's so fucking important it can't wait till tomorrow. Where the fuck are you? Call me back."

"Look at this," said Marcell. Next to the message light was a small window with a phone number. "She has one of those gadgets, tells you the phone number of the person who called you. Looks like we've found Rudy."

Frank stood over the bed, staring down at the dead woman, a small stain of blood on the sheet where it covered her neck. "Write it down," he said, almost in a whisper. "This isn't what I wanted. This is all wrong."

The drive back to Marcell's cabin was a somber one, both men still in shock. They had their windows rolled down, trying their best to cleanse themselves with fresh air. Frank drove down the freeway in the right lane, barely going fifty, Marcell staring out the window. After twenty minutes, Marcell broke the silence.

"Do you think it was Rudy?"

"Veronica? No. We've seen this guy's work before. That's Freddie's partner. Cleve."

"But why?"

"She's the link to him and Rudy, and whoever else is involved. People are getting nervous."

"Do you want to call it off?"

Frank rolled up his window and looked over to his friend. The sight of Veronica's lifeless body had really shaken Marcell. It was one thing to stand over the body of someone you hate, someone you could demonize, like Bartelli, but seeing a small, beautiful woman, curled up in a cold, wet death, that was something else, altogether. Especially the first time. "It's too late for that now. But if you want out, I understand."

"No, no, I'm with you, Frank, all the way. It's just..."

"I know, Marcell. Try not to think about it. One thing. When we find him, Cleve, he's mine. You understand?"

"Sure."

There were a few more minutes of silence and then. "It's our fault, isn't it?" said Marcell.

"What?"

"Veronica's death."

"It's everybody's fault."

By the time they got back to Marcell's house the sky had already begun to lighten from the rising sun. They had cleared an area not far from the house, out of view from the road, where Frank could leave his truck. Both men were exhausted but Frank decided to make the hike to his cabin and sleep there. Marcell's bed was comfortable enough, if you happened to be under five feet tall.

Frank took his time getting back to his place; he needed to be outdoors for a while, needed replenishing. This was his favorite

150

time of day in the woods. Everything was waking now, coming to life. For Frank, each day out here was a micro-version of a year. Morning was spring, heralded in by a multitude of colorful singing birds, their voices unique, yet harmonious. As the sun's light brought color back to the surrounding trees and prodded flowers to reveal themselves, it also brought hope to a tired soul like Frank. Most people slept right through this part of the day; most people lived without hope. Noon brought warmth and activity—summer. The woods were alive with thousands of creatures scurrying about, playing in the cool streams, grooming and petting one another in the warmth of the sun. As the sun fell lower in the sky, autumn began and the noise of the woods subsided as everyone sought shelter for the approaching night, gathering up their young, securing their nests. Night was winter, a short death of sorts. Flowers turned in on themselves, and why not? Who could appreciate their beauty now? Birds rested their voices; no need to sing for a sleeping forest.

Of course, there were some creatures still stirring about. Like men, some preferred the absence of light, the stillness and peace of darkness. It also provided a good cover for those who wished to prey on their sleeping brother. There was a certain element of terror added when one attacked their prey in the blackness of night, or the depth of winter, when death surrounds and points its icy finger in all directions.

Yes, nature had a rhythm, a pattern, and Frank had tried his best to become part of that pattern. Here it was the break of dawn and he could hardly keep his eyes open. He should be just getting out of bed. Everything was out of whack again, like in Vietnam, when he had to grab an hour of sleep three or four times a day, catch as catch can, or with the Service, never knowing what the schedule would be, and then with each election, a new President, a new timetable; it was all so maddening, so unnatural.

He'd come out to the woods and set his rhythm to the one he found in nature, and in doing so had freed himself from the concept of time, had in fact managed to stop time. Each morning

151

he awoke was a small rebirth; each day lived, a lifetime, followed by a sleep (a death?) and then another birth. Time was, after all, artificial. Life, reality, was circular, not linear. The earth rotated on its axis and circled the sun; it never passed it by. Things did not really age; they changed. Hair turned gray then fell out, skin dried up, muscles lost their elasticity, the heart grew weak and the fire that burned inside a man grew dimmer just as the sun did each time the earth spun around on it's axis.

In the peaceful midst of that existence he had lost himself, lost track of the world and its phony time. He kept no clocks or calendars, never dated his journal. He knew his checks were delivered every two weeks but no longer kept track of those deliveries either. He would go to town when his supplies ran low and whenever he went he checked his box; if there was a check, he cashed it, if not he would check on his next visit. Now, strangers had come into his world and brought their world with them—their greed, their cruelty, their time.

The thought of them now filled him with rage. He wished it didn't, wished he could put it aside but there was no way. Like pests, they had bored themselves into his life and he had no option but to dig them out, each and every one. He still had to deal with Rudy, had to put an end to Cleve, and he had to help Marcell with his problem. Maybe then he could return to the real world, to a true life. Maybe not.

As he came to the clearing by his cabin he noticed a dark figure tucked into the corner on his deck. There weren't any lights on inside the cabin but the front door was open. Frank never left the door open and he couldn't remember leaving anything sitting out on the porch. No sense taking any chances. He moved slowly back to the cover of trees then quietly circled the cabin to the other side. He checked his pistol to make sure it was loaded then crept along the far side of his cabin till he got to the corner of the porch where the figure had been. He cocked his gun, pushed away from the building and turned to face the porch. There, curled up in a ball against the porch rail was Mozart, fast asleep, one arm

152

draped over Frank's CD player.

"I'll be damned," he said and lowered his gun. Just then another figure appeared from the front door, startling Frank, and he quickly raised his gun. A sharp penetrating bark eased his fear as Bones crossed the porch to greet him.

"Bones, you found him. Good boy." Frank thought of calling Marcell, but figured it was best to let him sleep; he could use some himself. He fixed Bones a plate of food then made a quick entry in his journal.

Life is unpredictable at best. Tonight I saw a beautiful young woman cut down in her prime; a senseless, brutal killing. All I could hang on to as I lifted her lifeless body from the shower was my rage for the man who killed her. I know that rage; I understand it well. It can race through a man like a wildfire, burning up everything in its path. There are moments when I feel it taking over; I fear I will not be able to control it.

Mozart has returned. He's come home. I can only imagine the trauma he has experienced these last few days, not knowing what happened to his mother or brother, left alone out here to fend for himself. But he is alive. Bones has found him and brought him back to me. Perhaps his presence will help diffuse the anger within me. I hope so. I am so tired. ✒

THIRTEEN

Rudy woke up Halloween morning feeling a little bit strange. He wasn't sure if it was the small section of gall bladder he had made into soup and eaten the previous night or the full moon, but something had put him out of whack with his body. Rudy had never done any hallucinogens, but he imagined this was what it felt like; his body seemed to float a split second behind his mind so that he would perform some simple maneuver, say, opening a door, and then glance back and see himself doing it.

It was strange all right, weird.

He'd had sex with two of the girls from the Malibu house: Angel, who had brought along her collection of objects of entry—Rudy didn't usually go in for that kind of thing but he'd seen the lesbians across the way and he wasn't sure what was going to happen once he ate the bladder; better to be prepared—and Maple, a sixteen year old black girl he'd been doing since she was twelve—she knew everything Rudy liked and she had the greatest set of lips he'd ever seen. Rudy liked lips. One thing he'd made crystal clear to Veronica, if they didn't have nice lips, don't bother bringing them around. He could overlook any other flaw, but if a girl had a pair of skinny little lips and a tiny mouth in general, forget it.

As far as he could tell, the gall bladder hadn't really made much difference in the sex. Of course, he'd had a lot to drink and done a couple grams of coke; maybe they had counteracted one another. It was a funny thing about cocaine, how it always made him so horny but at the same time made it almost impossible to concentrate on the sex. You had to do just the right amount, which was easy enough to tell yourself before you started into it. After that first couple of lines there was no way you could just put the rest away and say okay, that's it for this, now let's have some sex. The only way to really test the bladder would be to use it by itself, no drugs or booze, and the only way to do that was to make sure there wasn't any of either of those in the house when he started. Maybe tonight, he thought. Maple was coming back to make a movie with O'Neill's client. If he could get that wrapped up early enough, he'd go another round with her.

Rudy fixed himself some coffee, making sure to move very slowly so as to eliminate as many of the trailers as possible. It was already noon and he hadn't heard from Veronica. First she calls up (twice!) sounding like she's in a panic—like Rudy was gonna climb down off Maple and answer the phone—then he finally calls her back and she's not home, and now here it is twelve o'clock, she's supposed to pick up the Chinese guy at the airport and he hasn't heard a word from her. She's been getting way too independent lately, he thought. Time to bring her down a notch.

He grabbed the phone and dialed her number. Three rings and the machine came on. "Leave a message," that was all it said, no music, nothing. Just, "leave a message," then that long silent period waiting for the beep.

There it was. "Veronica, pick up, it's Rudy. Goddamn it, you better be on your way to the airport. Call me back." He hung up. Well, hopefully she was on her way, if not, the jerk-off would just have to find his own ride to his hotel, cause Rudy sure as hell wasn't picking him up. Fucking O'Neill thinks I'm running some kinda baby-sitting service here, he thought. Damn, there it was again. He had his coffee cup pressed right up against his lips yet he could still see a trail of cups and arms leading from the table to his mouth. It was like looking into a mirror reflected into another mirror and seeing your image reflected into infinity.

Rudy got up from the table and slowly walked outside onto his deck. He was still in his Speedos but it was warm and dry, and the sun felt good on his skin. He set his cup on the ledge and gazed out over the city. He had to laugh. All those slobs down there, running around trying to make a buck just so they can turn around and hand it over to their wife and kids and here he was living large, all the girls he could handle, plenty of money, and never having

155

to lift a finger. Not bad for an ugly fat guy, he thought,.

"Not bad at all," he said as he grabbed his cup from the ledge and turned to go back into the house. He could see his reflection in the sliding glass door. All of them.

Kate Mallory was on the phone in her office arguing with a man about a tile job done incorrectly at her house. She was quickly losing patience. Something about being at Veronica's condo, seeing all the great furniture and beautiful tile and fabrics, had made her feel cheated. She had a habit of settling for second best. Not anymore.

"No, *you* don't understand. I ordered white, smooth grout and your people came out to my house with gray, sanded grout, and used that without telling me. I wasn't home. No, it's not your fault I wasn't home, it's your fault for using the wrong materials. Not only that, but the backsplash looks like the Pacific Ocean. I mean it's wavy!"

Tulary stuck his head inside her doorway.

"Just a second," said Kate to the man on the phone. "What's up?"

"Horton wants to see us. I think he's pissed off."

"Just a second." She returned to her conversation on the phone. "Look, I have to go. You have one week to rectify this problem. Hey, I'm a cop, mister. Believe me when I tell you, I don't need to sue you. This is the last time I'm calling."

Kate slammed the phone down and got up from her desk. Tulary had a big smile on his face. "What are you laughing at?"

"I'm a cop, mister. I don't have to sue you. That's good, I like it. What are you gonna do, shoot him?"

"If I have to." The two of them started off toward Horton's office. "What's bugging the lieutenant?"

"Hey, he's a lieutenant. That's his job."

"You don't have to take so much pleasure in it."

"I know Bill too well to derive any pleasure from his anger. But you, you brighten my day."

"I just don't understand these people who come and work in your home. The plumber left a mess all over the bathroom floor. He used one of my t-shirts to clean off the pipes; I have no idea what it is he got on it. It looks like baby shit. A guy came last week to work on my locks and set his greasy tools down on the carpet; and now these tile guys...what's with these people?"

"I think it's a law, Kate. Work on a house, leave a mess. It's some kind of code."

Captain Horton greeted them at his office door as they arrived. "Come in, come in," he said in an obsequious tone. He closed the door behind them, then walked around behind his desk and sat down. Kate and Tulary grabbed some chairs but Horton stopped them.

"Don't sit. You won't be here that long. Right now, as we speak, there's an attractive young Asian woman lying in her bed not four miles from here with her throat slit from one ear,"—he drew a line across his throat—"to the other." He shuffled through some papers. "Let's see, here it is. Her name is Kieu Ho, also known as Veronica Ho. That name ring any bells?"

Kate started to speak but Horton interrupted her.

"This, is miss Ho's rap sheet, mostly for prostitution." He held up a stack of papers. "But I guess you already know that don't you, Kate."

"I spoke to her, boss, but I didn't really have anything to bring her in on. She knew Diddlesby and the other guy, Pepperton, but so did a lot of people."

"Uh,huh. What kind of car do you suppose was seen leaving the scene? Give up? A red Toyota pickup."

"Was there a bear driving it?" said Tulary. Kate did her best to keep from laughing.

Horton stood up and leaned over his desk. "You think this is funny? You people are supposed to be my best. Now, this is the third killing in a little over a week. I want some progress on these cases and I mean like yesterday. Word gets out we got a serial killer on our hands I'm gonna have to start issuing rubber boots to get us through all the shit. Starting right now, you're off all other cases but these and you're both on overtime. Now get over to Miss Lee's apartment and find something, anything. I want these people off my streets. Understood?"

"We're on our way, boss," said Tulary.

As they left Horton's office, a clerk sitting at a desk called out to Kate. "Oh, detective Mallory. I have that information you asked for on the Secret Service Agent."

"Give me a minute," Kate said to Tulary. She went over to the woman's desk.

"Frank Noble. Retired a little over a year ago. Last known address is right here." She handed a sheet of paper to Kate.

"Eureka." said Kate. "That's right, I think his brother lives up there. Can you find me a phone number to go with this."

The woman grabbed the paper and pointed toward the bottom. "One step ahead of you, detective."

"Great, thanks a lot. It's Karen, right?"

"Right."

"Thanks for your help."

"Anytime."

A good night's sleep had done wonders for Frank. Mozart was back and unharmed. Even Bones seemed to sense the joy this brought to the quiet man. For the first time since that horrible morning when he found Gladys and Stumble's mutilated bodies lying on the forest floor, he had reason to smile. He had been listening to the same piece all morning, Mozart's *Oboe Concerto in C*, one that Mozart the bear had always favored. It was an exuberant, uplifting number and Mozart would often get up and dance to it. He was still asleep on the porch but Frank wanted it on when he awoke, sort of a welcoming home for the young orphan.

The happy music had put him in a good mood. The sun was out now and Frank moved his chair off of the porch so that he could feel the rays on his face. As he sat there feeling warm and

158

content in the knowledge that Mozart had returned to him, he contemplated taking him away, putting an end to the killing, starting over somewhere else. Then his thoughts turned to the young woman, Veronica, her throat split open, left there in the shower, the cold water still running. And now he pictured Gladys and Stumble, their bladders ripped from their bodies. Marcell had seen the man, that morning—it seemed so long ago—when the bears were killed, had described him to Frank, and when the time came, would point him out.

His reverie was disrupted by a familiar voice calling out. "Frank. Hey, Frank."

He opened his eyes. He must have drifted off to sleep. Marcell was standing next to him. He had a newspaper in one hand and a rifle over his shoulder.

"Marcell."

"Man, I tried calling you on the walkie-talkie but you didn't pick up." Marcell was out of breath and there was sweat dripping from his brow. He looked over to the CD player. "Now I see why."

Frank got up from his chair. Marcell was obviously upset. Frank put his arm around him. "Sorry, Marcell. Mozart's back. I was playing some music for him, I guess I dozed off."

"You're lucky it was me."

"Bones is here. He would have let me know if I was in danger. What's with the paper?"

Marcell opened the newspaper and handed it to Frank. "Look. This drawing, it looks like you, and the article mentions a witness who saw a bear driving a red pickup truck."

"We better get rid of the truck."

"I'll take care of the truck. What are you going to do with Mozart?"

"I don't know. I need to fix up a place for her, a den of sorts."

"What about that hole you were digging, for your cesspool. Could we keep her in there?"

Frank stepped up onto the porch and turned off the music. "You want something to drink?"

"I'm okay. What do you think of my idea?"

"I think that would work. We could put some leaves down in the bottom for a bed and I'll make a cover out of branches. Yeah, I think that'll work just fine."

Marcell looked down at the sleeping bear. "So, Frank, are we still going to the circus tonight?"

"Oh, yeah, I'm sorry, I forgot all about that. Sure, we'll go."

"Great. And I got a good idea, too. Tonight's Halloween, you know. We could wear the bearskins; nobody'd suspect anything, two bears at the circus on Halloween. What could be better?"

"Okay. I'm going to work on Mozart's den. I'll meet you at your place around sunset. We're going to need a car."

"I'll take care of that. Oh, one other thing. Our man. Rudy. His name is Rudy Carlyle, and I have his address."

"What were you in the circus, anyway, a magician?"

"Well, in a way. Actually, I was a clown, and a pretty good one at that. Of course, the beauty of being a dwarf in the circus, Frank, is that you don't have to be anything else."

Doing Arnie on the way to and from her trick was bad enough, and the old man of course was totally pathetic, but what Penny didn't realize was that things could always—and usually did—get worse. When she and Arnie returned to the Malibu house, Roberto was waiting in her bedroom. Penny had turned immediately to Arnie and told him no way, she'd had enough for one night without having Roberto slobber all over her, at which point Arnie just slapped her across the face and told her he'd decide when enough was enough.

The two guards kept her up all night. They both started into some cocaine. which only prolonged the ordeal for Penny. The more of the drug they took, the more perverse they became while at the same time the less able to perform fully erect. At one point, Arnie had to leave to pick up Angel and Maple from Rudy's place, leaving Penny alone with Roberto who went on and on about how pretty she was and how a girl like her shouldn't be no prostitute, while all the time he kept doing lines and turning her in every position he could think of. An hour later Arnie was back with the two girls and before long all five of them were tangled up on the bed. Sometimes it was hard to tell just whose parts belonged to whom.

For Penny, and the other two girls, the whole thing was ridiculous. The two men had them in every combination and position imaginable and were using everything in the house for penetration. It was absurd. Penny couldn't understand how someone could receive sexual pleasure from sticking an ashtray or a light bulb inside a woman. What were they possibly thinking? "Oh, if I just get this item in there, then I'll really get off." They were like children torturing animals or burning an anthill. It could be done, by God, so they were going to do it.

It went on till six in the morning, when the two men finally got so coked out their penises shrunk to the size of a soggy peanut. Angel had fallen asleep an hour earlier even though Roberto was still trying to fuck her. Everyone drifted out of Penny's room except her and the sleeping Angel. Penny put a blanket over the worn out girl, then got into bed next to her and sat staring out the window, waiting for the sun to come up, wondering how in the world she was ever going to get out of that house. A little while later she drifted off to sleep.

It was late in the afternoon when Penny awoke. She could hear voices coming from another room, angry voices and lots of them. She got out of bed and put on some clothes, then went out to investigate.

Rudy was screaming at Roberto, something about doing drugs on his own time, and look what had happened while they—Roberto and Arnie—were sleeping. Evidently both men had passed out, leaving the house wide open and Maple had taken off. It was bad enough she was gone, but it was particularly bad now, for it was Maple who was supposed to come to Rudy's tonight for the movie with the Chinese.

Rudy did not confine his anger to Roberto. Angel got her share for not watching over Maple, including a couple of well-placed punches; Rudy knew how to smack the girls around without leaving too many bruises.

It was obvious to Penny that Rudy was intimidated by Arnie, for during his entire rampage, he never once looked directly at him or implied that Arnie was directly responsible for the whole mess. This only further convinced Penny of her need to get out of that house.

"Jesus Christ!" said Rudy. "What the fuck am I going to do now? Veronica's nowhere to be found. I had to send a Goddamn limo to the airport to pick up some Chinese asshole, and now Maple takes a powder."

"I can make the fucking movie, Rudy," said Angel. She was still lying on the floor nursing her wounds.

"You can make the movie? You can make the fucking movie?" Rudy reached down and grabbed Angel by one ear, gave it a violent twist, and lifted her by it to her feet, then dragged her to a nearby mirror. "Take a good look at yourself, Angel, and tell me who the fuck wants to be in a movie with that."

Angel had definitely seen better days. She was only twenty, but she'd been doing a lot of coke the last few years, along with two packs of cigarettes a day and a diet of sweets and booze. Her eyes had huge bags beneath them, her skin was dried out; even her hair looked tired. She still had her purpose, hell, Rudy had used her himself just last night, but her days were numbered. All she had going was her specialty act with her objects. Nobody was going to lay out any big money to make a movie with her. Rudy released her and shoved her away.

"What about me?" asked Penny. Up until now, nobody had noticed her standing in the doorway.

"You're not ready, kid. You need more experience."

Penny looked toward Arnie. "I've learned a lot in a hurry, Rudy. Give me a chance. I can do it."

Rudy shook his head. "What about the red head, what's her

name...Connie?"

"She's with the senator," said Arnie, " and he only likes..."

"Yeah, yeah, I know. He only likes red heads. Jesus Christ. Would somebody tell me what's so fucking special about a red bush. Who else is there?"

"There's Candy."

"Candy? The little blonde? Yeah, yeah she'll do."

"You should know, Rudy, she's got the clap."

"Again?"

Arnie just shrugged his shoulders.

"Well, fuck, I can't take her. That's all I need. Give this fucking yellow monkey a good dose of the clap. O'Neill will have my ass." Rudy turned to Penny. "Okay, sister, you're it. Get some things together." He turned his attention back to Arnie. "You hear from Veronica, you tell her to get a hold of me, right away. Roberto, I want you to get out there and find Maple. Don't do anything to her, just bring her back. I'll deal with her later."

"What if I can't find her?"

"There is no 'what if I can't find her?' Roberto. You don't find her, then I'll find her. Then I'll find you, and when I find you, you'll wish you were lost. For your sake, I hope that sinks into your thick Mexican skull."

Penny retreated to her room and started gathering some clothes. She grabbed the red silk dress and a pair of heels for her big movie—though she was hoping to be long gone before that even got started—a clean pair of jeans, extra underwear and socks and a light weight jacket, being careful not to over pack; she didn't want to make it look like she wasn't returning. But she wasn't, that much was certain. Somehow between now and tomorrow morning she was going to get free of this place and everybody in it. If she had to kill, or be killed, in the process, that was okay, too. Anything was better than this. Even home.

Frank spent all afternoon working on Mozart's den. First he cut some small, green branches of pine and laid them across the floor of the hole, and then he gathered up numerous baskets full of leaves and distributed them over the top of the branches, making a comfortable bed for the young bear. Then he set out to make a roof. For this he cut some larger branches, long enough to span the hole, pared them down and tied them together like a raft, then anchored one end with stakes driven deep into the ground so, if necessary, the entire roof could be lifted open from the unanchored end. Over the frame, he tossed bundles of full, leafy branches, enough to keep out the sun and maintain a cool cave-like environment.

The hole was a good six feet deep so Frank had taken the effort of digging a trench at one end to enable Mozart easy access to his new home. He even stacked extra branches at that end to serve as a step from the trench to the hole.

When he finished. he returned to the cabin for Mozart, who was now awake and standing by the window, peering into the cabin. Frank approached slowly, making just enough noise to let him know he was there without alarming the young bear. He went inside and returned shortly with a pan full of berries he had collected earlier in the day. He tossed a few at Mozart's feet. Mozart gazed down at the berries then over to Frank, then he squatted down and grabbed them and stuck them in his mouth.

"Good boy, Mozart."

Bones started barking, a playful bark, and Frank knelt down to pet him. "Come on Bones, let's show Mozart his new home."

Frank headed off toward the cave, dropping a trail of berries behind him along the way, and Mozart quickly followed with Bones close beside him. When they got to the hole, Frank put some berries into the trench then set the bowl down into the hole and waited.

Mozart quickly grabbed and ate the berries in the trench but stopped short of entering the new home. Instead, he got up on top of it and began what seemed to Frank like an inspection of the roof. He pulled at the bundles of branches, then he poked his nose down into them like he was looking into the blackness below him. Frank was afraid the whole thing might collapse but it held up okay.

Seemingly satisfied with the roof, the young bear got off, circled the structure a couple of times, then slowly climbed down the trench and into his new residence. Frank could hear him scraping at the pan for the berries, then there was a long howl, like he would give while listening to music, a rustling of leaves, and then quiet.

Frank knelt down beside Bones. It had been a good afternoon. Mozart was back and happy in his new home and Frank had not given any thought to what lay ahead of him for hours. He sat there with his four-legged friend until the sun disappeared behind the hills and a warm breeze picked up out of the east. He got to his feet. "You keep an eye on him, Bones. I've got work to do." ✹

FOURTEEN

Frank was running late. He had promised Marcell he'd be there at dusk, but by the time he got started on his hike the only remnant of the setting sun was a reflected pink hue against the clouds; the pink quickly washed away to gray as the clouds merged with the evening sky. Frank had made the trek many times and could have easily done it blindfolded, still it was nice to see the moon creep over the ridge to the east; it was full tonight and would soon spread an amber sheet of light across the terrain.

How beautiful and peaceful it all was. A cool breeze massaged his face and teased the hair on his arms, while his ears bathed in the serenade of a hundred different creatures of the night. At one point he cut away from his trail and forged his way through the bushes down to the creek, where he took rest on a large boulder and soaked up the evening symphony. He considered the cricket, the frog, the nightingale. Did they understand each other? People would think he was crazy, having such thoughts, still, nobody really knew for sure. They have small brains and they look odd and so we project limitations on them. No one would hesitate to squash a bug, or worry himself over a flattened toad. Even Christians. But, my God, if there is a God, and He created us, didn't He create them, too?

Sitting there, considering all this, absorbing the sounds—the gurgling water gently sliding over the rocks in its journey to the sea, the night-owls never ending question, an unidentified rustling in the bush—he wished he were one of them. But just the wish itself kept him separate, and there was this voice in his head, this human voice, that kept prodding him, telling him he had work to do—God's work?—and it was that voice that still defined him. He rose unconsciously from his seat and continued on his way.

Marcell came out the front door just as Frank arrived. There was a strange odor in the air, strange out here in the woods but one not unfamiliar to Frank.

"I was beginning to worry about you, Frank. It's after seven."

"I had a lot to do. What's that smell?"

"Oh, that must be the paint. I can't even smell it any more. Come on, I'll show you."

Frank followed Marcell to the other side of the cabin. As they walked, Marcell mentioned once again that he was afraid Frank wouldn't show. He seemed anxious, or better yet, excited. There was a small pickup truck parked around back, right where Frank had left his, in fact it looked like Frank's, but a different color. He wasn't sure in the light of the moon but it appeared to be a light blue.

"You painted my truck?"

"I had paint left over from the house. You like it?"

"Well, sure, I guess. Is that oil base paint?"

"I think so."

"Is it dry?"

"Dry enough."

Frank touched one of the fenders. "It's still tacky."

"It'll be alright. Once we get driving, the air will dry it."

"Okay. You ready to go?"

"Everything's loaded. I put our outfits in a box in the bed; guns are behind the seat. I'll drive. We should stop along the way and switch plates. Have you ever been to the circus, Frank?"

"Once, years ago, when I was a kid."

"Did you like it?"

"I don't remember much about it, Marcell. I was only five or six. You know how that is, everything seems huge, overwhelming."

"Don't I ever."

The two men got into the truck and pulled away. Marcell had attached some blocks of wood to the floor pedals, rigged an extension for the gear shift and stacked a couple of pillows on the seat, making it easy for him to maneuver the vehicle. He seemed to be enjoying himself as he sped along the dirt road, taking the curves like he was in some kind of race.

"Our circus isn't real big, not a three-ringer or anything, but I think you'll like it. Especially Miranda."

"Miranda?"

"My mother."

"Oh, well, I'm sure I will. Do we have to go so fast?"

"Oh, sorry. I like to drive, and I really like to drive fast." He slowed the truck down a bit. "She's a direct descendant of Leitzel, you know."

"I'm afraid I don't know who Leizel is."

"Leitzel, Frank, with a 't. She's just about the greatest high-wire act ever, and beautiful. Of course, I never saw her; she was way before my time. Bohemian, you know. Lot of good circus people came from Bohemia. Anyway, she had this act where she would put her wrist through a loop that was attached by a swivel to a hanging rope and she would build up momentum swinging until finally she would hurl her entire body in a full circle over itself. They called it a full-arm plunge. Now, here's the thing. To do this, you have to dislocate your shoulder every time you come around, and Leitzel would sometimes do as many as one hundred circles. Can you imagine, the strength, the tolerance for pain, the sheer beauty, this woman suspended a hundred feet off the ground, going around and around in a circle, her long hair following behind her in a trail like a comet. And all this without a net!"

Frank was staring out the side window. He turned to look at Marcell. "Do you suppose she'll do it tonight?"

"What? Who?"

"Your mother. Do you suppose she'll do a full-arm plunge?"

"It's not my mother who does it. It was Leitzel."

Frank turned his attention once again outside. "Oh, sorry. I misunderstood."

"Are you okay, Frank?"

"Yeah, yeah, I was just trying to picture it. It's funny, really. Millions of birds fly by us everyday and we think nothing of it, but put a beautiful woman up in the air and spin her in a circle and we're amazed."

Marcell took a deep breath. He seemed slightly perturbed. "Birds have wings. It's no big deal for them."

"Yes, wings. And we don't. Sad, isn't it?"

Marcell turned off the dirt road onto the highway. There were quite a few dead bugs on the windshield so he turned on the wipers. "I don't know," he said. "I barely have arms."

It hadn't taken Penny more than five minutes to get ready to leave the Malibu house. Arnie had suggested to Rudy that he go along with them—maybe he was suspicious of Penny or maybe just jealous—but Rudy said no, he needed to stay put in case Veronica came by or called. Besides, Rudy was perfectly capable of controlling one teen-age whore. Rudy was getting a little tired of Arnie's attitude lately, forgetting just who it was exactly that ran this show. He didn't like the way O'Neill was pushing his weight around either, and Veronica getting so damn independent, and now Maple taking a powder. Seemed like everybody was getting all independent, treating him like a fucking chump. All that shit would have to change. Yes sir, there were going to have to be some big changes in the very near future.

Rudy dumped all this onto Penny during the drive to Hollywood, how he had built the whole business up from nothing, just a couple of street whores at first, twenty dollar blow jobs in a ten dollar room. He'd gone through plenty of girls the first couple years, some got pregnant and split, some went back to mommy and daddy, others found some jerk dumb enough to marry them and tried the straight life; one of his girls actually kept working for him on the side after she got married, said she needed the excitement. Yeah, they came and went but Rudy hung in there, saving his money, slowly moving up the ladder of commercial sex. The most important thing he'd learned of course was getting the girls while they were young, and only the cream of the crop. That's where Veronica had been so useful; she could find a girl dressed in rags, sleeping in doorways (like Penny), and spot the potential right off. Veronica had made him a bundle all right. It was she who showed him how to control the girls so they don't runaway or start selling a little on the side. Maple, man, she was really wrong to leave like that after all Rudy had done for her.

"It's okay, though," he said, "she'll be back, and she'll be sorry. One thing I won't tolerate is betrayal."

All the time he spoke, Penny kept nodding her head and saying yes, she understood, trying her best to appear sympathetic, maybe get Rudy to let his guard down a little, give her a chance to make her move. She even slid over closer to him in the car and started rubbing the back of his neck, telling him he was only man who had ever been nice to her, saying he was better to her than her own father.

"I need to stop at a drug store, Rudy."

"What for?"

"Female things," she said. "I'll only be a minute."

Rudy checked his watch. "Okay, but we gotta make it quick."

He pulled into a shopping center and parked in front of a Sav-on. Penny had her door half open before he even turned off the ignition.

"Hold on," he said.

"What?"

"I'm going with you."

"That's all right, Rudy. I'll only be a minute."

"Sorry. I've had too many things go wrong today. Close the door."

Penny pulled the door shut.

"Let me educate you a little. You look at me and see a fat old man, you think maybe I just fell off the turnip truck or something. You think you're the smartest whore ever worked for me? Listen, sister, I've heard it all. I ain't going for that 'you're the closest thing to a father' bullshit line. One thing I know. A girl takes off—like Maple—it can start a stampede. You're like fucking cattle or those little rats—what do they call them, lemmings—run themselves right off a cliff; you may not think that's what your doing when you take off, but when I find you, believe me, you'll feel like that's what happened."

Penny started to say something but Rudy cut her off. "Here's how it's gonna be. You need something in there we go in together and get it. Toothpaste, Kotex, whatever. But you pull any shit, I'll gut you right there in front of everybody and don't fucking think I won't. I ain't a violent man by nature, but I'm more than ready to do what I gotta do. Now, do we need to go inside or not?"

"It can wait," whispered Penny, gazing out the window.

"What, speak up."

She turned and looked him in the face. She was going to have to kill him if she wanted out, she understood that now and he could see by the look on her face that she understood it, and that's how he liked it. Lots of them got the idea, none of them had the balls to do it.

"It can wait," she said again.

"That's what I thought," he said and started the car. Neither one said another word all the way back to his place.

Marcell parked the truck at the far end of the dirt parking lot so they could change into their costumes without being seen. The paint had not quite dried to his expectations, and there were now hundreds of insects stuck to the hood and fenders, some of them still alive and squirming. He tried picking a few of the live ones off but only managed to rip their mangled bodies into little pieces. Under the parking lot lights, Frank realized now that the truck wasn't blue but more of a lavender and there were sections where the color was deeper than others, giving the paint job a swirled effect as if two separate colors had been haphazardly mixed together.

"You could have stirred the paint a little better."

"I didn't have all day. Besides, it gives it a little more character, don't you think?"

The two men donned their suits and started through the lot. The place was filling up with cars and a large crowd gathered by the entrance. Marcell was right about one thing: It wasn't a huge

171

circus. The whole operation was set up on less than a city block. There was a small Ferris wheel, a merry-go-round, a few other rides, and one rather imposing contraption appropriately entitled The Hammer.

The Hammer consisted of a long metal bar hinged in the middle to a metal post, enabling it to spin around vertically a full three hundred and sixty degrees. At either end of the bar was a caged metal pod where customers were strapped in; unlike the Ferris wheel, these pods did not spin on an axle (which would keep them in an upright position) but were permanently attached so that when the pod reached the apex of its path it, and the occupants, were upside down. Frank watched it swaying back and forth, building up enough momentum to complete the circle, at times balancing the inverted pod for two or three seconds before it plummeted down toward earth, the faithful inhabitants screaming themselves hoarse. It looked just like a giant sledgehammer about to rip apart a chunk of asphalt. Frank had never been good with height, had actually been diagnosed as acrophobic; watching that little basket teeter at the end of the pole two hundred feet off the ground made him nauseous. He had to look away.

There were other less threatening attractions; shooting galleries, gaming booths, concession stands, and one large tent where the animal acts and high-wire show were put on. It was more like a carnival than a circus, still, there were plenty of people there, mostly families, young children racing about with there cotton candy and snow-cones; hucksters trying to reel patrons into their booth for a chance at winning that special prize for their loved ones—a con game, yes, but a con accepted by the public; a time out from the real world. Everybody knew it would be cheaper to go out and buy that huge stuffed teddy bear than it was to try and win it, but where was the glamour in that? At the circus, or the carnival, miracles could happen. You could knock down the milk bottles with one toss, shoot all the ducks in the pond, gently deposit those baseballs into the bushel basket; and if you were big and strong enough, you could even ring the bell.

Many of the patrons were in costumes for Halloween, allowing Frank and Marcell to proceed unmolested through the festive crowd. Now and then a small child would stumble across the two bears and dart away in fear but their mothers would quickly grab them up and try their best to explain that the two bears were not real; although some seemed to be reassuring themselves as well as their children.

As they went along, Marcell pointed out various booths to Frank, giving him a little biographical sketch of some of the proprietors. To watch him move through the place, to hear the tone in his voice, one would think there was a child inside the mask making his first trip to the circus. Marcell was home.

"That man, there, running the dart game, his name is Jorsky; he's a gypsy, supposedly from Transylvania. If we had the time I'd introduce you and you could listen to his stories about the old country, and Count Dracula; he claims to be related. One thing for certain: he is a blood-sucker. He files down the points of his darts. Nobody wins anything from him; even Miranda."

"How's that?"

"I didn't tell you?"

"Tell me what?"

"Miranda's not only a high-wire expert. You should see her with a bow and arrow or darts. She's a crack shot. Remember in *Robin Hood*, when they have the archery contest and Robin splits another arrow right down the middle. Miranda could do that."

"Well then, why doesn't she win anything?"

"Because, Jorsky's got it all fixed. What he does is, he hands you the first dart by itself, and it's a sharp one. 'Go ahead,' he says, 'the first one is on me.' You throw it and pop a balloon and you get all excited, thinking you're going to clean up. Then you cough up the money and he hands you a bunch of filed darts. Works every time."

"Are there any honest games here?"

"They're not dishonest, Frank. They're just rigged. There's a difference."

"Oh, I see."

"No, really. It's like I told you about ringing the bell."

"You said it was all in the timing."

"Well, that's mostly true. But, there's another element, too. The plate you bring the hammer down onto is set up at an angle so that if you bring the hammer down square onto the surface, you're never gonna succeed, and that's what all these big muscle-bound boyfriends try and do, you know, show how clever they are, land a solid square hit."

"And you don't think that's dishonest?"

"No, not at all. Where's the challenge if all you have to be is strong to win? You see, one thing people don't realize about circuses and carnivals."

"What's that?"

"It's democratic, Frank." Marcell pointed a paw to his head. "If you don't have it up here, you're not winning anything. Much more fair than the real world, wouldn't you say?"

"Maybe so. Where's your mother's trailer?"

"We'll find it, it's a bus. Let's go in and watch some of the show first."

Frank had cut a slit in the side of his bearskin to access his clothing underneath. He reached in now and pulled out a watch. "Don't forget, we've got another appointment tonight."

"Just for a few minutes, Frank. We came all this way."

Frank pulled out some money and bought a couple of tickets and the two bears made their way into the large tent. It was full inside and noisy, children screaming and blowing on paper horns, vendors stalking the aisles, trying their best to be heard over the roar.

"Peeeenuts. Popcorn. Ice-cold Co-ca-co-la."

In the ring, a couple of clowns were busy juggling water balloons, every now and then intentionally overthrowing one onto an unsuspecting customer. Frank and Marcell found some seats close to the front. The clowns finished up their short routine then

174

hustled away as the lights dimmed.

An announcement came over the loudspeaker. "Ladies and Gentleman, America's favorite cowboy, Jack Daniels."

The crowd gave an apathetic applause and as the lights came back on, a man dressed up like a cowboy came running into the ring carrying a blanket and saddle, closely pursued by a white horse. The cowboy appeared to be drunk as he stumbled through the ring, dropping the blanket once, and then clumsily retrieving it. As the horse approached him, the cowboy placed the saddle on the ground and attempted to put the blanket on the horse's back, but the horse quickly turned his head and bit him in the ass. This drew some laughter from the crowd, mostly the children.

The cowboy turned to the horse and scolded him, then successfully placed the blanket on the horse. But when he reached down to grab the saddle, the horse removed the blanket with his teeth and tossed it to the ground. Two more unsuccessful attempts were made until finally the cowboy got the saddle on the horse. The cowboy then climbed onto the horse, but because of his drunkenness, immediately fell off. This brought a mild applause. The cowboy slowly rose to his feet, brushed himself off and with much feigned effort, climbed back onto the horse. As soon as he got situated in the saddle the cowboy removed his hat and waved to the crowd, at which point the horse reared up on his hind legs and bucked him off, the cowboy doing a somersault and landing on his feet. The horse then began to chase the cowboy around the circle till finally the cowboy left the ring and hid out in the crowd. The horse continued to run wild in the ring and every time the cowboy would try and re-enter, the horse would go after him and try to bite him in the ass.

There was a large woman sitting next to Frank and Marcell. She had four rather large children with her and the five of them were laughing hysterically throughout the performance, popcorn flying out of their mouths and spilling from their boxes onto the ground.

Marcell gave Frank a tug. "She's a plant. Supposed to get the crowd worked up."

175

In the ring, the cowboy, in an attempt to get away from the horse, fell to the ground. The horse then came up from behind him and started nudging him gently with his head, helping him up onto his feet. Once on his feet, the cowboy faced the horse and removed his hat. Then he and the horse bowed to each other and then to the spectators. There was a polite round of applause, the cowboy whispered something into the horse's ear, the horse appeared to laugh and then he chased the cowboy out of the ring.

Marcell sat shaking his head.

"What's wrong?"

"That's a good act. But these people don't care."

"People have television now, Marcell. They've seen everything."

The two men got up from their seats and started up the aisle for the exit. "But this is the circus, Frank."

"Well, I enjoyed it. Let me ask you a question. How does he get the horse to laugh?"

"He sprays pepper in his nose."

"Oh. You suppose the horse likes that?"

"I don't think it hurts him, and besides, it's the cowboy who's playing the idiot. And you should see his ass; that horse has taken more than one chunk out of him."

"Maybe he's trying to tell him something."

"It's a circus, Frank. It wouldn't *be* a circus without animals."

"Maybe not. Or maybe it would just be more—how did you put it?— democratic."

The two of them walked along the perimeter of the grounds, looking for Miranda's coach. Most of the vehicles used by the members of the circus were old and run down, a menagerie of pickup trucks with camper shells, customized vans, and a few large buses. Marcell recognized all but a few. "There it is," he said.

At the end of a row of vans, thirty yards away, parked directly under a bright streetlight, sat an old but attractive bus. It had a pleasant design to it, a somewhat rounded look with belly boxes down below for storage and huge white-wall tires. It was difficult to say for certain in the nightlight, but the side appeared to be painted a dark maroon. There was a man seated in a chair by the door.

"There's somebody by the door," said Frank.

"It's probably Howard, my mother's driver. I can't tell from here. You better go alone. If it's him, tell him who you are, he'll let you know if it's safe."

"How will I know if it's him?"

"Howard's a mute. He can hear okay, though, so whatever you do, don't start talking real loud or over enunciating. Really makes him angry."

The lights were on in the van and as he got closer, Frank could make out a woman's silhouette behind the drawn shades; she appeared to be dressing. He removed the bear head; it felt good to be rid of it.

"Are you Howard?"

The man made some signs, but Frank had no idea what they meant.

"I don't know how to sign," he said and realized that he was, indeed, over enunciating, and quickly corrected his speech. "My name is Frank. I'm a friend of Marcell's. We've come to see his mother."

The man eyed him suspiciously and pointed at the bear's head.

"We had to come in disguise."

He turned and knocked on the door. A woman's voice called out.

"What is it, Howard?" Shortly after, the door opened and she was standing there, half dressed, a towel wrapped around her waist. Howard made some more motions with his hands and she reciprocated. "Who are you?" she said to Frank.

"I'm a friend of Marcell's. He's come to see you."

"Marcell? Where is he?" She seemed excited.

"He's close by. He sent me to be sure it was safe."

"Howard, quick. Go and get Marcell."

Frank told him where to find Marcell, and then he went inside with the woman.

"I'm Miranda," she said, extending her hand. Frank took her hand in his. It was strong and muscular, yet soft and somehow still delicate. Marcell was right about one thing: she was beautiful. Her blonde hair hung down to the middle of her back and had a soft satin sheen. Her skin was white and, with the exception of a small mole on her left cheek—which tended to add to her beauty—unblemished. But it was her eyes that caught his attention. They were a translucent green and sparkled in their sockets like emeralds. He could not keep from staring.

"It's not safe for Marcell to be here. Bartelli's looking for him."

"We know. I saw him, in the woods."

"Then he's found Marcell's cabin?"

"No, I ran them off..."

The door opened and Marcell came in. He still had his bear head on but quickly removed it once inside the bus.

"Marcell..." At the sight of him, Miranda broke into tears and the two embraced.

"I'll wait outside," said Frank.

"No, no, stay," said Miranda, wiping away the tears. "Let me get some clothes on. Marcell, I've missed you so much." She kissed him. "I'll just be a minute." She went into another room.

"Your mother's very beautiful."

"Yes, she is."

"And this place; I've never seen anything like it."

The inside of Miranda's bus was more like a plush room in a hotel than any bus Frank had ever seen. The walls were covered in a rich velvety material and trimmed out in dark mahogany wood. There was an overstuffed couch and chair, beautiful Oriental rugs, numerous small statues and other art objects including a wall-sized copy of a Rembrandt Fresco. Against one wall there was a beautiful oak cabinet filled with books and records and on top of it an old RCA record player. It was like being in an antique store, but one of very fine quality.

"Miranda has exquisite taste," said Marcell.

178

"You know, Marcell, you are very much alike. This bus, it reminds me of your cabin. Perhaps a little more elegant, but very similar in style."

"I wanted to feel at home," he said. There was a tinge of sadness in his voice.

Miranda came back into the room. She had put on a pair of black silk pants and matching top and her hair was pulled back in a ponytail. Frank could not take his eyes off of her.

"You can't stay long, Marcell. If Bartelli finds you here..."

"He'll be busy for awhile. Daniels just finished his act. The crowd is apathetic tonight."

She looked at Frank. "You saw Bartelli, you said, in the woods?"

"Yes, he and one other man."

"That would be Peabody."

"Peabody?" said Marcell.

"That's right, you don't know, do you?"

"Know what, Miranda?"

"The Peabodys." She made a gesture with her open hand, like a knife cutting through a cake. "They've split up."

"What? They can do that?" asked Marcell.

"I'll tell you all about it. But first, let us have a drink. I'm so happy to see you again."

Miranda grabbed a crystal decanter and three small crystal glasses from a table and poured some brandy. Frank watched her every move with undying attention. So much grace and style, so much natural beauty. He had never met a woman like this before, had not felt the feelings that were beginning to stir within him since...well, not since Kate Mallory. She handed him a glass of brandy. She smiled and for just a second their eyes locked.

She reached over and tapped her glass to his. "To Frank, for bringing me my wonderful son."

"To friendship," added Marcell as he clanged his glass to theirs, "a sheltering tree." ❧

FIFTEEN

They arrived at Rudy's a little before eight. Mr. Soon, or so he called himself, was a middle-age man, well built, dressed in an expensive suit, his graying hair cropped short around the ears. He had with him two men, one Chinese, the other black. The Chinese was a huge man, his belly threatening to pop the center button of his suit coat. His hair was slicked back, revealing a major recession, and was tied in a braided ponytail. The black man was lean and muscular, his head shaven—he must have liked the way it felt, for he kept rubbing it—his eyes hidden behind very dark glasses. Soon did not bother to introduce either of his guards to Rudy, and neither man so much as acknowledged Rudy's presence. The black man carried a large leather bag and Mister Soon had a small box that he set on the kitchen table.

"Where is the girl?" asked Soon.

"She's in the bedroom," said Rudy. "Is it just gonna be you, or are these two in on the action? Cause if it's more than one, it'll cost you extra."

"Mister Black," he said, pointing to the black man, "will operate camera. Mister Brown, wait in here."

Black and Brown, thought Rudy. How clever. Chink looks more yellow than brown. Everyone who came to Rudy's place used a pseudonym, even public figures. Some movie star might show up, hell, fifty million people know his mug, and he tells Rudy his name is Jones or Smith and says it with a straight face. Rudy would just play along; as long as their money was green, he could play dumb, no problem.

"Okay," said Rudy, "she's right in there, waiting. I'm sure you'll be more than happy. What's that you got in the bag?"

Mister Soon did not bother to answer Rudy. He turned to Mister Brown. "Prepare tea." Then he and Mister Black headed for the bedroom.

180

Brown got a pan from Rudy then he opened up the small box and removed a large piece of gall bladder and placed it in the pan. He added some water and what looked to be some herbs from a small jar. Rudy watched carefully, hoping to learn something. The man kept the fire low and stirred the concoction every time it started to boil. After a few minutes he removed the pan from the stove and poured the juice through a piece of cheesecloth into a cup. Then he took it into the bedroom.

Rudy picked up the pan and gave it a whiff. It didn't smell quite as bad as when Rudy had prepared his, though one still couldn't say it smelled good—tolerable would be closer to the truth; maybe it was the herbs Brown had added.

Brown returned from the bedroom. "You have any beer?"

"Yeah, sure," said Rudy. He got the large man a beer and one for himself and sat across the table from him. After a couple of awkward moments, Rudy spoke.

"You Chinese?"

The man looked at him like Rudy was some kind of idiot, but said nothing. Another minute passed and Rudy tried again. "I tried some of that bladder stuff, myself, last night, but to tell you the truth, I don't know if it works or not. Sure felt weird this morning. You ever try it?"

The man quickly finished the beer, got up and went to the fridge and grabbed another.

"Hey, get me one, too, will you?" asked Rudy. "What was that you added, some kinda Chinese herbs or something?" No response. "You know, I'm the guy gets those bladders, not O'Neill. Your boss should talk to me, I could save him some money."

"He's not my boss."

Brown grabbed a second beer and brought them back to the table. Rudy checked his watch. They had been in there over ten minutes. The arrangement was for two hours. He opened his beer and took a swig.

"Who decorated your apartment?" asked Brown. There was an all too obvious smirk splattered across his chubby face.

"What's wrong with it?"

"Looks like a Mexican whore-house."

"Yeah, like you've been to Mexico." Rudy was quiet for a minute then he asked him again. "So what's the scoop on the bladder?"

"How the fuck do I know?"

"I thought maybe Mister Soon in there told you how to prepare it."

"That's rich. He just takes it back to Hong Kong and sells it. O'Neill told him to try some out. If you ask me, it's all mumble-jumble."

Rudy thought he heard a noise coming from the bedroom. He leaned in that direction and listened. This time it was louder, it was the girl, Penny. She sounded in pain. "Hey," he said, "what's going on in there? I don't want no rough stuff." He started to get up from his seat.

"Sit down."

"What?"

"You talk too much. The man paid for two hours, the man gets two hours. None of your business what he does."

"The hell it ain't. That's one of my girls in there. She gets hurt, I lose money."

There was another cry from the bedroom, louder than the others. Rudy got up from his chair but Brown also got up and blocked his path.

"Why don't you take a walk, come back in two hours. Maybe you won't worry so much."

Rudy sized up the situation. There was no way he was getting by this gorilla, and even if he could, what was he gonna do when he got in there? Nothing was going right, today, he might as well just face it. "Yeah, fine," he said. "But I'm telling you, anything happens to her, you guys are gonna pay."

Rudy opened a closet door and grabbed his wig from the shelf, then stood in front of the mirror adjusting it. He could see Mr. Brown out of the corner of his eye, smiling, and shaking his head. Rudy looked over at him at one point. "You got a problem?" Mr.

Brown just raised his eyebrows and swallowed some beer.

When he was happy with the fit, Rudy grabbed his keys and a light jacket from the couch and moved toward the front door. As he reached the door he heard a muffled scream and for a second he actually felt bad, not just about his property, but for the girl, for what she was going through, but he quickly put that out of his mind. Too late in the game to get sentimental. He'd make it up to her somehow. Maybe buy her a new dress.

Cleve sat on the bed in his hotel room playing with the key he'd taken from Veronica's condo. His fortunes had taken quite the turn in the last few days. He'd taken five hundred bucks off of Freddie's dead body, picked up twenty-five hundred from O'Neill for the second bladder, another five thousand for taking care of Veronica and then, as a little bonus for all his hard work, another eighteen hundred from the box in Veronica's closet. Yes sir, things were looking up and Cleve had wasted no time in making some changes. He moved out of the dump in Hollywood and got himself a nice room at the Sheraton, a hundred and twenty bucks a night. It wasn't the penthouse but the way things were going, Cleve figured that wasn't too far off. He'd also bought himself some new clothes, including a leather jacket to replace the one the bear had torn. He had come to believe that in order to keep the money flowing in, he had to live like he had money, had to believe all the nickel and dime stuff was behind him.

What about this key? Cleve had gone to the airport and the train station and checked the lockers but the keys were different. He hadn't bothered to check the bus station; he'd spent enough time in those to know this key didn't come from there. It probably fit some safe deposit box, but from what bank? There had to be a way to find out.

There was a knock on the door. "Room service."

Cleve stuck the key back in his pocket and opened the door. A young man pushed a cart into the room. "Where would you like it, sir?"

"Put it by the bed."

The man placed the cart by the side of the bed then turned and handed the check to Cleve who signed it and handed it back. Because he had no credit cards, Cleve had to leave a cash deposit with the desk in order to sign for expenses. It had pissed him off but he had shown great restraint at the time. It was all part of his new image. He had money now. He was somebody.

"Will there be anything else, sir?"

"No. Yeah, yeah there is. I want you to get me a woman."

"Sir?"

"A woman. A whore."

The young man stared blankly at Cleve. "I'm sorry, sir, I wouldn't know how to do that, and I'm sure the management wouldn't go for it."

"The management ain't supposed to know, asshole."

"I'm sorry, sir."

"Okay, here's what you do. You go downstairs and talk to your buddies that work here. One of them is bound to know what to do. If they don't, go outside and flag down a cab and ask the driver. If he can't help you, then go down to Hollywood Boulevard and get one, yourself. I want her young and built, understand?"

"But..."

Cleve grabbed him by the shirt. "Don't fuckin disappoint me." He released him.

"Uh, I'll need some money, sir, for the girl."

"You can't put that on my bill?"

"No, sir, that much I do know."

Cleve took his wallet from his jeans and grabbed some hundred-dollar bills. He also pulled out a small white plastic card, inspected both sides of it then tossed it onto the bed. He handed the man three one-hundred-dollar bills.

"Here. Two hundred bucks for the broad and a hundred for you. And listen, what's your name?"

"Kelly."

"Listen, Kelly, don't go bringing me back some twenty-dollar

184

hole, and try pocketing the rest. You fuck with me, I'll cut your nuts off. You understand?"

"Yes sir."

"Good, now get the fuck out of here."

The young man left and Cleve sat down to enjoy his meal. He took a couple of bites of his steak then reached over and grabbed the plastic card. What the fuck was it? He set it back down and tore into his steak again, every once in a while glancing down at the plastic card. Then it came to him, the couple he'd robbed that night he'd followed Veronica.

"Rudy," he said and quickly grabbed the card again. "I bet you know where she keeps her money."

He stuck the card in his pocket and continued on with his dinner. It was a quarter till ten. Soon as he finished his meal he'd go pay old Rudy a visit. He'd cut him a deal, maybe give him ten percent of whatever he found, and if Rudy didn't like those apples, Cleve had other ways of getting what he wanted. He took a long swig off a bottle of bourbon. Right then at that moment he was feeling better than he'd ever felt in his life. Things were going his way, no doubt about it. It was like rolling a series of numbers on the crap table. When it's workin, it's workin. You hit it and hit it hard before you crap out. He'd never seen Rudy before, but he knew damn well no fucking pimp was gonna be that bad roll. O'Neill, now he was a different story; he could be trouble. He'd ordered Veronica's death as if he were ordering up a cheeseburger. "Just make sure it's done well," he'd said. Those very words.

Frank and Marcell had kept their visit with Miranda short. Bartelli's act with the elephants only lasted about ten minutes, then the clowns would be back out and then Miranda was due up for her show. They wanted to stay and watch her but she convinced them it wouldn't be safe. Once the circus left Pasadena and she was certain Bartelli had left with it, she and Howard would stay behind and set up a rendezvous with Marcell.

Their truck, parked in the dirt, now had a fine film of dust

185

burnt into the paint job; the entire surface felt like sandpaper. They put their bear heads back in the box in the bed of the truck and headed for Hollywood.

Seeing his mother had put Marcell in a good mood. He was cruising along in the fast lane, whistling and tapping his fingers on the dash-board.

"You like my mother, don't you, Frank?"

"She's a beautiful woman."

"Yes, we've established that. But, you like her, don't you?"

"Sure, Marcell, I like her. Who wouldn't? She's extraordinary."

"Ironic, don't you think, that a woman like her should be saddled with me for a son?"

"I thought you were finished with that kind of thinking."

"I'm not being maudlin about it. I'm just saying, it's ironic."

"Maybe I missed something, Marcell, but your mother appears...content, maybe even happy, if that's even possible in this world. She's created a life for herself and you're a big part of it. You can see that in her eyes every time she looks at you. If it's irony you're looking for, try this on. I find it interesting that anyone fortunate enough to have a woman like that in their life would be going around looking for flaws."

Marcell pondered Frank's point for a moment. "You're probably right, Frank. But you know, I am a freak. Don't say it, I know, not to you, and not to my mother, but to everybody else, so you have to forgive me if it's had an effect on me. We are all of us, to a greater or lesser extent, products of our environment. Nonetheless, I shall try and temper my self-pity with cheerfulness and optimism."

"Good. Just don't over do it."

Marcell reached down and turned on the radio. He ran through a few stations but got nothing but static.

"What's wrong with your radio?"

"You know, Marcell, I've never turned it on before so I have no idea."

Marcell finally found a station. They were playing classical music. The reception wasn't very good but the piece sounded very soothing, mostly flutes and violins.

Frank quickly turned off the radio.

"What's the matter?"

"I'd rather not hear that particular piece right now, Marcell. Reminds me of Gladys."

"Oh, sure. I understand. Boy, I can't believe Karl. I mean, he was always a bit of an asshole, but to give me up to Bartelli."

Miranda had told them the story of the Peabody twins, most of which, of course, Marcell already knew, but for Frank it was fascinating. Karl and Tiny had never gotten along. Even as children they would fight constantly and it was always Karl who started the trouble. They were connected just above the waist and Karl was a good two inches shorter from the waist down, requiring him to wear lifts in his shoes so as not to be a drag on their connecting band. This aggravated Karl.

Tiny was interested in books and science while Karl liked guns and things mechanical, but because of their condition, they were able to discuss only one topic at a time and Tiny was possessed with the stronger will. He would go on and on for hours about the Universe and God and wasn't it all so grand, while Karl wanted nothing more than to read Hot Rod Magazine or someday get a rifle and go hunting.

By the time they were teenagers, Karl had taken to alcohol, which Tiny absolutely hated; it fogged his mind and kept him from studying. He would do his best to keep Karl from drinking but Karl would go to great lengths to get drunk, often waiting till late at night when Tiny had fallen asleep to start into a bottle. Tiny would wake from his sleep completely drunk and the two of them would start arguing. It was unbearable.

After Bartelli's death, his brother kept coming around asking everybody a bunch of questions. Karl was afraid Bartelli would do something to them and wanted to tell him about Marcell but Tiny told him if he said anything he'd stick a knife in his heart, kill them both. Finally, they came to an agreement, perhaps their first ever. They would be separated, take their chances apart. Anything was better than the life they were leading.

They spent eighteen hours in surgery, but the operation was a success. The doctor told them it was the easiest separation he had ever performed, that none of their vital organs were joined, that they could have been separated years ago.

Once he was on his own, Karl completely rejected his old friends at the circus and started hanging around with Bartelli. He told him everything, how Marcell had killed his brother, how they had all forced Karl to go along and, most importantly, he told him how to find Marcell. The time that Marcell had come to San Francisco, he hadn't seen his mother, but he did see Mary, and had told her where he was living. She of course shared this information with Miranda and the others, including the Peabodys. Everyone knew Tiny would never say a word of it to Bartelli and without his cooperation, neither could Karl. But, that was back when they were joined. Everything was different now.

"Well, they don't know exactly where your cabin is though, right?" asked Frank.

"No, all I told Mary was that I was living in a cabin in Santa Anita Canyon. And I gave her my P.O. Box number."

"Well, those woods run deep, Marcell. Bartelli could spend months out there and still not find you."

Marcell took the Hollywood Boulevard exit from the freeway. "The woods are lovely, dark and deep," he said. A huge grin crossed his face. "And we have promises to keep..."

"And miles to go before we sleep," added Frank. "Even I know that one."

Kate Mallory had placed a call to Eureka, trying to locate Frank's brother, but all she got was an answering machine. She left a message for either one of them to call her as soon as they got the message, then she and Tulary went to Veronica Lee's apartment. They talked to the neighbor who had seen the red truck and got a license plate number from her, though beyond that the

188

woman was no help. She hadn't seen who was driving; the only reason she took the license number was the truck kept leaving and coming back, like they were waiting for someone to show up.

The scene inside didn't make much sense. The girl had obviously been killed in the bathroom; there was blood on the shower curtain and more in the tub and a spotted trail leading to the bed. But why would the killer take the time to remove her from the shower and put her in bed?

"Maybe the guy's a necro," said Tulary. They were in Kate's office, trying to put the pieces together.

"Did you see the way she was covered up, like someone was trying to make her comfortable? Do you really think someone would kill her, have sex with her and then tuck her in?"

"The way I see it, a guy fucks a corpse, he's liable to do anything."

"I got ten bucks says there was no sex. And I'll tell you what else. I don't think it was our killer who put her in bed."

"I'll take your ten bucks. If our perp didn't move her, who did?"

"I wish I knew. But think about it. The girl's jugular was severed. Where's all the blood?"

"Down the drain."

"Right. But that's going to take some time."

"And."

"So, our killer just stands there and waits for all the blood to empty out before he moves her? Doesn't make sense."

"Maybe he wanted her clean, before, you know. Some people are very particular about cleanliness. Sheila was always using that one on me."

"Sheila? Oh, your ex. I guess that is a lot to ask. But it's not the case with Veronica. Somebody else came in, later, found her in the shower and moved her into the bed."

"Yeah, well, I got another ten says you're wrong."

"You're on."

There was a light tap on the open door, then Karen, the woman who had found Frank's address for Kate, came in.

"I've got those phone numbers for you, detective."

"Oh, great," said Kate.

"There were a lot of numbers to run, and I crossed referenced them to the other victims' records. Most only show up once or twice, but there were a few I think you might find interesting." She set some papers on Kate's desk. "This number here, it's not on either of the other two victims phone records, but it shows up most frequently on Miss Lee's. In fact, it's the last phone call she made; called it twice in fifteen minutes. Guys name is Rudy Carlyle."

Kate examined the phone records closely.

"I pulled his sheet," added Karen. "Couple of arrests in the late eighties for pimping, but nothing recent."

"That would be her pimp," said Tulary.

"One other thing. She had one of those gadgets on her phone, tells you what number a call comes from. Guess who called her last."

"Rudy Carlyle?"

"None other."

"That would explain the missing tape from the answering machine," said Tulary. "Mr. Carlyle calls up, leaves a message. She calls him back when she gets home, he goes over, does a little carving."

"Well, actually," said Karen, "she called him first."

"You got an address on him?" asked Kate.

"Right here."

Kate got up from her desk. "Let's give Mr. Carlyle a visit. Thanks Karen. Good work."

"You wanna pay me the twenty bucks now?" asked Tulary. He grabbed his jacket from the back of the chair and the two of them headed toward the door.

"Why would I want to do that?"

"Well, it's perfectly clear, Kate. Her pimp finds out she's been doing a little business on the side, so first he does her clients, then her."

"And he places her in her bed because...?"

"She's a whore. Live by the sword, die by the sword. So to speak."

"And what about the claw?"

"It's a diversion."

"No. You're way off on this, Tu. In fact, I'll bet you another twenty, Mr. Carlyle isn't our guy."

Kate pushed open the door and the two detectives stepped outside. It was getting late, past ten, the moon was straight over head and full and the streets were busy with cars and pedestrians, a lot of people in costumes, people blowing whistles and yelling out of cars.

"Based on what?" said Tulary.

"Well, for one thing, Carlyle is only five-feet seven and weighs a hundred and eighty pounds, which, unless he's still growing, makes him about five inches too short."

"So he hired a couple of thugs for the Johns."

"Remember Freddie?"

"Diddlesby?"

"He was gay."

They got into Kate's car, she started it and pulled away from the curb.

"How do you know that?"

"Do you remember the pizza boy?"

"Yeah, I questioned him, remember?"

"So did I."

"You went behind my back..." Tulary was upset.

"Hey, you were half lit up that night. I didn't want to miss anything."

Tulary pulled a cigarette out and lit it. The two cops looked at each other a couple of times, both waiting for the other to say something. Then Tulary reached into his pocket, pulled out two twenty dollar bills and threw them on Kate's lap.

"What's this?"

"You win."

Kate reached down and grabbed the two bills. She stuck one in her jacket pocket and handed the other one back to Tulary.

"Here. You never took the last bet."

Tulary took the money. "You don't miss anything, do you?"

"I try. By the way, how did it go with the animal rights groups?"

"Well, I'll tell you, it was a real education."

"So you got something useful for us?"

"Not about the case. But I'll tell you this. Those people, they've seen more blood than we have. Maybe they're right."

"About what?"

"Well, you know, they claim there is a direct correlation between the way we treat animals and the way we treat each other."

"Why Tulary, that's so sensitive of you."

"Yeah, well, don't get too excited. I ain't about to give up my hamburgers just yet. In fact, there's a joint right up the street...what time is it?"

"Almost ten."

"If we hurry, we can make it. I think they close at ten. You're buying."

Sixteen

Marcell cut the motor to Frank's truck and glided up to the curb in front of Rudy Carlyle's apartment building. The first thing he noticed when they got out of the truck was the full moon poised above the building like a beacon. He pointed it out to Frank. "It's like somebody was leading us to him," he said.

They grabbed the heads from the box and proceeded toward the front door of the building. Half a block away, a Halloween party had spilled out into the front yard of someone's home, the noise of rock and roll music and happy partygoers reverberating down the street.

"Wow, there's a party down there, Frank. Maybe we should crash it."

"Let's crash Rudy's, instead."

They reached the door, only to find it locked.

"Looks like you need some kind of card to get in," said Marcell.

"We'll have to find another way. You move the truck around back, out of sight. I'll check the sides of the building and meet you back there."

Marcell went for the truck while Frank made his way around the building on foot. Access from the north side of the building was out of the question. Rudy's building was connected to the adjacent one by an iron fence over ten feet high. On the other side of the building there was a large pool area encased by another wrought iron fence, a little lower than the first one but with pointed ends to discourage any would be trespassers. Frank quickly removed his bearskin, doubled it over and laid it across the top of the iron pickets, then proceeded to scale the iron barricade, being careful not to put too much weight on the pointed ends.

Once inside the grounds he put the suit back on and checked for an access to the building. All the windows on the ground floor had iron grates around them. There was an iron mesh door that led to a narrow hallway ten feet long, and another door at the other end of the hall that accessed the inside of the building. Frank tried the exterior door. Locked. He followed the walkway to the rear of the building where he ran into another iron fence, identical to the one he had just climbed.

Marcell pulled the truck up by the fence and got out. "Any luck?"

"This place is locked up better than the White House. Check the back door."

There came a clanging of metal as the side door to the building opened and a man and woman came out. Frank moved into the shadows. The couple was laughing and groping at one another. They sounded like they might have been drunk. As soon as they saw the pool was empty they removed their robes; they were both naked underneath. Reflecting off the water, the moonlight bathed the lovers in a silver blue light as if they were posing for a Maxfield Parish painting. The man grabbed the girl but she broke away giggling, then ran the ten feet to the pool and dived into the water. The man went right behind her.

"Meet me at the back door," said Frank.

"What are you going to do?"

"I'm going to get some keys."

There was a small dressing room between Frank and the pool and the robes were laying just five feet in front of the room. He ducked behind the dressing quarters then crept along the side, out of view from the young couple. Once he got the keys, he would have to cross an open area to the gate; timing would be everything. At the end of the building, he dropped to his knees and reached out for the robes, slowly pulling them toward him. Water splashed up from the pool and a small stream trickled down by Frank. He paused momentarily till the playful couple's laughter reassured him he was safe, then continued with his search. The pocket of the first robe was empty, but as he reached inside the second one he felt the cool edge of the metal key chain and ever so slowly lifted them out.

194

The couple appeared to be having a great time in the water; they were young and attractive and seemed without a care. For Frank, watching them frolic in the water was almost surreal, it was so foreign to his life. Was he ever that innocent? Here they were, surrounded by iron gates, prisoners in their own home, acting as though they hadn't a care in the world, while just outside those gates the world was falling apart. They didn't know, or else they didn't care. Either way, he couldn't help but envy them. They started into a game of tag and the young girl swam to the deep end to get away. She went under the water and the man went down after her. Frank was so enthralled with their excitement he hesitated but then, realizing his opportunity, he made his move for the door.

In less than ten seconds he was across the cement patio and through the metal door. He hurried down the short hall and through the unlocked wooden door. He was in. He went to the rear entrance and let Marcell in.

There were two elevators. One was on its way down and the other sat empty before them. They got into the empty one and started up to the seventh floor. It was hot and stuffy in there. Frank removed the bear head and wiped the sweat from his face. He looked pale and somewhat ill. "I don't like elevators," he said as the bell rang and the doors slid open.

The two men stepped out of the elevator into the hallway. There was nobody around. Frank paused for a minute and leaned against the wall to steady himself, then he replaced the bear head and the two of them started down the hall.

When they got to Rudy's apartment they found the door slightly ajar. They drew their guns and entered cautiously. The lights were on in the living room and kitchen and there was a foul odor permeating the apartment.

"Stinks in here," said Marcell.

"Check the bedroom. And be careful."

Frank followed the odor to the kitchen where he found a small burnt piece of meat inside a pan sitting atop a lit burner. He put

195

away his pistol, removed his bear head and set it on the kitchen table. Then he turned off the burner and examined the piece of meat; it was hard to tell for sure but he had a pretty good idea what it was.

Marcell came into the kitchen. "Nobody here," he said, "but I found something interesting."

They left the kitchen and entered the small alcove adjacent to the living room where Rudy had set up his office. Marcell tossed his head and paws on the floor, grabbed a pillow from the couch and placed it on the chair, then sat down at the desk and turned on the computer. "I'll bet there's a lot of good stuff in here," he said. He started typing. "Ah, Mr. Carlyle uses a password, I see. Some people don't trust anybody."

"Can you break it?"

Marcell took a deep breath and gave Frank a look of mild disgust.

"What I meant was," said Frank, "how long will it take you to break it?"

"Did you get a good look at the living room?"

Frank glanced over at the statue of the penis. "Hard to miss."

"What does it tell you?"

"I'd say the guy is obsessed with sex."

"Exactly. And that's how he chose his password, which should make it very easy for me to penetrate this machine, if you'll pardon the pun."

"I'm going to take another look around. Enjoy yourself."

Frank moved slowly through the living room, shaking his head in disgust at the decor. Behind him, Marcell talked out loud to the computer, trying to ease the secret word out of it.

The bedroom was somewhat disheveled, especially the bed; all the blankets had been ripped away and tossed onto the floor. On closer inspection, Frank found what looked like blood on the sheet, small spots scattered upon it like somebody had had a bloody nose they couldn't contain. There was something red sticking out from under one of the blankets. He reached down

196

and picked it up; it was a red silk dress that had been ripped down the front.

He heard a sound coming from behind a pair of closed louvered doors. He pulled his gun out from its holster and moved slowly toward the doors then stopped directly in front of them and leaned in to hear better. There it was again. It sounded like pieces of metal clanging. He slowly opened the door, searched the wall for a light switch, found one and turned on the light. It was a walk-in closet, six feet wide and a good ten feet long and packed with clothing—men's on one side, women's on the other—from the looks of it, not cheap. He slowly made his way through the room till he reached the far end. On the rod to his left were some empty metal hangers swaying just enough to barely touch each other. Beyond the hangers were some dresses that hung down almost to the floor. Frank reached in and pulled back the dresses. There in the corner, trying to hide herself behind a fur coat, was a young girl, hyperventilating, a look of horror on her bruised face, her naked body shivering behind the coat.

He bent down to the girl. "It's okay, I'm not going to hurt you."

She recoiled from his touch. He had no idea what to do. He had always been good with animals, but humans, that was another story— especially children.

"Don't be afraid. I'll be right back. Don't worry, you're going to be alright."

He hurried back to the living room where Marcell was deeply involved in his work. "Marcell, I need you in here."

"I got it, Frank. You won't believe the word he used."

"That's good, but I need you in here. Now."

Marcell got up from his seat. "What's the problem?"

"Come into the bedroom with me."

At the sight of the girl, Marcell nearly broke into tears. An array of black and purple bruises plagued her soft, white skin; her bottom lip was cut and a trail of dried blood meandered from it all the way up to her ear like an old scar; one eye was practically swollen shut. They helped her out of the closet and sat her on the edge of the bed, then wrapped a blanket around her.

"I think she's in shock," said Marcell. "Jesus, what kind of guy is this?"

"Quiet," said Frank. "Somebody's here."

Rudy didn't like being kicked out of his own house, but he figured there was nothing he could do but make the best of it. So he had put on his wig and jacket, grabbed some blow and headed out to the streets of Hollywood, see what kind of action he could stir up.

Things were jumping in Hollywood. Everybody was in costume—kind of like every other night—music blasted onto the streets from the different clubs, cruisers, and hand held stereos, setting up a hierarchy of sound; rock overpowered country, metal drowned out the rock and rap obliterated them all, its overpowering bass lines pulsating through the streets like an earthquake keeping time.

Rudy could see the headlights stretched out for blocks down Hollywood Boulevard as thousands of eager thrill seekers lurched their way slowly toward the epicenter of activity. Where that epicenter was, nobody really knew for sure; one just kept moving till something caught his eye, a particular crowd outside a club, perhaps, or something a little more personal: a good looking girl smiles at a car full of young men and the driver starts the hunt for a place to park.

Rudy watched the parade with a smile. All these people, all that money to spend, most of it driven by sex. He was in the right business, all right, and business was good. He ducked into a small club, stood at the bar and ordered a Jack Daniels, straight up, quickly downed it then made his way back to the bathroom, closed the door to the stall and did a couple of bumps.

That's how it went for over an hour, jumping into a bar for a drink, doing a bump, stopping along the way to talk to the freaks, fuck with their heads. It was a little after nine, Rudy figured one more drink then he'd head home. He went back into the first bar he'd visited that night, only this time he sat down at the bar and ordered his drink. There was a small television hanging from the ceiling at the end of the bar. Rudy sat sipping his drink, watching the TV, the sound off. Then he saw her picture.

"Hey," he said to the bartender. "Turn up the volume."

The bartender grabbed the remote and turned up the TV. The newsman said the dead girl's name was Kieu Ho, that she had been murdered early that morning, and that the police were following up on some clues.

Rudy was shocked. He paid for his drink and hurried out of the bar. This was O'Neill's work, he was sure of it. Goddamn. What the fuck was going on? He headed back toward his place. A party had started up down the street from his apartment and there was a crowd of people outside on the lawn. Most of them were in costumes but Rudy could tell they were all pretty young, late teens, early twenties.

A young girl ran up and grabbed Rudy's arm. "Are you Elvis Presley?" she asked. She was dressed like an Indian. Rudy figured, Pocahantas.

"Yeah, sure, kid," he said. He hadn't tried, but it was one of his best Elvis's yet.

"Come on into the party," she said.

Rudy took a close look at the girl. She couldn't have been over sixteen and man, what a looker. She had her long black hair tied in braids, her face was tan and her eyes a light blue. But mostly, she had those lips that Rudy loved so much. She didn't look much like an Indian, but Rudy could give a shit about that. He checked his watch. Soon wouldn't be finished for another half an hour. Might as well go inside, have some fun. Veronica was dead, nothing he could do about it tonight.

The girl wanted to know if Rudy had any blow and he said yeah, he did, and the two of them made their way to a bedroom in the back of the house. They spent about ten minutes alone, snorting up half of Rudy's stash, Rudy laying a rap on the girl about how much money she could make as a professional; then the girl got up, told Rudy she'd be right back, and left the room.

She was only gone a minute, and when she returned she had another girl and two guys with her. She told Rudy to draw out some more lines for her friends. Didn't ask, told. Rudy had been sitting on the edge of the bed waiting for her to return, thinking maybe he was gonna get some action, but at the sight of the whole gang standing there with their tongues hanging out, thinking they were gonna cop a few free snorts, he figured it was time to move on. He stuck the spindle of coke into his shirt pocket and got up from the bed.

"This is Halloween, not Christmas, and I ain't fuckin Santa Clause," he said and started to push his way past the group.

The two men with Pocahantas were not small. One, obviously the girl's date—he kept rubbing her neck—was dressed in buckskin, like Daniel Boone. The other one wore a police uniform. They moved together now to block Rudy's path. Daniel Boone spoke. "Come on, Elvis. Give it up."

"Hey, why don't you go outside and fuck yourself a possum," said Rudy. "It'll help you get into character."

The man started to grab Rudy, but before he could make his move, Rudy reached behind his back and pulled out a .38 and stuck it in the man's face. "Now what, Hillbilly, you gonna fuck with me?" Rudy was pissed. He'd been shoved around enough the last couple of days. Maple had run away, O'Neill had treated him like dirt, Veronica, his number one girl, was dead. It was time to draw the line. "Get down on your knees, motherfucker!"

The guy tried to back off. "Hey, come on man..."

"I said, get down on your knees. The rest of you, over here." Rudy waived the gun toward the wall and the others grouped together. Daniel Boone dropped to his knees.

"We just wanted to get high," said the cop.

"Yeah, come on, mister, take it easy," said Pocahantas.

Rudy pointed to Daniel Boone. "This your boyfriend?"

Pocahantas nodded yes.

The tip of the pistol was touching Daniel Boone's face. "How'd you like it I blow a hole through his head?"

Daniel Boone started whimpering. Rudy turned his head from the group and stared down at the frightened young man. He wasn't planning on shooting him, but he sure was enjoying scaring the piss out of him. The thought occurred to him that he might even run Pocahantas through some motions, right there in front of her boyfriend, teach them all a lesson. But then he caught a glimpse of something out of the corner of his eye and as he turned his head back to the group, he recognized the cop's billy club, then felt the full impact of it as it cracked into the side of his head. There were a few seconds of unbearable pain, then there was two of everything, and then the whole room started spinning in circles until Rudy collapsed to the floor.

When Rudy awoke, the room was empty, his stash was gone, along with his gun, and his left eye was swollen shut. His head felt like it was a barn door and a horse was trying to kick it in. He reached up and grabbed it with both his hands. Something was wrong, something missing. His wig, it was gone! He staggered out of the bedroom and made his way through the house; the party still going, louder than ever, everybody either drunk, stoned, or both. Rudy didn't see Pocahantas or the others anywhere, but he really didn't care. He just wanted to get back to his place and lie down. He checked his watch. At least, he tried to. It was gone, too. It was so ridiculous, he almost laughed. How else to end a perfectly fucked up day—rolled by a bunch of kids.

He made it outside and started for home. He could see his building just fifty yards away. Soon he would be in his elevator, then the comforts of his apartment. Hopefully, Soon would be finishing up and Rudy could get to bed, get some sleep. Tomorrow would be a better day. How could it not?

The front door opened and somebody stepped into the apartment. A voice called out. "What the fuck. Where is everybody? You left the door unlocked."

At the sound of the man's voice, the girl started breathing heavy again. Marcell did his best to calm her down.

The man stepped into the bedroom and Frank stuck the end of his pistol in his ear. "You must be Rudy."

"Who the fuck are you? What happened here?"

"Stay with the girl," said Frank to Marcell. Then he pushed Rudy through the doorway into the living room. He smacked him once upside the head with his gun. "You like to beat up little girls!" He hit him again, knocking him to the ground.

"Hey, take it easy, will you? I didn't beat up nobody. Who the fuck are you guys?"

Frank kicked him in the groin. "Shut up. I'll ask the questions. I want to know about the gall bladder, who you got it for, and I'm only gonna ask you once."

Rudy was lying on the floor, writhing in pain. "I don't know what you're talkin about."

Frank reached down and grabbed him by the shirt and jerked him to his feet. He noticed Rudy's swollen eye and figured maybe the girl had gotten in a punch. He shoved him into the kitchen, grabbed him by the hair and stuck his face in the pan.

"Wrong answer." He pushed harder.

"All right, all right, it's mine. I got it for me and my girlfriend."

"You're lying." He pulled his head up from the pan and slammed Rudy up against the wall. He noticed the sliding glass door and pushed Rudy toward it. "Open the door."

"What for?"

"Open the door!"

Rudy opened the door and the two men stepped outside. It was a clear night and the full moon looked close enough to reach out and grab it. The party was still going on down the street; the music had gotten louder. Frank noticed the telescope. He picked it up and tossed it over the side.

"Hey, man, that's a very expensive piece of equipment."

"Not anymore." Seconds later it exploded against the sidewalk below them.

"Who'd you buy the bladder for?"

"I told you, I got it for me and my girlfriend."

"Yeah, I suppose that little girl in there is your girlfriend, huh? What happened to your eye?"

"You wouldn't believe me if I told you."

"Okay, let's do it the hard way." He grabbed Rudy and bent him over the ledge.

Marcell came out onto the patio. "I got her dressed. Found some of her clothes in a bag. Don't drop him, yet, Frank, I want to get some information from his computer. Hey, those are nice shoes." He was referring to the black loafers Rudy was wearing. He bent down and examined them closer. "You got pretty small feet for a man your size. What are they, about a five?"

"Fuck you, you runt."

"I'd like to have those shoes, Frank." Marcell walked away.

"One last time. Who'd you buy the bladder for."

"I got it for my mother. She's gonna make a stew."

Frank pushed Rudy a little further over the edge and began lowering him down until he was completely upside down, Frank holding on to him by the ankles.

"Can you see your telescope down there? Maybe you should go down and see if you can piece it back together." He let go of one leg.

Rudy started to panic. "Hey, fuck, Jesus Christ, let me up!"

"The bladder."

"Okay, okay. His name is O'Neill. Patrick O'Neill."

"Where does he live?"

"He has the penthouse. At the Bonaventure. Let me up, will you, my head feels like it's gonna explode."

Frank pulled Rudy back up onto the deck. "What about the girl?"

"What about her?" said Rudy. He was brushing himself off. He really looked like hell.

Frank grabbed him by the front of his shirt and pulled him in close. "What about her? I want to know what happened to her and who she is, or maybe you'd like to take another look at the scenery."

Rudy smirked. "Hey man, she's a whore. What difference does it make. You want her, take her. Just leave me alone."

What happened next happened so fast, that later on that evening Frank would hardly be able to recall the occurrence. Maybe it was the smirk on Rudy's face, or maybe something he said, or maybe it was everything up to that point, but before he realized what he was doing, he was holding Rudy above his head and Rudy was screaming something, Frank couldn't say what it was, and then he tossed him.

Marcell came running out onto the patio. "What the fuck. You threw him over?"

Frank just gazed out at the moon.

Marcell tried to look over the edge but he was too short to reach. "What about the shoes, Frank?"

"What?"

"The loafers. I told you I wanted the loafers."

"I'm sorry, Marcell, it must have slipped my mind." Frank leaned over the balcony and looked down to the street. He was still slightly dazed. "We better get out of here."

"I need one more minute on the computer. I got his records on a floppy but I just want to transfer some funds."

Frank pulled away from the edge. "Make it quick."

"Okay. What about the girl?"

"The girl. I guess we'll have to take her."

Frank went into the bedroom for the girl. She was sitting on the edge of the bed, dressed in a pair of jeans, t-shirt, and a pair of old sneakers. He tried to get her to walk but she couldn't even stand on her own two feet. He picked her up and carried her into the living room.

"Let's go," said Frank.

"Okay, I got it." Marcell jumped up from the computer, grabbed his head and paws and ran to the front door.

"You sure nobody will be able to follow that money."

"Frank, I sent it all the way around the world. By the time anyone traces it back to us, I'll be six feet tall."

They hurried down the hall and onto the elevator.

"So what was it?"

"What?"

"The password."

"Fuck, me," said Marcell.

"What do you mean?"

"I mean, that was it. Fuck. Me. Those were the words."

"Oh."

The elevator reached the bottom floor and the doors pulled back.

"Well," said Frank, "he certainly got his wish, didn't he."

Rudy's final moment went something like this. He heard his last words, "you want her, take her," come out of his mouth and something told him immediately he had said the wrong thing. He actually hadn't intended to be so flip—he really just meant if you want to take the girl, take her—but he was exhausted and beaten down and the words just came out that way. Then he felt himself being lifted up into the air. The thought occurred to him that he should say something quick, something like, "I'm sorry," but Rudy had never said he was sorry for anything his whole life; he didn't know how. All he could do was scream, as if maybe he could snap the guy out of his trance, get him to let him go, but before he knew it, the man did let him go—only not like Rudy had wanted—and he was free falling down the face of the building.

Rudy had always enjoyed the sights from up on his deck, so it was rather ironic that tonight he would see more things clearer than ever before but get absolutely no enjoyment out of it. Each passing window held behind it light and safety, couples nestled together, an old man watching television, an empty room with a large white couch (so comfortable). He even noticed the individual bricks in the building—just beyond his reach—how no two were exactly the same. And there were a few quick glimpses into his past. His mother, drunk, chasing him down the street; his older brother, in the cellar with the girlie magazines; girls, so many girls, each passing through his mind in a mini-second, some smiling, some angry, but none able to reach out and grab him, save him from his fall.

Then his entire world turned red and he realized he was about to hit the canopy above the doorway, and for an instant he thought he was saved. He felt the heavy canvas in his hand, then felt it— and his hopes—pull away as he ripped through it and slammed down onto a cold, hard surface, where his entire body collapsed in pain.

Cleve had been driving the streets of West Hollywood for fifteen minutes, trying to remember where exactly it was that Rudy lived. He knew it was a large building and not too far from Lankershim and Hollywood Blvd., and it had a large red canopy outside the front door; he'd recognize the place if he saw it, he was sure.

He had stopped and picked up a six-pack of beer on the way and was half way through his third beer as he turned the corner and headed north from Hollywood Blvd. The street looked familiar to him and there were plenty of large apartment buildings on both sides. His would be on his right, the east side of the street. He slowed down a little, and then he pulled over to the curb in front of a high, modern looking apartment building with a bright red canopy. This could be it. There was a new Jag in front of him with custom plates that read YNG GRLS. Cleve tried to decipher the meaning of the letters.

"Yinga Girills," he said, then "Yung grils. Girls. Young girls. Rudy."

He lit a smoke, got out of the car and started toward the building. There was a lot of noise coming from down the street, people laughing and screaming and music blaring, but there was something else, somebody else was screaming but it was closer and seemed to be coming from above. He looked up just in time to see something, someone, come flying over a balcony. It was a man and he was screaming his lungs out and flapping his arms like a large bird with busted wings, trying to grab hold of something, anything; but there was nothing there but air. Cleve stood there on the sidewalk and watched the guy rocket down toward earth, till he finally hit the red canopy. There was a tearing sound as the canopy gave way and then a loud thump as the man landed on the cement walk.

"Wow," said Cleve. He moved closer to the guy. He was lying there on his side, moaning. Cleve couldn't believe he was still alive. The canopy must have slowed him down a bit. Cleve looked back at the Jag, then down at the broken man. "Are you Rudy?"

"Help me," the man whispered. He looked like a bag of broken bones.

Cleve bent down to him. "Are you Rudy?"

The man tried to speak. He seemed to be mouthing the word "yes."

"Okay, Rudy, I'm gonna help you, man, but first I gotta ask you a question. Where did Veronica keep her money?"

Rudy's eyes had been closed but he opened them now and stared up at Cleve. He had a look of total bewilderment on his face, what was left of it. "Whaaa, What?" he whispered.

"Veronica. You remember Veronica? What bank did she use?"

Rudy's breathing was very erratic. He seemed to be searching his mind for an answer; his eyes kept closing and opening. "Fff, fir, firs inner..."

"Firs Inner," mimicked Cleve. "Go on."

"T, t, tir," said Rudy. "Help. Me."

"Firs Inter," said Cleve. "Never heard of it." He stood up. Something caught his eye inside the building and as he looked in he saw the backs of what appeared to be two bears leaving the elevator and heading toward the back door. One of them was carrying a girl in his arms.

"Help..." said Rudy.

"Yeah, yeah, sure," said Cleve, then he pulled out the little derringer he had taken from Veronica's house, examined it briefly, then pointed it toward Rudy. "This oughta do it." He squeezed the trigger. It wasn't much louder than a cap gun but when the smoke cleared away, there was a neat little hole in Rudy's forehead.

"There, that's the best I can do." He turned to leave, and seeing the Jag sitting there, had another thought. He went back to Rudy, rummaged through his pockets and found his keys, stood up, flicked his half-spent butt onto Rudy then ran out to the Jag. It was a match, all right. Now, if he hurried, he should be able to catch up with Goldilocks and the two bears. ❧

SEVENTEEN

Frank was very quiet during the drive back to the cabin. The girl was fast asleep, her head resting on his shoulder. After giving it some thought, he had come to the realization that it probably wasn't Rudy who had beaten her up—at least not literally—but he had put her in harm's way, had been using her, God only knew for how long, selling her youth to anyone with the right amount of cash. He watched her now, fast asleep, and wondered what was in store for her down the road, just how much damage had been done, not so much to her face—bruises disappear in time—but inside, in her heart.

At one point, Marcell tried to lighten things up, complaining about the loafers and how Frank could have easily removed them before tossing Rudy over the side.

"I just tossed a man to his death, Marcell. It's not that funny."

"Exactly when is a man a man? Rudy may have had all the physical qualities of one—though you must admit he wasn't a very good example of the species—but what else did he have to qualify? He wasn't smart enough to keep his mouth shut and save his own life and worst of all, he was one hundred percent morally bankrupt. If you have any doubts about that, just take another look at this kid."

"Don't get me wrong, Marcell. I don't feel bad about Rudy. It's just not very pleasant work."

"Well, Frank, I have to tell you, I kind of enjoy it, myself. Feel like a gardener, cleaning out the weeds, making room for the flowers to grow."

By the time they arrived at Marcell's cabin it was after midnight. Frank carried the girl inside and put her in Marcell's bed—even she was too big for it. She was young, fourteen or fifteen, but lying there in that tiny bed, bruised and battered, and looking fragile in her sleep, she could have passed for ten. Frank pulled a blanket to her chin then tiptoed out of the room, closing the door behind him on his way out.

Marcell was sitting at the kitchen table, a bottle of whiskey before him, shot glass in hand. "I think we could use a drink," he said.

"I think we could use a lot of drinks."

Frank set his pistol on the table and filled a shot glass with whiskey. "I lost my head," he said.

"Frank, you have to forget about Rudy. He had it coming."

Frank downed his shot of whiskey. "I'm talking about the costume. I left it in Rudy's apartment."

Marcell thought for a moment, scratched his head. "We could go get it."

"I don't think so." He grabbed the bottle and poured them both another drink.

"We've really stirred things up, haven't we?"

Frank downed his second drink. "You know, I can't help but wonder how different things might be if I had gotten up an hour earlier that first morning..."

"They probably would have just come back another day, or found another bear to kill. Besides, what about the girl? Who knows how much longer she would have survived with the likes of Rudy. There are probably hundreds just like her."

Frank took another drink. "Yeah, your probably right. It's just... I had a good run there for a while, six months of peace. I should have known it couldn't last."

"He makes a solitude and calls it peace," whispered Marcell.

"What's that?"

Marcell filled both their glasses. It occurred to him that in two years he had been living in the cabin, Frank was the only person to visit him, the only one to share a drink and conversation. He'd had a good run of peace himself, but he missed being around people, talking about books and movies or just sharing a good bottle of wine. He had put his own little hideaway at risk the moment he'd signed on with Frank, but it was worth the risk. He

210

was back in the world.

"Nothing. Here, a toast. To peace."

"To peace," said Frank.

"And the power of good."

The two men tapped their glasses together and finished their drinks, then Marcell got up from his seat. He was feeling the effects of the drink and had to brace himself on the table. "Whoa," he said. "That's pretty good stuff." He went to a closet and retrieved some blankets, and set them on the couch. "I guess you'll have to sleep on the floor, Frank."

"We should take shifts, so one of us can keep watch."

"You sleep. I've got work to do."

"I am tired. But first I want to make an entry in my journal."

Frank found a spot on the floor and curled up under the blankets. He opened his journal and began to write. He could hardly keep his eyes open.

Tonight we moved another step closer to finishing this business. My emotions are running wild. I go from hate to remorse to love in a matter of seconds. I threw a man off of a roof to his death. Did he deserve it? Did I have the right? I don't know. I only know that when I did it, I wasn't thinking at all, but merely responding. It may have culminated in a man's death, but in retrospect I can honestly say during those few seconds I felt as though I was in a state of grace, much like a musician must feel when he is in the middle of a piece and his mind is completely free of thought. It was pure emotion, for better or worse.

We found a young girl at Rudy's house. She was beaten up and in a state of shock. Perhaps we saved her life. Perhaps it is too late. Marcell. He is like a son to me. I truly love him. Very tired. Must sleep.

Rudy was about as bad a looking corpse as Kate Mallory had ever seen, and she had seen plenty in her seven years on the force. They came in all shapes and sizes: beaten, burned, decapitated, riddled with bullet holes; a sorry looking bunch, to be sure, but none quite as pitiful as this. Rudy's pain was plastered all over his deformed face, as if wherever his soul was now residing, it was still experiencing that critical moment of impact.

"So, what's the verdict?" asked Kate. She was standing over Rudy's flattened remains with Ken Fuji, the Medical Examiner, Fuji probing Rudy's head in search of the bullet, Kate finishing off a bagel.

Fuji was a small, lean man with short graying hair and black-framed glasses, which he constantly removed from his face so as to rub his eyes. He was in his fifties and had held his position as Examiner for twenty years.

"Dead. Most definitely."

Kate swallowed the final bite of her breakfast, wiped her mouth with a napkin and tossed it into the trash. "Well, now I know why you guys make so much money."

"That's true, however, we never get to shoot anybody. Your vic died from the gunshot wound, not the fall. Death was instantaneous; bullet went right through the cerebrum." Fuji tapped at the hole in Rudy's forehead with his tweezers and continued his probe.

"So was he shot before or after he was thrown off the balcony?"

Fuji stopped his work and removed his glasses. "Assuming he was thrown, you mean."

"I'm pretty certain he didn't jump."

Fuji rubbed his eyes and then placed his glasses back on his face. "Well, either way, he was shot while on the ground." He reached over to a table and picked up a piece of red cloth. "I took this out of his hand."

"From the canopy."

"Our friend here was trying desperately to grab hold of something. This is all he got, meaning, if he had been shot first he would have been dead long before he reached the canopy, and, of course, would have been much less likely to grab hold of it."

"So, if he isn't shot, does he survive?"

"Define survive. Technically, he might have lived. Every bone in his body was broken, his spleen was ruptured along with

212

numerous other organs. And that's the good news. There was spinal cord damage that would have left him paralyzed from the neck down, and there was enough trauma to the head to suggest he would probably not be receiving any Nobel prizes in the near future. Basically, what you would have had is your garden-variety quadriplegic idiot."

"But alive?"

"If you ask me, whoever pulled the trigger, did this guy a favor."

Kate's beeper started. She reached down to her belt and turned it off. "Mind if I use your phone?"

"I only work here," he said and continued his search.

Kate dialed her office. "This is Mallory. Mrs. Noble? Okay, do you have the number handy? Just a second." She turned to Fuji. "Do you have a pencil?" Fuji pointed to a desk and Kate retrieved a pencil and paper. "Okay, go ahead." She started writing down the number. "Three, seven, two. Got it. Thanks, Karen."

She hung up the phone and dialed another number. "Mrs. Noble, this is Detective Mallory, in Los Angeles. I'm trying to reach your husband. Oh, I see. When do you expect him back? Well, maybe you can. I'm a friend of your husband's brother, Frank, and I need to get hold of him. It's very urgent. Do you have an address? I see. Sure, I'll hold."

Fuji removed his glasses and started rubbing his eyes again. "You're going to stretch the skin out," said Kate, then she quickly turned her attention back to the phone. "No, I was talking to someone else. Go ahead." She jotted a number down on the piece of paper. "And this cabin, there's no address on that. Santa Anita Canyon. Uh, huh. What about a map? I see. And the campground in Colorado; what's the name of it? Rifle Falls. No, your husband's not in any trouble. I can't really discuss that with you. I understand. Yes...yes. Thank...thank you for your help." She hung up.

Fuji pulled a small bullet out of Rudy's head. "Here's your culprit. Tiny little thing. I'm no ballistics expert but I'd guess it's from a Derringer."

Kate was deep in thought. "Oh, great," she said.

"What's the matter, bad news?" said Fuji.

Kate looked over at the dead man. "It's like a bullet in the head. Sometimes it's both."

Frank had quickly drifted off to sleep. Maybe it was the exhaustion or maybe the booze, but he had no dreams. When he awoke the following morning, Marcell was working at his computer.

"You been up all night?"

"Ah, you're awake. Good. I made some coffee. Frank, you won't believe what's on here." Marcell was referring to the disc he had taken from Rudy's apartment."

"I can imagine. How's the girl?"

"She's still asleep. He's got names, dates, the particular sexual proclivity of his customers."

Frank got up from his makeshift bed and slowly made his way to Marcell's desk. His back was stiff from lying on the floor and he had a mild headache from the whiskey. The information on the computer screen seemed to be in some kind of code. "How are you making anything out of all that?"

"It's in code, but most of it is real amateur stuff. Like this. He puts down Mr. S., January 2, 95. Five dollars and fifty cents for a fifteen ounce bag of brown coffee—Maple flavored. Likes to grind his own."

"And you get..."

"Well, I'd say Mr. S. paid five-hundred-fifty dollars for a night with a fifteen year old black girl named Maple. I'm guessing on this last part, but I think maybe this Mr. S. is into playing with himself while Maple performs some kind of act."

"That's all interesting, Marcell, but unless you know who Mr. S. is."

"I'm working on that. I've got all his files copied. Somewhere in here there has to be a list. This guy is too stupid to remember everyone's tag. I'll find it. Another thing, this guy, O'Neill. His name is all over the place. Rudy calls him Mr. O. They're into

214

everything, Frank: animal parts, child porn, even weapons. Looks like Rudy did all the middleman stuff. A lot of money. I moved close to two-hundred grand from his account to mine, and he's probably got more in other places."

"Well, he won't be needing it now, will he."

Marcell stopped his work and spun his chair around. "You know, this changes everything, Frank. I got a feeling when I break this code we're going to find the names of a lot of men who would rather remain anonymous. Some of the things I've been finding..." Marcell glanced toward the bedroom and lowered his voice. "They've been into some pretty ugly stuff with these girls."

"Anyway they can tell you made copies?"

"It's possible. Depends on how good Rudy was with the computer. He could have tagged everything. I didn't have time to run a check."

"Let's assume the worst, which means they'll be looking for us. We'll finish our business with Cleve and O'Neill, then we'll turn this stuff over to the police."

"The police?"

"I told you before, Marcell, once I took care of my own business, that was it. O'Neill is the end of the road. As soon as the girl wakes up, I'll move her to my cabin. You need to get rid of the truck. There's a place not far from here where you can dump it."

"Frank, what happens after we get O'Neill?"

"I'm going to take Mozart and leave the area, maybe go into the Sierras, someplace away from people, someplace where I can find some more peace; or shall we say, solitude?"

Lieutenant Horton was just finishing up his lunch, sucking the last ounce of milkshake from a styrofoam cup, when Kate Mallory barged into his office.

"Do come in," he said. He took a final slurp from the cup and set it on his desk.

"I need to talk to you, about these killings."

215

"Yes, I see we're up to four now, Kate. Are you going for some kind of record, because if you are, let me tell you, you won't like the prize, believe me."

"I think I have a lead."

Horton got up from his desk. Kate was still standing on the other side. "A lead, wow, that's terrific. Four dead bodies and two weeks later you've got a lead. I'm impressed. Ecstatic. So why are you here and not out following up this lead?"

"I'm working on it. The thing is, this person I think might be involved in these killings is a Secret Service agent, or he was one. But it's more than that."

Horton sat on the edge of his desk. "I'm listening."

"We met a couple of years ago. You remember that group that made the botched attempt on the President when he came to L.A. Well, Frank—that's this agent's name—he was assigned to the President and I was working with him."

"I remember. I put you on it."

"Well, what you don't know is, we kind of had this thing..."

"This thing your talking about, it would involve sex?"

"Let's just say it was personal. Anyway, we spent some time together, things were going along great, then we finished up the case and he just disappeared."

"Well, Kate, maybe he just changed his mind. It happens."

"Yeah, I know that, Billy..."

"You want me to pull you off the case?"

"No. No, I want to see this through. I put a call in to his brother, talked to his wife. There's a cabin in the Angeles Forest where I think Frank might be living..."

"Where's the brother?"

"Fishing."

"Fishing?"

"His wife said he's gone fishing. Colorado. Place called Rifle Falls."

"Well, when will he be back?'

"She says that depends on how they're biting. Could be tonight,

216

could be in a week. I called the ranger station, they're going to try and locate him, but the ranger said a lot of these guys set up their camp and then disappear up the river for a couple of days."

Horton ran a hand through his hair. "Now, that's the life, isn't it? The whole world is falling apart and this guy is out fishing. What did I do wrong?"

"I never really thought of you as the outdoor type."

"That's not the point, Kate. Okay, so, in the meantime, assuming the fish don't bite, what are we doing?"

"I've got a P.O. Box on Frank. I'll put somebody on it, but, knowing Frank, if he's involved in these murders, he's probably not using it anymore. And I'm checking with the forest department, see if I can get a list of cabins in Santa Anita Canyon, and we're running the list of red Toyota pick-ups again, see if his P.O. number comes up."

"The guy's Secret Service, he's not about to have the cabin registered in his own name."

"It's a shot."

"Check with Secret Service, get his mother's maiden name. Maybe the cabin's been in the family."

"Sure. Listen, Billy, when I go in, I want to go in alone."

"Absolutely not. No way. This guy's killed four people, Kate."

"I know, I know, just hear me out. First of all, I don't think he killed the woman. Second, he's not out randomly murdering people. All these people are connected, and none of them are exactly pillars of the community..."

"Well, then, I guess we should thank Mr. Noble for eliminating them."

"I'm just saying, if we go in there with a SWAT team, there's likely to be more killing. If I go in alone, maybe I can convince him to come out. He won't hurt me, I'm sure of that. The man saved my life."

"Look, Kate, maybe he will and maybe he won't. The guy you knew two years ago isn't necessarily the same guy today. You don't know *what* he's going to do."

"I'm willing to take that chance."

"Well, I'm not, Kate. The answer's no. I'm sorry. When the time comes, the squad goes in with you. You'll have your chance to talk him out, but you're going in with full back up."

"I figured you'd say that."

"Then you should have spent this time finding this guy instead of wasting it in here with me."

"I had to try."

"Sure you did. Kate. This guy, Frank, whatever it was between you, you're over it, right?"

Kate hesitated. "Yeah, of course."

"Good. Let's get him off the street."

Kate left Horton's office. She didn't feel good, lying to Horton, but there was no way she was going to get herself pulled off this case. She wasn't sure what it was she felt for Frank at this point in time, but she was certain, if given the chance, she could bring him in. No matter what he had done, he deserved that. The SWAT team had its function, but they were like musicians, always practicing their chops. When a gig finally comes along, they can't wait to play. Kate couldn't let that happen. Not that tune. Not to Frank. ❧

EIGHTEEN

Cleve Cuttridge stepped into the elevator at the Bonaventure Hotel and put his key into the slot to access the penthouse. For most guys, having that key would have been a big ego boost, but not Cleve. When the day came that the key belonged to him, then it would mean something, but for now it just reminded him of everything he wanted but didn't quite have; but he was getting closer by the minute.

A week ago he was broke, now mister big shot O'Neill had given him a key to his floor, he had plenty of money and, with the demise of Rudy Carlyle, another opportunity to take a giant step forward. Somebody would have to run Rudy's operation and as far as Cleve could see, he was the perfect man for the job. No way some maniac from the forest would be throwing him over a balcony. Rudy was fat and weak; Cleve could see that just by looking at his broken body lying there on the cement. No wonder Veronica was such a bitch; Rudy probably let all his girls run him that way. Not Cleve.

As he stepped into the foray, he was pretty sure that was exactly what O'Neill had called him about, taking over for Rudy. Actually, it wasn't O'Neill who'd placed the call, but one of his flunkies— someday Cleve would have people making his calls, too. The guard outside the door let him in, and the second he stepped inside the door, a large black man grabbed him and put him up against a wall, while another man frisked him. They took away his knife and pistol, then the two men grabbed him by the arms, carried him into the living room and dumped him onto the sofa.

"What the fuck...what's goin on?"

The black man leaned down and pointed his finger in Cleve's face. "Best you keep your mouth shut, little man."

Cleve quickly sized up the opposition. The two men were both gigantic and heavily armed, one black, and one some kind of

Asian, maybe a Sumo wrestler for all Cleve knew. Cleve decided to do what he was told.

A minute later, O'Neill came in, dressed in one of his silk robes, smoking a cigarette in one of those sissy plastic pieces like some British fag.

"Mister Cuttridge," said O'Neill, setting the cigarette in an ashtray. "I thought we had an understanding. Evidently I didn't make myself clear."

"I don't..."

"Don't, speak. It really infuriates me when people interrupt. Nobody has any manners anymore. It's very upsetting. But, back to the point at hand. I believe the arrangement we had was for you to take care of Veronica but to keep your hands off of Rudy. Does that sound like an accurate summation of our conversation?"

Cleve started to answer but O'Neill quickly cut him off. "Now I find out that Mister Carlyle has had a horrible fall—imagine it, seven floors up; gives me the willies just thinking about it; must have been a terrible thing to see. So my good friend Rudy has his bones rearranged and the next thing I know, you are driving around in his car. Now, maybe I'm wrong. Rudy's a generous guy, maybe he gave you his car. But then, you don't know Rudy, so, I'm wondering, why would he do a thing like that?"

O'Neill picked up his cigarette and moved closer to Cleve. He motioned to the two guards and they each grabbed Cleve by an arm. Then O'Neill bent over to him and put the hot cigarette right up to his face. "You really have no idea what you're dealing with here, do you? You think because you go out and cut up a bear, or kill some whore, you're some kind of tough guy. Now, Rudy's dead, and that bothers me, it really does. Rudy and I, we were like, well, like brothers. But, you know, people die, life goes on. Shit happens. But you see, in Rudy's case, there's a little more to it. Rudy had a lot of information in his computer, information that I wouldn't want to see fall into the wrong hands."

The cigarette was less than an inch away from Cleve's eye. "I can explain."

O'Neill pulled back from Cleve and told the guards to let loose of his arms. "Okay," he said, very flippant. "I'm a reasonable man. You explain it. If I like your story, I'll kill you quick. If not, I'll let Mister Black and Mister Brown play with you. You got one minute."

"First of all, I don't know nothin about no computer and second, I didn't kill him...that is, well, I shot him, but I was just putting him out of his misery..."

"An act of kindness. That makes sense. You seem like the benevolent type."

"Hey, the guy was busted up in a million pieces." Cleve was trying to come up with an angle, and quick. "I figured, if the cops got to him, he might do some talking. I was just trying to cover you..."

"You did it for me. You were probably going to bring me the car, too. Right?"

"Hey, take the car. I just was using it, you know." O'Neill looked to the two guards. "Take him." The two men started to grab Cleve. "Wait. Wait, I'm telling you, I didn't kill him and I don't know about no computer. I've never even been inside his place. But I do know who did kill him."

O'Neill motioned to the guards and they dropped Cleve. "What were you doing at Rudy's in the first place? And, a word of advice: think carefully before you answer."

Cleve could tell O'Neill was running out of patience. He told him about the key he'd found at Veronica's, how he was going to Rudy's to find out where she did her banking.

"Did he tell you?"

"Hey, the only thing that came out of his mouth was his teeth. But I saw the guys leaving the building that threw him out. They were dressed up like bears and one of them was carrying a girl, a blonde."

"Like Goldilocks?"

"Yeah, yeah, that's just what I was thinking. I followed them back to their cabin. It's out in the woods."

"Well, where else would a couple of bears live?" O'Neill took a drag off his cigarette.

"I swear it's true."

"Could be the girl that we left there," said the black man.

"They're the same guys killed Freddie," said Cleve. "Couple of whackos, pissed off about the bladders. One of them is one of those little people, a midget."

"A midget or a dwarf?" said the black man.

Cleve looked at him like he was an idiot. "The fuck do I know."

"Okay, here's what were going to do," said O'Neill.

"First, you go over to Rudy's place and find out if anybody's tampered with his computer."

"I don't know nothin about computers," said Cleve.

The black guy slapped Cleve in the back of the head. "Don't interrupt."

"Mister Black and Mister Brown will go with you. They'll handle the computer. Then, I want you to pay a visit to these bears, and the midget or dwarf, whatever he is. If they took any information from Rudy's computer, get it back. Now listen, Cleve, very closely. Make sure, before you go cutting anybody up, that there aren't and discs floating around that belong to me. You understand?"

"And what about me?"

"What about you?"

"What's in it for me?"

O'Neill looked down at the wound on Cleve's arm. "How about I don't open up that wound of yours and stuff it full of maggots."

Cleve stared down at his arm then up to the two huge men on either side of him. Then O'Neill broke out laughing and the two large men followed suit.

"Just kidding, Cuttridge," said O'Neill. "You take care of this problem for me, I'll take good care of you."

"And how do I know that?"

O'Neill smirked. "Well, I guess you're just going to have to trust me. Oh, and one more thing. Get rid of Rudy's car."

Penny was awakened by the chatter of birds, the report so noisy she thought perhaps they were right there in the room with her. She had no idea what type of birds they were, though she assumed there must be numerous species to fit the various tunes. There was something very soothing about the chaos of melodies flooding her brain, as if they were protecting her from some other unidentified intruder. She felt, intuitively, if she could just keep focused on their songs, she would be safe, she could hold back whatever it was that wanted in. She began mimicking the different tunes, first in her head, then in a quiet whistle. After a while, she came to realize there were not so many birds as she had imagined, but rather a few, each blessed with a large repertoire of songs, and it occurred to her that they might be mockingbirds.

He's gonna buy be a mockingbird, she thought, and the image of a man sitting on a porch step with a guitar in his hands flashed before her. He was a handsome man, dressed in jeans and a t-shirt, his muscular arms tan and mapped with thick, night-crawler veins. There was a girl there, too, a young girl, maybe five years old. She wore a flowered dress and had her long brown hair pulled back in a ponytail. The girl sat with her back against a post, her knees tucked under her chin, her small arms wrapped around her legs, her eyes glued on the man as he sang his song.

...and if that mockingbird don't sing
he's gonna buy her a diamond ring.

Penny watched the scene play out before her as if it were on a screen. A yellow taxi pulled up to the house and the driver honked the horn. Then the man stopped playing his guitar, waved to the driver and stood up. Now the girl stood and the man leaned his guitar against a post, reached down and picked her up. She wrapped her arms around his neck and he kissed her gently on the cheek. He had to pull her tiny arms away from his neck, then he set her back down on the porch, picked up his guitar and a small suitcase and walked out to the waiting cab. The girl ran out toward the cab as it pulled away. The man rolled down his window, smiled and waved to her and she waved back and continued waving until the cab disappeared in the distance. Then she wiped the tears from her face with her arm and walked slowly back to the porch.

Penny sat up in bed as the vision disappeared. The birds were still singing but she was not with them now, she was in the room, lying in a tiny bed, dressed in unfamiliar clothes. The walls were covered with strange looking black and white photographs of animals, clowns and people dressed in bizarre costumes. There were bruises on Penny's arms and a dull aching in her head, and there were voices, men's voices, coming from beyond the closed door. Then her mind returned to the little girl on the porch, no longer a vision, but a memory. She hadn't thought of that day in years, had never seen it so vividly, and the thought of it now filled her with sorrow as a ground swell of anguish pushed its way up from her gut. She tried to hold it down, tried to erase the picture in her head, concentrate on something else—whose voices were those? what were all these pictures on the wall?—but it was too powerful. For years it had sat there waiting to get out, had come close at times only to be shoved back down, but now somehow it was being released and there was nothing Penny could do to stop it. Tears poured freely down her face as the image of the man became more and more clear. Why had he gone away? Why hadn't he stayed to protect her? Her tears turned to sobs, then a crying out loud, so loud she didn't hear the bedroom door open, didn't know the two men were in there until she felt the hand on her shoulder.

"Hey, hey, it's all right." The voice sounded like a coffee grinder. Penny pulled her hands away from her eyes. An odd looking man with a large head and bad complexion was gently patting her shoulder. She stared at him inquisitively, too distraught to be alarmed. "It's okay," he said again. "You're safe, now."

There was another man, much bigger, standing by the door. Both of them looked somehow familiar, but she couldn't place

224

them. "Who are you?" she said, trying her best to bring her sobbing under control.

"I'm Marcell," said the smaller man, "and that's Frank. How are you feeling?"

"I don't know. Confused. Hungry."

"Hungry. That's good," said Marcell. He turned to Frank. There was excitement in his voice. "She's hungry, Frank." He turned his attention back to Penny. "You just stay here and rest, I'll get you something to eat."

"No. No, I want to get up."

"Okay, that's okay. The bathroom's right there. You can wash up and come out to the kitchen. What would you like to eat? I've got pancakes or eggs, cereal."

"Pancakes, I guess. Where am I?"

"Well, what did you say your name is?"

"Penny. My name's Penny."

"Well, Penny, this is my home and outside is the Enchanted Forest. You'll like it here, I promise you. And you'll be safe."

The three of them sat at the kitchen table, Penny working on her second plate of pancakes. She told them about the previous year, how she had left home because of her mother's boyfriend, taken a bus to Hollywood and had been living mostly on the street since then, till she met Veronica. She gave them the whole story right up to the previous night. She remembered going back to Rudy's house, thinking she was going to get away from all of them, but after that it all got very hazy. She had a few questions of her own.

"I don't understand why I'm here."

"We took you from Rudy's," said Marcell.

"Why, what happened? Where's Rudy?"

"Rudy...had an accident," said Frank.

"Yeah, Rudy fell," said Marcell, "and he can't get up."

Penny set her fork on the plate. "What do you mean?"

"Rudy's dead, Penny. He won't be bothering you, anymore,"

said Frank. "As far as last night goes, my guess is one of Rudy's customers got rough with you. You were in pretty bad shape when we found you."

"But you're okay, now," said Marcell. "We'll take good care of you."

"When you're done eating, I think we should move to my cabin," said Frank. "You think you're up for a hike."

"I think so. What's going on?"

"I'm staying here," said Marcell. "I still have a lot of work to do on the computer."

"I don't think it's safe, Marcell. This place is too accessible."

"I'll be fine. We've got the cameras and the walkie-talkies."

"Will somebody please tell me what is going on here?" asked Penny.

"What's going on, Penny," said Frank, "is, you've fallen into the middle of a war"—he looked over at Marcell—"and the enchanted forest may soon be under siege. So, until we can figure out what to do with you, I'm afraid we're stuck with each other. Finish your food and we'll get going. Marcell, stay in touch, and as soon as you finish your work, get out of here, okay."

"Sure. I want to make you some copies of Rudy's discs before you leave. It'll just take a minute."

Marcell slid off his chair and made his way to the living room. Penny waited until he reached his desk before she leaned over and whispered to Frank. "Is he a midget or a dwarf?"

Frank glanced over at Marcell. The two of them had come a long way since that very question first entered Frank's mind. "That man over there," he said, "is a giant. You may not realize it yet, but you will, believe me. You will."

Cleve sat quietly in the front seat of an older white Cadilac, stuffed between Mister Black and Mister Brown, trying his best to get comfortable, his long legs doing battle with the hump from the transmission. Mister Brown was driving. He and Cleve had

226

followed Mister Black to South Central L.A. where they dumped Rudy's Jag in a field of tall weeds behind a boarded up church. Then Mister Black jumped into the front seat and the three of them took off for Rudy's place.

"It's kinda tight up here," said Cleve to Mister Black. "Why don't you sit in back?"

Mister Black scowled. "Homey don't play that back seat shit, cracker."

"Then I'll sit back there," said Cleve. "It's too fuckin crowded up here."

Cleve started to turn and climb over the seat but Mister Black grabbed him by the shoulder and jerked him back. "You stay up here where I can keep an eye on you."

"What the fuck you think I'm gonna do, jump out of the car?"

"Let him sit in the back," said Mister Brown. "He smells."

"Hey, fuck you," said Cleve. "Ain't me that smells, it's O.J. over here."

"Man, you got some kinda death wish, white boy." said Mister Black.

"You been eating too much of that Campbell's soup."

"Motherfucker," said Black. He grabbed Cleve by the neck and began to squeeze.

"Let him go, Horace," said Brown. "Put him in the back seat."

Cleve's face had begun to turn blue. Horace let go of him. "Better watch your mouth, skinny, or I'll finish the job. Get in the back."

Cleve was gagging for air as he climbed over the front seat and plopped down in the back. A minute went by and then he spoke. "You don't got much of a sense of humor, do you...whore ass?"

Horace looked over at his partner. "I'm gonna rip his fuckin heart out, he don't shut up."

"Take it easy, Horace. We got a job to do."

"Hey, stop the car!" said Cleve.

"What the fuck's the problem?" said Brown.

"That bank back there, First Interstate, that's it."

"What about it?"

"Nothing, I just, I need to stop there."

"Yeah, well, do it on your own time, asshole."

Cleve thought about telling them why he needed to stop and quickly decided that was no good. They'd probably just take the money and hand it over to O'Neill. Best to keep his mouth shut, finish up his business and come back. He was going to have to figure out some way to get loose of these two, though. No way O'Neill was going to just let him walk. He knew too much.

Getting into Rudy's place was easy enough. Cleve still had the plastic card, which got them into the building, and Horace and Brown had the muscle to get them into Rudy's apartment. Mister Brown went to work at the computer while Horace and Cleve kept lookout just in case the cops should return.

Brown couldn't tell if the files had been copied or not, but most of them had been deleted, which suggested they *had* been copied. The question was, who did the copying, Rudy's killers or the cops. Either way, it wasn't good. Brown searched the entire system but could find nothing of value. Just to be sure nobody else could come along and discover something he might have missed, he took out his pistol, put a silencer on it and quickly put a few bullets into the hard drive.

"I've always wanted to do that," he said as he stuck his pistol back in its holster. "Let's get out of here."

"What now?" asked Cleve as they exited the apartment and started down the hall.

"Now, we go and pay a visit to your friends in the woods."

"It's gonna be dark before long," said Cleve. "Maybe we should wait till tomorrow morning. The place is hard enough to find during the day."

The three men got into the elevator. "Maybe he's right," said Horace. "I don't want to be crawling around out there at night with a bunch of wild animals."

"Yeah," said Cleve, "it's real...spooky."

228

Horace was gritting his teeth. He wanted to tear into Cleve so bad it was driving him crazy. Cleve was loving every minute of it.

"I guess that's okay," said Brown. "I better call O'Neill, let him know what's up."

They got back to the car and Cleve hesitated getting in, thinking maybe Horace would climb into the back seat.

"Get in, peckerwood," said Horace, as he gave Cleve a shove.

"You guys can drop me at that bank," said Cleve.

"Where thou goest, we goest, motherfucker," said Brown.

"Whatever you say, Chang."

"The name is Brown."

"Yeah, right," said Cleve. "Brown and Black. Give me a break."

"My mother was Chinese, asshole."

"Yeah, yeah, that's real interesting. Forget about the bank. Let's get a drink. You guys are getting on my nerves."

Brown pulled away from the curb and Horace turned to Cleve, a big grin on his face. "You ain't gonna have to worry about us too much longer, Barney."

Tulary came into Kate Mallory's office and dropped a manila folder on her desk. "You want the good news or the bad?"

"Start with the bad," said Kate.

"We've got it narrowed down to fifty or so cabins," he said, "stretched out over a couple hundred square miles."

"We can eliminate all those outside of Santa Anita Canyon."

"That's what I'm talking about, Kate. It's hard to narrow down the locations. And you won't believe the situation out there. The permit fees are good for ten years. Some of these people buy the cabins and wait till the previous owner's permits expire before they bother getting new ones, so it's hard to know who's living where. And you won't believe the deal they get. Two, three hundred bucks and you're all set up in a little cabin down by the babbling brook."

"Maybe you should get one, Tu, get back to nature."

"My luck I'd get Lyme disease, or get eaten by a bear. Anyway, some of these cabins will be relatively easy to find, others are way off the road; hell, there are probably cabins out there nobody even knows exist."

"Did you run the mother's name through the computer."

"Yeah, big zero on that. Speaking of computers, somebody paid a visit to the late Rudy Carlyle's apartment, and shot his."

"Now that's a homicide I can understand. I thought we had a black and white out there."

"Whoever got in must have had a card to the building. Just passed through, unnoticed."

"Our people get anything off the computer before its demise?"

"Nothing of value, but I got a feeling whoever did Rudy found some juicy stuff. This thing has gotten much bigger than a couple of animal lovers chasing down a bear killer."

"So, you mentioned something about good news."

"We've got the license number on the truck. It was registered to the P.O. Box in Pasadena. Your Mister Noble used his own name."

"Well, evidently that was back before he started into a life of crime. You got a map of the area?"

"It's in the folder."

Kate opened the folder, pulled out the map and studied it for a minute. "Let's put a team on each of these roads," she said, pointing at the map. "There must be somebody out there who has seen that truck."

"Any word from the brother?"

"Not yet. Let's hope the guy knows how to fish. Listen, Tu, I have to ask you a favor. When we find the place, I want you to give me a head start going in. Can you do that?"

Tulary pulled a cigarette out of his pocket, lit it and took a deep drag. "I think you may have already burnt that bridge."

"Meaning?"

"Meaning—and try not to take this too personal—for a bright, young detective, you're not too smart. You go to Horton, tell him you had this thing with your prime suspect, and what, you think he's gonna believe you when you say it's over?"

"So much for privacy."

Tulary shook his head and laughed. "Listen Kate, Billy likes you a lot, but he's no dummy. You go in alone, start feeling that old familiar pang in the chest...anything can happen. The word's out, everything comes through him before it gets to you on this one. So unless you find Mister Noble's place by yourself, you're gonna have a lot of company bringing him down."

Kate opened her desk drawer, pulled out an ashtray and slid it across the table. She was a little perturbed. "Because I'm a woman, you mean."

Tulary flicked his ashes into the tray. "I don't want to go down that road. Believe what you want, I'm just telling you, you blew it."

"You got all the answers. What should I have done?"

"You should have come to me. I'm your partner."

Now it was Kate's turn to smile, one full of irony. "You're not always that easy to find. I'm not that familiar with all your watering holes." She regretted the words the instant they left her mouth.

Tulary snuffed the half-spent cigarette into the ashtray and blew out the last bit of smoke from his mouth. Then he put his hands on the desk and leaned over into Kate's face. "I probably had that coming. But let me tell you something, sister. If I was you, I'd rather have me watching my back, stone drunk, than you, picking lilies down lover's lane."

Kate stared up at the worn looking detective. She wanted to apologize but it was all too obvious, too easy; better to sit there and take her punishment quietly. Her phone rang and Tulary reached down and grabbed the receiver and handed it to Kate.

"Mallory," she said, her voice low and a little shaky. "Can you speak up a little, we've got a bad connection. Yes, yes, Mister Noble. Where are you?"

Tulary took a seat on the edge of Kate's desk.

"I'm in Colorado. What's this all about?"

"It's Frank, Mister Noble. Frank, your brother." She was practically yelling. She looked at Tulary and shrugged her shoulders. "He's in a lot of trouble and I need to find him as soon as possible. Can you get to a fax machine?

"A fax machine? For what?"

"I need a map to your cabin."

"In Eureka?"

"No, the one in Santa Anita Canyon."

"That would be difficult."

"What?"

"I said, that would be difficult. I haven't been there in twenty years."

"Just do the best you can. I need to get out there." There was a long pause on the other end of the line. "Mister Noble?"

"Exactly what kind of trouble is Frank in?"

"I can't go into that right now, sir, just, all I can tell you is, I'm a friend of his and I want to help him. I need you to send me a map. Will you do that?"

"I guess, if it's important."

"Good. Take down this number."

Kate gave Daniel Noble her fax number and hung up the phone. "He's sending me a map."

Tulary picked up the map from Kate's desk. "I better get started on those cabins...first thing tomorrow."

"Tu..."

"I wasn't here when this call came in."

"Thanks."

"Don't thank me yet. I want a copy of the map and I want to know when you go in. That part of it is not up for debate."

"Okay, but I go in alone."

"Absolutely." ❧

232

Frank got up early the following morning and went out to check on Mozart. The Santa Ana winds had gotten stronger overnight and he had to retie some of the bundles of pine branches to the roof of the young bear's den. The winds always made him nervous, especially the Santa Anas, and particularly this time of year. No rain in six months, a long hot summer to dry up all the chaparral, the entire forest and every living creature in it kindling; all of it just waiting on a spark.

After securing the roof, he hiked to the top of the hill and checked the horizon for any signs of fire. Everything looked clear, in fact, he could see for miles. All the smog in the city had been blown out to sea. The thought crossed his mind that the prettiest days out here were often times the most dangerous; all those acres of chaparral, baking in the hot sun. His grandfather had seen two fires come close to their property. It was the only thing that frightened him all those years out here by himself; it was the reason he had built his cabin out of stone.

On his return to the cabin, Frank found Penny in the kitchen putting together a plain breakfast of oatmeal and black coffee. They enjoyed a quiet meal together, then Penny cleared away the dishes and wiped off the table and Frank got out one of his rifles and started cleaning it.

"What if I just stayed out here with you?" Penny was standing by the window staring out at a couple of squirrels scurrying up an oak tree as if they were playing tag.

Frank attached a cloth to the end of a metal rod and jammed it down the barrel of his rifle and then pulled it out again. "I don't think so."

"Why not? I could help out. I could cook for you and clean." She turned from the window and came over to the table, close to Frank. "If it's the other thing you want..."

234

Frank stopped cold and set the rifle down on the table. He looked up at the young girl. He was angry she would think that about him. How could she? But then, how couldn't she? Probably every man she'd ever known had led her to believe her only value was one of sex, much like Freddie and Cleve could see no value in Gladys and Stumble aside from their parts. Selfish, greedy men, using up the world to satisfy their immediate needs, no matter who gets hurt. "Don't be so quick to offer yourself up to every man that comes along. We're not all like Rudy, you know."

"That's what you *all* want." She sounded bitter beyond her years.

"Not all of us. Not like that, and not with children." He couldn't believe he was having this conversation with a teenage girl. It made him strangely uncomfortable. Was she right? Was there anything to it at all? She was a very attractive girl, fully developed, and he had been alone for a long time. Still, he couldn't quite see her in that way. Maybe it was his upbringing, or maybe that other part, that biological drive, had died, but when he looked at her he saw only a child. Whatever the reason, he was thankful for that; he knew they were both better off that way.

"I'm not a child."

He glanced up at her then quickly returned his attention to his rifle. "Yeah, I know, you've seen the world." It came out more flippant then he had intended.

"I've seen a good piece of it."

Frank paused work and stared into Penny's eyes. She *had* seen a lot, he could see that. He softened his tone. "I know you have and I feel bad about that, I really do. But you still can't stay here. I'm not going to be around much longer, myself."

"Then take me with you when you leave."

"Look, you don't understand what's going on here. People have died and there's likely to be more bloodshed. You're not safe here; you're not safe with us."

"Marcell said I was safe."

"Marcell...Marcell thinks we're invincible. He has a romantic notion about all this. I should never have let him get involved in the first place. I deceived myself into thinking he knew what he was getting into. How could he? He's not that much older than you."

"Maybe it wasn't up to you. Maybe Marcell is old enough to make up his own mind."

"Maybe, maybe not. Either way, I feel responsible for him, and I've got Mozart to look after. Even if we manage to avoid O'Neill's people, I've still got the police to deal with."

"Right, well, you don't need any more baggage then, do you?"

Penny's eyes started to fill with tears. Frank got up from his seat and Penny turned to walk away. He grabbed her by the shoulder and turned her around to face him. She was crying now, tears running freely down her face. She buried her head in his chest. "I don't know where to go," she said. "I don't know what to do."

Frank slowly lifted his arms and placed his hands gently on her shoulders. Things were getting way too complicated. He should have never gone after Freddie in the first place, never started down this road. He could have just taken Mozart and left, kept things simple. Now he had a dwarf and a young girl to take care of. It was not what he had planned. "We'll think of something," he said. "Come on, I'll take you out to see Mozart. Would you like that?"

Penny wiped the tears from her face. "I thought he was hibernating."

"He is, but you can get a look at him. Besides, it's a beautiful day. You should get out for awhile."

"When's Marcell coming?"

"Soon, I hope. Then the three of us will sit down and make a plan, something we can all live with."

Kate Mallory got her fax from Daniel Noble at six o'clock in the evening. As eager as she was to find Frank, she knew there was no way she could make the drive from Hollywood to Santa Anita Canyon and then search for the cabin, all before dark. She was going to have to use some of that patience she had learned

236

so long ago while still living at home watching her father self-destruct. She called from the station and ordered a pizza, then drove home, arriving a little before eight, just in time to greet the delivery boy. She showered, slipped into her cotton pajamas, poured herself a glass of white wine and climbed into bed to watch a movie. When she was seeing Frank, she had imagined the two of them sharing that bed, lying around at night like other couples, watching old movies, drinking wine, sharing small talk. But it had never come to fruition. Now, here she was preparing to go after him, bring him in to face justice. What if he wouldn't come? Was she prepared to use force? Was he?

Her sleep was anything but restful. She tossed and turned all night, waking every hour or so to check the clock. Around four-thirty, she pulled herself out of bed, got dressed, left a note for the tile guy—assuming he'd actually show up, this time—and headed out for the Canyon.

Daniel couldn't remember any of the street names leading out to Santa Anita Canyon but his directions were easy to decipher along with the county map of the area. Once she got into the Canyon, however, things got a little trickier. There were directions like: take the second (or third) dirt road to your right; there should be a small stone cabin fifty yards or so off the road. Follow this road about two miles until you cross a small, one lane bridge— the bridge might not exist anymore, so watch for a dry creek. Shortly after you cross the bridge there should be another dirt road to your left—maybe to your right.

Kate spent an hour running down a couple of dead ends, but eventually she came to what she believed to be the point marked on Daniel's map where she should leave her car and start in on foot. If getting this far was difficult, the rest of her journey would be all but impossible. Daniel's map had an X indicating where Kate's car should be and another one where the cabin was located. How to get from one X to the next would be up to her. She had the foresight to bring along a compass, so if she could somehow manage to maintain a northwesterly path, she might just stumble onto the cabin. It sounded easier than it was. Sometimes she would have to hike a hundred yards due east just to find a point where she could turn and proceed north, other times she would have to go south in order to go west. She jotted down notes in a small pad of paper, trying her best to keep a record of her sidetracking.

After an hour and a half of hiking up and down hills, plowing through head-high bushes—including some that appeared to be poison oak—bruising herself on rocks and taking a couple of nasty falls, she arrived at a small clearing, out of breath and sweaty, her tennis shoes covered with mud, one sleeve of her jacket torn from a run in with an unyielding branch. Directly in front of her, less than fifty yards away, stood a stone cabin with a wooden deck. She glanced down at the picture Daniel had drawn. This looked like it.

Kate figured there was no sense in trying to sneak up on Frank. If this was indeed his cabin, he would already know she was there. She started across the clearing, slowly at first, then gradually picking up speed, the tall grass in the field brushing up against her jeans and then quickly falling away in a gentle swishing rhythm, as if her legs were two finely honed scythes clearing a path to some long sought after treasure.

She heard a rustling close by and stopped momentarily to try and pinpoint the origin of the sound. It stopped, and then started again. Whatever it was, it was moving away from her and it wasn't large; probably a small rodent. She continued on toward the cabin, wondering if Horton could be right. Would she find a Frank she no longer knew? Would she even make it across the clearing?

The last ten yards seemed like miles and as she stepped onto the deck, the old planks creaked beneath her feet and Kate came to an abrupt halt. There were no sounds coming from within the cabin, but the front door was open. She stood there (she had no idea for how long), staring into the small dark space, wondering if someone was inside staring out at her. She stepped forward, gave a gentle push on the door and stepped inside. The place was empty.

238

The president made his tour of L.A. today, and all my fears about an assassination attempt came true. Fortunately, he escaped unharmed—again. He must have an angel on his shoulder; he's had so many brushes with death and each time he manages to walk away untouched. I think he thinks I'm that angel. Maybe he's right, maybe I'm just good at my job.

Others were not so lucky. At least four people were killed in one of the explosions, including a talk-radio celebrity. I forget his name. He was one of those obnoxious, reactionary types who are always trying to stir up the public. Still, even he didn't deserve his fate. The limo he was riding in was torn in half by the explosion and the radio personality—what was his name?—was thrown out. When we found him he was impaled on the end of a metal post. It must have been an excruciatingly painful death. Kate was wounded in a shoot-out with one of the terrorists, but fortunately it wasn't too bad. She is an incredible woman.

Thousands of dollars and hundreds of man-hours went into securing the president's safety and I suppose one could say we did succeed. But what about the others? Innocent bystanders hoping to catch a glimpse of their beloved leader, their lives snuffed out in an instant. Who was looking out for them?

There is too much violence in this world, too much cruelty, and I've come to realize that no matter how hard I try, I cannot have any significant effect on that. I don't think anyone can. Mankind has made so many advances over the years but it still cannot get over that last hurdle; we are so quick to kill—and I include myself in that—so eager to tear down what others build. I am no longer a young man, and I do not want to spend what years I have left surrounded by the carnage of madmen, so from this day forward I shall remove myself from it. Tomorrow morning I am turning in my resignation. I'll go up to Eureka and see Daniel for awhile but I think ultimately I'll need to find a place where I can be alone, some place where I can find some peace; maybe Pop's cabin.

Where have all the years gone? It's an old cliché but it does seem like only yesterday I was chasing a football around a field. Where did that person go?

I should send Kate a note. If I see her I might change my mind and that would be disastrous for both of us. I wouldn't be any good for her. I'm no good for myself right now. Perhaps...some day.

Kate Mallory flipped through the pages of the journal and began reading another entry.

We busted a ring of counterfeiters today. They had set up shop on a small cattle ranch just outside of Austin. It was a large operation; their machinery was very sophisticated, their product top quality. The bust went easy enough, nobody was hurt, but I found something that literally made me ill. During our days of surveillance of the property we could smell something horrible coming from the ranch. We discovered the source of that stench the day we went in. Whoever owned the ranch had been raising calves for veal. Under the best of conditions these creatures would have a pitiful existence.

They live out their short lives in total darkness, their cages so small they can't even turn around. As it turns out, the counterfeiters had paid off the ranchers, who had then disappeared, leaving the calves in their cages without fresh food or water. Whenever our suspects felt like having a steak, they'd just go out to the barn and grab one of the healthier looking calves and cut him up. Nobody ever bothered to give them any water or food. Nobody cared.

Most of the calves were dead by the time we arrived, those still alive were too weak to stand, their frail bony bodies covered in their own drying feces. I cannot for the life of me imagine anyone walking into that barn and seeing what I saw and smelling the rotting flesh, ever...

Kate heard voices outside the cabin. She set the book down and pulled out her pistol. The front door swung open and a young girl came in, followed close behind by a tall, well built man. He turned and faced the bedroom. It was Frank, all right, but he looked different. He'd lost the little paunch that had begun to develop back then. This Frank was slim and muscular, more compact. Kate stepped into the bedroom doorway and her and Frank's eyes met. Neither said a word.

"Who are you?" asked Penny.

"How are you, Kate?"

"I'm not good, Frank. I've had a long hike and I've got a shitty job to do."

Frank stared down at her gun. "Did you really think you'd need

240

that?"

"You've left a pretty bloody trail. How was I to know *what* I'd need? You want to tell me what happened?"

"Penny," said Frank, "why don't you go outside for awhile." He looked to Kate. "Is that okay with you?"

"Sure, that's fine. Go ahead."

"What's going on?" asked Penny.

"It's okay," said Frank. Kate's an old friend. We need to talk."

Penny went outside.

"Should I put my hands up, Kate, or are you going to put the gun away?"

Kate slid the pistol back into its holster.

"Mind if we sit?" said Frank.

They went into the kitchen and sat at the table. Frank said he didn't have much to offer her, but he'd make her some coffee if she wanted. Kate said she'd settle for a glass of water and some answers.

"Yeah, I guess I owe you that. But first, let me ask you, how did you find me?"

"Your brother."

Frank laughed. "Daniel? I can't believe he still knows how to get here."

"Well, I'm not so sure he does. I have been out in those woods all morning. Point is, I'm here, and I'm waiting."

Frank got Kate her water and sat down across the table. "What do you want to know, Kate? Why I left?"

"Frank, it's not your leaving that has me concerned right now. It's Freddie Diddlesby, and the others."

Frank looked slightly embarrassed. It was a little presumptuous of him to think she still cared after all this time. "Oh, sure, of course. I just wanted you to know, that it was me, not you, for whatever that's worth."

Kate smiled. "I appreciate that. Really, I do. Listen, maybe I should read you your rights."

"It doesn't matter. For the record, though, if it will make you feel more comfortable, let's just say I waive them. You're going to catch a lot of heat, coming out here by yourself, aren't you?"

"Not if I take you in with me."

Frank leaned forward and stared into Kate's eyes. "You came by yourself because you figured you owed me, for that day in L.A. You

took a big chance."

"Did I?"

"People can change."

"How much have *you* changed, Frank? Did you kill those people?"

"I didn't have anything to do with Veronica's death. Freddie and Pepperton, I guess you could make an argument for self-defense, but the truth is I did have murder in my heart when I went to see them. And Rudy, I'm not really sure what to say about him. Something took over inside me...it all happened so fast."

"What about your partner?"

"There is no partner."

"We know there were two of you."

"There's knowing, and there's proving."

"You murdered three people, over a bear?"

"I don't expect you to understand, Kate."

"Try me."

Frank put a hand to his face and began rubbing his forehead. He seemed tired, worn out. "When I first came out here, I had no idea what was going to happen. I just knew that I had to get away, be by myself. I couldn't care for anyone; I didn't care about myself. I just figured I'd sit it out, you know, sit on the porch, watch the sun come up in the morning, watch it go back down at night. I didn't expect anything more than that. Then the bears started coming around, poking into the trash, stealing food right off my table, and before you know it, they started accepting me into their lives. I played music for them, Kate, some of the most beautiful music ever made, and they loved it. I sat as close as I

242

am to you sharing a basket full of wild berries. I've watched them chase each other around in the woods, like children, seen the joy on their faces when they reach into a cold stream and pull out a trout. Kate, they brought me back to life. I was starting to feel something again.

"Then they came, Freddie and Cleve. They came out here with their knives and guns, and greed in their hearts, and they butchered two creatures that I loved dearly. They cut out parts of their bodies to sell to men like Rudy Carlyle, men who use young girls like Penny, out there, for their entertainment."

"You could have come to me, Frank. You could have let the law handle it."

"The law! The law doesn't care about Gladys or Stumble. By the time the law was to get around to Rudy Carlyle, Penny could be dead. We're way past the law here, Kate. This is much simpler than that. This is about justice."

"What if everybody thought like you?"

"I can't concern myself with everybody. These men took something from me and I'm settling our account. It's a personal matter, doesn't involve anyone else."

"But I thought you came out here looking for peace."

"I did come looking for peace, and for awhile I found it. If you could have seen the bears, Kate, watched the way they lived..."

There came a crackling sound from the bedroom and then a voice. "Frank, Frank, are you there. We got trouble."

"What's that?" asked Kate.

Frank got up from his chair and moved toward the bedroom. Kate had put her gun away but now she put her hand on it again. "Hold it."

"Wait."

The voice came again. "Frank, get out here quick. I got company." There was panic in the voice.

"Who is that?" asked Kate.

"I don't have time now, Kate. I gotta go."

Kate drew her pistol. "I don't think so."

"I'm going to pick up my rifle now, Kate, and I'm walking out that door. I give you my word I'll come back, but the only way you're going to keep me from leaving is to use that thing."

Frank moved for the rifle and Kate pointed the gun at him. "Frank." Frank stopped momentarily then slowly reached down and picked up the rifle. Kate lowered the gun back into her holster. "I'm going with you."

Penny was waiting outside the door when the two of them came out.

"Stay here," said Frank. "We'll be back."

"What's wrong? It's Marcell, isn't it?"

"There's a rifle in the bedroom. Lock the door and stay inside." Frank and Kate took off running. "Who's Marcell," asked Kate.

"He's my friend. I pray I haven't gotten him killed."

Cleve had hoped to get Horace and Brown drunk enough to enable him to slip away during the night. Now that he had located what he believed to be Veronica's bank, he could see no percentage in continuing on in Mr. O'Neill's employ.   Veronica had money in the bank; Cleve could almost smell it. The thing to do was to get the money and clear out of California as soon as possible. Unfortunately for Cleve, Horace and Brown were not about to accommodate him. After a couple of drinks at a local bar the three men drove to Pasadena and checked into a motel. They got adjoining rooms and Horace and Brown took shifts keeping an eye on Cleve.

They left the motel around eight the following morning. It was already getting warm out and a brisk wind was blowing out of the east. Cleve sat in the back seat and directed them to the Canyon where he and Freddie had killed the two bears and to the cabin where he had followed the men who killed Rudy. Once they got their hands on what they were looking for, Cleve was certain his companions would dispose of him along with the dwarf and his partner. He'd have to be on his toes, be ready to make his move the minute they lowered their guard.

244

After moving the truck away from his cabin and doing his best to cover it up, Marcell had gone back to his cabin and continued working on Rudy's files. It had taken him half the night, but eventually he managed to locate the file that contained the key to the code. What he found was astonishing. Many of the names on Rudy's list were unfamiliar to Marcell, but others were household names; actors, politicians, corporate executives. Rudy had compiled enough information to bring down some of the most powerful people in the country. It amazed Marcell that men with so much to lose would risk everything just to spend a few hours with a young girl. Marcell, of course, was still a virgin, and he wondered if perhaps he too would become a slave to sex if and when he ever managed to experience it.

What other explanation could there be? It must be like some potent drug; once you've had it, it becomes an addiction. Some of these men were in their sixties, they had children, grandchildren!, important positions in the government. Every day they were making decisions that affected thousands, millions, of people. All of this was put on the table every time they lowered their fly.

Now that he had this information, the big question for Marcell was, what to do with it. He could easily turn it over to the media and watch the heads roll, and didn't these men deserve it? After all, most of Rudy's girls were just children, being used up and discarded after his clients had their pleasure. But what about the families of these men? What would happen to them when they learned what their husbands and fathers, grandfathers, were doing? People—innocent people—would be hurt.

Frank would have to decide. He understood these things better than Marcell, understood the ways of the world. All these years, Marcell had lived in the circus, had thought of himself and his companions as freaks, living on the edge of society, misfits, unable to conform to the rigors of normal life. Now he had to wonder, what exactly was normal life? Who were the real freaks?

After printing up a copy of the files, he deleted them from his hard drive, then grabbed a pack from his closet and started putting together a few necessary items to take with him, his magic wand (for difficult reaches), shoelace fasteners, back scratcher. Life was funny. For Marcell, and others like him, every day was filled with challenges. Simple things, things that most people took for granted, like tying a shoelace or cleaning oneself after using the toilet, were chores that had to be met with ingenuity and special tools. And there were the medical complications: backaches from improper spinal alignment, hip and joint abnormalities—he'd known dwarfs who'd had their hips replaced—premature arthritis, severe myopia (one of his own problems), the list went on and on.

All these things that made his life more difficult he had come to terms with, had come to accept as his cross to bear, and yet, he couldn't help feeling especially angry at those who had been blessed with the looks, the good health, the money, and still weren't satisfied, still had to go out and have more, had to have their fun, no matter who it hurt or what it cost. Now here he was being driven from his second home, perhaps never to return. Damn them. Damn them all to hell.

He went into the bedroom and grabbed a couple of shirts and an extra pair of shoes for his pack. There was an irritating buzzing sound coming from the living room; he didn't recognize it at first and then it hit him. It was the alarm from the equipment Frank had set up. He raced to the computer and checked the screen. There were three of them and they were close. He grabbed his walkie-talkie.

"Frank, Frank are you there? We got trouble."

There was no answer. He tried again, still no response. He glanced over at his front door. It was unlocked. Then he searched the room for his rifle. It was leaning against the wall, clear across the room. He turned and moved toward it and was only steps away when the front door pushed open and they poured in.

"Touch it and you're dead, little man," said the giant black man. Marcell had never seen him before, or the Asian looking man that

246

came in behind him. But the third guy, the tall skinny one, he recognized from that morning in the woods. It was Cleve, Freddie's partner. If I get a chance, thought Marcell, I'll at least take him out with me. That much I'll do. ✍

TWENTY

Brown was busy at work on Marcell's computer but had found nothing pertaining to Rudy Carlyle or to his boss. While Brown did his work, Cleve chain-smoked and raided the refrigerator, dumping stuff out onto the floor, taking small bites of foreign looking foods and then spitting them out. He was having a hard time finding something he was willing to eat.

"What kind of bullshit is this?" said Cleve as he took a bite off of what looked like a meat loaf, then spit it out and dumped it and the plate it was on, onto the floor. "Tastes like mud."

Marcell was sitting in the kitchen, glaring at the skinny intruder, wishing he could get him in a headlock, choke the life out of him. Horace was standing over Marcell, asking the same questions over and over again, getting impatient with his uncooperative attitude. All Marcell could do was hope that Frank had heard his call for help and that he would get there before these cretins got too bored coming up empty handed.

"Hey, dwarf," said Cleve, "ain't you got any alcohol around here." Cleve had abandoned the refrigerator and was now pilfering whatever he could find in the cupboards.

"I'm an abstemious drinker," said Marcell.

"I don't care what kind of drinker you are. Where's the booze?"

"What I mean is, I only use alcohol in moderation, kind of like you and your brain. I'm out at the moment. Perhaps we could go to a liquor store."

Cleve slammed a cupboard door shut and walked over to Marcell. "You better watch your mouth, freak." He reached for his knife but his holster was empty. A large ash dropped from his cigarette onto the floor.

Marcell looked down at the ash then cast a disapproving eye toward Cleve. "I'd prefer it if you wouldn't smoke in my house," he said.

Cleve made a move toward Marcell but Horace placed his huge arm between them and gave Cleve a little shove. "Back off, let me do my job." He returned his attention to Marcell. "Now listen, what did you say your name is?" His tone was all buddy, buddy.

"I didn't say. In your haste to extract information from me, you seem to have neglected your manners."

"Well, I'm asking you now."

"It's Marcell."

"Some French faggot," said Cleve.

"Hey," said Horace, "will you get the fuck away from us!"

Cleve backed away.

"Marcell, all we want is the discs. We know you got them."

"I may be little," said Marcell. He glanced over at Cleve. "But I'm not a moron. If I did have some discs and I was to give them to you, I'd be dead and you know it. So all three of you can kiss my rather large ass."

Horace slapped Marcell so hard he knocked him off his chair. Marcell hit the ground and his head slammed against the cabinets.

"Hey," said Cleve. "Something smells. You guys smell that?"

"It's smoke," said Marcell, rubbing the painful lump that was forming on his head. "It's what you get when you smoke cigarettes. I guess they should write it on the package. You could have somebody read it to you." He got up from the floor and sat back down at the table.

In the living room, Brown was busy cursing at the computer. He got up from his seat and walked into the kitchen. "There's nothing in there," he said. "Might as well shoot the little fucker." He walked to the sink and got himself a glass of water. "Jesus Christ!"

"What?" said Horace.

"Look out the fucking window. There's a fire out there."

Horace ran to the front door and stepped outside, leaving Marcell unattended as Cleve and Brown gathered at the kitchen window. Marcell made a break for the front door and actually got a couple of steps outside before he felt Horace's large hand on the collar of his shirt. Horace picked him up off the ground and stepped back inside the cabin. He tossed Marcell down to the ground like he was some cat that had been climbing up an expensive piece of furniture.

"We gotta get out of her, pronto," said Horace.

"What about the midget?" asked Brown.

"Finish him."

"Fine by me."

"Hey, wait a minute," said Cleve. "Remember what your boss said. Don't do anything until you get the discs. This guy's got a partner. We should take him with us. Maybe we can make a trade."

"What do you think?" said Brown.

"Fine, bring him. Let's just get the fuck out of here. It's gettin hot out there."

Marcell had no idea why Cleve had interceded for him but he was not about to question their decision. The fire was raging and would be on his cabin in minutes. Horace reached down and picked him up, tossed him over his shoulder like a leg of lamb.

"Hey, I need to get some things," said Marcell.

"Sorry, pal," said Horace.

They didn't give him time to take anything with him, not one thing. He got a final ten second, upside-down look at his home, tried his best to take it all in, his books, pictures, a lifetime of memories, all about to go up in smoke; and then they were out the door. As they raced through the woods he raised his head and watched through the tears as his cabin disappeared behind a cloud of dark smoke.

Frank moved through the woods like a mountain lion on the chase, his knowledge of the terrain apparent with each and every step. Where others might go around an outcropping of boulders, Frank went over them with grace and ease, sometimes committing himself in his momentum to a blind leap, but always landing on his feet and rarely losing stride. Kate was having a difficult time keeping up. It was one thing to get on her treadmill everyday and walk five or six miles—she was in great shape; she had the legs to prove it—but being out here, running up and down hills, dodging branches, catching a few in the face, that was something else altogether. Ten minutes into their run she momentarily lost sight of Frank as he disappeared over the top of a small ridge. Moments later, as she reached the top, she found him waiting— he wasn't even breathing hard—staring off to the east.

"Do you smell that?" he said.

Kate was pouring sweat and trying her best to catch her breath. "That's me, dying."

"It's smoke." He pointed toward the east. A small funnel of smoke ascended from the trees half a mile away. "Marcell's cabin. We have to hurry, Kate. Stay up with me."

"I'm trying."

They ran for another five minutes or so, Kate somehow managing to stay close to Frank. By now the smoke was getting thicker and closer. Frank stopped. "I'm going up on that ridge. I can see Marcell's cabin from there. You better get out of here before this whole place goes up in flames."

"I'm sticking with you."

"Suit yourself. But be careful." He started up the hill. It took them about five minutes to reach the top. What they found on their arrival only confirmed his worst fears. The fire was raging out of control, giant flames gobbling up acres of forest, and worst of all, large embers caught in the strong winds were starting additional hot spots hundreds of yards away.

"Oh, God," said Frank.

"What is it?"

He pointed toward the middle of the fire. "Do you see it? Marcell's cabin, it's right in the middle."

"What do we do?"

"We're too late. There's nothing we can do except get out of here. In this wind...we gotta move quickly, Kate."

They started back down the hill. It was rocky and very rough

251

going. Half way down, Kate tripped and started tumbling down, coming to rest at last against a large boulder. She screamed in pain and Frank ran back to her.

"Are you okay?"

Kate was holding her ankle. "I think I broke it."

Frank gently grabbed her foot and tried to move it. Kate recoiled from the pain. "Ah! Careful."

"I don't think it's broken, Kate. See if you can stand on it."

He helped her up on her one good foot. She tried to take a step on the other one, but she couldn't do it. The smoke was getting thicker by the minute and they could hear the crackling of the branches now as the fire moved closer. Frank picked her up and put her over his shoulder. "This is getting to be a habit with us," he said as he carefully sidestepped down the hill.

In fact, the last time Frank had seen Kate, she was lying on the street about to be crushed by the remains of a blown apart limousine. He had gotten to her just seconds before the twisted hunk of metal slammed down onto the pavement, then slid another fifty feet into the side of a building. Two others had not been so lucky as Kate.

They reached the bottom of the hill and Frank stopped for a second to get his bearings. He couldn't see more than fifty feet now and it was getting hard to breath.

"You're never going to make it with me to slow you down, Frank."

"We'll see about that." He heard a clicking sound. At first he thought it was a branch snapping but then a voice called out.

"Hold it right there."

Frank turned and faced the man. He had a gun, and it was pointed right at Frank."

"Tulary," said Kate. "What are you doing here?"

"All right, set her down."

Frank hesitated. Tulary cocked the gun. "Put her down. Now."

Frank lowered Kate to the ground. "We don't have time for this," he said.

252

"Tu, how did you find us?"

"I can follow a map, too, you know."

Frank looked him up and down. Tulary was wearing a suit and tie and black dress shoes. "We're wasting precious time here, people. Let's go." He reached for Kate.

"Not so fast, pal." said Tulary.

"You wanna carry her?"

"Put the gun away, Tu. He's right, we have to go."

A large flaming branch broke from a tree and crashed to the ground just feet away them. Tulary looked down at the burning limb. "I'll take the rifle," he said.

Frank handed him the rifle. "Can we go now?"

Tulary stuck his pistol in his holster and pointed the rifle at Frank. "Okay, you lead with Kate."

Frank slung Kate over his shoulder and the three of them headed west. The fire seemed to be coming at them from all directions but Frank kept plowing through, almost as if he could predict where it would hit next. After a few minutes, they came to a clearing. The smoke was a little thinner here. Frank stopped and waited for Tulary to catch up. He dropped Kate down onto her good foot and she leaned against him for support. "This is where I get off," he said.

"Meaning what?" said Tulary. He was tired and out of breath. He raised the rifle up and pointed it toward Frank.

"Meaning, the road is due south of here just a couple hundred yards. You take Kate and get to your car and get the hell out of here." He looked to Kate. "I have to go back for Penny."

"I let you go, we'll never see you again," said Tulary.

"You've got no other choice," said Frank. "If you don't get moving, you're not gonna make it to your car. Now what's it going to be?"

"Let him go, Tu."

Tulary lowered the rifle. Kate looked up at Frank.

"Kate..." said Frank.

"Next time it won't be me comes after you, Frank. I can't stop them."

Frank pulled her to him and kissed her, long and hard. "I'm sorry," he said, and took off running toward his cabin.

"Okay, detective," said Kate. "Which shoulder am I on?"

Penny sat on Frank's deck watching the smoke drift closer to the cabin, a rifle across her lap, Bones pacing nervously in front of her. Frank had said to wait, but she was getting nervous and frightened by the approaching fire. What if he didn't return? She gazed across the open field into the thicket of trees, searching for some movement, wondering how much longer she should wait before she cleared out of there.

And where exactly would she go if she left? This was wilderness to Penny. She'd been to a State Park before when she was little; her aunt and uncle had taken her camping. Her most vivid memory of that trip was one of fear. Fear of the darkness, of the strange sounds at night, fear of being left behind. And that was in a park; they had roads and bathrooms and showers and other campers just feet away. There was nothing out here as far as the eye could see, nothing but trees and rocks and sky. Right now that sky was turning an ugly gray. Pretty soon she'd have to make a move.

Something caught her eye in the trees. She stared at the spot and waited. There it was again, a figure, a person moving toward her. He came out of the trees and into the clearing; he was running. Penny raised the rifle and stood up. Then Bones bolted across the field toward the intruder. Penny had him in her sights, had her finger on the trigger and then quickly lowered the rifle as she recognized Frank's face. She didn't know why, but somehow she knew she would be safe now. Or maybe she just wanted to believe it.

She ran out to greet him. "Did you find Marcell? Is he okay?"

Frank slowed to a fast walk. "I don't know, Penny. His cabin's gone."

"What do you mean, gone?"

"Just that, burnt to the ground."

"Oh my God. What about Marcell? Is he..."

"I don't know. We have to get out of here."

They reached the cabin and went inside.

"Can't we just stay here?"

There was panic in Penny's voice. Frank grabbed her by the shoulders and shook her. "Listen to me. In just a few minutes this whole area is going to be an inferno. There's no time to waste. There's a plastic jug in the kitchen, fill it with water and put whatever food you can in a bag."

"But the cabin's made of stone."

"Yeah, like a fireplace, and we're the kindling. Now hurry, do as I say. There's no time."

Frank grabbed a duffel bag from the bedroom and started putting some items in it: his journals, the notebook from the rifle shop, the floppy discs, some clothing. Then he pulled out a wooden crate from the closet and opened it up. Inside the box was another world. In one corner, neatly folded, was his dress uniform from the marines, adorned with various medals, including two purple hearts and the Medal of Honor. Frank ran his fingers over the medals and then lifted the jacket out of the crate. He started to place it in his bag but then paused briefly before finally returning it to its corner of the wooden box.

There were also some weapons in the box, a knife, a few hand grenades, and his M-14. These he took with him, along with a couple of small canisters of oxygen. When he returned to the living room, Penny was waiting with the water and a bag of food.

"Where are we going?"

"Out of here."

They stepped outside. They could see the flames now, mostly to the east but some had jumped to the other side of Frank's cabin.

"I saw a show once, about fire fighters," said Penny. "Sometimes they dig a hole and put a fireproof blanket over themselves."

"That works great, if you have the blanket and the fire moves by quick." Frank paused and thought for a minute. "Maybe..."

"What?"

"There may be a place for us. It just might work. Come on."

"Where?"

"Into hibernation."

Penny was a little reticent about crawling into the hole Frank had dug. First of all, there was a bear down there, a cub, yes, but a bear, nonetheless, and if he woke up, anything could happen. Plus, it was dark and dank and all the talk about firemen digging holes and pulling blankets over their heads was one thing, but when it came right down to it, the idea of burying oneself underneath a raging fire was frightening, at best. They would be trapped, no way out, their only hope in the wind, that it would blow the fire past them quickly enough so as not to bake them like a couple of loaves of bread.

"Aren't you coming?" said Penny.

"You go in with Bones. I'll be down in a minute, just as soon as I put some dirt over the roof. I'll hand you down the bags as soon as you get in. Go on, now. Don't be afraid. There's a flashlight in my duffel bag."

"You sure we shouldn't try and outrun it?"

"Penny, in this wind the fire can leap hundreds of yards and before you know it, you're surrounded. Now go on, we'll be all right, I promise." What he didn't tell her was that he might have tried to outrun it if he were alone, but with her to slow them down, they didn't have much of a chance; no sense adding guilt to her fear. What he also didn't tell her was just how limited their supply of oxygen was and what would happen if the fire should hover above them too long.

Penny slowly crawled into the dark hole along with Bones, and Frank handed in his duffel bag and food and water. Then he grabbed his shovel and began digging through the mound of dirt he had removed when he dug the hole. The dirt on top had dried out over the past few weeks, but deeper into the hill it was still

256

slightly damp. He used this moist dirt to cover the branches on top of the roof, piling it a good six inches thick. Hopefully, the whole roof would not collapse on top of them, leaving them exposed to the heat and the flames.

By the time he finished he could hear the flames lapping away at the nearby trees, the air hot and thick with smoke. It wouldn't be long now. He did his best to clear away any branches from around the hole, then, figuring he'd done everything he possibly could, he crawled down into the cool earthy sanctuary. Penny and Bones were nestled together against a wall, Penny nervously directing the beam of light from the flashlight first onto Frank and then to the far end of the room where Mozart lay curled up, fast asleep, dreaming of spring.

There were a couple of loud booms outside, like bombs going off in the distance. "What was that?" asked Penny.

"The fire's hot, real hot. Sometimes the Pines can explode. It's okay, we'll be all right."

"What if one falls on us?"

"Then we won't be all right. Try not to think about that." He dug into his duffel bag and pulled out the canisters of oxygen.

"What's that?"

"Oxygen. Just in case."

Penny picked up one of the canisters. A tube ran from it to a small facemask. She quickly set it back down. "We're gonna die, aren't we?" She started to cry.

"Nobody's going to die."

Outside they could hear the roar of the fire now as it swept overhead. Branches crackled and the wind cried out almost as if it were searching for them, searching for more fuel to keep itself alive. Anything and everything would do; a firestorm will suck the moisture out of a rock and boil a man in his own fat.

It started getting hot down there and the air grew thicker with each breath; it had a sweet sticky smell, like the sap of pine trees. Frank handed Penny the mask. "Put it on."

"We're gonna die. I know we are. I know it."

257

Frank sat next to Penny and held the frightened girl in his arms. He had done everything he could for all of them, had tried his best to keep Mozart and Gladys and Stumble safe, had rescued Penny from the clutches of Rudy Carlyle, had warned Marcell not to get involved. Now, he had run out of ways to protect anyone; Marcell was most likely dead and he and the remainder of his family were lying in their own grave, just waiting for the final amen. It was up to God, now. Or the whims of fate. ❧

TWENTY-ONE

"No, I *want* to hear it all again, detective," said Lieutenant Horton. He was seated behind his desk, leaning back in his chair, his arms folded across his chest. "Every little detail. Maybe you'll tell me something, anything, that will convince me the two of you should keep your jobs."

"Well, Billy..." said Kate, her voice soft and apologetic.

Horton unfolded his arms, leaned over his desk and waved his large black hand in Kate Mallory's face. "No, no 'Billy.' Right now I'm Lieutenant Horton to the both of you. I'm your very pissed off boss who's been cajoled, lied to and disobeyed, so don't try to sneak in the back door with some cheap sentimentality."

"Sure, Lieutenant," said Kate, glancing over at Tulary, who just shrugged his shoulders. He'd known Horton over twenty years. He'd never seen him this angry before today.

Horton looked over at Tulary. "Go ahead, smirk. I'll get to you next."

Kate retold the story. They had barely gotten out of the woods alive. Tulary was a reasonably strong man, but he was overweight and out of shape. (At this point in the story, Tulary had looked down at his stomach then shot a disapproving glare toward Kate.) They had to stop every fifty yards or so for him to switch Kate to the other shoulder and take a minute to catch his breath. By the time they got to his car, they were encircled by flames, and thick dark smoke. A large burning branch had fallen onto the road in front of the car, forcing Tulary to move it out of the way, and burning both his hands in the process. (Tulary raised his bandaged hands in the air as evidence.) The car doors were red hot, the leather seats burnt their asses, their lungs were torched from the smoke. It was a miracle the car even started.

They raced down the dirt road, half blinded by smoke, unable to breathe, dodging frightened animals and falling debris, plowing through the occasional wall of fire, not knowing what lay waiting on the other side, or even if they were still on the road. It felt like the end of the world, at least theirs. Tulary interrupted. "We've been to hell in a Toyota and it's still running."

"I know you told me not to go in alone," Kate continued, "and I know I was wrong to do it, but, it all happened so quick, I guess I didn't stop to think."

"Bullshit," said Horton. "You knew when you were in my office what you were going to do. Don't make it worse than it is."

"Well, Billy...er, Lieutenant, that's not entirely true. I wasn't sure. I didn't make the decision until I got the fax from Noble's brother. I don't blame you for being angry..."

"Angry! I'm not angry, I'm furious!" Horton took a deep breath and then let it out in a show of desperation. Then he spun his chair around, momentarily turning his back to the two detectives.

Kate looked over at Tulary who just shook his head and looked up at the ceiling. Horton turned around and faced them again. He began shaking his head in disappointment. "What am I going to do with you two?" There was total disgust in his voice.

"Well, boss," said Tulary, but Horton cut him off.

"You, don't say anything. I understand her motive, here. But you, you should know better. What if you hadn't found her out there. You'd have a dead partner on your hands, not just a dead suspect."

"We don't know that he's dead, Lieutenant," said Kate.

Horton ignored Kate and kept staring at Tulary.

"Look, Billy, you do what you gotta do, but understand this. Detective Mallory is my partner. I did what I had to do for her, right or wrong. You would have done the same thing in my shoes and you know it. You been sitting behind that desk for so long, playing politics with the big boys, you've forgotten all about being a cop, so as an old friend let me just say, cut the crap and get to the point."

"Get to the point. You want the point. Right now, my black ass is the only thing between the two of you and the unemployment line, so okay, here it is. You got twenty-four hours to bring me Frank Noble, char-broiled, pan fried or walking on water, I don't really give a damn what condition he's in. This time tomorrow, this case isn't wrapped up, you're both on suspension. Now, is that direct enough for you?"

"Sure," said Tulary. "Should I assume tonight's dinner invitation is off?"

"Get out of my office. Both of you."

Tulary got up first and headed for the door. Kate was still seated.

"Was there something else, detective?"

"I, I just wanted to say, I'm sorry."

"Yeah, me too, Kate. Now go find your man."

Kate got up from her seat and grabbed her crutches, then hobbled to the door where Tulary stood waiting, both hands wrapped in gauze, a pack of cigarettes in one and a book of matches in the other. He got a cigarette into his mouth, but he was having difficulty extricating a match from the pack.

Kate leaned one crutch against the door then grabbed the matches from Tulary. "Let me get that for you." She pulled out another cigarette, and stuck it in her mouth. "Let's see what the big attraction is," she said as she struck the match and lit the two cigarettes.

Frank wasn't sure how long they had been down in that hole; he figured two, maybe three hours. You lose track of time when you're dug in like that. Once, in Vietnam, he and a young corporal by the name of Eddie Hapsburg got cut off from their platoon behind enemy lines and had to hide out in a small cave, no water or food, no light. The two of them sat there in complete darkness, afraid to speak for fear of being heard, the frightened corporal unable to stop the incessant chattering of his own teeth to the point where Frank had to actually hold his mouth shut to keep from giving them away to any passing Viet Cong. That night passed slower than a funeral, and when the two men crawled out of there at first light, Frank didn't really care if they were killed, captured, or got away, as long as they were free of that coffin.

He took his shovel and poked through the entry to Mozart's den and then ever so slowly stuck his head out. There was a light smoke drifting over the area and a few hot spots still burning themselves out, but for the most part, the fire had moved on to fresh terrain. Penny had fallen asleep during the ordeal. Frank pulled back into the hole and gave her a nudge.

"Come on, Penny, we're going out."

The young girl opened her eyes, at first confused and then surprised to still be alive. "Is it over?"

"It's safe, we made it."

The three of them, Frank, Penny, and Bones, eased their way out into the smoky aftermath. The area was devastated, most of the trees burnt beyond saving, a thick layer of hot ash covered the ground. The smoke limited visibility to a hundred yards at best and Frank feared what he might see once it lifted.

All that remained of his cabin was the stone frame. The roof, porch, everything inside, was torched. He and Penny rummaged through the refuge searching for any little article that might have survived. Penny found a black skillet in what used to be the kitchen along with the partial remains of a few utensils. Structurally, the place was fine. Put on a new roof, redo the floor and add some windows and you have a cabin. But right now, Frank had more important things on his mind.

"Time to go," he said.

"Where to?"

"First we go to Marcell's, see if he made it out or not. After that, I don't know, but we can't stay here."

"What about Mozart?"

"I'll come back later and check on him. I can't believe this has happened."

It was strange, to say the least, making the hike to Marcell's place. What used to be an enjoyable trek through the woods was now a painful, depressing ordeal, the smell of ash and smoke, the

262

occasional half-burnt carcass of an animal reminiscent of the jungles of Vietnam so many years ago, jungles so thick you needed a machete just to walk through them, reduced to a moonscape after a splattering of napalm bombs. That was their land and he had taken part in destroying it. He had always been sympathetic with their situation, had thought he understood their defiance, their enormous capacity for punishment, but only now, as he walked through the burned out ruins of his own world, did he truly understand the depth of their commitment. No wonder they couldn't be defeated.

The only landmarks that remained between Frank's and Marcell's cabins were the outcroppings of boulders and the few small rises of land. Not that Frank needed them to find his way; the hills, the creeks, the rocks, the slope of the earth, the patches of blue sky between the stand of trees, all this and more was part of him, it flowed in his veins. It would take a nuclear bomb to remove all that.

Marcell's cabin was made of wood, not stone like Frank's. There was nothing left standing but the chimney. Frank and Penny searched the rubble for a sign, anything that might reveal Marcell's fate. The kitchen sink, the timy bathtub, a heap of plastic that used to be a computer, all guided them through the house. In the bedroom, buried beneath a piece of flashing that had fallen from the roof, Frank found a picture of Marcell standing next to an elephant—probably Dinky—still in its frame, completely untouched by the fire. He put the picture in his duffel bag and continued his search. What he was looking for was a corpse but after searching every inch of the place he found no traces of one, not an ounce of flesh, not one bone. Marcell had not died in this fire.

"They've taken him," said Frank.

"Who?"

"Whoever O'Neill sent out here."

"Do you think he's still alive?"

"That depends on whether or not they found what they were

looking for."

"What do we do now?"

"I'm going to take you someplace safe, then I'll try and find Marcell, if it's not too late."

They hiked down to the dirt road by Marcell's place. To the east of the road the hills were untouched by the fire. It had started somewhere between the road and Marcell's cabin, most likely by the men who had taken Marcell. As they followed the road down toward the highway they could see a clear point of demarcation where the blue sky ended and the huge cloud of smoke began. The winds were still blowing out of the east and Frank figured the fire department would be busy with this one for quite a while.

"Hey, can you slow down a little bit?" said Penny. Frank had been keeping a good pace and she was dragging behind.

"You're young, keep up."

Penny ran after him. "God, where's the fire?"

Frank stopped for a second, gave her a dirty look and shook his head, then continued on.

"What happened to your girlfriend?" she said. She was walking right beside him now.

"What?"

"The woman, the cop that came to the cabin. What happened to her?"

"She ran off with another man."

"Did you two have a thing?"

They came to the end of the dirt road. All along the highway were parked cars, thrill seekers come to watch the fire. Most of them had left their cars and hiked up the road to a vista point.

"You ask too many questions.'

Frank began checking the empty vehicles.

"What are you doing? said Penny

"Getting us some transportation."

Most of the cars were locked but at last he found one, an older Chevrolet. It was black and shiny and lowered to the ground. Most importantly, it was unlocked and the keys were in the ignition.

"Get in," said Frank.

They got into the car, Frank and Penny up front, Bones in the back. Frank turned the key and when he did, the music blasted out from the speakers like a bomb going off. Bones starting barking.

"Jesus, turn that shit off," said Frank.

He swung the car around and headed down the hill. Penny reached over and turned down the music.

"How do people listen to that stuff?"

"It's rap, Frank. It's cool."

"It's cool, huh. It's a bombardment of the senses."

"So's the world," said Penny, slightly agitated by Frank's attitude.

"You're right, Penny, it is. And when I turn on some music I don't want to be reminded of it. I'd rather hear something beautiful. Try not to take it personal."

"You're such a jerk," she said, half under her breath, then reached back and started petting Bones. Frank just smiled.

"I know where they've taken him," she said, sounding coy.

"You what?"

"Marcell. I think I know where he'll be. But you have to promise me something."

"Oh, really. What's that?"

"Promise you'll take me with you."

"What! Forget it. This is not a game, Penny. These are very bad people. Do you understand that?"

"Yeah, Frank, I understand it. Better than anyone. I've got my own score to settle, so you either take me with you or you can find him yourself."

Frank hit the brakes hard, pulled the car over to the side of the road and turned off the engine. A cloud of dust enveloped them. "Now you listen to me and listen good. I don't sleep with children and I don't take them into battle with me. So if you want to sit there and think of yourself and let Marcell die in the meantime, you go ahead, you live with that."

"You don't know what I've been through!" she screamed. "You

265

don't know what they did to me." Penny started crying. "I hate them! I hate them all. I want them all dead!" She was getting hysterical, now, the tears pouring out. She opened the door and jumped out of the car and started running down the road. Frank watched her go then he started the car and followed slowly behind her. After a few minutes her run slowed to a walk. He pulled the car a little ahead of her, stopped and opened her door. She got in and closed her door, wiped the tears from her eyes with her sleeve.

"You feel better now?"

"They have a house in Malibu," she said, very deadpan. "That's where they keep the girls."

"Penny, I promise you, they'll pay for what they've done, but you've got enough to deal with already, without worrying about trying to get their blood off your hands. You'll just have to trust me on that."

"You don't have to save us all, you know."

Frank pulled the car back onto the road. "Sometimes it sure feels like I do."

After a half-hearted attempt at finding Maple, Roberto had returned to the Malibu house where he and Arnie were currently winding down from three days of drunken, drug induced debauchery, including an impromptu film staring Roberto, Connie, and Angel, wherein boy has girl, boy and girl get in argument, boy leaves girl, girl has sex with girlfriend, boy returns and has sex with both girls. Roberto kept asking Arnie if he thought Rudy would put the movie on the market, and if so, if Roberto would get any money for his part. Arnie told him, yeah, yeah, he was gonna be a big porno star and he should be thinking of a showbiz name, advice Roberto took to heart, coming up with one lame idea after another.

"How about Peter Dragon?" he said. "You know, you spell like it like dragon, d-r-a-g-o-n." He and Arnie were out on the rear deck sucking down a couple of beers. Connie, Angel, and Candy were all in the house, passed out.

266

"Yeah, Roberto, I get it. Are you a total fucking moron, or what? Forget about being in the movies, okay. You may not have noticed, but neither Rudy or Veronica have been around for the last three days. What the fuck does that tell you?"

"I don't know."

"Something's going on, man. Something big."

The phone rang. Roberto took a swig off his beer and lay back on his lounge chair. "Don't get up, Peter," said Arnie, sarcastically. He got up from his chair and went into the house.

Roberto gazed out at the surrounding hills. He imagined himself owning this house, could see himself sitting down by the pool, lots of girls—young, attractive girls—hanging around, important people coming by to see him, trying to get him to star in their movies, and not just pornos, real movies with big named directors—he couldn't think of any of their names off-hand—and large budgets. He was deep into his reverie when Roberto kicked him in the leg.

"Hey, get up, we got work to do."

Roberto removed his sunglasses. "What? What kind of work?"

"That was mister big on the phone. They're coming over here with some guy, and they want us to get rid of the girls. Oh, and by the way, your pal Rudy is dead, and so is Veronica."

"Dead? How?"

"What am I, a fucking information booth. They were murdered, what do you think."

Roberto got up from his chair. "What do you mean, get rid of the girls?"

"Just like it sounds, Einstein."

"Hey, wait a minute, Arnie. I didn't sign up for no killing."

Roberto was wearing a short sleeve Hawaiian shirt with bright red and yellow flowers. Arnie grabbed hold of it just below the collar and pushed the bigger man back against the railing. "I didn't sign up for no killing, Arnie," he said, in a mocking, whining tone. "What the fuck do you think this is, a fucking Ferris-wheel? I'm tired of this ride, I think I'll get off now. It don't work like that, stupid. When the man says get rid of the girls, you get rid of the girls. If that don't fit into your plans then you better find a hole somewhere on the other side of the planet and get in it, pal. Do you understand me?"

"All right, all right. Let go of the shirt, man."

Arnie released him and tidied up his shirt. "You gotta get smart, Roberto."

"I just don't see why we have to kill them, Arnie. Jesus, man, that's serious shit."

"You think I like it? This O'Neill's a heavy hitter. We don't have any choice."

"Maybe we could just tell the girls to disappear."

"They're whores, Roberto. In a couple of days, they'll be working the streets in L.A. First time they get popped they'll start shooting off their mouths and you and me will be the ones who pay the price. Is that what you want? You wanna spend the next ten years is prison. Now come on, wake them up, tell them we gotta go somewhere."

"Where?"

"Tell them they have a job, a party at a big ranch. Tell them to wear some nice clothes."

When Maple left the Malibu house she had it in her mind to make a new start. She was only sixteen years old; it wasn't too late to turn her life around. She had been with Rudy for four years, and all she had to show for it was a few hundred dollars and a couple of very low budget pornos with some very old men. She had never bothered to watch them, it was all just whoring with a camera, small money, no art. Tired stuff.

She decided to go back home, to South Central, stay with her mother—if her mother was still alive—maybe find a job. She could even go back to school; she'd made it through the seventh grade before she started turning tricks. Got pretty good grades, too.

Things didn't turn out exactly like she planned.

It was good to be back in her old house, same old worn out furniture, paint chipping off the walls, the familiar smell of her mother's kitchen. Nothing had changed, except maybe her mother. She was happy enough to see Maple, but she was back on the pipe, and from the looks of her, she was hitting it hard. She was twenty-nine when Maple took off four years ago; now, at thirty-three, she looked fifty. And there was one other problem. Corrina, Maple's mother, had her a new man. When Maple told her what she had in mind, she popped the bubble.

"Uh uh, girl. I got me a man, now. He take one look at you, he be all over your ass like sweet on honey."

Maple told her she could handle herself, but her mother said there weren't no way she was staying there, not one night. Then she asked Maple if she could loan her ten bucks so she could score a couple rocks. She'd pay it back, she said, just as soon as Thomas, her man, came around. Maple gave her mother fifty bucks, suggested she do it all up at once, get it over with, then she gathered up her things and split.

She had close to eight hundred dollars on her and decided the best thing to do was to find a small apartment somewhere and go it alone. That night, she checked into a homeless shelter and the following morning she put on a clean white dress and went looking for a job. Her plan was to start at the top and work her way down, so her first assault was on Beverly Hills, hitting every fancy boutique and restaurant on Wilshire Boulevard; she could sell clothes or steaks, didn't matter to her. A very long day of yes m'am and no sir brought her two tired feet and zero results. She returned to the shelter, exhausted from the long day, but determined to try again tomorrow.

When she awoke in the morning, her purse was gone and with it, the eight hundred dollars. The folks that ran the shelter seemed genuine in their concern but what could they do? That night she went back to what she knew best.

By midnight she had already brought in a hundred bucks. Three or four good nights, she'd have a decent stash of money, she'd give the straight life another shot. Around two in the morning a car pulled up to the curb and Maple walked over to it. The guy driving was young and good-looking and Maple was eager to pull one more trick before calling it a night.

"You want a good time?" she asked and the man opened the door. Five minutes later they were in a motel room, Maple was down to her bra and panties and she was quoting him prices. The minute money came into the deal, he reached into his jacket and pulled out a badge.

"You're under arrest," he said.

"Oh, man, listen. How about I do you for free, honey, you give me a break?"

"I'm already giving you a break by getting you off the street. How old are you, fifteen? You shouldn't be living like this."

"Why not, it's good enough for your mother."

"Come on, get your clothes on."

"You're really fucking everything up, you know that. I'm just trying to make enough money to quit this business."

"Sure you are."

"You makin a big mistake, passing this body up, cause I still ain't going to no jail. You coulda had yourself a good time."

Maple pulled on her skirt and grabbed her blouse from the bed. She still had one more ace up her sleeve. She hated to do it, but damn if she was gonna spend one night in prison—any kind. ❧

TWENTY-TWO

All the way to Malibu, Cleve had to sit in the back seat of the Cadilac with the dwarf, listening to his insults while Horace and Brown sat up front laughing at the little man's jokes. Cleve tried giving it back to him, but he was no match for the quick- witted prisoner with the voice that sounded like it was filtered through coal. And to make matters worse, Horace and Brown wouldn't let him touch the little asshole.

"Hey, Cleve, couldn't your mother have given you a picture of herself instead of making you wear that tattoo?"

"At least I had a mother," said Cleve.

"You probably had her more than once. Or is that your sister? It's my mother. It's my sister. My mother. My sister," said Marcell.

Cleve just looked at him like he was crazy. Brown turned around in the front seat. "What's the matter with you," he said to Marcell.

"Nothing. Don't you guys ever go to the movies? Chinatown? Faye Dunaway? She's my sister, she's my daughter...forget it. I'm sure ignorance has its benefits."

"Watch who you're calling ignorant, little man," said Brown.

Marcell sat up on the edge of his seat. "Well, I certainly wasn't referring to you, sir. I can tell you're an intelligent man just by the company you keep."

Brown reached over and slapped Marcell with the back of his hand and sent him bouncing off the back of the seat.

"Now there's a man who knows how to debate," said Marcell. "I'm keeping track of all your rebuttals, you know. When my friend shows up, you will be asked to account for each and every one of them. Did I fail to mention he's a green beret?"

Marcell looked over at Cleve, who was smiling now, delighted to see Marcell get slapped around a little. "Must be your night in the barrel, huh, Cleve."

Horace started rubbing his shiny head and laughing out loud.

"Yeah, that's a good one. Ol Cleve's goin in the barrel tonight."

Cleve reached over and popped Marcell in the chin, for which Mister Brown abruptly smacked Cleve. "I told you to keep your hands off of him."

"It was worth it," said Cleve. Blood began to drip from his lip. Cleve wiped it off with his sleeve.

Marcell sat back up on the edge of his seat. "So, I guess you guys work for O'Neill, huh? Let me ask you, how much do you get paid to beat up on young girls?"

"We didn't beat up no young girl," said Horace.

"Really. I suppose Penny tripped and fell."

"You ask too many questions," said Brown.

"Just curious. I know it wasn't Cleve who did it or she'd be dead. I've seen his work up close. He's very good with a knife, as long as he's fighting a girl or a dead animal. Of course, I'm rather handy with the cutlery, myself. Maybe I'll get the chance to show you. How about it, Cleve, you and me mixing it up in the kitchen?"

"I'd love that," said Cleve.

"You hear that, Mister Brown? I've challenged your associate to a duel and he has accepted. So what do you say?"

"Yeah, sure, whatever. Just can it for awhile."

"You know, what I really don't understand is why the two of you are hanging around with Dracula, here, especially considering the way he feels about, you know, people of color."

"What's he talkin about?" said Horace.

"He's talking out his ass," said Cleve.

"I'm just going by what Freddie told us. Did you boys get a chance to meet Freddie? Looking back on it, I have to say, perhaps we were a little hasty in our dealings with him. Compared to the rest of you, he was a pretty decent fellow. Anyway, he mentioned—just before I put a bullet in his head—how Cleve was always using that word, you know, the N word. N this, N that. Said carving up the bear reminded him of the time he cut up a big black N down in Georgia. Personally, I don't care for that word, never have. It's kind of like calling a dwarf a runt. What are your feelings on it, Horace?"

Horace turned completely around in his seat and just glared at Cleve.

"Watch the road, Horace," said Brown. "You wanna get us killed?" He reached over and grabbed the steering wheel. "And that's enough out of you, runt. Just sit back and keep your mouth shut. You'll get plenty of chance to talk when Mr. O shows up."

"I'm gonna do my own carving," said Horace.

"He's just trying to start trouble," said Brown.

"Hey, you guys," said Marcell, "you want to see a trick I learned in the circus? A magic trick?"

"As long as it doesn't involve flapping your gums," said Brown.

"Okay, now you have to watch closely." Marcell pulled his legs up onto the seat, then pulled them tight to his chest as he rolled onto his back.

Cleve leaned in to get a closer look. "Big fucking deal," he said.

"I'm not done yet," said Marcell. Quickly, he turned to the side so that his feet were just a foot away from Cleve's face, and then like a tightly coiled spring, his legs sprung out, both feet smacking Cleve in the face. It was a solid blow to the head, sounded like a hammer on a piece of lumber, and sent Cleve's head crashing into the side window.

"That's for Gladys," asshole.

Cleve rebounded off the window and grabbed Marcell by the neck, lifted him off the seat and started strangling him. Marcell's tiny body dangled freely in air, enabling him to get in another kick, this one square into Cleve's Adam's apple.

"That's for Stumble," he said, his words barely audible.

Cleve started gagging and released one hand from Marcell and used it to try and block any additional kicks, until Brown finally reached back and separated the two of them.

"One more outbreak between you two and we're gonna pull this fucking car over and I'll put a bullet in both of your heads, I don't give a fuck what O'Neill does about it. You understand!"

The two of them retreated to their separate corners of the back seat. Cleve was now bleeding from his nose and his lip; Marcell's face was purple from lack of oxygen. As soon as he got his breath, he started right back in.

"Let me ask you this," said Marcell. Brown just shook his head. "When we get to wherever it is we're going, which one of you will be in charge of extracting information from me?"

"That pleasure will be all mine," said Brown.

"That's what I thought. Here's what I was thinking. So far, you haven't been what I'd call a gracious host, slapping me around and all, but that's your job and I have a certain amount of respect for that. The important thing is, you haven't done any permanent damage and I'm sure, with a little effort, I could persuade my partner to forgive and forget. He's a little hot headed—you know how those Vietnam vets are, guy goes ballistic, wants to kill everything in sight—but at this point it's really only Cleve and O'Neill he's after, so if you were to let me go, I'm sure you and your darker brethren could both look forward to a long and prosperous criminal career. I have to tell you though, and it's very important you listen carefully now: this is a one time offer. Once you start pulling out my fingernails and such, there will be no more deals. You look like a couple of K-Mart shoppers. Think of it as a blue light special"

The car pulled to a stop in front of an open iron gate.

"Wonder why the gate's open?" asked Horace.

"Arnie and Roberto had to take care of some business. Go on in." He turned around to Marcell. "You know," he said, "I'm actually going to enjoy working on you. I like a challenge."

"Really. Well, I look forward to it, myself. But you're going to have to do better than these little pats on the face you've been giving me; I'm not your girlfriend, you know. Maybe you should do Cleve first, get yourself in the mood. Just promise me I get to watch."

Cleve looked at Brown, who now had a huge grin on his face. Cleve, on the other hand, didn't look happy at all.

Once they got out of the hills, Frank quickly ditched the car and he and Penny caught a cab to Pasadena. They were both a mess, covered in soot and dirt, but the driver paid them little mind, just charged them extra for Bones and told them to keep the dog on the floor. Frank had him drop them a few blocks from the circus and they finished their journey on foot.

They didn't get there any too soon. Workers were finishing pulling up stakes as the circus prepared to leave town. Frank located Miranda's bus, told her about the fire and Marcell.

"But who are these people? Why do they have my son?"

"There's no time to explain that to you right now, Miranda."

"You're going after him by yourself?"

"He thinks he's Rambo," said Penny.

"I'll need a car," said Frank.

"You can take mine," said Miranda. "It's the Yugo. I'll have Howard unhook it from the bus. Is there anything else you need?"

"I could use some rope and maybe a hook of some sort. And I need to use your bathroom so I can change. Penny, I want you to write down everything you can possibly remember about the house. Don't leave anything out."

Frank was in the bathroom for fifteen minutes. When he came out, Miranda and Penny were sitting at the table working on her list for Frank. One look at him and their mouths fell open. All his hair was shaved off his head, red stripes ran across his forehead and cheeks, and his eyes were encircled in black. He looked frightening, like a man gone out of his mind.

"I borrowed some of your make-up," said Frank.

The women just stared, unable to speak.

"Sorry if I startled you, but that's basically the idea."

Miranda got up from her seat. "I got the things you asked for. Frank, I could get you some help. You don't have to do this alone."

"I can't go in there with amateurs, Miranda. They'll just get themselves killed. It'll be dark soon. I better get going. Penny, you got that information for me?"

Penny got up and handed the paper to Frank. She was having

a difficult time holding back the tears. Frank hugged her. "Don't worry. Everything's gonna be all right. Now, do me a favor and let me have a minute alone with Miranda."

Penny put her arms around his neck, pulled his head down where she could reach it and kissed him softly on the cheek. "Please come back," she said, then she let go of him and ran out the door.

"How soon do you pull out of here?" said Frank

"We leave at midnight, but I'll wait."

"No. If we're not back by then, we won't be coming back. You can do me one favor though, take care of the girl. She's been through a lot."

"Don't worry about her. What about your dog?"

"I'll take Bones with me. Well, I guess that's it then." He stood there, timid, like a schoolboy. "I better get going."

Miranda moved in close. "Just one more thing, Frank." She put her arms around him and kissed him on the lips, long and hard. "When you get back, we'll try that again, without the makeup."

The three girls were not very enthusiastic about going out on a job that afternoon, not after two days of partying with Arnie and Roberto. And where was Rudy, by the way? He hadn't told them anything about a party. Arnie just said fine, stay here, don't get dressed, don't go to the party. When Rudy comes over later you can all explain to him how you didn't feel like working today. And so they got dressed, bitching and moaning the whole time.

All five of them climbed into Arnie's black Chevy Blazer, Arnie behind the wheel, Roberto riding shot-gun, the girls in the back seat in their tight dresses and high heels, doing up lines, trying to get themselves up for their job.

They had been driving a good forty minutes, the sun was about to go down, and Roberto hadn't said a word the whole way.

"What's the matter with you, Roberto?" said Angel.

"Nothing," said Roberto. He wouldn't even look at her.

"He's probably embarrassed cause of the movie," said

276

Connie.

"You never been in a porno before?" said Candy.

Roberto looked over at Arnie. The guy looked cool as a cucumber. Not Roberto. His stomach was going crazy; he felt like he was gonna throw up, and he couldn't stop the sweat from pouring down his face.

"Leave Roberto alone," said Arnie. "He's shy."

Angel reached up and ran her fingers through Roberto's hair. "Oh, that's so cute, Roberto. Don't worry about it. Ain't like your mother's gonna see it."

Roberto knocked her hand away from his head.

"Wow, don't get sore, okay?"

Roberto started biting at his nails, every now and then glancing over at Arnie. They were out in the sticks now, miles from anything.

"This is wrong, man."

"Shut up," said Arnie.

"What's the matter?" said Candy. "*What's* wrong? Are we lost?"

"No, we ain't lost. It's just right over this next hill."

"It's dark out here," said Connie. "I'd sure hate to be out here by myself. Scary. What an asshole Rudy is, making us come all the way out here. You guys gonna stay for the party."

"Yeah, sure," said Arnie. "For awhile."

They came over the ridge and Arnie turned the car onto a narrow dirt road and followed it about a half a mile, then he turned onto yet another road, went a hundred yards or so and pulled the car over under some trees. He left the motor running.

"Where are we?" said Candy.

"Yeah," said Connie, "I don't see no ranch."

"This is it," said Arnie, "end of the road. Everybody out."

"What's he talkin about? Roberto, what's goin on?"

"Just, get out of the car," said Roberto. "Come on, it'll be all right."

Connie and Angel got out but Candy stayed put.

"Come on, Candy," said Arnie. "Let's go."

"Fuck you, there ain't no ranch out here, and I ain't gettin out of this car."

"Get out of the car, Candy. Now!"

Candy refused to move.

"Get her out, Roberto." Arnie pulled out his gun. "Get her out of the car."

Connie and Angel were huddled together, whimpering like small children. Roberto leaned inside the car.

"Come on, Candy, get out."

Candy was crying. "Please, Roberto, don't do this. I'll do anything. Don't let him hurt us."

"I'm sorry..."

"Jesus Christ!" said Arnie. He pushed Roberto aside, then reached inside, grabbed Candy by the hair and pulled her out of the car, kicking and screaming. Once he got her outside, he slapped her across the face. "Shut the fuck up. All right, now let's everybody take a walk."

They started through the bushes, the girls leading the way, stumbling through the brush in their high heels, branches scratching their faces and ripping their dresses, all the while the three of them crying and pleading with Arnie to let them go. Every time one of them would start to lag, Arnie would give her a shove.

They came to a narrow creek. Arnie told them to stop and get down on their knees. Angel tried to break away and run but Arnie grabbed her and tossed her to the ground. Then he turned to Roberto.

"Okay," said Arnie. "They're all yours."

"What do you mean?"

"I mean, do it. You gotta be part of this."

Roberto stared down at the three hysterical women. Just a few hours earlier they had all been in bed together, stone drunk, laughing, making total fools of themselves; Roberto had felt like a king. Now here he was standing over them with a gun in his

278

hand.

"Come on, Roberto, we haven't got all night."

Roberto raised his gun and pointed it toward the girls. His hand was shaking, his legs felt like they were going to buckle under any minute. He had done a lot of things in his life he wasn't proud of—one thing always seemed to lead to another—but this, this was the bottom. Once he pulled that trigger, there would be nowhere else to go.

"For Chrissake, Roberto, do these bitches and let's get out of here."

Roberto cocked the gun. There was only one thing to do, and he knew it. Just count to three, he thought. Count to three and get it over with. One, two, three.

Karl Peabody had been searching frantically for Bartelli for ten minutes. He had checked by the animal cages, gone to Bartelli's bus, even tried Shanna-The-Sword-Swallower's bus—she and Bartelli had a thing going—but she hadn't seen him all day. The only other place he could think to look was the bar down the street, a run down joint called The Pasadena. When he wasn't doing his act or chasing Shanna around her bus, Bartelli was usually drinking. Mostly he drank alone, but now and then he liked sitting in a dingy bar, conversing with the locals, playing the role of the world famous animal trainer. He never mentioned he'd gotten the job by default, that it was actually his dead brother who had made the name Bartelli famous. Insignificant details.

The Pasadena was built in the forties and nobody had changed a brick or a stool since; it even had its original neon sign. The city council had placed it on the endangered species list. To most people, it was just an eyesore. Karl parked his car out front and stepped inside. Bartelli was sitting at the bar, all alone, a dozen empty shot glasses in front of him, his head bobbing inches above them.

Karl shook him by the arm. "Bartelli. You gotta come quick. He's here, the guy from the woods."

Bartelli slowly turned his head. "Hey," he mumbled, "it's half-a-man. Have a drink."

"No, listen. That guy is here. He's with Miranda. I heard them talking about Marcell."

Bartelli perked up a little and gazed about the room. "Where is the little fucker. I don't see him." He picked up one of his empty shot glasses and tried to drink out of it, then realized it was empty and started checking all the rest, picking them up and slamming them back down onto the bar.

"No, he's not here," said Karl.

Bartelli slapped his hand on the bar. "Barkeep, another drink."

Karl waived the bartender away. "The bar's closing, but we can go to another one, my car's right outside."

Bartelli tried to focus on Karl. "Hey, how come there's two of you? Tiny?" He reached out to where he thought he saw Tiny's face but there was nothing but air.

Karl grabbed him by the arm and helped him off his stool, but Bartelli was a large man and his weight was too much for Karl to handle. He went crashing to the floor.

Karl leaned down to him. "Come on, Bartelli, you gotta get up." He grabbed him by the shoulders and tried lifting him to his feet but could only get him up onto his butt.

"I want a drink," said Bartelli

"We'll get one, but you gotta get up."

"Hey," said the bartender. "You better get him outta here, fore I call the cops."

"What do you think I'm trying to do?"

Karl tried once again to lift Bartelli to his feet, but there was just no way he could lift all that dead weight. He looked around the room, thinking maybe somebody would help, but everyone just turned their heads away as if they didn't even see him. It took him awhile, but he finally managed to drag his drunken friend out the door and get him into his car, Bartelli mumbling all the way about wanting another drink.

The street was busy with traffic and it was not yet dark. Bartelli was very confused.

"Where's everybody going? The sun coming up?"

"Yeah, that's right, the sun's coming up, everyone's going to work. Why don't you get some sleep."

Bartelli closed his eyes and laid back in the seat, his bearded chin resting on his chest, drool running from one corner of his mouth. After a couple of minutes, he popped his head up and opened his eyes. "I'll kill that little fucker," he said, then he passed out. ❧

TWENTY-THREE

Marcell recognized the room in the film as his current prison. He was tied to the very same bed, was sitting on the same dirty sheets. Brown had given him a pretty thorough beating but, true to his word, Marcell had not given in. Exasperated and afraid he might kill him if he continued, Brown had cleaned him up and tied him to the bed, then gone outside for some air.

There was a strange odor emanating from those sheets, an odor, Marcell assumed, left behind by the people in the movie. It was a sickening aroma, as if someone had sprayed perfume in a locker room, and it pained him to think it was the smell of sex; in his mind he'd always imagined sex would smell as clean and fresh as his tiny friend, Mary. The smell seemed to fit the movie, which only served to disturb Marcell even more for, like the pungent odor filling his head, the display of sex before him was not at all like he had imagined it would be.

He had never really contemplated the specifics of sex, the body fluids, the tangled hair, the distorted expressions, the animal sounds. His was a lofty fantasy, always Mary, her golden hair fanned out on a pillow, her gentle face smiling up at him. They were both naked, of course, but their bodies were clean and soft and each and every touch was filled with wonderful sensations, each caress a loving expression of their souls.

What he saw before him now was nothing like that at all. There was no love on the girls' faces, there weren't even any signs of pleasure, their features contorted into a fusion of wickedness and pain. Their eyes looked like dark holes, exits through which their souls were draining forth. He wanted to turn away, for he felt naturally repulsed, and yet somehow he couldn't. He tried closing his eyes but the sounds kept pulling him back. He had to know, had to understand what this force was that had the power to both repulse and arouse.

The camera moved in for a close-up as the man entered one of the girls. Cleve was sitting on a chair next to the bed, drinking a beer. He yelled at the screen. "Yeah! Give it to her, man."

The filmmaker had taken a precious thing, an act of love between two people, and reduced it to its lowest form. This is the penis, this is the vagina, watch now as they fill the screen. The mystery of love, the splendor of two lovers joined together, all this was gone. It was like watching a magic act and knowing how all the tricks work, only worse. This wasn't about pulling a rabbit out of the hat or turning a white glove into a soaring bird. To Marcell, it was the killing of the human spirit. The fact that the girls in the movie were just children made it all the worse.

He watched as Cleve made obscene gestures toward the screen. Sex to Cleve no longer involved the soul. It was just another way to manifest his power. He could cut the bladder out of a bear and sell it for money, slice a woman's throat and leave her dying in a pool of blood. All that was good in a human being was missing in Cleve. He was like a rabid beast running loose on the street, no, much worse, for unlike the diseased animal, Cleve thrived on the pain and suffering of *his* victims. The philosophers and the psychiatrists might look at him and see a tragedy, consider his youth, the traumas he had most likely endured; that was their job. In the meantime, someone had to put Cleve, and all the others like him, down. Marcell would be more than happy to do that. As far as he was concerned, lying there on that bed, his wrists bleeding from the tight ropes, his face bruised and battered from being knocked around, it all came down to making a choice; Cleve made his a long time ago.

Marcell closed his eyes. He would not look up at the screen again. Cleve and the others would get nothing from him. He would think only of Mary, smell her sweetness, touch her soft skin, bathe in the kindness in her eyes.

Brown came into the room and turned off the movie.

"Hey," said Cleve. "I'm watching that."

"Not anymore you're not. Mister O is here."

O'Neill came in a few minutes later. He was wearing an expensive looking bright blue suit, a light blue shirt and a yellow tie. He had a couple of men with him. The two men wore black suits and dark sunglasses and carried rifles over their shoulders.

"Why isn't there anyone at the gate?" asked O'Neill. He sounded very angry.

"Arnie and Roberto never came back," said Brown.

"Never came back? Jesus Christ, what kind of organization is this, anyway? I send the bums out on a simple mission...where's Horace?"

"Sleeping."

"Sleeping? Sleeping? You go wake that nigger up and tell him to get his black ass out of bed and get out there."

Brown started to walk away but O'Neill grabbed his arm. "Wait a minute. He pointed over at Marcell and let out a short laugh. "This is it, This is the creature that's been causing me so much grief. He's a fucking midget for chrissake, and you guys can't get any information out of him?"

"He's a tough little fucker, boss. He won't crack."

Marcell watched his every move, the way he tugged at his tie and ran his hand along his hair as if he were preparing himself to step before a camera. So vain, so arrogant. This is the man, he thought, the man who pulls the strings. This is the man I want to kill.

"What's his name?" asked O'Neill.

"Marcell," said Brown.

"Okay," said O'Neill, "go get Horace." O'Neill stepped closer to the bed. "So, Mister Marcell, you've been running around Los Angeles being a tough guy, meddling in my business and now, look at you, here you are all bloody and tied up. Right now, you have to feel like a complete idiot."

"You'll have to come closer," said Marcell, "I can't hear out of this ear."

O'Neill leaned in toward the bed. "You've got something that belongs to me, and I would really appreciate it if you would

284

cooperate a little more."

"Sure," said Marcell. "How's this." He spit in O'Neill's face. Some of it went on his tie; it was mostly blood.

O'Neill looked down at his tie then used it to wipe his face. He tasted the blood then smiled at Marcell. "I like the taste of your blood. Before I'm through with you, I'll make a meal of it." He turned to the men he had brought with him. "I want that information out of him. I don't care what you have to do to get it. Understand? Take him upstairs, out of my sight."

"Why don't you come up, do it yourself?" said Marcell.

"Get him out of here, before I put a hole in him," said O'Neill. He turned to Cleve. "Cuttridge, I want you outside the front door."

"They took my weapons."

"Tell Mister Brown I said to give them back to you. And unless you want to change places with the midget, don't try anything clever. Now, move it."

O'Neill's men untied Marcell and one of them picked him up off the bed. Marcell reached down and grabbed the guy by the balls and squeezed.

The man bent down in pain. "Christ! Get him off of me."

His partner grabbed Marcell's arm and tried to break his grip but Marcell would not let go. He had the first man on his knees now, water running from his eyes.

"Do something!"

The second man took out his pistol and smacked Marcell over the head and he passed out.

You take a guy, a guy that ain't so smart, and you try and help him out, get him into a good situation, good money, lots of pussy, best thing he's ever gonna run into and what does he do, he turns on you, out of the blue. And for what, three washed up bug-ridden whores, don't give a good shit about him.

Arnie was walking down the dirt road, the full moon peaking through the tall trees, trying to make sense of Roberto's behavior,

285

thinking how he was gonna fill him up with lead as soon as he caught up with him. His head was throbbing from where Roberto had smacked him with his pistol. That was bad enough, but then the guy takes his shoes and doesn't even leave him his gun way out here in the middle of nowhere.

He had been hearing something out there in the bushes for the last ten minutes, something following him, he was sure of it. Every time he would stop, it would too. If he had been wearing shoes he would have started running but without them, even walking was difficult. The only good thing was the full moon lighting his way down the rock-strewn dirt road, and even with that, both his feet were bleeding.

He found a large piece of branch by the side of the road and carried it with him. It was heavy and would work well as a club, just in case. In the distance he could see the lights from passing cars on the highway. It was hard to say how far away they were, maybe three or four miles. Another hour and he'd be safe, then he'd flag somebody over, take their car and get after Roberto. At least, that was the plan.

The rustling started up in again off to his left. He paused for a second and waited, only this time it didn't stop but got louder instead. Then he saw the figure, low to the ground and moving fast. It came out of the bushes not fifteen feet away from him, its yellow eyes fixed on him, its mouth wide open and full of long, pointed teeth. Arnie paused for a second, unable to totally comprehend the picture before him. The creature sprung from the ground and Arnie raised the club over his head and started into a swing, but the cat was quick, too quick for a frightened city boy. He felt the teeth sink into his neck and the razor sharp claws ripping away at his face. He tried his best to push the strong animal away from him, but it was too late. The cat had his neck in a vice like grip. It would all be over soon.

A hot shower and a meal had made Penny feel much better and Miranda had been very reassuring; just the tone of her voice was enough to make you relax. Marcell was tough, she said, he wasn't afraid of anything; never was. Once, when he was around six years old, he wandered away from their camp in the middle of the night. They didn't find him until the following morning, sleeping under a tree out in the woods. He hadn't been afraid out there, he said, because the animals kept him company.

Penny told Miranda about Rudy and how Marcell and Frank had rescued her from him and that life and how gentle Marcell had been with her. Then she asked the question that had been utmost on her mind since meeting the beautiful Miranda.

"Why is Marcell...I mean, you're so pretty and..."

"Why is he a dwarf?"

Penny felt awkward. "I'm sorry, I don't mean..."

"It's okay, you're not the first, believe me. It's a natural reaction. People look at Marcell and they see a freak. He has suffered a lot for being what he is, for how he looks, but then, look at you, look what you've been through already in your life. You're a beautiful young girl but your beauty got used against you. In some ways, you've probably suffered more than Marcell; he's never had any other expectations. But to answer your question, you don't need to be a dwarf in order to give birth to one. In fact, most are born to average size parents. The doctors call it a random gene mutation, but I think there's something more to it. I think Marcell was sent to me, like he is, for a reason."

"Reason? What reason could there be?"

"The day Marcell was born, I thought I was being punished for something. I was very young and pretty, like you, and my definitions of beauty and love were very narrow. How could I, a beautiful young girl, be burdened with such a freak? Those were my very thoughts, Penny, about my own child. I'm ashamed to say it, but, those first few days in the hospital, I used to lie in bed and pray he would die in his crib. My heart felt like it was breaking."

"What happened, to change your mind, I mean?"

"One night the nurse brought him to me to feed him. He lay there sucking at my breast—I wouldn't even look down at him—

and at some point, I fell asleep. When I woke up, his face was underneath my breast and he wasn't breathing. I looked down at him, Penny, and...I'm not certain I can explain to you what happened. All I know is, at that instant all I could see was a beautiful baby boy, dead, or close to dead, I wasn't sure which, and I was struck with horror at the thought of losing him. I picked him up and started breathing into his mouth. I was in a panic. I prayed to God, please give me another chance. A few seconds later his eyes opened and then he began to cry. It was the most beautiful sound I had ever heard and the happiest moment of my life. I never again thought of Marcell as a burden or saw him as a freak. He was perfect, just the way he was, a brand new life that had come into the world. He was a blessing; my blessing. God had sent him to me to save me from myself, my ignorance."

Penny didn't know what to say. Life was funny. Marcell is born a dwarf and gets Miranda for a mother. Penny was a beautiful, normal child and her mother turns her away. There was a knock on the door. It opened and a man stuck his head in.

"Excuse me, Miranda, I didn't know you had company."

"That's okay, Tiny, come in."

Tiny came into the bus. He was tall and thin and walked with a slight limp, but he was handsome in his own way. There was gentleness about him. Penny couldn't take her eyes off him.

"Tiny, this is Penny, she's a friend of Marcell's. Penny, this is Tiny Peabody."

Tiny nodded to Penny. He seemed very shy. "I just wanted to ask, that is, I saw a strange looking man drive away in your car a little while ago, looked like he was all painted up."

"That's okay, Tiny, he's a friend of mine."

"Well, what concerned me was, Karl and Bartelli took off right behind him in Karl's car."

"Who's Bartelli?" asked Penny.

Miranda got up from her seat. She seemed anxious. "You're sure they were following him?"

"They were parked on the street and as soon as he left they

started their car and went right behind him."

"Tiny, go and find Howard, tell him we have to go somewhere in the bus. And get Turk, too. Hurry."

Tiny hurried off on his mission.

"What's wrong, Miranda?"

"We have to go to Malibu, Penny, and quick."

"Who is Turk?"

"Turk is a friend. In case we need some muscle."

The drive to Malibu had been a slow and uncomfortable one for Frank, chugging along in the right lane at fifty miles an hour, his long legs crunched into the tiny space beneath the steering wheel, his neck bent over to keep his head from hitting the roof.

People passing by were looking at him like he was some kind of a maniac. And why not? His face all painted up, his head shaved, his large body crammed into the tiny automobile.

Penny's directions were perfect, and after an hour and a half he pulled up to the dirt driveway that led to the house. He parked the Yugo on the side of the road, spent a couple of minutes unwinding his sore body, and then grabbed his rifle and bag from the back seat. Bones jumped out of the car, ready to go.

Frank bent down to him. "Sorry, boy, not this time." He put the old dog back into the car, rolled up the windows most of the way so he couldn't get out, then took off into the woods.

It was just like Penny had said. At the entrance to the house was an iron gate. Directly inside the gate, Frank could see the silhouette of a man. There were cameras mounted on either side of the gate and a high wall that ran in both directions. Staying behind the cover of the trees, Frank followed the wall to where it turned a corner and ran down the side of the house. There was another camera mounted at the corner. He studied the angles of the cameras. There appeared to be a small area half way down the wall, a blind spot, where neither camera covered. It was here he would make his entrance.

On the other side of the wall, not far away, stood a large oak tree. Frank pulled the rope and hook from his bag. If he could catch the hook onto one of the larger branches, he could easily scale the wall. He rolled up the rope and gave it a toss. The hook banged into a branch then crashed down onto the ground. Frank leaned up against the wall, waiting for some kind of response. Evidently, nobody had heard him. He grabbed the rope and slowly dragged it back over the wall. Once again he curled it up and tossed it. This time it caught on a branch. He gave it a couple of tugs to make sure it was secure, then he threw his bag over his shoulder and began his climb.

Half way up the wall, he heard something snap, like a small branch. At first, he thought maybe his rope was going to break free from the tree limb, but then he heard the voice and knew it was much worse.

"You can climb down, or I can shoot you. Makes no never mind to me."

Frank paused. He was too far from the top to make it over the wall. The man spoke again.

"I ain't gonna wait all day."

Frank lowered himself to the ground then turned around to face the man. He had seen him before, in the woods by his cabin. It was Bartelli, and his friend Karl was with him. Bartelli had a double-barreled shotgun pointed right at his chest.

"So, we meet again," said Bartelli. "This time, I got the gun." He was four or five feet away, but Frank could smell the booze. The man stunk.

"What do you want?" said Frank.

"Why, hell, I want the same thing as you, and he's right inside that house. I got me a feeling, I could make a little trade with the folks inside, and that's just what I'm gonna do."

Frank saw something coming out of the trees in a full run behind Bartelli. At first, he thought it was a bear, it was so large. Bartelli heard the rustling of branches and started to turn. When he did, Frank grabbed the shotgun and pulled it from his hands. Before Bartelli realized what was happening, a giant man grabbed

290

him in one arm and Karl in the other and smacked them together. The two men fell to the ground, unconscious.

"I'm Turk," said the man. "I'm with Miranda."

Frank had never seen anyone so big in his life. The man was at least three hundred pounds and yet he moved with the grace of a ballerina. He wore a pair of sweat pants and a spaghetti strap t-shirt, his chest and arms covered in thick black hair.

"Where is she?"

"In the bus, back on the road."

"Let's get these two out of sight," said Frank.

Turk threw Bartelli over his shoulder as if he were a small child. Frank carried Karl. They carried them through the woods and down to the dirt road where Howard had parked the bus.

Miranda, Penny, and Tiny were standing outside the bus, along with Bones. When they saw the men approaching, they ran to greet them.

"I was afraid we wouldn't get here on time," said Miranda.

"Another minute and you wouldn't have," said Frank. He dumped Karl onto the ground.

"Did you find Marcell?"

"They've got him in there somewhere. I don't know how many of them there are, but the place looks pretty secured."

"We can help," said Penny.

"What I need," said Frank, "is a diversion. And I think our friends, here, are just the ones to do the job." He looked to Tiny. "If you want, Tiny, we can leave Karl out of this."

Tiny looked down at his brother. "Karl and Bartelli came here to kill Marcell," he said. "I say to hell with the both of the them."

"What do we do?" asked Turk. He still had Bartelli over his shoulder.

"Get some rope. Miranda, get the Yugo. The keys are in it."

"What about me?" said Penny.

"I want you and Miranda to stay in the bus with Howard. And keep Bones with you. Do that for me, okay? I don't want to be worrying about any of you."

The fire that had burned Marcell and Frank's cabins destroyed over ten thousand acres before it was brought under control. The fireman told Kate Mallory if it hadn't been for the wind dying down, it could have been a lot worse. It seemed unlikely that anyone in the area could have survived that inferno, still, Kate couldn't believe Frank had perished. She wanted to go back out there, herself, but finding the place now would be next to impossible, not to mention her bad foot.

A secondary search of Rudy Carlyle's apartment had uncovered some pornographic films, many with very young girls, but there was nothing to go with them, no names or dates. It seemed as though she had run out of leads, and Horton was just about ready to take her badge.

Kate sat at her desk, her bandaged foot propped up on a trashcan, wondering what to do next, when the phone rang. It was Tulary. Hobble on over to South Central, he said, right away. A friend of his in vice had picked up a girl last night and she was looking to make a deal.

"What's that got to do with us, Tu?"

"The girl's pimp was Rudy Carlyle."

"I'm on my way."

"I want it all in writing," said Maple. She was sitting across a table from Kate Mallory, drinking a Coca Cola, putting on her toughest front. "And I want the D.A. to sign it, else I ain't got nothin to say."

"Rudy's dead," said Kate. "You could be looking at obstruction of justice."

"Obstruct my ass," said Maple. "I already told this other cracker, either I walk, or I don't talk." The other cracker she was referring to was Tulary, who was sitting on the edge of the table having a smoke.

Kate was getting exasperated. "Okay, Maple, I give you my word. You tell me about Rudy and his operation. If you weren't involved in his death, I'll recommend the D.A. drop all charges against you. That's the best I can do. If that doesn't work for you, then you can take your chances in court."

Maple looked up at Tulary. "Can I have one of them?"

It took some doing with his hands all bandaged up, but Tulary managed to get the pack of cigarettes out of his pocket. Maple grabbed a cigarette from the pack and Kate lit it for her.

"I sure as hell didn't kill the motherfucker, but I ain't sorry he's dead. And I don't know who did kill him. All I know is, Rudy worked for a man named O'Neill; I was with him a couple times. Real scary white dude; I think he liked boys better than girls. He coulda done it. They got a house out in Malibu where they make the movies. That's where we all lived."

"Who's we all?" asked Tulary.

Maple looked at him like he was stupid. "The girls, Rudy's girls. Keep us all out there like a prison, making movies and doin tricks. Four years I worked for Rudy, all I end up with was a few hundred dollars. Somebody gone and stole that from me."

"You know a girl named Penny?"

"Penny? I don't know, maybe. Know a lot of girls."

"Fifteen, sixteen years old. Blonde hair."

"Got the earring in her nose?"

"Yeah. You know her?"

"Yeah, she the new girl. Arnie got his eye on her. She dead, too?"

"We don't know, Maple. This house. You can tell us how to find it?"

"I don't know the names of the streets, if that's what you mean, but I know how to get there. Been livin there for four years. Rudy's dead, huh?"

"That's right, Maple, he's dead."

"Just like Elvis."

"What?"

"Rudy. He thought he was Elvis Presley. Now he's dead too. Serves him right. Never did nothin for me." ❧

TWENTY-FOUR

Marcell felt something cold where his face should have been. He had been dreaming and in his dream he had fallen into a deep hole, only, it was just his soul that had fallen; his body was still up there, at the entrance. It was dark down there but it felt safe; no one could see him as long as he stayed in the dark. He could hear voices in the distance. They were touching his body again, he was sure of it. He was afraid to look up, afraid the men would be staring down the hole at him, would pull him back up, put him back in his body and hurt him some more. Then he felt the cold again and realized it was his skin that was transmitting the feelings to his brain. They had found him, he was back on top, reconnected to his body. Cold water ran down his face. He opened his eyes.

He was on a chair, his clothing stripped away, his hands bound behind his back. There were wires connected to his testicles. Standing before him were two men. They were dressed alike, all in black. One of them was tall and very pale, the other was short and stocky. Marcell had seen them before, somewhere. He tried to recollect. Three words kept rushing through his head. Tell them nothing.

The stocky one leaned down to him. The man was in need of a shave and his eyes were all bloodshed. "You ready to talk now?"

Marcell traced the wires from his body down to a small box with a lever. The second man, the sick looking one, had his hand on the lever.

"Talk," said Marcell. His voice was very weak and raspy. "Bullshit talks...let's choose executors and talk of wills."

"He's delirious," said the man with the contraption. Throw some more water on him"

The man picked up a bucket and tossed more water in Marcell's face.

"Pour not water on a drowning mouse," said Marcell.

The man with the empty bucket grabbed Marcell by the hair and pulled his head back. "He's faking. Give him another jolt."

The skinny one grabbed the lever on the box and turned it. There was a high-pitched buzzing sound and Marcell sat straight up in his chair as the current shot through his body. All he could see now was a brilliant white light. The only thing stronger than the light, was the pain. Or was the light the pain? It was hard to tell. It seemed to start down there, where the wires were connected, and radiate out over his entire body. It seemed to go on forever, but in fact it only lasted seconds. The white light vanished and Marcell plopped back down into the chair.

"Where are the disks?" The words echoed through Marcell's head. Hundreds of floppy disks floated in space before him. He opened his mouth and tried to speak. Nothing came out.

"He's fried, man. We gave him too much. Better tell O'Neill. We ain't getting nothing out of this one. I'll gather up this stuff."

"You have to give the little fucker credit."

"Try explaining that to O'Neill."

The shorter man left and the other one took the wires off of Marcell and dropped them onto the floor. Marcell just sat there in the chair, drool flowing out of his mouth. The man was about to pick up the box with the switch on it when an explosion went off outside. He let go of the box and turned toward the bedroom door.

Marcell opened his eyes. The wire that had been connected to him was now lying in a puddle of water and just inches away from him sat the box. He wanted to lift his leg, he told it to but it didn't budge. Concentrate. Have to reach the switch. He tried again. This time his leg began to move. Ever so slowly he stretched his tiny leg as far as he could until his toes reached the switch. The man must have heard something, for he quickly turned around now and faced Marcell. Then he saw Marcell's foot on the switch and then realized he was standing in the puddle of water. Their eyes met.

"The...horror," said Marcell as he flicked the switch with his little toes. The man just stood there shaking, a glow of white light encircling his body. When smoke started coming out of his eye sockets, Marcell switched off the machine. The man dropped to the floor.

"Can we talk? Can we? Can we talk?" said Marcell. Now if he could just free his hands.

When Bartelli came to, he was seated behind the wheel of Miranda's Yugo, his hands tied to the steering wheel, the steering wheel tied to the window post. Next to him, in the passenger seat, was his good friend Karl who was also tied to his seat. The car was running. Fifty yards in front of them Bartelli could see the large iron gate.

Tiny was standing next to the car, talking to Miranda. She checked her watch. "Thirty seconds," she said.

"What are you doing? What's going on?"

"You said you wanted, Marcell. He's right inside that gate."

Karl struggled, trying to loosen the rope that secured him to the seat.

"I tied those myself," said Miranda. "You're wasting your time."

"Tiny! Don't do it! I'm your brother, Goddamn it."

"You've never been my brother," said Tiny. "Just an appendage."

"Ten seconds," said Miranda. "You might get lucky, Karl. It's more of a chance than you would have given Marcell."

Tiny turned his attention to Bartelli. "Your brother was an evil man, Bartelli, but compared to you he was a saint. He got what he deserved and now you're gonna get yours."

"Time," said Miranda.

Karl was crying now and pleading to Miranda and Tiny to let him go. "Bartelli made me go along with him," he said. "I didn't have a choice."

Tiny reached inside and set a brick on the gas pedal. "You don't have one now, either," he said. Then he stuck the car in gear and off it went, straight at the gate.

296

Bartelli tried desperately to reach down with his chin and turn the wheel but it was tied tightly to the post and wouldn't budge. He looked down at the speedometer. They were up to thirty now and just yards away from the gate. He could see a man just inside the bars. He was pointing something at them, a rifle. He was pointing a rifle right at them! And then he saw another man, outside the gate. It was Turk. He had something in his hand, but Bartelli couldn't tell what it was. Then Turk lofted the item toward the gate.

Bartelli looked over at Karl. "You son-of-a-bitch! This is your fault. Your fault."

At first, it had sounded like a chain saw and Horace Black figured maybe somebody was out there cutting down a tree. But the noise started getting louder and then he could see two small white lights moving toward the gate. He raised his rifle toward the lights. It was a car, he could see that now, and it was coming on fast. He wasn't sure if the gate could withstand the impact of a car and the thought occurred to him that he should get out of the way. Then he heard a thumping sound. He glanced down through the bars of the gate. They looked like pine cones, three of them, tied together. It wasn't until it was too late that he realized they weren't pinecones at all.

There was an explosion and the man inside the gate disappeared, along with the gate. Small chunks of concrete bounced off the car but it kept going, gliding through a cloud of smoke, and for a moment Bartelli thought they were going to be all right. Then he heard something heavy crash down onto the roof and he watched as a large section of the gate tore through the roof and compressed itself over Karl's head, ripping both his ears off in the process. Karl screamed in agony and then slipped into a state of shock.

The car kept moving. There was a statue dead ahead and behind the statue were two men. The men had rifles and were firing toward the car. Bartelli could hear the bullets striking the glass, could see the holes as the windshield began to shatter. Karl took a round to the face and his head jerked back against the seat and then Bartelli felt the impact as one of the bullets struck his forehead. The last thing he would see was the head of the statue flying up into the air as the battered Yugo struck the statue and burst into flames.

Brown had been standing right outside the front door when the explosion occurred. O'Neill had told him to stay close to Cleve, make sure he didn't try and make a run for it. When the bomb went off, Brown sent Cleve in to get O'Neill and he ran out to the driveway. A minute later he was joined by one of the two interrogators. The two of them took their positions behind the Venus de Milo statue and began emptying their guns at the runaway car until it exploded and blew the statue into a thousand pieces.

The interrogator started to run back toward the house but when he looked next to him, Brown was just standing there, motionless, his hands up by his neck.

"Let's go, Brown, move it."

Brown pulled something from his neck and then dropped his hands to his side. Blood poured out of his neck as he dropped first to his knees and then fell face first onto the ground. When his hand opened up, a piece of concrete the size of a pencil rolled out.

At this point, the interrogator figured his job was finished. O'Neill's Mercedes was parked less than twenty feet away and he could see no reason why he shouldn't get in it and get the fuck out of there. He made it to the car door, even got it open, before he felt the man's hands around his neck.

"Party's over," said the man. Then there was a loud snapping sound. It was quick but not painless.

When Cleve heard the explosion he figured the time had come for him to make his move. Brown told him to go inside, get O'Neill, but Cleve had other plans. His first thought was to go around back, scale the wall and get out of there as quick as possible. But then he saw someone coming over the wall and had another idea. He ran back into the house, and almost got knocked over by one of O'Neill's men as he came running out.

O'Neill was nowhere in sight. Cleve figured he had gone out the back door, which was fine by him. He raced up the stairs, expecting to find the dwarf still being guarded by O'Neill's goon. Cleve pulled out his gun. He was going to come in shooting, get rid of the guard and take Marcell with him.

Cleve burst through the door ready for action, but what he found was one very dead man lying in a puddle of water. Then he felt something sharp hit his arm and he dropped his gun. The pain was excruciating. He looked down at the blood gushing from his freshly healed scar as the dwarf removed his knife. He was standing there in his underwear looking like one of the undead, a big smile on his face.

Cleve pulled out his own knife from its holster.

"Let's carve this turkey," said Marcell.

Cleve's right hand was no good to him at all, and Cleve was not exactly ambidextrous, but he did have quite a reach on his smaller opponent. His wound rather leveled the playing field. Cleve rushed the smaller man, taking long wild swipes with his knife, but Marcell simply dived to the floor and went into a somersault, slashing Cleve's ankle as he went by.

"That the best you can do, Cleve." Marcell exposed his neck. "Come on, come and get me."

Cleve ripped away a portion of his shirt and wrapped it around his bleeding arm to try and slow the loss of blood. He limped across the room toward Marcell who was doing a small dance like a boxer, tossing the knife from one hand to another.

"I'm gonna gut you like a fish," said Cleve.

"Here I am, come sink your hook," said Marcell. "What a happy day this is. When I finish you, Cleve, I'm gonna do it so you die real slow. Now come on, tough guy, show me what you got."

Cleve picked up the wooden chair and used it like a lion tamer, prodding Marcell toward the corner of the room. His back against the wall, Marcell stuck his knife into the bottom of the chair then grabbed hold of the chair with both hands, twisting it and putting as much torque on Cleve's bad arm as possible until Cleve was forced to let go. Then he swung the chair at Cleve, knocking the knife out of his hand. It hit the ground and slid across the floor. Cleve turned and limped across the room for his knife.

He was half way across the room when he felt something land on his back and then he saw the short, muscular arms reach around his neck. The dwarf was riding him like a horse!

"Is this how it was with Veronica?" said Marcell. Cleve could feel the cold steel of the knife against his neck. Then the sharp edge sliced him, but not deep and then the dwarf wrapped both arms tightly around his neck.

Cleve tried to pull Marcell's arms away but Marcell was too strong. He spun around and smashed the little jockey up against the wall. Marcell hung on.

When Cleve moved away from the wall, the dwarf stuck him in the ass with his knife. "Giddy-up," said Marcell.

Again Cleve rammed Marcell against a wall, but once again he couldn't shake him. Now he felt a deep sharp pain in his back and then the pain was in his chest and when he looked down he saw the tip of Marcell's blade sticking through his shirt. Then the blade vanished as Marcell pulled it out and dismounted.

The pain was crippling. Cleve took a couple of steps toward Marcell, made a couple of weak jabs with his knife then dropped it to the floor.

He fell to his knees. "Finish it," he said.

Marcell reached down and picked Cleve's knife up from the floor and handed it to him. "You want it finished, do it yourself. Go on, you know how it works. One quick slice, right across the jugular."

300

Cleve put the knife up to his own throat. The pain in his chest was unbearable and yet he couldn't do it, couldn't put an end to his own suffering. He held the knife at his throat for a few seconds then dropped it to the ground.

"That's what I figured," said Marcell. I gotta go now. Thanks for the entertainment. You have a nice death." He grabbed his pants off the floor, stopped momentarily at the doorway and looked back at Cleve. Their eyes met, but only for a second, and then Marcell was gone.

Marcell hurried down the steps and into the living room. The house looked deserted. He proceeded cautiously toward the front door. He hadn't seen Frank yet but he figured he had to be the cause of all the explosions going on outside. Something cold touched the back of his neck and then he heard the obnoxious sound of O'Neill's voice.

"How nice of you to survive. You're my ticket out of here."

O'Neill picked him up with his left arm and pressed the pistol into his face. "We're going outside now. One move from you, and your complexion is going to get a whole lot worse."

They stepped outside. Marcell was still dressed only in his underwear, his pants draped around one arm. Just steps from the door lay Brown, a pool of blood gathered by his head. Marcell saw the burning car in the driveway and recognized it immediately. Then he noticed the figure slumped behind the wheel and his heart dropped. Was it Frank?

O'Neill carried Marcell across the driveway towards a parked Mercedes. The driver's door was open and there was a body lying next to it. Then a man stepped out from behind the car and pointed a rifle at O'Neill. Marcell didn't recognize him at first; his face was all painted up like an Indian. Then the man stepped into the light. It was Frank.

"End of the line, Mister O'Neill."

"Well, well. It must be the midget's partner. I'd suggest you drop that rifle before I finish this little monster."

Marcell started kicking and squirming. "Shoot him Frank! Kill him!"

"Yes, by all means, shoot me, Frank, and watch him die." O'Neill cocked his gun. Marcell could feel the barrel pressed into his temple.

Frank kept the rifle pointed toward O'Neill. "Let him go and you can drive away."

O'Neill laughed. "I don't think you're in any position to make a deal. But before I go, I am curious," he said. "You did all this over a lousy gall bladder, from a bear?"

"Among other reasons. Nothing you would understand."

"No, I don't suspect I would. Of course, you realize, right now your precious gall bladder is half way to Hong Kong. So it was all for nothing."

"Not completely. I put you out of business."

"This. This is nothing. This whole operation is just a toy, something to keep me entertained. I'll have another one like it up and running in a week."

"You're forgetting about the disks."

"Ah, yes, the disks. Those could prove to be embarrassing. Tell you what I'll do. I'll take our little friend here with me and I'll give you till tomorrow to bring me the disks."

"Don't do it, Frank."

"Drop your gun now and move away from the car. Do it! Or will end this right now."

Frank slowly lowered his rifle to his waist and O'Neill pulled his gun away from Marcell's head. "That's a good boy. See how well everything works when we cooperate. Now, move away from the car."

Frank backed away from the car. As O'Neill reached the door, he turned toward Frank. "On second thought..." he said and then pointed his pistol at Frank. Marcell reached out for the gun but there wasn't time. It went off and the bullet tore through Frank's shoulder and his rifle fell from his hands. "...to hell with the disks."

302

O'Neill moved a couple of steps closer to Frank and pointed the gun at him again. "It's been a pleasure, " he said as he cocked the gun. Marcell saw something shiny in the distance, just a speck of light reflecting off a tiny distant object. Then he heard a vaguely familiar swishing sound. It all happened in a matter of seconds, the reflection, the swish and then a crunching sound, like a walnut cracking open. He felt something warm and wet drip onto his face, then O'Neill loosened his grip and Marcell fell to the ground along with the gun. When he looked up he saw an arrow protruding from O'Neill's forehead. There was a look of disbelief on the man's face as his eyes focused on the colorful feathers at the end of the arrow. He reached up and grabbed the arrow with both hands and then collapsed face first onto the brick driveway.

Marcell got up and brushed himself off. In the distance he could hear the familiar voice of his mother calling to him and he rushed to meet her. When they met, she dropped the bow and they embraced. Bones ran right past them toward Frank.

"That was a great shot, Miranda."

"I would have shot sooner, but you kept squirming, I was afraid I might hit you. Oh, look at you. What did they do?"

"It's nothing. They're a bunch of wimps."

They could hear sirens in the distance and then Marcell felt a hand on his shoulder. It was Frank. "I have to go."

"Frank," said Marcell. "Man, for a minute there I thought you were dead. I saw the Yugo...who is that?"

"Bartelli, what's left of him."

"And Karl," said Miranda. You won't have to worry about them anymore."

"You're hurt," said Miranda.

"It's just a flesh wound, I'll be fine."

"I took care of Cleve," said Marcell. "I know I promised I'd save him for you but he didn't really give me much choice. Boy, you know, Bartelli's about your size."

"What are you thinking?"

"With the right identification..."

Frank reached behind his neck and unclasped a small metal chain. "Here, try these," he said.

Marcell took the dog tags, ran over to the burning car and tossed them onto Bartelli's charred remains.

"Better melt them down a little before the cops get here," he yelled out, but neither Frank nor Miranda heard him. They were in the middle of a long kiss. The sirens were getting louder now as the police cars drew closer.

Marcell returned from the car. "Frank, we gotta get out of here," he said.

Frank let go of Miranda and got down on his haunches. "I have to go now, Marcell."

"What do you mean, I'm going with you."

"Marcell, you're life is with the circus. You can go back there now, be with your mother, your friends."

"But, you said all the way."

"I know I did, and we took it all the way, and you were great. I couldn't have done it without you. You have to take care of your mother now and Penny."

"What about you? Who's gonna take care of you?"

"I'll be all right. I've got Bones and Mozart. Do me a favor. Whenever you set up the show, take your hammer and ring that bell once for me. One day I'll hear it and come and see you."

"You come and do it," said Marcell. "You could travel with us."

"I can't Marcell, it's not for me. Listen, the detective who's on her way here is no dummy. Sooner or later she'll figure out it's not me in that car. Besides, you have to know the right angle to make it ring, remember?"

"I made that all up, Frank."

"Well, give it a good ring for me anyway."

"I'll do it, Frank. I'll knock it clean off the post."

The two men embraced, then Frank stood, gave Miranda a quick hug. "I wish…"

Miranda stopped him. "You don't have to say anything. We'll meet again. I'm sure of it. Now go on, get out of here before I start to cry."

"Goodbye," he said and then turned to Penny. She started to cry and Bones jumped up and began licking her face. "He likes you. You've got a home now, Penny. Make the most of it. And take good care of Bones." He petted the dog's head. "See you, old friend."

Frank started running toward the back of the house. He got about twenty yards, then stopped and called out to Marcell.

"Marcell. Friends are like melons, shall I tell you why?"

"To find one good, you must a hundred try," said Marcell.

Frank waved, then turned and ran away. Bones watched his friend moving away and quickly began wimpering and pacing.

"Go get him, Bones" said Penny. "He needs you."

The tired old dog jumped up and placed his paws on Penny's chest, licked her face and then jumped back down and ran off after Frank. By the time the first police car arrived both he and Frank had vanished into the trees.

"What are we going to tell the police? asked Miranda.

"Let me do all the talking," said Marcell. "I got it all figured out."

"You might want to put on some pants first."

"Marcell looked down at his boney legs. "What's all the fuss?" he said. "They're only legs. No reason to be embarrassed. No reason at all." And with that the little man put his hands in the air and walked out to greet the police.

"Don't shoot," he said. "I'm unarmed." ❧

www.ingramcontent.com/pod-product-compliance
Lightning Source LLC
Chambersburg PA
CBHW031549240626
47153CB00002B/433